A Rose Remembered

Michael Phillips

The Secret of the Rose

A Rose Remembered

Tyndale House Publishers, Inc.
Wheaton, Illinois

Cover illustration copyright © 1993 by Jim Griffin
The black and white map of East/West Berlin copyright © 1994 by
    Hugh Claycombe
The map of Lebenshaus was originated by the author, Michael Phillips.
The artistic rendering is by illustrator Hugh Claycombe.

Published in association with the literary agency of Alive Communications, P.O. Box 49068, Colorado Springs, CO 80949.

Library of Congress Cataloging-in-Publication Data

Phillips, Michael R., date
  A rose remembered / Michael Phillips.
    p.   cm. — (The Secret of the rose : 2)
  ISBN 0-8423-5960-5 : (hardcover)
  ISBN 0-8423-5929-X : (softcover)
    1. Man-woman relationships—Germany—Berlin—Fiction. 2. Fathers
and daughters—Germany—Berlin—Fiction. 3. Young women—Germany
—Berlin—Fiction. I. Title. II. Series: Phillips, Michael R.,
1946- Secret of the rose : 2.
PS3566.H492R67   1994   94-4351
813'.54—dc20

Printed in the United States of America

99   98   97   96   95
 9   8   7   6   5

To the woman who has walked beside me
these last twenty-three years—my wife,

Judy Margaret Phillips,

with whom it has been my joy, privilege,
and honor to discover many of the mysteries
and secrets of love.

To you, Judy, I say,—*I'm so happy that God
allowed me to discover the secret of the rose . . .
with you.*

Acknowledgments

Thanks to Melinda Allen for her help. Appreciative acknowledgment is given for use of her poem—conceived and written by her for A Rose Remembered—in "A Fairy Tale Ride."

Acknowledgment is also made for use of the following books and magazines: Germany Between East and West: The Reunification Problem, by Frederick H. Hartmann, Prentice-Hall, Inc., Englewood Cliffs, N.J., 1965. Blockade: Berlin and the Cold War, by Eric Morris, Stein and Day, New York, 1973. Berlin: Success of a Mission?, by Geoffrey McDermott, Harper and Row Publishers, New York, 1963. National Geographic: "Berlin, Island In A Soviet Sea," by Frederick G. Vosburgh. "Life in Walled-Off West Berlin," by Nathaniel Kenney and Volkmar Wentzel, December, 1961.

Thanks also to Dr. Manfred Kober for his helpful insights into the situation in Germany during the cold war era.

And especially to my editor—a fine one—at Tyndale House, Ken Petersen, for his most helpful suggestions, assistance, and the overview which allows a book to become something more in the end than an author dares hope it can be.

Contents

. . .

Part III: Dangerous Mission ~ July/August 1961

Part IV: A Rose Remembered ~ August—December 1961

Part V: Behind Enemy Lines ~ January 1962

Part VI: The Secret of the Rose ~ February/March 1962

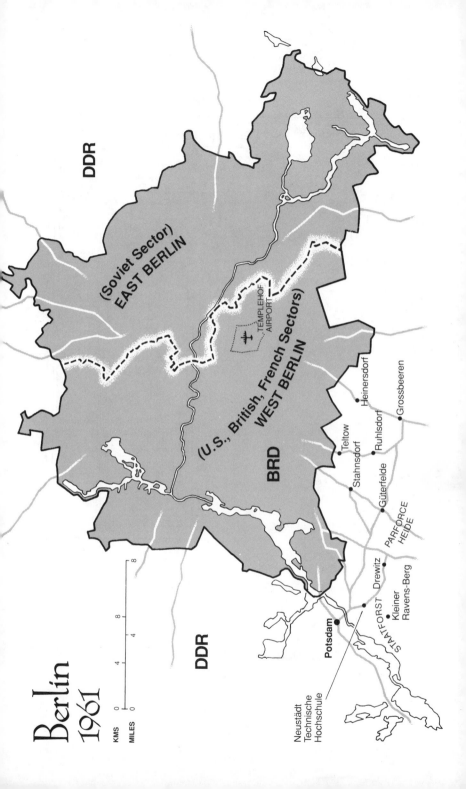

Berlin
1961

KMS
MILES

DDR

(Soviet Sector)
EAST BERLIN

(U.S., British, French Sectors)
WEST BERLIN

BRD

DDR

TEMPLEHOF
AIRPORT

Heinersdorf

Grossbeeren

Teltow

Stahnsdorf

Ruhlsdorf

Güterfelde

PARFORCE
HEIDE

Drewitz

STAATFORST

Kleiner
Ravens-Berg

Potsdam

Neustädt
Technische
Hochschule

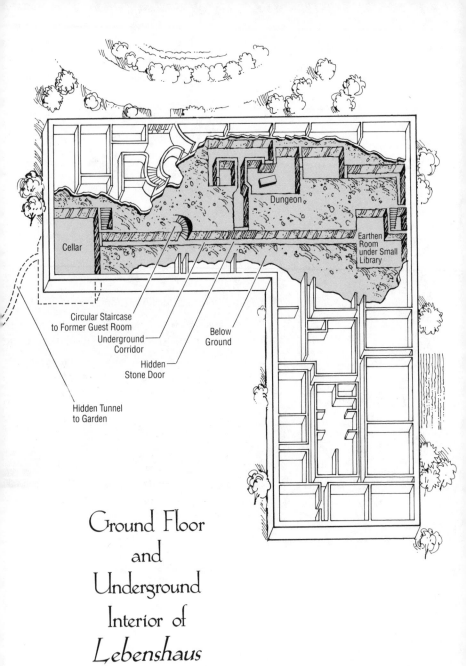

Cellar

Dungeon

Earthen
Room
under Small
Library

Circular Staircase
to Former Guest Room

Underground
Corridor

Below
Ground

Hidden
Stone Door

Hidden Tunnel
to Garden

Ground Floor
and
Underground
Interior of
Lebenshaus

Prologue

• • •

1950s

Everywhere was fragmentation.

Only a generation earlier this fair and energetic people had been told they were the greatest race on earth, whose empire would reign a thousand years.

Now they stoically went about their affairs at the convergence of a self-created matrix of brokenness.

Theirs was a sundered nation in the center of this ruptured continent, spinning on a globe of disconnected humanity.

Its great capital stood as the worldwide symbol of a fractured people, split as by capricious bolts of lightning into four random and unequal chunks. The lines of division, in many places invisible yet a while longer, snaked their way along streets, up sidewalks, through backyards and parks, over buildings, and across rivers.

The great city was now four cities—or two cities—it hardly seemed to matter. The huge metropolis of nearly four million no longer possessed claim to an identity it could call *its own*.

It was little wonder these were a fragmented people and that this was no happy time in their national soul.

Theirs was also a pedigree cut off from its spiritual roots. This was the land of the Reformation, the land where Protestantism was born and given life, the land of Luther, Barth, and Bonhoeffer. This was an erudite people, known for the wealth and breadth of their theologic heritage, a land noted for the vibrancy and personality of its thought and faith.

But the church of such foundations had closed its eyes to ungodliness. Its leaders and the masses had chosen a path of evil. An entire culture had embraced nazism, and thus the flame at its core had slowly been extinguished in a slow, silent, flickering death. The organized church became, as a result, but one more arm of the state.

Such it remained a generation later, though national socialism had long since faded into history.

That ancient German institution, the *mighty fortress* of God founded by Luther, now gave allegiance to two governments, as distinct from one another as white from black.

Though the democracy to the West was humane, the alliance with Bonn gave back the West German church no more of its essential vigor than was contained in its East German counterpart, whose lifeline stretched to Moscow. What had been lost in the 1930s by a policy of compromise had never again been recovered on either side of the line separating the BRD and the DDR.

Luther's fortress, like Berlin's great cathedral, lay in ruins.

Spiritual numbness accompanied political, national, and personal fragmentation as the embodying characteristics of the time.

At all levels, this was a domain, and these were its citizens, in need of restoration, healing, and a rebuilding of the foundations of their spirituality and destiny.

Those on the one side did their best to ignore the schism. They could do nothing about it anyway. The wealth that poured into their land in the 1950s made possible the fiction that the division did not exist. They learned again to walk with a stiff pride that belied the cracks in their national personhood.

Those on the other side tried to find consolation in routine.

But for neither could there be resolution. The national character, the identity of this fractured populace, had not been determined. Those fortunate ones laughed and spent their abundant deutsche marks to carve out a good life for themselves. But inside even prosperity could not erase the memory of how things really stood.

When would come the healing for this seen and unseen disconnection?

If it came at all, it would take many years.

And it would have to originate in the infinitesimally invisible regions of human hearts, rather than in the drafting of treaties between nations. It would come as prayers began to drift heavenward, as from Job's dusty heap of misfortune, for God to have mercy upon them, heal the pain of their souls, and restore health and vitality of spirit to their land.

PART I

Toward A New Dawn

June 1961

1
The Land

· · ·

IF ANYTHING COULD BE CONSIDERED TIMELESS AMID THE passing of life's fleeting hours, surely it was the land.

There were spiritual considerations, of course, that possessed deeper claims to immortality. She knew that.

But on the physical plane, the earth and the fruit it brought forth out of the ground—according to the ancient parable recorded by the gospelist Saint Mark—possessed, like no other aspect of the created universe, links to eternity.

The armies of six millennia of Nebuchadnezzars and Caesars and Alexanders and Napoleons and Hitlers tramped across it, changing its borders, subduing its nations, and slaughtering its inhabitants. But never had they altered by so much as a speck its miraculous power to produce, to recreate, to regenerate itself in the midst of what chaos the men above it wrought upon one another.

Generations came and went. Tribes, clans, families, and races all rose and fell. Life passed into life, as men and women, the great as well as the obscure, returned to the earth as they came.

Yet the land abided, an enduring reality under the gaze of the heavens. Over it the inexorable march of history passed, father to son, mother to daughter, one conquering dynasty giving way to the next—while the earth remained, surviving them all.

Karin Duftblatt let her eyes wander across the countryside out the windows in every direction.

Expansive fields of slowly ripening grain, extending right and left from her gaze, were beginning now to lose the green of their youth in preparation for the deep golden brown of their old age, which would arrive with the harvest later in the year.

It was a tranquil scene, broken here and there by green pastureland or trees, and now and then an uncultivated hillside. How could it now be so peaceful where bombs and blood had such a few short years ago filled the air and covered the ground? How could the land bear such abundant fruit where so much death had once been?

Didn't the land know what holocausts, what crimes against God's creation, it had witnessed?

Oh, but she loved this land! She could not help it, though there were places farther to the north she avoided. Some memories were too painful, even after all this time.

It may not have been the most beautiful of the world's landscapes. But she would always love it, mostly for what the black soil was capable of producing from out of the God-imbued riches of its subterranean depths.

Love the land and its growing things she did, though neither did she begrudge the present focus of her activities in the city. As much as she enjoyed an occasional drive into the countryside like this, she doubted she could live here again. The city may have tended to make its inhabitants cynical and callous, but it also helped her forget the past. Her work was there as well, and because of its importance, she needed to remain in the city.

She glanced about again as she drove, breathing in deeply and then exhaling a melancholy sigh.

Conquering dictators had indeed fought over this particular segment of Eastern Europe's geography. The Huns and Franks and Magyars and Mongols had all tried to subdue it. Napoleon had stretched the reach of his domination this far early in the last century, as had their own mustached Teutonic madman in this. By many names had it been known, this Prussian, Pomeranian plain between the two great and ancient powers of Germany and Russia.

Never, however, had this land been fully its *own*.

Now it possessed borders and a name that hinted at the racial individuality of its people. No one in the world was deceived, however, into thinking that the territory to which had been affixed the name "Poland" was anything but a subject of the new power that had arisen to the east, in the same autocratic tradition of the worst of the world's ancient conquering empires.

Out of the rubble of fascism's defeat had arisen the spectre called communism, whose shadow now, sixteen years later, blanketed half of two continents. Its persecution was not so visible. No less lethal, however, were the results.

If a handful of brave souls could not by themselves prevent the silent and insidious carnage, they might at least be able to make it known to the rest of the world.

Such was the mission to which she and the man she was on her way to meet had given themselves.

Ordinarily she would have sent another of her people. It was a long drive from her home in East Berlin, halfway across Poland. But word had come that this delivery was unlike any before it, and it must be managed by as few hands as possible.

Thus she had decided to make the pickup herself and return personally to the city with the evidence they had so long sought.

2

Secret Holocaust

• • •

IT WAS PROBABLY FOOLHARDY FOR HIM TO CROSS THE border to make the contact himself.

For a normal delivery he wouldn't even consider it.

But this was a special package. This time there were actual photographs. Along with the data they had recently uncovered and sent through last month, these pictures could help expose the entire Stalinist lie.

This envelope had to reach West Berlin!

As dangerous as it would be, and as well known as he was, he would take it himself into Poland, where he could place it directly into her hands. The fewer people involved in this transfer, the better.

She would get it safely the rest of the way. She always did.

Slowly the old man rose from the knees of prayer—his first order of business before any such undertaking—removed the *talit* from around his shoulders, and stood. Methodically he undressed, laying aside the traditional garb of his heritage, his calling, his very life, in order to don the costume of a working peasant. This had been the most difficult part at first. It had felt like he was denying the very culture he was trying to preserve.

But he had through the years gradually acclimated himself to the necessity of it. What sacrifice should he not be willing to give if even the single life of one of his people could be saved from the invisible holocaust of this terrible regime?

One by one he pulled off his vestments, reflecting over the time since this had all begun during the war. Who could have foreseen what it would lead to? Many years had passed. He was far from a young man. He had always known that he could not remain here indefinitely. His destiny lay toward the south. There were other things of importance besides photographs.

It was likely, he thought wearily, that there would not be many more such missions for him. Others could carry on the work in his stead.

If only they could locate Joseph. How happy that would make him! The continuing uncertainty over the young man's whereabouts was no doubt one of the factors that had kept him in Russia so long. The others looked to him for leadership, it was true, but he knew they could continue the work without him.

It was nearly time to emigrate for good. To do so was only fitting, and he knew his poor wife longed for it. Perhaps, he thought, pulling up his peasant trousers, after this one last delivery—after he knew the photographs were safe.

At last he was ready. He rose and left the room.

Two hours later he stopped at the border. The guard held up his hand to stop him. He rolled down the window of the small car.

"Passport and papers."

He handed out the documents of his false identity.

"What business do you have in Poland?"

"I have been transferred to a collective in Bialystok," he answered contritely.

"Out of the car, please."

He opened the door and stood before the uniformed official.

The guard searched him.

"What is this?" he said, discovering the valuable envelope inside the traveler's coat pocket.

"The documents of my transfer."

The guard opened the envelope, pulling out several papers, which he examined hastily.

"Proceed," he barked as he returned them.

Stuffing the sheets back inside, he pocketed the envelope, got in the car, and sped past the border and into Poland.

The would-be bearded farmer breathed a sigh of relief. At the first opportunity, he would replace his personal documents with other papers so as to eliminate any incriminating links between himself and his contact.

As many borders as he had crossed in his life, the experience always made his heart pound a little more rapidly than he enjoyed. Especially, since he would do it again tomorrow at another border station, when he had to cross back *into* the Soviet Union.

Well, he thought, very soon he would cross that hated border for the last time, never to return. Then *he* would be the "package" to be transferred safely to Berlin. But not until he was satisfied he had done all that was in his power to ensure the future safety of his people.

3

Secret Police

• • •

THE ROOM WAS NEITHER SPACIOUS NOR LUXURIOUS. ITS Spartan appointments fit to perfection the objective to which its occupant was dedicated.

Plain walls, grey paint, drab carpet, and uncomfortable chairs comprised what might sarcastically have been termed the "decor" of the office where the section chief of the East German Secret Police made his headquarters.

Most of the work of the *Stasi* did not occur in offices but rather in back alleys, on street corners, in homes and offices and factories and wherever else its feared and dreaded agents could gather and extort the information they sought against anyone considered an enemy of the state.

The door behind the chief opened.

Brisk footsteps crossed the floor. The chief turned as his assistant approached him.

"*Mein Herr*," said the younger of the two men, "an informant has just alerted me to a possible exchange involving the smuggling of information between some of the people we have been interested in."

"Jews?"

The young man nodded.

"A troublesome lot. One would think they would have learned by now. Where is the handoff supposed to occur?"

"Somewhere in Poland."

"Poland! How am I supposed to monitor a whole country that size? Let *your* people deal with it. Why do you bring it to me?"

"He says it concerns information that is coming to Berlin—important information."

"I see," mumbled the chief, pausing to allow his thoughts to wander in a new vein. Only two days ago Moscow had ordered them to double their surveillance on all known connections between Russian and German Jews. There was damaging evidence attempting to be passed from Russia to Berlin that could prove extremely compromising to several higher-ups at the Kremlin. It must be intercepted at all costs, they had said. The order came from the highest possible sources.

There must be a connection between that and this most recent information, thought the chief. Here was an opportunity to gain favor, if he could personally foil the delivery of whatever it was the Kremlin was worried about.

"Yes, perhaps then we ought to see what might be done on our end," he said thoughtfully to the young man, pausing once more.

"Get one of our men familiar with the Polish connections on it immediately," he went on. "Who do we have in that sector?"

The young man answered.

"A Pole . . . hmm, I don't suppose it can be helped at this stage. But I don't want to take any chances. Go out there yourself if you have to. If there is anything going on, I want to know about it. I'll see what I can find out through my contacts here in the city."

"Yes, *mein Herr.*"

"In the meantime," added the chief, turning to his desk and picking up a single sheet of paper, which he handed to his assistant, "there are some reports I want you to draw up the moment you return . . . on several individuals."

The young man glanced over the sheet.

"I need the complete files," the chief went on, "so utilize . . . ah, whatever techniques of persuasion you may require to obtain the information. Most of them should be on file with the Bureau of Records. It only remains for us to, shall we say, *acquire* them, even should we have to go through unofficial channels to do so."

"I understand."

"They will hopefully shed light on our ongoing search for the woman I have spoken of."

"I am still looking into the lead you gave me last week as well."

"Good. These new files on several men and women whose names have recently come to my attention may have just the connections we need. It is of the utmost importance that she be located."

4
Warsaw Newsstand

. . .

WARSAW WAS NOT A FRIENDLY CITY DURING THESE UNCERtain times. She had only been here twice before, once for a meeting with the rabbi, and two years ago to personally escort a small band of Jews through the network and to the safety of West Berlin.

There was always some danger this far from her own surroundings. And for some reason, on this day she was more nervous than usual.

She had the odd sensation of having been followed.

Karin glanced again at her watch. It was 4:12.

She had waited long enough. Something was wrong. She was certain this was the right place. Why hadn't he come?

Heart pounding, and still with the uncomfortable feeling that unwelcome eyes were upon her, she stepped away from the building and began walking down the sidewalk.

There was the newsstand just ahead.

She had been watching it, but there had been no activity. She stopped and absently asked the vendor for a paper.

Suddenly her eyes were opened. There, less than a meter from her, was the man she had been waiting for all this time.

Involuntarily her mouth opened in would-be greeting.

"Shh," murmured the vendor under his breath as he saw her about to exclaim. "Take the paper calmly."

She did so.

The portentous drop had been made.

Doing her best to keep tears from overflowing her eyes at the sight of her old friend, she dug in her pocket and handed him a few coins.

"I am sorry," the man said in reply, speaking barely above a whisper, "but you must not tarry."

"Would to God there was more time!" she replied.

"One day there will be time for all. Give her my love."

"You may be assured I will!"

"Godspeed, my dear friend."

Slowly she moved away from the newsstand, though she could not tear her swimming eyes from him, then finally turned abruptly away and continued on down the sidewalk, clutching the paper he had given her. The two of them had begun this work together, yet sometimes their self-imposed constraints could be so cruel. She had to remind herself that the cause was more important than her own personal feelings.

Sometimes she wondered what kind of a life she had carved out for herself. Mistrust was the stock-in-trade of her existence. There were so many—even Americans—whom she could not trust. Those of her people who possessed contacts at the British and American embassies in the West had to walk warily, for even in those bastions of freedom there were those who were unsympathetic to this fringe cause among all the world's more significant ills.

This is a weary life I have, Karin thought. *What happened to the girl I once was?*

She reached her car a block away and got in. It would not start. One more advantage to the communist system, she thought—everything was old, and nothing worked more than half the time.

She got back out, wondering what to do. Her uncertainty, however, was short-lived. A man and woman were happening by. He had seen her attempt and now came forward to assist her, while the woman looked on dispassionately.

A short push and the car sputtered to life. She stopped, thanked the man with a wave and greeting through the open window of the car door, then drove off.

Perhaps, thought Karin, she had been too quick to judge mankind untrustworthy.

It was not until she was in her car once more and safely speeding along the two-lane road back the way she had come that the sight of the face at the newsstand returned with poignancy to her memory.

He looked too old, she thought. *What burdens must he be carrying?*

Now at last she allowed her tears to flow. But even then they came only in a trickle. Living under the Communist shadow not only took away one's freedom, it also dried one's tears.

In truth, there was not much left to cry for.

• • •

Several hours later a phone rang piercingly in the evening stillness. It was late, and all the adjacent offices were quiet.

He had been expecting this call.

Even if there had been no business to detain him, he still might have been here. He had nothing to go home for. There was little in his existence that could be called a personal life.

The section chief grabbed the phone and listened intently.

"Why did your man miss the drop?" he asked at length. By the tone of his voice he was obviously far from pleased.

Again he listened as his assistant related the circumstances of the incident as best he understood it. Slowly his face reddened into the color of rage.

"The fool waited for *two* people to appear simultaneously! Did it not occur to him that the newsman himself could have been a plant!"

With extreme effort he forced himself to pay attention yet one more time.

"Describe the woman," he barked.

Silence.

"And then . . . ?

"The imbecile did what?!" he exploded. "The fool should have followed the girl, not continued to watch the stand!"

Another brief pause.

"If she hesitated and they appeared to exchange words, then that *was* the drop! Especially if a newspaper traded hands . . . how could he have been so stupid to miss it! Get a full description and do your best to locate either one of them. Although I doubt there'll be any trail left to follow by this time!"

He slammed down the phone, cursing as he did the moronic people they sometimes had to use.

As he paced about the room, the brief description he had just heard of the newsman's likely accomplice began to play tricks around the edges of his brain.

It couldn't be, he thought. His overexcited imagination must be mixing the various threads of his secretive endeavors.

Before jumping to any premature conclusions, he had better wait to see what he could discover from the new files after Galanov returned from Warsaw.

He turned, walked back to his desk, and pulled out the bottom drawer. From it he withdrew a half-empty bottle of scotch and a glass. He poured out a generous portion, then swallowed it in one gulp.

Fools! he muttered to himself, then sat down and poured another.

. . .

Arriving at her apartment the next evening, Karin Duftblatt's first thought was to hide the manila envelope that had been wadded inside the newspaper she had brought across western Poland here to East Berlin.

This was the most dangerous time in any mission: possessing valuable information until she could get it safely transferred into the right hands. She would pass it along two days from now, after her day at the office.

Yesterday *Poland* . . . today her home in *East Berlin* . . . tomorrow she would return to her work in *West Berlin*—how long could she go on living in such varied and diverse worlds?

Every day as she twice crossed the border separating this divided city, the emotional fabric of her being stretched nearly to the limits of its tolerance. Would the day arrive when it would tear across her own soul and finally rip it apart, as the line had split this city?

Would she one day reach the border and find something rising up within her crying out, "I can be a divided woman no longer"?

What was she thinking?!

She was tired. This line of thought could do nothing but depress her.

It had been a long and exhausting two days. All she needed was some sleep.

Slowly she began to get ready for bed. She lay down on the bed and gently eased her head onto the pillow.

Tired as she was, however, sleep eluded her.

Her thoughts returned again, not to the hubbub of life in West Berlin that she would face again tomorrow, but to the envelope she would deliver in two days.

Why had she not looked inside it before now? Sometimes lately she found herself not even wanting to know. Yet . . . she *had* to know.

Especially now. This might finally be what would get the world's attention.

She rose and retrieved the envelope from its hiding place.

She opened it and peered inside.

Only a few nondescript papers, laundry lists, and receipts that had replaced the rabbi's identification documents after he was safely inside Poland.

Gently she felt about, running her fingers along its inside creases.

Ah, just as she suspected, a hidden flap.

She folded it back, feeling inside. Her fingers pulled out two photographs.

The sight was unmistakable and sickening, even by the dim bulb of the light on her nightstand. Her stomach lurched and she had to turn away momentarily.

Naked bodies in heaps.

The piles of clothes nearby were of unmistakable ethnic origin. Several men stood by, one of whom she recognized. Despite the passage of years, the whole world would know that face!

The other she thought she had seen before too, but she couldn't be sure, nor could she affix a specific date to the memory. What a grisly and hideous smile on the unknown man's face!

In the distance, the road sign was unmistakable: Moscow 57 km.

This was more explosive than anything that had ever fallen into their hands before!

Slowly she replaced the contents of the envelope, rehid it, and returned to bed. It was time she began making preparations for tomorrow's transition back into the dull routine of her *other* life.

5

A New Era

. . .

A CLICKING FOOTFALL ALONG THE CONCRETE SIDEWALK echoed wearily in the morning chill.

The pace, though rhythmic, felt lethargic, echoing a listless cadence that contrasted with the surrounding urban bustle. The metronome of its beat had been turned down rather too slow to match stride with the crisp tempo of city life with which it seemed utterly disassociated.

There was public transportation Karin could have taken. But the walk was only two kilometers on this side, perhaps a little more. And, notwithstanding the spiritless appearance of her carriage, it was a trip she enjoyed making on foot. She felt greatly refreshed after her night's sleep, and the morning walk to her job in the western sector always made her thoughtful, though in a weary sort of way.

That impersonal thing people called *life* had not been especially kind—to her or anyone on the other side—and in truth had nearly worn her former natural radiant optimism to the bone. Fatalism had not quite set in, as it had for so many of her unfortunate comrades, although holding out hope for a better life became increasingly futile with the passing of each grey, unchanging day into the next. Most had nothing to live for, caught in the weary, purposeless cycle of merely *going on*. The dulled expression of their countenances gave visible proof that the human spirit—notwithstanding that it thrived as always among the more fortunate in the West, and was once so alive in these people—was here, degree by degree, man by man, woman by woman, child by child, slowly dying to all that had once seemed good and worth living for.

As she walked along in the cold morning air, however, plain scarf pulled over her hair, well-worn coat tight around her shoulders, Karin Duftblatt was yet enough a believer in what was true *Life* not to be altogether despondent with her lot. She well knew what the upward flying sparks signified, and she knew she had it far better than some.

She held a reasonably purposeful job in the Agency for the Aged, a job she liked even though her secret work managed to take most of the pay she received for it. It was just as well, for the government placed so many restrictions on what they could and couldn't buy with western-earned wages, that, along with taxes, it was hardly worth it. The hypocrisy of the Communist regime revealed itself in its willingness to allow its people to cross into the western sector to work, while its leaders dealt with the higher wages paid by the "evil" capitalistic system in the simplest of all possible ways—by devising ever more clever ways to keep the excess for themselves.

What gave her purpose in the midst of the greyness were her other responsibilities: night work, weekend work, middle-of-the-night work—the kind of work that had taken her to Poland for the last two days. It brought in no deutsche marks from either the Deutsche Demokratische Republic (DDR) of the east or the Bundes Republik Deutschland (BRD) of the west. But it was yet more urgent than helping the elderly of West Germany. The fact that it was clandestine increased the danger but in no way lessened its importance. It kept her far too busy trying to save life much less worry about the state of her own. If what the moviemakers and novelists of the West considered "happiness" had not been her allotted portion, it would accomplish nothing to lament that fact.

The dream had ended for her sixteen years ago. There were no more fairy tales in this part of the world.

Das Märchen lived on here, however, on all sides of her as she walked. Such was clear, not just from the lights and activity, the sounds of traffic and industry and commerce, the new buildings rising daily, and the constant construction and lavish wealth being poured into the city's future. Nor was it evident merely in the pace of life in the western two-thirds of this divided city, which was almost frenetic in the tumult of its twenty-four-hour-a-day madcap rush to reassert itself as one of Europe's most progressive and modern metropolises.

Everywhere were evidences that modernity had arrived at this place and that from the bitterness of defeat would rise prosperity, glamour, and even, they might hope, leadership again in the community of the world's nations.

Foreign visitors to Berlin gazed at such external signs with wondering awe that such a thorough transformation could have been accomplished in so few years. Out of the ashes and rubble to which Allied bombs had reduced the last Nazi stronghold in 1945 had emerged what the Bonn government called *Wirtschaftswunder,* or the postwar "economic miracle," taking rather more credit upon itself for the success than even George Marshall and his European Recovery Plan, a monstrous financial foundation already fading from sight in the new self-affirming West German consciousness. The subtle art of persuasion upon a new generation of Germans was even now at work. (The *other* side used "propaganda"; in Bonn events and developments of the last twenty-five years were merely "interpreted" on its own behalf in an increasingly favorable light. Revisionist history was quick to be written when the healing of a nation's psyche depended upon it.)

To a German, however, who was born after the War to End All Wars, raised during the tranquil period between it and the war which followed, came to adulthood under the Nazis, and now lived out that adulthood under the long and cruel Bolshevik shadow from the east, there was more at work here than the mere economic triumph of American dollars.

Karin Duftblatt's inner sight beheld, not new streets and buildings and highways and parks and libraries and agencies, but rather a reassertion of the quintessential ingredient of *Germanness* within those who walked the street beside her—*energy* . . . vigor, pride, even a certain arrogance toward a world that would never keep them down for long.

All about them was proof that things could and did turn out well in the end. Even a holocaust did not last forever. There *were* happy endings to life's tragedies, even ones so bitter as that, and they had brought about this happy ending substantially themselves. Their hard work and determined spirit had triumphed, as they always did. They now lived out the gratifying ending to a nightmare that was becoming easier and easier to forget had ever happened at all.

Germany was Germany again! To call oneself a *German* was once more a thing of pride, to which their sprightly, vigorous, and energetic gait gave ample testimony.

When one gazed upon this rebuilt island of a city, one saw in its people fortitudinous mettle, a timbre of confidence, spunk, tenacity, and a puissance in everything about how they bore themselves. Only one from the other side—one such as Karin Duftblatt—whose veins pulsed with the same Teutonic blood of the ages, could feel the irony in such countenance of energy in those all about her, almost despising it and yet lusting to lay an equal claim to it. Longing had to share the emotional stage equally with the caustic anguish of having been ill-used by the American, British, French, and Russian authors of this fairy tale, which had resulted in wealth and opportunity for some, endless drudgery for others. Even worse was the gnawing sense of having been forgotten by their German brothers and sisters on the western side of this new jigsaw-puzzle Germany.

Those who crossed back and forth daily from the bleak and quiet side each came to terms in his or her own way with their lot. But the ache of buried pain was evident on their faces.

All were separated from one another, severed from their kinsmen, detached from the commonality of their blood and heritage, cut off from their spiritual roots . . . separated from themselves.

The undercurrent of fragmentation persisted. No one, however, could comfortably look at it, talk about it, or even think about it. It was a new era, they tried to convince themselves—time to cast the gaze forward, not back.

With each passing year this schism in the national German psyche grew wider, deepening the schizophrenia of envy and bitterness between the two halves of the collective German consciousness.

● ● ●

The hour was 7:50 A.M.

Karin Duftblatt arrived at length in front of the six-story brick building housing the office of her daytime activities. She engaged none of the others present in conversation, but rode the elevator up to her floor in silence.

6
Memories from Long Ago

. . .

KARIN DUFTBLATT WALKED BACK ALONG POTSDAMER-
strasse toward Potsdamer Platz and the border crossing by which she
would reenter the eastern sector.

Evening had come. Another day of work was behind her.

The city she left behind still resonated with an atmosphere of
vibrancy, and its activity would last long into the evening, continuing
in some spots all night long.

It was a metamorphosis she had to move through twice daily, and
she had done so for more than a dozen years, emerging every
morning from out of the past, spending the day surrounded by the
urgent pace of the West, only to find herself returning at day's end to
the listless, hope-denying weariness of the East.

The portion of the city she now entered, though known by the
same name, may as well have been located on another continent, or
come from another century. Truly it was a city of another time.
Between the one end of her day's walk and the other yawned a gulf,
not merely of years, but seemingly of eons. For the contrast was
between the new and the old, the living and the dead.

As she made her way eastward along Leipzigerstrasse, no voices, no
sounds of life, few other pedestrians met either her gaze or her ear.
What sounds could be heard of automobiles mostly came distantly
from behind her. Here and there a storefront, closed for the evening,
boasted nothing of interest. There were no taxis or buses, no parks,
little grass growing around houses or buildings, few flowers or trees.

The air was still, vacant of life.

Though others, like Karin, likewise made their way home, either from a day in West Berlin or from some work nearby, they did so methodically and quietly, as if in this part of the city one might be imprisoned for making too much noise—an observation not altogether without basis in fact.

Indeed, legalities here, like activity and business and everything else, functioned with different rules and on a different plane altogether than in the West. One could not be too careful. The Gestapo may have been long gone, but the secret police, known as the *Stasi,* had taken its place, and the difference between the two was not easy for an ordinary citizen to discern. There were also the *Vopos,* or so-called people's policemen, though, as in the case of the *Stasi,* there was no mistaking whose side they were really on.

The most singular distinction between the Berlin of the West, where Karin spent her days, and the Berlin of the East, which was her home and where she spent the rest of her time, was a visual and auditory one. In the East there had been no Stalin Plan, no Khrushchev Plan, to rebuild, but only Moscow's design to dominate and control and exercise its power with tactics of fear and repression.

The Russian sector of Berlin looked much as it had in 1945 when its tanks and troops had rolled in from Poland to join the Americans and British. Piles of bricks and rubble still lay strewn about unmoved. The streets had been cleared, but dozens and dozens of half-buildings loomed as silent sentinels in the evening sky, reminders of a war long past but ever present in the memory. No evidence existed anywhere within her vision of a board, a brick that was new. Not so much as a fresh stretch of concrete underfoot or a brightly painted fence met the eye. The streets were pitted and full of holes, the sidewalks along them cracked and sprouting weeds. What buildings had survived had been put to use as they were. The rest of the city still looked like a quiet battlefield after the bodies had been removed and everyone on both sides had gone home.

The somber quiet, the bombed-out relics of a time long since gone but visually as fresh as when fire and smoke and the sounds of planes and explosions filled the air, all sent her mind back, as they often did, to the last days of the war.

It must have been terrible to have been here in the city, she thought. Not that it had been pleasant in the country! She had heard reports of what it had been like in their neighborhood. How lucky she had been to get out before the final darkness had fallen over the land.

Once she had considered hatred an emotion impossible to feel. Her natural sanguine buoyancy had always been able to see the good in any situation, in any person.

Her faith had been shaken during that year in exile, without that one whom she had always depended upon for so much. The equilibrium of belief on which she had always relied had been convulsed to its core. If her belief had survived, it had not exactly done so intact.

She had changed. A realism had entered her being sixteen years ago that she despised but couldn't help. Whatever her youthful ideals and optimism had once been, they were but distant memories. She had discovered that she too was capable of hatred.

She could not deny it—she had *hated* them, those of her own blood, hated the barbaric inhumanity they had allowed themselves to become part of.

And now, though the intensity of those emotions had moderated, there remained enough effects from it directed toward their new oppressors to worry her.

What kind of Christian was she if she could not forgive? Would she ever again know the peace and happiness of her youth, or were they gone forever? She went about what she saw as her duty. She tried to help people, and indeed they had helped thousands. But could she forgive? She didn't know if she would ever be capable of it.

She had asked herself such questions, and hundreds like them, a thousand times.

And the biggest question of all. Was *he* still alive?

She was confident he had survived the final year of the war. But had he survived Stalin's quiet purging since? That purge was the object of their efforts, what she hoped the photographs still hidden in her apartment would expose. Yet even they knew so little about it. Once the Russian shadow had engulfed them, secrecy and darkness ruled the land.

It was the question that had plagued her for sixteen years. Even as she carried on the private work of *Das Netzwerk,* the inner turmoil of her own personal quest remained unresolved. She could not rest until she knew for certain. Yet she could not bring danger upon the others, or upon him.

Where could she turn for help?

She was alone. The system had become so polluted with informants and KGB spies and *Stasi* that she didn't know whom to trust. Nothing had changed since the war. The most inviting smiles could hide the most sinister motives.

And if they discovered her true identity, the entire network at this end of the lifeline could unravel. Khrushchev was called a moderate, but she still didn't trust him. Especially after what she had seen last night. Whatever the propaganda said about a new tolerance these days in Russia, she was not deceived. Stalin's persecution would never be altogether over for those of God's people living under the dark cloud of the Kremlin.

Coming to no more conclusions than she did every evening, she arrived at length at her small apartment, unlocked the door, and went inside.

7

Face from the Past

• • •

THE NEXT MORNING SHE ABSENTLY WALKED ONE OF THE same routes she did every day, turning at length onto Kurfürstenstrasse.

It was difficult not to feel things she did not like to feel toward those whom fate had smiled on and who, by sheer chance of geography, were fortunate enough to call themselves *West* Berliners. The daily metamorphosis was accompanied by a daily battle to quiet the ugly head of envy constantly ready to rise in her bosom.

They felt like strangers. They spoke her language. Their veins pulsed with the same Aryan blood of the centuries. But there had already become two distinct and separate peoples occupying this ageless Celtic empire, long ago so fragmented, finally united under Bismarck, and now fractured again. The scission between them was the ancient cleavage of the ages—that between East and West, between the past and the future, between light and darkness.

Thus absorbed in her thoughts, Karin Duftblatt made her way along the busy sidewalk toward the building where she spent the working hours of unreality in the West.

Absently her eyes moved about the activity around her, seeing but half-consciously, hazily inattentive to those brushing by her along the crowded walk.

Suddenly her heart leapt!

Her glance had fallen upon a face crossing the street in front of her, whose owner then fell into pace with the stream of sidewalk traffic. Her entire frame snapped into focus, all the fog clearing from her brain in an instant. The envelope she carried inside her coat for this afternoon's transfer was suddenly as distant from her thoughts as the men Russia was sending into space.

She could not believe her eyes!

It . . . it couldn't be!

With faltering step she stumbled forward, gazed fixed on the figure moving now ahead of her. All she could see was the back of the shoulders and head.

Unconsciously she began to hurry, gradually breaking into an uneasy run, bumping through the crowded morning throng. If only she could catch up . . . see the face again!

Her heart pounded within her.

Already her mouth was dry at the very thought of finding the right words.

He was just ahead. . . . She had nearly caught him now. . . .

He turned and strode quickly up the steps of a governmental building.

Karin followed, running now.

He reached the door.

She opened her mouth to call out—but only a dry croaking silence came from her lips.

The man opened the door and briskly disappeared inside.

Karin stopped at the bottom of the steps, eyes staring at the door as it closed. She stood immobile, heart still racing, eyes wide, not knowing whether or not to follow inside.

Suddenly she remembered her appearance.

Though they were the best she had, her clothes were old. The scarf and coat were hand-me-downs from the forties.

She could not go in there. What would they think? They would throw her out for a tramp!

Slowly—dejected, frustrated, bewildered, uncertain—she backed away, then continued toward her own place of employment. She tried to tell herself that she had been mistaken, that it had only been a delusion, a fancy in the midst of her reflections about the past and the war.

Throughout the morning she did her best to convince herself that her brain had played her a cruel trick. Hallucinations were common among war survivors. Yet she could not keep the incident from playing itself over and over in her memory.

As it did, the assurance grew stronger and stronger that it had not been a phantasm of wishful thinking at all!

She could not keep her mind on her work. The distraction grew to a feverish pitch by midafternoon.

8

Forgotten Appointment

* * *

AT FOUR FORTY-FIVE KARIN BEGAN CLEARING HER WORK space in readiness. At five till five she put the last of her things away and went to find her coat. If they relieved her of her job for her mental absentness, it was a risk she was willing to take!

At exactly five o'clock, she slipped from the office, then ran for the stairs. She would not even wait for the elevator!

She bolted down the four flights, hurried through the lobby and outside, then tore along the crowded sidewalk of Kurfürstenstrasse, the gathering scent and feel of approaching evening in the air.

An observer would never take her for an Easterner now!

Her eyes glowed with a fire they hadn't felt in years. Her footfall was precise and quick. With rapid, purposeful stride the equal of any West German, she hurried back to the Bundesamt building. She took a position about half a block away, from which she could see the doorway and steps clearly . . . and there stood waiting.

She glanced down at her watch. It was eleven minutes past five.

Her heart beat wildly, even after the exertion from the fast walk had subsided.

What would she say!

What if she went up to him and began to talk . . . and had made a mistake?

Worse yet, what if it *was* him and he didn't remember!

He might not even be in this building at all! He might have only gone in for five minutes. Or if he was inside, maybe he wouldn't come out for hours.

This was a fool's errand, she thought to herself. What was she thinking? There were no fairy tales! This was 1961 . . . she lived in the Communist sector . . . twenty years had gone by!

She turned and began walking away. She was behaving like a little girl! It was time to go home and forget all about this morning!

Her footsteps, reluctant and slow now, could only take her half a block in the opposite direction before they stopped.

She had to know . . . she had to find out!

She returned quickly to the same spot, eyes again fixed on the building ahead. What did it matter if she made a fool of herself! What was there to lose—her brain would snap if left forever in doubt whether she'd been dreaming, or if—

The door of the Bundesamt opened!

Feverishly her eyes scanned the four or five persons who came out and walked down the steps. They walked toward her. She backed to the edge of the sidewalk as the three men and two women passed.

No, he was none of them.

She sent her eyes back toward the door. It opened again. An elderly gentleman emerged. He walked down the sidewalk in the opposite direction.

For several minutes the door to the building showed no activity.

She glanced at her watch.

Five-twenty-seven.

It was no use. It was much too late. What had she been thinking! Grown women couldn't survive on daydreams. What kind of fool was she to think—

Five-twenty-seven!

Suddenly the significance of the hands on her watch exploded upon her brain!

Instantly she spun around and ran back along the sidewalk in the direction she had come twenty minutes earlier, heedless of the elbows and shoulders bumping against her as she veered recklessly through the afternoon's heavy pedestrian traffic.

How could she have committed such a lapse!

So much depended on her, yet she had forgotten altogether about the photographs in her coat. She had been scheduled to pass them to her West Berlin contact at precisely twenty minutes past five!

Everything was carefully planned down to the last detail. This had been the arrangement they had used for years, ever since they had each decided to take up separate residences in the two halves of the city.

She herself had been the one to establish the ground rules: After three minutes, if the other had not come, leave the site. Watch from a safe vantage point half a block away or across the street for another three minutes, just in case. If after six minutes there was no sign of the other, then leave—quickly and immediately. If something had gone wrong, then only danger could result from waiting any longer.

She reached the cafe, sweating profusely. She slowed to a walk, breathing in deeply.

She walked inside, attracting a few stares by her disheveled appearance, and cast her gaze hurriedly around. The clock on the wall confirmed what she already knew—five-thirty-six.

Much too late!

She turned, left the place, and began the long walk home, disconsolate at her blunder.

She felt inside her coat.

At least the photographs were still safe, though by now they should have been on their way into hands that would know how best to use them.

Chastising herself as she went, she knew there was no alternative but to make the attempt again at the soonest available opportunity.

How soon that would be, however, she didn't know.

9

Meeting

• • •

IT WAS THE MOST SLEEPLESS AND MENTALLY TORMENT-
ing night she had spent in years.

When she did manage to doze off, her slumber was interrupted by
weird phantasms of half-recognizable faces . . . of her contact with
packet in hand and arm outstretched, running toward her but never
reaching her . . . of two men standing watching her and laughing at the
futility of it . . . and of dead corpses piled high, but where no grave
could be found to allow the bodily half of their souls at last to find rest.

She crawled out of bed the following morning, exhausted but
determined to put the previous day behind her.

She would hide the envelope securely in her apartment. She
would go to work by a different route so as not to pass the Bundesamt
building at all. There was no sense stirring *those* memories into
hallucinating daydreams again. On her way home she would use a pay
telephone to try to make contact again and confirm a new time to
meet.

The day passed drearily.

Try as she might, she could not stop the flow of memories.

It was ridiculous, she told herself at least fifteen times. It could not
possibly have been him!

When five o'clock came, she had again worked herself into an
excitable state against her own volition.

She could not help herself!

When she exited the building, her footsteps began hurrying by
yesterday's exact route along Kurfürstenstrasse. The need to locate a
telephone to reach her colleague had been completely forgotten.

Just as she had done the day before, she slowed as she reached the Bundesamt building, then stopped and took up a position about a third of a block from its entrance.

Heart pounding, she watched as now one, now another left the building, scanning each one with feverish eyes of anticipation.

Oh, but it couldn't be, she kept saying to herself—what am I doing here!

Yet she was powerless to move. She had to know!

Was this pulsating of the blood in her veins the result of her exhaustion over the last few days, from the lack of sleep, from the danger and intrigue over the matter of the photographs? Or was it from seeing someone she thought was—

The door opened.

A man stepped out, descended the steps, and headed toward her.

She gasped, squinting to focus the intensity of her gaze.

He came closer, then passed not more than a meter away.

What was she thinking? It had been a perfect stranger! Her brain was playing so many tricks on her that she was having delusions about reality!

This was idiotic. She was going home.

With resolution she began walking again along the street toward the Bundesamt. Her way would lead her past it and on toward East Berlin.

She could not help glancing one more time up the steps toward the door.

Suddenly she caught her breath.

The door opened again.

A man stepped out.

It was the *same* navy blue three-piece suit she had seen yesterday morning!

She stopped, involuntarily clutching her chest as if the action would produce more air in her suddenly constricted lungs.

What a handsome figure the man cut! Oh, but he was so much older, with grey around the edges of his well-groomed brown hair.

It couldn't--

No, but . . . it . . . it *had* to be him!

She could see his face now! Yes, the similarity was total . . . it couldn't . . .w . . . what if . . . but—it *had* to be!

He walked down the steps. He was coming her way!

Her heart pounded violently! What if . . . but he would never remember her! Why . . . why hadn't he written all those years . . . why now!

Oh, God, what should I say? she thought. *Oh, what a mess I look . . . and him so dashing and impressive! This was a mistake!*

In a torment of conflicting emotions, she suddenly spun around to avoid being seen, then turned to the edge of the sidewalk, one hand covering her face.

She stood, immobile as Lot's wife, her back toward the Bundesamt, quivering as she heard the footsteps on the concrete approaching her position amid the late-afternoon flow of men and women returning home after their day's work.

She felt a presence pass along the sidewalk behind her. Her whole body grew hot with the emotion of disbelieving certainty.

As the sound of the footfall now receded behind her in the other direction, her hand fell from her face. She slowly turned and left her momentarily self-imposed cocoon.

Without consciously willing it, she followed, staring as one in a trance at the back of the form some ten meters in front of her. So drained was she already from the emotion the incident had cost her that she could not keep up the brisk pace. Within two blocks she had fallen thirty meters behind.

He approached one of the buildings attached to the American consulate and began jogging even more rapidly up the wide concrete steps of the entryway.

With great effort she quickened her step, then tried to cry out. But her throat was dry, and she succeeded in producing no more than a rasping choke.

Suddenly, ahead of her, she saw the man pause. Something had arrested his stride, compelling him to look behind him.

Immediately she stopped, though this time she did not glance away.

Why had he stopped? she wondered.

He was standing there now, in the middle of the steps. He had seen her!

His face had now gone pale as hers. A look of question and disbelief flooded his countenance.

She tried to move.

Her feet were stuck in the concrete! Her mouth struggled, but there was no voice. It was a bad dream—she could utter not even a peep!

He was walking again now, still staring at her with incredulity. He was coming straight forward!

Then he was running toward her, and a radiant knowing dawned over his face.

He stopped, only inches away, a thousand expressions of joy and wonder and disbelief passing across his face in a second.

She struggled for her tongue.

A few mumbled incoherent words reached her throat, then died. Only a tear or two found their way out from inside.

The two sets of eyes met.

They had seen those depths before. Nothing could make them forget.

Several long seconds passed.

"Sabina!" he whispered. "Is . . . is it *really* you?"

She melted in laughter and weeping all at once, her tongue and tears loosed together.

Suddenly, neither knew how, they were in each other's arms, both weeping. The ratty old scarf had fallen, and tenderly he stroked her greying hair.

"Matthew," she murmured. "I . . . I was so afraid you might not remember."

"Not remember *you,* Sabina," he said. "I have not forgotten. I could *never* forget."

"Neither could I," she breathed softly, then laid her head contentedly against his chest, feeling safer and more at peace than she had felt in sixteen years.

10

Together Again

• • •

NEVER HAD TWO HOURS PASSED SO QUICKLY.

It was seven-thirty, the evening still balmy though gradually chilling. Matthew McCallum and she whom he had met as Sabina von Dortmann at a garden party in this same city twenty-three years earlier sat together across the table of a sidewalk cafe.

The light of dusk would not descend for several hours and, even in this northern region in late June, would never utterly extinguish the hues of the sunset until they gradually gave way to the early sunrise a few hours later. Neither of the two were heeding the passage of time, however, nor the gathering chill in the air any more than they had paid much attention to the light supper they had finished long before. They had been talking, sometimes rapidly, occasionally their words broken by lengthy silences, and had barely managed to scratch the surface of catching up on the years.

They now sat sipping coffee, but their thoughts were occupied only with one another.

"Oh, Matthew," sighed Sabina at length, "you cannot imagine how good it feels to talk like this again. But I fear I must not be much longer."

"Why?"

"It would not look right. There are eyes everywhere."

"Do they really regulate you so tightly?"

"Not specifically, though it is becoming tighter all the time. But I meant with neighbors, acquaintances. People watch one another."

"I've read the reports. I suppose I never personalized it."

"It is a different world over there," answered Sabina with a nod of her head toward the east. "You should know that—I still can't believe it. An attaché to President Kennedy—your dream came true!"

"My dream?"

"You always said you wanted to follow your father's footsteps into politics."

"I didn't realize I had my course set so early."

"You were a diplomat even then," laughed Sabina. "Don't you remember trying to talk us out of that trouble with Gustav, my neighbor?"

"That I could never forget," said Matthew, joining her in laughter. "I wasn't too successful, either."

"No, but you were so chivalrous and brave, protecting me from that brute."

"I don't know about that. But I agree with your assessment of the fellow."

"And from your humble beginnings, now you are an important man working for the American president."

Matthew nodded thoughtfully. "Jack's election didn't do my diplomatic career any harm," he said.

"What exactly do you do for your president?"

"Mostly I've been involved in the negotiations and discussions over Khrushchev's proposed independent peace treaty with the DDR. I'm working not exactly *for* our State Department, but in conjunction with them, sort of a private liaison and troubleshooter and mender of fences. Essentially I do anything the president or the secretary of state want me to do."

"Is there going to be a treaty?"

"You mean between Russia and the DDR—I certainly hope not. It would seriously threaten the free status of West Berlin."

"I don't see how."

"It would legitimize a divided Germany. Adenauer's goal, and ours, is the eventual unification of the two Germanys in a free and democratic state. Everyone, from Chancellor Adenauer to Berlin mayor Willie Brandt to the British, and of course we Americans, are all agreed that Khrushchev's proposal will doom our attempts to keep discussions open toward unification."

They were silent a moment.

"I really think I ought to go home," said Sabina. "Thank you for the supper, Matthew."

"May I see your work papers?" he asked.

Uncertain why he had asked, Sabina hesitated a moment. He saw a strange expression cross her face.

"Never mind, if you have some objection," he said. "I was only curious."

"No . . . no, it's all right," Sabina said, then opened her purse and a moment later handed Matthew her identity card and work permit. He glanced them over hurriedly.

"Karin Duftblatt," he said with a puzzled expression. "Who is this?"

"I'm afraid it's me. Karin Duftblatt is my new identity."

"But why?"

The same inexplicable look crossed her face. "It's a long story, Matthew," she answered, again after a brief hesitation. "There's not time now."

"That's what you've said to half my questions all evening," he rejoined. It had not been intentional, but his voice contained a hint of frustration.

She smiled a melancholy smile but said nothing to alleviate his bewilderment.

Matthew rose from the table, paid the waiter, and they left the small cafe.

"I'll walk you to the border," he said. "You can tell me as we go."

"It's too long a story for that," she said, keeping to herself the fact that she couldn't tell him. Not yet anyway. How could she possibly know what his reaction might be to the secret life of Karin Duftblatt? Many Americans still denied there was a Jewish problem in Europe nowadays, just like their friends the West Germans. To look at the recent Jewish problem in Russia could only focus the spotlight all the more grimly on Germany's past—a reluctance of accountability shared by both West and East Germany.

"Then I'll see you tomorrow. I insist on hearing every one of your so-called long stories."

At the words Sabina's heart fluttered, while her brain told her she must exercise caution.

"I didn't dare hope you would want to see me again," she said.

"Are you kidding! Sabina, I've been waiting—what has it been—nineteen years, to see you again!"

"But look at me. I'm . . . I'm just a poor working woman now. I'm not the kind of woman—"

"Sabina, please," interrupted Matthew.

"But just look at how you're dressed. Everything's changed now. You're an important man. You shouldn't be seen with me."

"Now that I've found you," insisted Matthew, "I'm not about to be satisfied with one short visit."

"But wouldn't you be embarrassed—"

"Sabina, Sabina," said Matthew, cutting her off again, with a peremptory but tender tone. "Embarrassment could not be further from my mind. Meet me at that same building, the consulate, tomorrow at five," he said.

"I don't get off work until five."

"Then a few minutes after. I'll wait for you. We'll have something to eat again, and then plan for the weekend."

"Weekend?"

"Of course! I have the whole weekend free."

"But, Matthew, you don't have to—"

"*Sabina,*" said Matthew, interrupting her yet a third time. "I *want* to see you again."

She nodded and looked away. They were nearly to the border by now and walked the rest of the way in silence.

Their parting words were few, Matthew reminding her to be at the American consulate the next evening and securing for his own satisfaction the name of her place of employment.

Sabina walked the remainder of the distance to her apartment, her heart filled with thoughts and her eyes with tears that she could have explained to no one.

She hardly understood herself from what depths they had arisen within her.

It did not occur to her until much later that she had completely forgotten about the photographs.

1 1
Brief Visit

• • •

THE FOLLOWING AFTERNOON, MATTHEW AND SABINA met again for a light supper. Though their time together was brief, Sabina found herself feeling gradually more comfortable sharing and talking about things she had not thought about for years.

After ordering and talking about the next day, their conversation drifted backward in time.

Sabina was relieved Matthew did not bring up her new name again. As long as she could avoid her current activities, she didn't mind telling him anything else.

He had just asked about the war years and how it had affected her family.

Sabina was silent a long while, her countenance clearly faraway and pensive as she quickly relived the time since she had last seen Matthew. When she finally spoke, her voice sounded heavy and tired again, burdened with the weight of the intervening years.

"The war was terrible here, Matthew," she began at length. "Everything you and your father were worried about in the Nazis came true, and more. We made every effort to help those less fortunate. My father and mother dedicated themselves to trying to protect both Jews and Christians whom we could shelter, but the tide of evil was too strong. Those who helped were always in danger themselves, and finally we had to get out too."

"Get out—you mean out of the country, out of Germany?" asked Matthew.

"We were warned—"

"When?"

"It was in '44. We were warned that my father was in danger. We left *Lebenshaus* in the middle of the night. That's when my father was arrested, though mother and I made it safely to Switzerland."

Briefly she told him of the events of that fateful night, of her father's arrest, and of their journey to Switzerland.

"But you told me yesterday that your mother didn't survive the war."

"She died just as the war was ending," said Sabina sadly. "And it had nothing to do with the war, just one of those fluke viruses that came through the region. Of course medical help and doctors were in short supply, even in Switzerland. Oh, how I wished for our Dr. Abrahams during those days! Losing my father to prison and my mother's dying—it was nearly more than I could bear. Though those last hours with my mother were some of the most special hours in my life."

"What became of your friend the doctor?"

"We fear he was imprisoned and probably killed in one of the camps. He was too well known—and his name made it impossible for him to hide his Jewish blood. He was my mother's cousin—had you known that?" Sabina asked.

"No, I hadn't," answered Matthew. "You only told me your mother herself was Jewish."

"Does it bother you that I didn't tell you before?"

"Of course not. Back in those days it was not the kind of thing you told even friends."

"I was afraid you might not understand."

"You said your final hours with your mother were special?" said Matthew.

A sad smile came over Sabina's face as she thought again of the last day of her mother's life.

"Even as she was dying—and we both knew it because several others in the village had preceded her—a strength seemed to come over her. Not a physical strength, of course, but a spiritual one. It isn't that my father exactly overshadowed her, but he was such a dynamic and forceful man, and she was so lovingly content to always defer to him, that she had no desire to be other than his helpmeet. Even after Papa was arrested, for the rest of the trip down to Switzerland she trusted Rabbi Wissen and Jakob Kropf as the leaders of our little band.

"But during the year in Switzerland, especially in the rabbi's absence, others of our group, and even those in the village, including both Jews and Christians and Jakob himself, began, I think, to look to Mama in perhaps a motherly way—for help and sustenance, and even spiritual strength. My father's arrest seemed almost to elevate her to a loftier level, even in her grief. It is hard to explain, Matthew, but I came to see a stature in her face and an expression in her eyes that reminded me of Papa. When she spoke, it was like listening to Papa himself.

"I suppose it was not until that year in Switzerland that I fully realized what a depth of oneness had existed between them. Though Papa was the most outspoken and the one everyone had looked to as the spiritual guide at *Lebenshaus,* I came to realize what an equal part Mama shared in it too, though in the background."

Sabina looked away wistfully.

"You don't have to go on if you'd rather not," said Matthew.

"Oh, I want to. As sad as the memory is in one way, in another it was wonderful." Sabina laughed lightly. "Here I am telling you of my mother's death and I say it is wonderful! You must think me peculiar."

"No more so than when I first met you," rejoined Matthew. "You *are* always full of surprises!"

He glanced at his watch.

"I'm sorry, but I have to go. I've got an evening meeting in fifteen minutes."

They rose from the table and left the small cafe.

"Tomorrow morning, then," said Matthew, "as agreed?"

12

The New Regime

• • •

THE RAVAGES OF WAR MADE STRANGE BEDFELLOWS.

The unexpected fortunes of peace, however, threw together even stranger and more ill-suited allies. He would never be intimate with these people. But then intimacy was hardly the stock-in-trade of the new regime. Expediency demanded that one know where the power lay and nothing more.

So if those he secretly looked down upon were his colleagues and collaborators in this stay-alive, boot-licking business of trying to scratch your way gradually up through the system, well, it was just the latest challenge, he reflected, in a life that had had its share of them.

He had grown up despising the Russians. Now they were his cronies and his superiors. They called *him* comrade!

Sometimes he hated it. Sometimes it made him smile inside at the irony.

Comrade, indeed!

There were no "comrades" in this deadly game of loyalty roulette the Russians played. Suspicion, self-preservation, fear, and pretended allegiance to the system—they were the grease and gears that kept this bulky contraption called the "communist state" functioning, albeit inefficiently and unproductively.

All his life he had been adapting to one thing or another. Why should now be any different? First it had been his mother's doting, then his father's lofty expectations, then the demands of the Gestapo upon his whole being.

He had survived it.

He had grown rugged and hard, strapping around his character the steel coat of armor called dispassion. And it had protected him well during these bumpy postwar days when you needed some protection if you wanted to stay alive.

He looked down again and briefly scanned the papers on top of his desk.

No, there just isn't anything here, he said to himself. *Another dead end.*

Just then the door to the section chief's office opened. A crisply attired young lieutenant strode in, a brown manila folder in his hand.

"I have the dossiers you requested," he said.

"Very good, Galanov. You had, ah, no *difficulty* obtaining them?"

The young lackey betrayed the hint of a boyish though cunning smile. He appeared to be in his early twenties.

"Only those you anticipated."

"The offer was sufficient?"

"Along with the mention of the KGB, yes, he was only too happy to give me the files."

"You have looked them over?"

"Only briefly."

"Any word on the girl?"

"Which one, *mein Herr,* the woman that was seen in Warsaw, or the other whom you have—"

"Either one!" interrupted the chief angrily.

"Nyet, Comrade Schmundt."

Whatever reply left the lips of the older of the two men was lost in the sound of his fist crashing down upon the desk in front of him, sending the papers he had recently been examining flying in all directions.

The young Russian lieutenant did not ask for the words to be repeated, but stood stoically awaiting his next orders.

The chief slowly regained his composure.

"Has your Polish contact learned anything further concerning the botched surveillance earlier this week?" he asked testily.

"He interrogated witnesses in the area. Someone saw a lady we think is the same woman getting into a car. He is still in the process of investigation."

"The origin of the auto?"

"They were German plates."

"The region?"

"Berlin."

"As I thought. By now the information has probably been passed into the West. But have him continue."

"We are attempting a more thorough description of the car, and we have a number or two of the plate."

"How is it possible witnesses saw anything when your man saw nothing?"

"Apparently the woman in question was very beautiful—not the sort that Poles see every day in Warsaw. Even as poorly dressed as she was, she made an impression. There was a man who helped her get her car started who has been helpful."

The chief brooded over the information briefly, not exactly sure what it might mean. However, he kept his conjectures to himself.

"Continue to comb the area," he ordered at length. "Use whatever means you must. If we can put together a partial license number and can learn the make or model of the car, we may yet be able to regain even a cold trail."

"Yes, Comrade Schmundt. I will see that your instructions are carried out."

"Keep me informed personally. I want all reports kept between you and me, Galanov, is that clear?"

"Yes, Comrade."

"That will be all for tonight then."

1 3

Remembering *Mutti*

• • •

"WE'LL GO FOR A NICE LONG DRIVE," SAID MATTHEW THE next morning as he drove Sabina through the barren streets back toward the western part of the city in his late-model BMW with diplomatic plates.

During supper the previous evening, Matthew had said he would pick up Sabina at her apartment building in the eastern sector a little before eleven. Embarrassed that he should see where she lived, Sabina reluctantly had given him her address and the directions necessary to find it. Now that they were driving out of that part of town, Sabina was able to relax. "Do you want to know what feels good?" she said.

"What?"

"Having something to *look forward* to. It's been longer than I can remember that I felt any sense of anticipation toward something."

"Well, I was hoping for that, for both of us. I canceled all my appointments for the day."

"Matthew, can you do that?"

"I did it, so I guess I can."

"But why?"

"Because I want to spend the whole day without interruptions, with no phone and no appointments. I want to know more than just what you briefly told me last night, about your life, your father, and everything you've done since the war."

"I'm just as curious how you have spent the years," said Sabina.

"Then I'll answer your questions too," laughed Matthew. "But I *would* like to hear the whole story. Your parents occupy an important part in my life too—more than you perhaps realize, even if it was brief."

Sabina turned away, staring out the window, collecting her thoughts.

As they drove, Sabina was hardly aware of the thinning homes and buildings of West Berlin's suburbs passing by, regions of the city she had never seen.

At length she sighed and continued with the story she had begun the previous evening.

"After Mama became ill, I spent every available moment with her. We talked when she felt well enough. We spoke of Father and the things we both imagined he would have been saying to us. And when she began to have feverish spells, I would read to her from the Psalms or the Gospels."

"There was no hope for a recovery?"

"I prayed, of course. But there was nothing the doctor or anyone could do."

Matthew looked over at her. "I'm sorry. It must have been very difficult for you."

"We actually had a very rich time together those last few weeks," Sabina went on. "We talked a great deal about Papa. He could not help but be on our minds. Something would be said at a meal, and we would look at each other across the room and our eyes would meet. We both understood that we were reminded of him.

"The night before she died, I had a dream that was so lifelike. I saw Jesus walking through our garden at *Lebenshaus.* He rounded a bend in the path, walking beside the plants Papa had planted for Mama from Palestine, then disappeared. I followed along the path. But when I caught sight of his back again, there was another figure at his side, though I could see neither of their faces.

"He sensed my presence and knew the anxiety in my heart. He turned and cast upon me a tender smile, full of an expression I knew it was not my time yet to fully comprehend. Then he turned around again and walked on with the other and out of sight once more. This time I knew I could not follow.

"Gradually I drifted back to sleep.

"When I woke later, though there had been no more coherence to the image of my dreams, I was filled with a sudden sense of apprehension. I felt as though something or someone was calling to me, but I couldn't hear or tell what it was. I lay there for what seemed a long time. Then I heard Mother speak softly to me out of the darkness in the room.

"'Sabina.'

"'Yes, Mama,' I answered.

"'I dreamed your father was calling to me. He said he had something new to show me in the garden.'

"In spite of the darkness I could tell Mama was smiling. Soon she was sleeping again.

"I lay awake for a long time.

"I prayed and thought about my mother and father and all they meant to me. I finally went back to sleep once more just before dawn."

Sabina sighed and stopped. It had been taxing to remember, and she needed to rest her thoughts on the scenery for a while.

1 4

A Matriarchal Blessing

• • •

MATTHEW DROVE SOUTHWARD TOWARD LUCKENWALDE. It was better, he thought, to enjoy the countryside in that direction, rather than north, where Sabina might have been reminded too much of her old home. Once, upon leaving the city, they nearly managed to forget the overpowering Russian presence that existed over this easternmost corner of the former Third Reich.

"Do you feel comfortable finishing what you were telling me about your mother?" Matthew asked.

Sabina nodded.

"I'm sorry I got so quiet. I just needed to collect my thoughts," she sighed.

Again it was silent between them, but only for a moment.

"When I awoke the morning after my dream," she began again, "the day was well advanced. Mother was still in her bed, but she was awake.

"'I am feeling weak, Sabina,' she said softly.

"'What is it, Mama?' I asked anxiously.

"We both knew the end was near. She was so peaceful. . . .'"

Sabina's voice trailed away.

She shook her head slowly back and forth with a sigh, then glanced over at Matthew.

Sabina smiled with poignant nostalgia. Matthew could see that her eyes had begun to water.

"She called me to her bedside," Sabina went on. "I knew her time was short. I could not help crying. I had already lost a father, and I could hardly bear the thought of Mama's dying. I felt so like a little child again, so vulnerable and alone, even though we had become very close to the Kropfs and the rabbi's wife and daughters.

"I was crying. Mama reached out a frail hand from the bed and laid it on my head. 'My child,' she said, 'you mustn't think this is the end of it. Life is now ready to begin for me.'

"Oh, Matthew, I could hardly bear it!

"'Sabina,' Mama said softly after a few minutes. I could almost hear the life draining out of her voice. 'Sabina, there are things I must tell you. Our time is short.'

"'Mother, you should rest. We can talk in the morning.'

"'No, Sabina. It is time. There are things your father and I planned to tell you when you married. But we do not know where your father is—whether he is even alive. So I must give you the blessing he would have. I am confident you will see him again. When I am gone you must look for him. Tell him I have loved him so much. And that I am so grateful to him for making my life here on this earth one of such contentment and wonder. Your father is special, Sabina. Do you know why?'

"'I know, Mother. He always made every situation so meaningful and fun and rich.'

"'Do you know how he was able to do that?'

"'I never thought of why or how. That was how he was. He was just Papa.'

"'I will tell you what we learned in our long journey together. It is the secret of a contented and fulfilled life with God. It was the secret of your father's very existence. It is so simple, yet few people make the discovery. It is the life of service, Sabina. It is what Jesus taught during his time on earth. I know you have heard it many times and seen your father practice it since before you can remember. But we often miss things that are right before us. There is no other way to live, Sabina. Your father always spoke of enabling you to start a little further along the road of self-denial, so you would be able to exceed what we did.'

"'Oh, *Mutti*,' I said, 'no one could be more selfless than you and Papa!'

"For a moment Mama seemed to be tracing back memories with her mind like she might a pattern with her finger. Her eyes were closed and her breathing became so faint that I was anxious. I took her hand. The touch seemed to revive her back to the present, and she went on.

"'This is the charge I must give you. Live to serve others, Sabina. Give yourself in every way to those God puts in your path. You have within you the spirit of a long line of descendants of the children of God. That is your greatest gift and your deepest privilege. You must keep this family line alive and constantly renewing itself—if not by your own flesh and blood, then by the new children of God who will become heirs and adopted sons and daughters by your life being lived for them.'

"Mama's eyes were glowing as she spoke, conveying the intensity of how much she felt what she was saying.

"'I will remember, *Mutti*,' I said. I could feel the choking in my throat of the sob wanting to escape.

"'*Mutti,* you should rest now,' I said.

"'It is nice to hear you call me *Mutti*. That is what you called me when you were young. I can hear you calling through the halls looking for me—searching for me with your voice more than your eyes.'

"'It was always easier to make noise and let *you* find *me* than for me to find you,' I said.

"We both smiled, although it was difficult for me to smile through my tears, and for her to smile through her weakness.

"'I will treasure the things you have told me,' I said quietly.

"'There is one more thing,' Mama added. 'I hope your papa may speak to you more of these things. But I must now do my part. You know I was raised with the traditions of the Torah. So many of the old Jewish ways are still good, even for Christian Jews. Many forget in these modern times about the blessing. When a father died, he gave his blessing to his sons. So this mother will give her blessing to her daughter.'

"The sob that had been rising up finally escaped my lips. I laid my head on her hand, which I had been holding. She put her other hand on my head and stroked my hair like she did when I was young and came to cry on her lap over some trifle which would seem so large at the time.

"'I know we cry and weep and we feel sad when our loved ones leave us,' she said. 'But you must remember how happy I will be to be with our Father in heaven. And you know we will be together again, you and I and your papa. Our Father is so good, Sabina! Trust in that goodness, my daughter. I know you may grieve for me to leave. But you must not grieve *for* me.'

"She paused a moment, and then when she next spoke her voice was serious and solemn, and I imagined that I was listening to one of the Old Testament prophets.

"Her voice had been weak as she spoke, but at the same time it possessed a commanding quality.

"'You are one of the chosen, Sabina,' she said. 'Not because the Hebrew blood of our father Abraham flows in your veins, but because you are a child of almighty God. You are a Jew in the full and truest sense of the word, and a Christian because you are a follower and servant of Jesus Christ, our Messiah and the world's Messiah. You are privileged like few others, Sabina, as I myself have been.

"'This is the inheritance I leave you, my daughter. It is the inheritance of a people whose destiny is to reflect the goodness of God our Father to all the nations of the world. For such was our father Abraham called and set apart. For such did God make his covenant with him. For such was Israel set apart. And for such did our Lord Jesus live and die—that the world might know his Father, who is our God and our Friend.'

"Her voice by this time was soft and barely audible, yet she spoke with an urgency I could feel. I remember her words almost as if she had said them yesterday.

"'As this great heritage is yours,' she said, 'so is a responsibility to faithfully walk as God's woman wherever he may lead you. I have tried to do this at your father's side. Now we have had to walk apart for this last season of my life. But I still count myself blessed to have shared life with him. Remember, my dear child, that the inheritance your father and I leave you is not an inheritance of wealth, nor of houses and possessions made by hands. Our beloved *Lebenshaus,* and the wealth of the Dortmann family, they have all passed beyond us now, and we may never see them again. There were always those who looked down on your father and me for how we lived our life and how we tried to bring you up in the things of God. But you are a daughter we could not have been more proud of. You have made us both very happy.

"'I bless you, my precious daughter,' she said. 'You have been a constant joy to me. You have made my life richer. God go with you, my daughter. I love you.'

"'Thank you, *Mutti*. I love you so much.' I was weeping as she spoke.

"'Find your father, Sabina. Tell him that I love him, and tell him thank you. He will understand.'

"'I will, *Mutti*,' I sobbed. 'I will.'

"Whenever she mentioned Papa, Mama's voice became tender. She stopped briefly now and smiled. I think she was reliving many pleasant memories. When she finally spoke again, it was as the wife speaking one last message to the husband she loved.

"'When you see your father,' she said after a few moments, 'give him a message from me.'

"'Of course, Mama,' I said, weeping again. 'What is it?'

"'Tell him for me that I know the secret of the rose.'"

"'I will, Mama,' I said."

It was silent.

Sabina said nothing for a long while, remembering to herself the remainder of the conversation.

Matthew glanced over, expecting her to continue. When he saw the expression on her face, however, he knew it was time for quiet.

Will I ever know the secret of the rose? Sabina remembered asking her mother.

Sabina smiled, recalling to herself what had been her mother's reply. *Yes, I'm certain you will, my child . . . when you meet the one God has chosen to tell you of its mysteries.*

When finally Sabina spoke again to Matthew, her voice was soft and full of emotion.

"After our lengthy talk, we both grew quiet," Sabina said. "I sensed a peacefulness wrap itself around us. For the rest of that day, time seemed altogether insignificant. I thought about all she had said and prayed that God would help me to live up to the blessing she had given me."

Sabina paused, but only briefly.

"Mama died the next afternoon," she went on. "Her hand lay in mine as I sat at her bedside. She had been sleeping peacefully for some time, so I was not expecting it.

"Suddenly her fingers tightened around mine in a grip so strong I did not know where it had come from. Her eyes opened wide, though she did not seem to see me. They were full of light, like the sunshine itself were pouring into them. She half sat up in the bed, her lips moving as if struggling to speak.

"'It's . . . it's the Father,' she mumbled faintly. 'My Father is coming—'

"Unconsciously I found myself glancing away, in the direction of Mama's gaze, as though expecting to see someone. The grip of her hand clutched at me even more. Then a great sigh went out of her mouth.

"I turned toward the bed.

"Her head had sunk back into the pillow, and the light had gone out of her eyes.

"She was gone.

"I knew the Father had taken her with him, and that they were walking together in *his* garden now.

"I glanced down at my hand. Her fingers were limp, still resting in mine."

Sabina glanced out across the peaceful setting and exhaled a long sigh that contained dozens of unspeakable emotions.

1 5

Connective Links

• • •

"BE AT THE USUAL NUMBER. I WILL CALL IN EXACTLY TWO hours."

Without further ceremony the line went dead.

An hour and fifty minutes later, he stood waiting in readiness. Ten minutes more and he picked up the receiver on its first ring.

"There is a matter of great importance you must look into for me," said a voice.

"Unofficially?" replied the young man Galanov into the mouthpiece of the telephone. "Is that why you called to my apartment on Saturday?"

"Perhaps at first, though your *Stasi* connections have been notified as well, though not by my office. For now, I want to see what you are able to find out and then report back to me."

"I understand."

"There has been a serious information leak."

"Yes, we did hear of it."

"Certain documents have been smuggled out of the country."

"There were no details in the report my chief received, but we have been looking into the matter."

"Berlin is the likely destination."

"What kind of documents?"

"Photographs."

"Damaging?"

"Extremely. They could compromise everything our premier is currently engaged in over the Berlin question."

"How?"

"If these photographs reach the wrong hands and are exploited fully, it would turn world opinion against us, and would also damage, er . . . my own position here, and therefore yours as well. My people were supposed to drop a net on the organization, when suddenly the photos were gone."

"The organization?"

"Jews."

"Any leads that would help me on this end?"

"Only that the trail led to Poland . . . Warsaw, we think."

Galanov did not reply immediately.

"Hmm . . . ," he said after a moment. "We received word ourselves concerning an exchange in Warsaw just this past week. We had the site under surveillance—"

"Was the drop made?" interrupted the other hopefully.

"Yes, but my man lost them."

A loud imprecation sounded in Galanov's ear.

"We are attempting to piece together the make of a German automobile that was observed leaving the scene."

"Then I am instructing you to make it a top priority. If there is any chance the incident you speak of is connected with the photographs, you *must* do what you can to locate them. There is no price too high to be paid. Bribe if you have to. Kill if necessary . . . but get to the bottom of it!"

"I understand."

Galanov hung up the phone and began the walk back to his apartment.

It wasn't easy working for two men, he mused, especially when both were so passionate, even psychotic, about the individuals they sought.

He wondered how long he would be able to keep walking the tightrope between what each expected of him.

16

A Thoughtful Walk in the City

• • •

MATTHEW HAD WANTED TO SEE HER ON SUNDAY TOO, BUT Sabina had declined.

As much as she had enjoyed their Saturday drive, once she was alone that evening she found herself reflecting on the day from a more introspective and gloomy vantage point.

Matthew's presence had all at once sent so much confusion into her mind that she had to step back and try to sift through it and make sense of it all.

Her previously one-dimensional life had suddenly taken on twists and turns and complexities she didn't quite know how to handle. She hadn't realized all the implications when she was with him, but now they came assaulting her from all directions.

After a cloudy and chilly morning, the sun came out between noon and one. Sabina decided to go for a walk, probably a long one.

There was much to think about.

She bundled up, for the wind threatened to be cold in spite of the sun. In Berlin the fact that the calendar indicated June was no guarantee of warmth.

As she left the house she turned east instead of west. She was not in the mood for West Berlin's activity and vibrancy. Today the melancholy and quietness of the eastern sector suited her pensive mood.

Matthew was on her mind as she set out. So were the photographs still stashed away back in her closet.

She had made arrangements to meet her contact again on Tuesday. But the thought had continued to plague her since their first two hours together—might *Matthew's* be the perfect hands in which to place the evidence, rather than the regular channels?

They always had to struggle to get much attention paid to their evidence. Now here Matthew was, as high up in diplomatic circles as they came. If *he* made the photographs known in the right places, the whole world would know what Stalin had done and what was still going on in isolated parts of Russia. Running into Matthew might be just the break they had been hoping for.

Yet could she take such a risk? How much did she really know about his life now?

She was not the same person she had been when they knew one another before.

She *was,* of course . . . but time had brought so many changes.

Could she ever again find room for someone like Matthew? Then came the even deeper question—how far could and how far *should* she trust him?

Germany was divided, and she had landed on the side where freedoms such as Matthew enjoyed did not exist.

Evidence of the division was all around, Sabina thought as she walked. Was she free to *feel* without asking the State's permission? Were her emotions still her own . . . or did the geography of her existence place borders and fences around them, just like it did around this place where she made her home?

As much as she liked Matthew, as wonderful as it was to see him again, and as much as part of her wanted to abandon herself to the joy she felt in his presence, there was one factor which at this moment outweighed all others—he was an American.

She, on the other hand, was a German—an *East* German living in the Communist-controlled DDR.

Between them there was an invisible and insurmountable wall that it seemed could never be scaled or torn down.

He was not merely an American—he was an *important* American diplomat.

Matthew possessed loyalties that had to remain inviolate, no matter what might be their potential feelings for one another. What if the secrets she held did not suit the purposes of his government?

She had *heard* things about the Americans. Half of them she could not make herself believe. She did not trust the Communists to tell things from an altogether unbiased perspective.

Yet there was so much in their news these days about the United States preventing world peace for its own selfish ends. There could be no doubt that tensions in Berlin were rising daily. They said the young American president was a warmonger, pushing Europe daily closer to the brink, just waiting for an excuse to press what they called the nuclear button. Matthew couldn't possibly work for such a man, yet it could not help but make her wonder.

What if it *was* true?

Could she risk giving her information to people like that?

Even if it wasn't true, even if Matthew *was* sympathetic to her cause, he would be obligated by loyalties higher than those due an old teenage friendship to turn over anything he discovered to other American agencies. What if she confided in him, and then someone else in his government found it necessary to try to shut down their operation?

And who was to say Matthew *would* be sympathetic?

She couldn't know that. As much the same as he seemed, perhaps he had changed too.

And where did the bounds of *her* loyalties lie? If she had to make a choice between Matthew and *Das Netzwerk,* it would not be as simple as she would have thought two weeks ago.

Oh, there were too many questions!

As much as she wanted to see Matthew again, his very presence threw her into such conundrums of confusion that she didn't know whether she could endure it.

When Sabina returned to her house three hours later, she was no nearer a resolution to it all than when she had set out.

Making Contact

• • •

IT WAS THE TUESDAY FOLLOWING THEIR DRIVE.

Matthew had attempted to contact Sabina again, but unsuccessfully. He had suggested they get together on Sunday as well, but she had been vague and evasive, saying she would be busy most of the day.

He had thought it strange at the time, given how dull and uninvolved she had represented her life.

He had meetings and obligations most of the week, but was free until seven-thirty this evening. Hoping that they might have supper together, he went to the building where the Agency for the Aged was located, and waited on the sidewalk near the double glass doors.

Sabina emerged at two minutes past five.

"Matthew!" she exclaimed as he approached, her tone registering both astonishment and nervousness. Unconsciously she pulled her coat just a little more tightly around her, although it had warmed up considerably since Sunday.

"I got away a little early," he said. "I've got a meeting at seven-thirty, but thought we might have supper together again."

"I'm sorry, Matthew," she replied. "I . . . I can't tonight."

"Don't tell me you have a pressing engagement too!" he said, laughing.

Sabina did not reply. They began walking down the sidewalk together.

"Surely you can spare an hour," said Matthew. "Do you really have to get home so soon?"

"I just can't, Matthew. I . . . I have to meet someone."

"Will it take long?"

"No . . . not long."

"Then I'll go with you, and we'll have supper afterward," he suggested.

"Please, Matthew—it's something I have to do myself . . . alone— maybe another day."

"Thursday, then?"

"Yes . . . yes, that would be fine."

"Good. I'll come here again at five."

Matthew stood puzzled, watching as Sabina hurried off down the sidewalk. She did not once look back.

• • •

As she left him, Sabina's heart pounded with conflicting emotions.

Why had he had to appear right then?

The envelope inside her coat had suddenly felt hot, like it was burning a hole in her pocket, the moment she had set eyes on him. It was as if the photographs were calling out to be put into *his* possession!

She didn't want to get confused about it all over again, not just now, after she had decided to turn them over as always.

She entered the small cafe at 5:19, sought a table in the far corner, and sat down, her renewed quandary about what to do far from resolved.

At 5:21 another woman entered, some six or seven years younger, approached her table, and sat down across from her.

"*Guten Abend,* Ursula," said Sabina quietly.

"How are you, my friend?"

"Well, though with too many things on my mind."

"Unpleasant things?"

Sabina nodded.

"I wish you would reconsider moving to the West. Life is so much better here."

"The work must go on. Someone must remain behind."

"But there is not even enough food there."

"I manage. God is faithful, and I have no complaints."

"There are others who could take your place."

"Not who care about it as I do. Perhaps in time I will join you, but not until God makes clear such is his purpose."

"I miss you terribly."

"And I you."

There was a brief pause. Their meetings were always too short, but the sacrifice of a cherished friendship was the price both had agreed must be paid when they arrived at this arrangement several years earlier. Happiness in this life was not a commodity given all to enjoy.

"You have a delivery for me?"

"I did . . . but . . ."

Sabina hesitated.

"But what?"

"I think now it might be best . . . that is, a new channel might be open to us. I . . . I think I should wait."

"Wait for what . . . ?"

"Until we can put the information I have to better use than our own people here in the West are able to."

"I don't understand you."

"I cannot explain," said Sabina, suddenly resolving to hold on to the photographs for the moment. "Please, you'll have to trust me."

"I do trust you, of course, but—"

"There may be more effective means than those avenues we have tried previously. I cannot say more than that until I know more myself. But we have been long enough—I must go."

Sabina rose.

Her friend looked up into her eyes with a bewildered expression. This was not like Sabina at all.

Sabina saw her confusion. She reached down and clasped her hand, giving it a tight squeeze.

"Have no worry," she said. "We will be shown what is best. I will tell you all at the right time," she added, smiling.

The warmth of Sabina's look alleviated the other's anxiety for the moment. She returned the squeeze, and the smile.

"Your father sends his love," Sabina said.

"You saw him!"

"He is the one who gave me the packet."

"He is well?"

"Very well."

"Thank God."

"I must go. Bless you, my sister."

"And you."

18

Another Visit

• • •

THURSDAY NIGHT WAS THE FIRST FULL EVENING OF THE week Matthew had had free.

This time he went to the place of Sabina's employment well before five, took the elevator to her floor, and there waited in the hallway.

Whatever it took, he was determined to see her for supper at the very least. He would not take no for an answer this time. His schedule was too demanding, and he would not be free again until Saturday. He didn't want to wait that long!

But he needn't have worried. Though she remained uncertain what to do concerning the photographs, Sabina had no one to meet today. Besides that, she had had two days to anticipate their time together. During that time she had found herself looking forward to it and chastising herself for being so jittery earlier.

Matthew was Matthew, she thought. Whatever other doubts she had, she was certain that *he* was no warmonger.

She therefore resolved to enjoy whatever moments she was given with Matthew, whenever and wherever they came. For the immediate present, she would put off any major decisions about trust. She would say or do nothing to involve him in her other life.

On his part, Matthew was delighted to find Sabina's spirits improved. He said nothing about their previous awkward meeting, and soon they were talking freely over supper.

Matthew asked about the baron, and Sabina began relating to him more details of her father's plight than she had before.

"There were reports we hoped were reliable saying that the Nazis hadn't executed my father," she said. "Therefore, after the war, I hoped to find him when he was released from prison."

"You hadn't had any further contact with him?"

Sabina shook her head. "We only continued to hear that he was alive, but nothing more. No, we had no direct contact with him. When the Allies reached Berlin and the war ended, naturally I assumed he would be released. That was a very difficult time, you have to understand, Matthew, in 1945. Germany had collapsed. There was great confusion and uncertainty. Nobody knew what was going to happen. Russian soldiers were everywhere along with Americans and British, and we were as afraid of the Russians as we had been of the Gestapo."

"Did you find your father?"

"I went to the prison where I had reason to think he had been held, but there was no record of him there."

"What did you do?"

"I then went to the Allied authorities—first the Americans, then the British and French, and finally even to the Russians. I was told that all religious and political prisoners of that kind had been released. I searched everywhere, talked to prison managers, and requested prison lists, but nowhere was there a trace of him."

"There would have had to be some record."

"Things were very confused. The country had fallen apart."

"There must have been some trail left."

"Not that I could find. He had disappeared. No one knew anything. They all told me the same thing, that the Nazis had undoubtedly killed him before the war had ended."

"But you didn't believe them."

"I didn't know what to believe, Matthew. They *had* killed so many. Why not Papa too? Our friend Dietrich Bonhoeffer was hanged just two months before the end of the war. Oh, it's so gruesome and awful I can hardly say the words! They were such a cruel people, I can hardly think of them as Germans like myself!"

"We heard of the atrocities they committed in '45 when it was all caving in. I had heard about Bonhoeffer too."

"The authorities assumed my father met the same fate, but you're right—no, I couldn't believe it. I had to believe he was still alive. I *did* believe it. But alive or dead, the fact remained that he had vanished and I could find no trace of him."

"What did you do?" asked Matthew.

"I kept searching, kept asking questions, kept talking to people and following what leads I had."

"What kind of leads?"

"We had met many people during the war who were involved in hiding people from the Nazis. They are the ones who helped us escape to Switzerland. They had contacts with the underground resistance. Many of those same people continued to actively search for people. There were thousands like me trying to regain contact with relatives who had been lost, though it was such a chaotic time."

"And?"

"It took some time, but eventually I did find out what had happened."

"You found your father?"

"No, I only found what had become of him."

"Was he . . . alive?"

"Yes, thank God. And that was something to be thankful for. But the rest of it wasn't so happy."

"What had happened?"

"He was still being held, secretly, in the Russian sector."

"Who was holding him?"

"That's where it became even more confusing. I couldn't find out why they were so interested in him, but it was the Russians who were behind it."

"You tried to find out?"

"Of course, for over a year, but there was such a veil of secrecy over the case. Wherever he was, he was being kept under tight security."

"You were sure he was alive?"

"In my heart, yes—and the people I was in touch with knew of my father and were themselves also certain of it."

"What people?"

Sabina was silent and glanced away. She had not meant to open that door! She could not tell Matthew about what she had been involved in since the war . . . for either of their sakes.

"People who . . . knew things . . . who had contacts," she finally answered hesitantly, her doubts from two days ago assailing her all over again. "What we finally learned," Sabina went on after a moment, "is that my old friend and neighbor Gustav was responsible for my father's plight."

"The Schmundt fellow!" exclaimed Matthew in disbelief.

Sabina nodded.

"How in the world did he ever get such clout in the new regime?"

"That was unclear for a long time. I still find myself puzzled by it, in fact. Gustav was not the sort of man I would have expected to rise high anywhere. But somehow he'd found favor with the Russians, and when they set up their new East German puppet government, there was Gustav in the heart of it."

"And you say he was the one responsible for keeping your father in prison when the war ended—why?"

"I imagine there are a dozen reasons a small nature like Gustav's would have. Revenge is probably at the top of the list. The day my father was arrested, he challenged Gustav and that other man—"

Suddenly Sabina stopped.

A gasp escaped her lips and her face turned pale. That was where she had seen the face before!

"Sabina—what is it?" asked Matthew in alarm.

"Uh . . . nothing," she fumbled. "The memory of that day is just . . . so vivid and, uh, painful. Papa challenged them to their faces. It was like nothing I've ever seen. He *told* them to let all the rest of us go."

As she spoke, slowly the color returned to Sabina's face, and she went on as before.

"They were Gestapo agents, Matthew—yet they were powerless to resist him. They were so small and pitiful at that moment. Even though they arrested my father, no one could have witnessed the scene and be mistaken who the real victor was. I'm sure the encounter ate at Gustav for the rest of the war, being made to look so helpless, so like a boy again, in front of his superiors. If I know Gustav, and I do, he probably vowed to get even with my father if it was the last thing he did."

"Why would he have kept him alive? If he had that much influence, he could have had him executed like so many others."

"That remained a mystery to me for quite some time too," replied Sabina, "until I finally received a message from my father."

"Then he *was* alive?"

"Yes."

"And you finally saw him?"

"No, I didn't say that. I finally received word from him. It turned out that he knew more of what was going on, and why, than I did."

"So *did* you see him?"

"No, but at least contact was established. For two years we were unable to locate my father at all. Just when my contacts got close, it seemed all the information would dry up and we would lose all trace of him. We later learned that Gustav was moving him from prison to prison to keep his location from being discovered. My father was a well-known political prisoner in some circles by then, and there were many persons in the underground and other organizations assisting me in my search to find him."

"Your friend Schmundt had that kind of power?"

"No friend of mine! But yes, apparently so."

"But eventually you found him?"

"Not me personally, but yes, others did."

"How?"

"Actually, all of a sudden, it was as if the veil was lifted and no longer was there a secret about it at all. It was as if Gustav suddenly *wanted* my father found, which, as it turned out, was exactly the case."

"He *wanted* you to find him?"

"Yes. He hadn't got what he'd wanted by hiding my father, nor from beating and interrogating him and keeping him in confinement, so he suddenly changed his tack."

"What was it he wanted?" asked Matthew.

Sabina looked away, a distressful expression of anguish on her face. She remained silent several minutes.

At length Matthew sought to relieve the obvious heaviness his question had caused.

"I'm sorry," he said, "I didn't mean to pry."

"I . . . I just don't think I can talk about it anymore right now," said Sabina. "I'm sorry too . . . perhaps you should take me home."

"Tell you what," said Matthew, trying to lighten the mood, "let's go for a picnic on Saturday—what do you say?"

Sabina attempted a smile.

"And I promise—no deep questions. We'll just have a good time!"

"I appreciate what you're trying to do, Matthew. Yes . . . yes, I think I'd like that."

19

Matthew's Reflections

. . .

DRIVING BACK TO HIS HOTEL THAT EVENING, MATTHEW could not help growing pensive over the sudden change in Sabina's countenance.

He knew hers had been a difficult life since the war. Had the incident been isolated he would have thought no further about it. After their very first meeting, however, she had seemed to grow increasingly uneasy around him. He couldn't help but wonder if down deep she would rather not see him again.

It would be a blow if he discovered that was the case.

Not so much a blow to his masculine ego. He was strong enough as a man to deal maturely with it if that was how she felt.

The blow would simply come from disappointment. He had thought about Sabina for so many years. He had never forgotten her and had prayed on and off—as impossible as such an event seemed— that somehow, in some way, he would be allowed to see her again.

Now suddenly, here she was!

Yet . . . something was wrong. He could sense it. The bond they had known as teenagers still existed—he knew it. He was sure she felt some of it too!

But there was another ingredient in the mix of their relationship as well, something he could not identify. Whatever it was, it was not friendly to their coming more closely together.

If he had to isolate it, attach a name to it, he would say that she seemed occasionally secretive.

There was nothing wrong with an individual keeping certain things in his or her life close to the vest. He knew well enough from his years in government that you couldn't tell every person you met your whole emotional life's story. One had to remain guarded at times.

But such personal circumspection had not been part of the Sabina he had known. She seemed different, more so than the mere passage of years or hardship of life would account for.

What could be the cause?

How he longed to see the playfulness and childlike innocence of the former Sabina erupt in smiles of delight and musical laughter.

If only there was a way he could unlock that part of her personality again!

She seemed too world-weary and careworn. He wished he could wash away some of the burden with the waters of shared happiness.

She was a woman being pulled in two directions at once, as if part of her wanted a closer renewal of their friendship, while another part—the secretive side that she had closed off to him—did not want to open the door to happiness.

Might there be another man in her life?

Why shouldn't there be? She was attractive. More than merely attractive, she was stunning. No years could change that fact. She must have had suitors through the years.

Suddenly another fact struck him.

The change of name—he had thought it odd from the beginning. What was it all about?

Here was another secretive corner in the once clear and openly visible personality of the one whom he had once known as Sabina von Dortmann.

What if there was more to it than she let on? Could she have been married? Could she *still* be married . . . separated . . . husband in prison, or perhaps in hiding . . . ?

So many possibilities suddenly leapt into Matthew's brain to account for the secrecy surrounding the peculiar name *Duftblatt,* a name that, though he was positive he had never encountered it before, yet had an oddly familiar ring to it.

Arriving at the Steinplatz, he parked his car, then walked slowly inside and up to his room on the second floor.

Well, he thought, he was not going to resolve all the mysteries surrounding Sabina tonight. He probably ought not to try to resolve them at all!

If Sabina had more to tell him, she would do so in her own time and in her own way. If he was not content to allow her to do so, what kind of friend was he anyway? They hadn't seen one another in twenty-one years and ten months. He had no right to pry or push.

He would see her as much as his schedule permitted and she seemed to want. Other than that, he would only do his best to show her a good time, demonstrate that he cared for her, and make her comfortable enough with him that perhaps, in time, the playful exuberance that had attracted him to her in the first place would begin to emerge once more.

20

Sad Memories and Laughter

* * *

TWO DAYS LATER, ABOUT TEN AS ARRANGED, MATTHEW picked up Sabina at her house and, as he had a week earlier, headed out of the city, this time in a northwesterly direction.

He could tell immediately that her smile had returned, which was enough to nearly alleviate altogether the doubts and uncertainties with which he had wrestled since seeing her last.

"I asked my landlady to pack us a picnic lunch," he said.

Sabina smiled, thinking how long it had been since she had even thought about such things as picnics.

"Though she was too curious for her own good whom I would be sharing it with!" added Matthew.

They drove across the border separating West Berlin from the rest of East Germany—stopping for a brief inspection of their papers—and on for some distance through the countryside. They then enjoyed the scenery for a time in relative silence.

At length Matthew slowed, then turned the car off the pavement and onto a dirt road leading into the lightly wooded forest through which they had been traveling. When they were out of sight of the rest of the traffic, he slowed and stopped.

"Well, we came to get away from people and the city," he said. "How about a walk in the woods—for old times?"

"That would be nice," replied Sabina.

As they walked through the forest, it was Sabina, to Matthew's surprise after his own resolve, who brought the conversation back around to where she had left it two days earlier.

"Matthew," she said, "I'm sorry I was so abrupt the other day. You must think me dreadful, with all my changing moods."

"Don't even think such a thing."

"I've had so much on my mind. And to be honest, meeting you again has added to the complexity of it all, stirring up so many things from out of the past that I thought I had dealt with."

"I know. Please—think nothing of it. I shouldn't have pressed so hard."

"No, it wasn't your fault. I hope you don't misunderstand what I just said—it's got nothing to do with you. What I'm trying to say is that I want to finish what I was telling you. I . . . I *want* you to know how things were with Papa . . . and Gustav. I think I'm finally ready to answer the question you asked me."

"You mean about what Gustav wanted?" said Matthew.

Sabina nodded, then was silent for a time, gathering her thoughts and emotions together.

When Sabina finally spoke again, it was with a heavy sigh of silent torment.

"What he wanted . . . ," she said, "was me."

"Gustav wanted . . . *you?*" asked Matthew, doing his best to keep his voice calm, though angered at the very thought. "He wasn't still intent on marrying you after all that time?"

"Apparently so," said Sabina. "He had been trying ever since my father's arrest to use him to get information about my whereabouts."

"If your father was in prison, what did he expect to learn from him?"

"He was certain my father was responsible for our escape to Switzerland and would be well familiar with the names and contacts that would lead to me."

"But he found out nothing?"

"My father would never betray me to Gustav no matter what they did to him."

"What about *Lebenshaus?* Why did you not go back?"

"I did . . . but only once."

As Sabina spoke, an involuntary shudder swept through her at the memory. Matthew saw it but said nothing, waiting for her to continue.

"It was all so changed, Matthew," she went on after a moment, in a poignantly forlorn tone. Both of them could not help remembering

Lebenshaus as it had once been. "What the Nazis didn't destroy that was good and wonderful in our country, the Russians took, and either destroyed themselves, or else twisted and perverted and communized it. It was terrible to see what they did to our beloved land. You must forgive me if I sound bitter. . . . I suppose I am. We all could not help hating the Russians. They were equally as cruel to us as any of Hitler's storm troopers."

"Are you saying they took *Lebenshaus?*" asked Matthew.

"During the final days of the war, when Germany was collapsing, the Russians came through from the east, marching toward Berlin, committing foul atrocities to the German people, raping and pillaging, trampling farms, taking their revenge upon us however they could. Of course my father's property, and all of Pomerania and Prussia, stood right in the middle of their path. They confiscated *Lebenshaus* even while Berlin was still in flames."

"The thought of it turns my stomach," said Matthew with revulsion.

"I have done my best to forget," sighed Sabina. "The passage of years is good at least for that."

"But you said you did go back once?"

Sabina nodded. "My friends all warned me against it," she said. "But as soon as I returned to Berlin I couldn't help wanting to see the house again. With the war over—this was months later, it had taken me some time to arrive back in Berlin from Switzerland—I assumed that the Allies would be agreeable, including the Russians.

"I was so naive, until I learned the true state of affairs! After the Nazis, I assumed all the Allies wanted to help in every way they could.

"In any case, I was taken up at first with trying to locate Papa and wondering what had happened to him and why none of the Allied authorities knew anything. By the time I did see *Lebenshaus* again we had received reports of what was going on with my father. After that, any further doubts I had were put forever to rest. If I had to pinpoint a moment when the hope drained out of me, that would be it."

"What happened?"

"They told me I shouldn't go, that I needed to forget how it had been before. I suppose I realized the danger, it being so close to Gustav's old house. I didn't know what had become of him. For all I knew his father had bought the place like he always wanted to. Don't go, my friends said. No good can come of it. You've got to put that part of your life behind you. It is the only way to survive in the new Russian-controlled DDR, they said—you must look ahead to the reality of how things are now, not how they were before the war."

"But you couldn't?"

"Not without a piece of me dying in the process," answered Sabina. "How do you content yourself with wrong and injustice? How could I content myself with everything my father lived for and that my mother had died for, and that I had learned to love? How could I content myself with never looking upon those things again? No, I *had* to see *Lebenshaus* again."

"Did you?"

"With the help of friends I managed to sneak onto the grounds, through the woods to the south—you remember."

"How could I forget—where I had the most memorable horse-back ride of my life!"

"And the most memorable fall," added Sabina.

Matthew laughed. "It seems so long ago. And yet . . ."

"Like only yesterday?" suggested Sabina.

"How did you know?"

"That's how it seems to me too—oh, Matthew, seeing you again brings it all back so fresh! I thought I had put it all behind me, but now . . ."

"I know," he said. "I know exactly what you mean."

They walked on awhile in silence.

"Look, that seems to be a clearing up there," said Matthew. "What do you think—good enough for a picnic?"

He broke into a light run, and Sabina followed him.

Puffing and laughing a few minutes later, they both collapsed on the green grass of a small clearing, surrounded by pines.

"Not so difficult to squeeze our way into, at least!" said Matthew. "Are you hungry?"

"Not too much," replied Sabina. "Not yet at least."

"Then we'll wait for lunch, and you can finish telling me about your visit back to your home."

The fleeting flush of happiness drained again from Sabina's face, but she continued with what she had been saying before.

"By the time I got there," she went on, "as I said, a couple years had passed. They were using *Lebenshaus,* as they did many of the nicer estates, as a military headquarters. But there were not many soldiers around. It was for officers, mainly. It was so painful to see the destruction about the place. Some of the barns had been destroyed altogether, and though repairs had begun on the main house, many of the windows were still broken out, and all about the walls were evidences of bullet holes and gunfire. It was obvious the whole place had been ransacked. They were in the process of setting up the new military oversight for the area at the time and so it was a mixture of both Russians and Germans. Everything was tense between '47 and '49. Your people were in the process of creating the BRD and giving it its independence, while on this side, the Russians were setting up their satellites—isn't that what you call them?"

Matthew nodded.

"They were setting up the countries within their sphere of influence much differently."

"Much differently!" repeated Matthew with deliberate emphasis. "Without any freedom."

The more they spoke together, the more Sabina found her previous hesitations regarding America, its policies, and its government diminishing. It was obvious that theirs was no policy of war and repression. She knew that . . . she had known it all along. She should never have let such doubts infiltrate her thinking.

Of course she could trust Matthew. Whether she *should* entrust the photos to him was another matter.

She would have to wait on a decision that important. What were a few more days or weeks . . . even a month? The situation was not going to change overnight. They had been fighting this silent war for years. She had to be prudent, until she knew what was the right course to follow.

"You weren't afraid to be so close to the Schmundt estate?" asked Matthew, intruding into Sabina's straying thoughts.

"I don't know," she replied. "I don't suppose I considered it that great a danger. If the reports we had heard about Gustav were true, and that he was already rising to prominence, I think I assumed he would be elsewhere."

"What did you do?"

"I came in through the woods, into the lower part of the garden—"

"How was the garden?"

"Oh, Matthew!"

Sabina looked away, and her eyes filled with tears at the memory.

"It was awful," she said softly after a moment, "devastated, over-grown, trampled down, hardly recognizable. The Rose Garden was the worst. It broke my heart to walk through it. I cried, to think of all the old happy times, to hear my father's voice in my memory as he had spoken to me there so many times. But I had to make haste. I could not be seen."

As Sabina spoke, she silently wondered how much she should tell Matthew of her family's activities during the war.

"I managed to sneak into the cellar—"

"How?" interrupted Matthew.

"Through the hidden door to the garden."

"What door? Did your father find the door you always spoke of?"

"Yes, there was a passageway that led from the cellar to the sloping ground of the garden, on the opposite side of the house from the underground room where you and I used to go. He eventually found the hidden dungeon too."

"He did!" exclaimed Matthew.

"Right where he always thought it was."

"I'm curious about the door to the outside. How did it open?"

Sabina explained it and where the keys to the inner doors were kept.

"They hadn't destroyed the hedge and discovered it?" asked Matthew.

"Some parts of the garden, though wild and overgrown, had not been trampled down, so the door was never found. Everything was well concealed. My father always made sure of that. I don't think the Russians, when they later came to the place, were interested in anything but the house, to which they quickly started to make repairs. I doubt if they had even gone into the garden. By then the hedges and shrubbery had grown up around the door. Nobody could have seen it without knowing just where to look. No, they hadn't found it, and I was able to get inside. You cannot imagine all the emotions and thoughts that went through me as I crept through the underground passages. I thought of you, Matthew, and all the fun we had. But when

I found myself climbing up the dark, narrow stairs into the room you had occupied with your broken leg, suddenly all my happy memories were shattered."

"What happened?"

"Oh, what I wouldn't have given to have heard your voice again on the other side of that wall where I played the trick on you with the noises. But it wasn't you I heard."

Again Sabina shuddered.

"There were people in the room?"

Sabina nodded.

"You could hear them?"

"Very clearly, when I put my ear to the crack. The door was still there, closed, and concealed from view. They had apparently moved right into the house to make use of its many rooms, but without much investigation beyond that. It was clear nobody had been in the basement passages since the night of our departure. We had closed all the hidden doors behind us, and they still hid everything from view."

"Who was it you heard, Russian soldiers?" asked Matthew.

Sabina shook her head.

"It was a voice I would know anywhere," she replied.

"Whose?"

"It was Gustav."

"What was *he* doing there?"

"He was speaking in a tone of command. I knew immediately that whoever was with him in the room—and it sounded like they were using your old room as an office or headquarters. I never understood that—why would they not have been using my father's old office, or one of the other larger rooms? In any case, Gustav happened to be there, and I strained to listen. At first when I heard his voice, the old childhood fondness tried to trick me into divulging my presence and rushing into the room, and pleading with Gustav to tell me where Papa was. Surely the things I'd been hearing couldn't be true. Surely Gustav would have compassion on us for the sake of old times. We had been childhood friends. He would not do me harm. Perhaps God had led me here to see him, for the very purpose of finding Papa.

"But then I remembered the warnings of my friends. I remembered Gustav's face when Papa was arrested. I remembered how much he'd changed.

"All this passed through my brain in a second or two when I heard his voice. Then my brain began to register the words he was speaking, and a cold chill of dread stole over me. Once again I couldn't believe what Gustav had allowed himself to become. I could feel the coldness in his tone and knew what kind of a look was in his eye on the other side of that wall. But what he said was even worse. It confirmed what we'd heard from several sources but that I was reluctant to believe."

Sabina trembled again at the memory. Matthew waited.

"'I want extra precautions taken,' I heard him say. 'Extra guards around the estate, and plainclothes agents in the village. She's bound to appear eventually. If she shows up here, I tell you, detain her and get word to me immediately. In the meantime, I'll get the information as to her whereabouts out of that fool father of hers one way or another. She'll not escape me forever. She's mine, and once I have her she'll never get away from me again.'"

She closed her eyes and shook her head.

"To think of it is more than I can stand, Matthew," she went on. "He was talking about *me!* He was still determined to get me into his clutches after all this time."

Unconsciously Matthew's fist tightened and his teeth clenched at the very thought.

"After that I knew I would probably never see *Lebenshaus* again. I crept back out, terrified that they might hear me, back through the desolate garden, careful to leave the doors concealed as my father had, through the woods and back to Berlin. I found permanent lodgings in the city, and have been here ever since."

A long silence followed. At last Matthew broke it.

"I appreciate your telling me," he said. "I know it must have been difficult for you."

"I appreciate your listening."

"What are friends for!" Matthew smiled.

Sabina returned the smile.

Their eyes met, just as they had on that first day in Otto von Dortmann's garden so many years ago. Their stations and fates may have changed, their features aged, their temples now showed shades of grey, and neither quite yet knew how far to extend trust into this renewed friendship that meant so much to each.

But the eyes had not changed. In that moment it seemed not a day had passed since their first meeting.

Both seemed to sense that a threshold of renewed confidence and hope had been crossed. Perhaps the time had not yet come for everything to be disclosed. But at least one or two barriers to further levels of intimacy had fallen.

21

Rising in the New Eastern Elite

. . .

GUSTAV VON SCHMUNDT, SECTION CHIEF FOR THE EAST
German Secret Police and one of many liaisons between the DDR
government and the Russian KGB for the region of Potsdam and
Berlin, was running out of patience. He had half a mind just to kill
the old man, forget Sabina altogether, and get on with his life.

Even with all the resources of the *Staatssicherheitsdienst* that he had
available, the search had proven altogether futile. In this building they
had files of more than three million men and women, in both East
and West. The *Stasi* knew everything about everybody. Yet he had
been unsuccessful at the one vital information link he wanted more
than any other, and this latest disappointment was the last straw.

The office, at whose lone window he stood, looked out upon a
dingy section of East Berlin not far from the border. Of course, he
thought, all parts of East Berlin were dingy. Had he been on the other
side of the building, he could have cast his gaze down upon the
lime-tree-lined thoroughfare known as *Unter den Linden.* Here was
the center of the city where Germany glittered and shone during the
1930s. He was not yet to the very highest rungs within the *Stasi* to
merit such an office, though such a day was not far off.

His eyes scanned the scene below him, a quiet street without
much activity. It was a wide enough boulevard to have handled
DeGaulle's triumphant entry into Paris in 1944. As it was, the
cobblestone thoroughfare, now known as *Lenin Allee,* had instead felt
the tramp of Russian boots a year later, which accounted for both its
new name and for the fact that not a stone of it, nor any of the
buildings that lined it, had been changed, washed, swept, or repaired

in all the time since. Only its name spoke of those who now claimed authority over everything east of the Brandenburger Tor, all the way to the Bering Sea half a globe away, even if the visual evidence did not lend much credence to the practical credibility of their founder's grand vision of proletariat power.

Schmundt turned from the window and slowly walked back to his desk and resumed his seat. The face was remarkable for nothing, other than how similar it looked to all the others of like motive in this faceless, impersonal bureaucracy. This was not a place that defined character but rather suffocated it. Personality was frowned upon, individuality held in suspicion, integrity given no soil in which to grow.

In truth, however, he was not a man who lamented such features of this new society to which he had given his allegiance. Like all those who found themselves comfortably flowing with the tide of the world surrounding them, he had long ceased to feel the downward current of that tide. Though he felt nothing of the process, honorability, courage, and uprightness were steadily being leached out of him, and all who likewise made conforming to the system's standards the ruling idol of their conduct.

In Gustav's case, the slight squint that came to his eyes as he sat down and the tepid light that shone from them were the result of what a long declension of poor and selfish choices had made of him. He would have ordered instant prison for any individual, man or woman, who hinted of such to his face. But the undeniable fact was that his countenance grew more every year to resemble his mother's, the unfortunate widow of Count Ernst von Schmundt, whose life the final year of the war had claimed. The pitiful countess now spent her days in one of the DDR's homes for the elderly, boring her unlistening companions with stories of past imagined glories that had never been. Gustav had not seen her for three years. Visiting her always depressed him, and he found excuses for avoiding it easier and easier to make. Every time he walked away from the place he vowed never to return, and he was well on his way this time to fulfilling that callous pledge.

His cheeks had taken on a rather sallow hue, accentuated all the further by the drab brown uniform he wore. What had once been a tolerably handsome face was now, as he approached his forty-second birthday, sagging in all the wrong places. His fleshy jowls were all too visually reminiscent of his mother after a lifetime's habit of far too many dainty Swiss chocolate rolls. Dark bags sat under his eyes. His hair, though retaining its darkness of color, was thinning all over. An especially worrisome small patch at the back had worn off completely, like the eye of a growing storm that portended ill, as its swirl gradually claimed more and more of the outlying regions.

Age was creeping toward him at an ever accelerating pace, and still the prize he had so long sought eluded him. Events had conspired to prevent his gaining control of the coveted adjoining estates. Nobody these days "owned" property. The state had seized both houses and parcels of land long ago. But even bureaucrats and KGB agents and governmental officials had *wives.*

And he had waited far too long to claim his!

He scanned again the papers the young lieutenant Galanov had brought him.

He knew that to kill the baron would only be to give his former neighbor the final victory. The fool was mad enough not to fear death, and he would take pleasure in not having betrayed his daughter.

No, thought Gustav, he could not kill him yet.

If he was to kill him, it would be with Sabina watching. Then he would have his revenge on them both!

But something had to be done. This had been going on far too long, and he was sick of the whole business.

. . .

Emil Korsch had seen the handwriting on the wall well in advance of the end. As the war had closed in upon them, thinking it might prove useful later to do so, he had taken Gustav with him. Korsch managed to slip into the ranks of the advancing Russian army, providing them with sufficient information so that, by the time Berlin was in their hands, he had so thoroughly ingratiated himself and made them believe he was a loyal Russian himself who had been acting the part of a spy in Germany, that he quickly became indispensable in the new regime.

They worked together in the Russian zone of Germany for a time, but soon went their separate ways. Gustav had slowly risen through the ranks of the Communist DDR after its creation in 1949 in response to the new Bonn Federal Republic, while Korsch had moved eastward toward the seat of power. Their contact with one another these days was minimal, though a common mission still bound them in an odd relationship of mutual disgust and mistrust.

They had been through too much together to have any mutual regard left. Friends they could hardly be called. In this region of the world, however, the concept of "friend" had fallen on hard times. Everyone was a comrade these days, and the new term worked well enough to define the relationship between them.

Their comradeship had one strong binding feature that preserved the link between the two. Each had a score to settle with Baron von Dortmann, for his own reasons. Gustav still wanted the baron's daughter; Korsch still sought Rabbi Wissen's holy box, with its valuable Old Testament Jewish relics—priceless in any age to whomever held them, whether for religious reasons or purely economic. Hitler's fascination with such things was twistedly occultish. His, now, on the other hand, had but one foundation. Possession of the sacred jewels and gold and silver artifacts would make him rich! But they had not had more than a sniff or two of a warm trail since the end of the war.

Baron von Dortmann remained the only link that might enable them to regain the scent. For this sole purpose had he been kept alive and under close surveillance.

As their paths diverged, Korsch wound up in Moscow, working in the KGB, while Schmundt had come to occupy his present position in Berlin. Korsch had no interest in the girl for her own sake, but only as a means, through her father, to locate the rabbi.

Quite simply, Sabina von Dortmann was the link for both men to the fulfillment of their long-cherished dreams.

Korsch, meanwhile, had his own informers in Stalinist Russia keeping track of Jewish affairs and relics. His personal passion against the Jews found fertile soil in which to grow. He had developed his own department within the KGB to track the movements of important Jewish figures, and he became an important figure in the silent Stalinist purge of Abraham's sons and daughters.

Meanwhile, he remained ready to move the moment word surfaced that anything had been learned from the prisoner regarding the rabbi or when his own sources gained some word that the stones themselves had surfaced.

At first Gustav and Korsch had conspired to hide the baron from the Allies, thinking they would be able to lay their hands on both girl and box quickly. The baron, however, divulged nothing. Eventually getting angrier and angrier, Gustav took to moving him around, questioning and torturing him to find out where Sabina might be.

Where is she . . . how did she escape . . . who helped you . . . who were her contacts . . . where did she go in Switzerland? The questions tormented him.

But her father would say nothing. Gustav became more and more determined to find Sabina and eventually changed his plan. Allowing the baron's whereabouts to become known, he was certain that Sabina would immediately try to make contact with him. When she did not, and one more of his ploys seemed doomed to failure, his anger finally spilled over toward her. Though he was no less determined to conquer her, the motive of revenge was now equally directed at Sabina as at her father.

Nothing he thought of turned up a single lead, nor had any of his spies been able to locate anyone by the name of Sabina von Dortmann anywhere in East Germany. He had questioned all their known relatives. No one knew a thing. It appeared Sabina had vanished off the face of the earth.

• • •

This was the last straw. It was time to change his tactics again.

As much as he loathed asking for help, and as much as he resented owing him for his present position, perhaps it was time to see if anything had turned up elsewhere.

He reached forward, picked up his phone, and barked into it with a voice of command.

"Fräulein Reinhardt, get me the private number in Moscow." The next moment he set down the receiver and leaned back in his chair to await completion of the call.

Knowing the inefficient Russians, he thought to himself, it would probably take an hour.

22

A Reflective Picnic

• • •

SABINA AND MATTHEW HAD AT LENGTH OPENED THE picnic basket and were now slowly munching their rye bread, cheese, and apples.

"What did you do after returning to Berlin?" Matthew asked at length.

"I didn't know what to do about Papa. The thought of him remaining in prison was dreadful. There were times I seriously considered finding out how to contact Gustav, and tell him I would see him if he would release Papa."

"He wouldn't have let your father go without your marrying him, would he?"

"I even thought about that too," sighed Sabina.

"Marriage!" exclaimed Matthew.

"That's how desperate I was to get Papa out."

"You couldn't have seriously considered becoming the man's wife?"

"Oh, Matthew, I don't know. I had nowhere to turn! I didn't know what to do. Papa had sacrificed himself to give the rest of us freedom during the war. Why should I not be willing to do the same for him?"

"Why didn't you, then?" asked Matthew.

"It was Papa himself who prevented me," answered Sabina.

"Your father—how?"

"It was sometime after the incident I just told you about when, as I said, suddenly Gustav changed his tack. All at once it became known where my father was. There was even a small article in the Berlin paper with the headline Former Land Baron Held for Treason. When

I read it my heart sank within me. Oh, you cannot imagine my distress. Time after time, I was within a hairbreadth of casting caution to the wind and going to the prison, just to try to have a moment with him."

"But you didn't?"

"My father, even where he was, apparently knew much of what was going on. He realized Gustav was trying to learn of my contacts in the city through him, and realized that now, frustrated and having failed to learn anything, Gustav was trying to lure me into making contact with Papa. My father was not in total solitary confinement, so he had developed contacts of his own too."

"Do you know how?"

"Not really. Prisons have a whole life of their own. There were multiple levels of intrigue and loyalty in Germany after the war, on the Eastern side I mean—Communists, Germans loyal to Allies but finding themselves in the eastern sector, the whole gamut. Papa shared his fate in prison with former Nazis, with Jews, with political and all kinds of prisoners in the newly evolving Communist state within the DDR. Though from what I gather he had a cell of his own, he was allowed certain privileges."

"Like what?"

"Being able to write, access to the prison library, mixing every several days with other prisoners. From what I could find out from the Allies, there were certain prisons where the conditions weren't too intolerable. In this environment, Papa came to know people who could get a message out to . . . to people I knew."

"So you did finally hear from him?"

Sabina nodded. The melancholy was visible on her face.

"It was not what I wanted to hear," she said. "Though knowing Papa as I did, I suppose it was exactly what I should have known to expect."

"What did he tell you?"

Sabina smiled. "All these years since, it's been one of the only tangible things I have to hang onto from Papa. I've replayed the words probably a thousand times in my mind. I know them so well they've worn a deep groove into my brain."

"Was the message written?"

"Oh no. It came memorized, probably passed through at least

three or four persons before it came to my ears. But it was unmistakably from Papa. There could be scarce a doubt of that."

She paused, remembering the words again, then opened her mouth once more and spoke them, almost reverently, to Matthew.

"'My dear one,' the young man bearing it said to me, 'you must not try to see me. I am safe and well. The Master is using me to help tend the forsaken flowers in this corner of his garden. It is time now for you to till your own soil. We will pray for one another, but our eyes must not meet until the Father wills it. Remember, the thorns as well as the petals have fragrance, for those who truly know roses.'"

Tears by now had risen in Sabina's eyes.

"Then he told me to change my name, and to do what I could to forget the past. He reassured me that he was fine, not to worry about him, but to beware of Gustav."

Sabina paused, then took a bite of apple and chewed it slowly. They were both quiet a few minutes, nibbling at their food more for something to do than from hunger, looking around at the peaceful countryside all about them.

"You can imagine that I was heartsick to have to heed his words," Sabina went on finally. "There were times I would plead with Papa, in my mind of course, to let me marry Gustav—for his sake. Then I would think back to all the times he told me to ask, not what I would want to do, but what the Lord would want me to do. I have learned to apply that truth over the years just as often by asking what Papa would do, and what *he* would want me to do."

A smile came to her lips as she thought of her father.

"He would probably disdain to hear me say it," she said, still smiling, "to compare him in any way with Jesus. But I couldn't help it. As much as I wanted to make whatever sacrifice I could for him, I knew at the same time that he would not want me to. I would have done anything to help him. But I knew that it would be going *against* his will to do so. In a way, I suppose, it was a sacrifice I had to make, though backwards. A sacrifice, if you can call it that, of *not* sacrificing myself for him, knowing such to be his preference."

Again she paused reflectively.

"In the end I knew I had no choice but to heed his wishes. That's when I became Karin Duftblatt, and essentially went underground . . . and left my past life behind me."

Sabina let out a big sigh, then glanced over at Matthew with a pensively melancholy smile.

"You see," she said, "it *was* a long story."

"I'm glad you felt free to tell me all of it," he replied. "Have you heard from your father since?"

"Occasionally. But I have still not seen him in seventeen years, and he remains in prison."

"He is . . . healthy?"

"As far as the reports that reach me, he is healthy and content."

"Does he know about your mother?"

"Yes. I'm sure Mama's death contributes to his contentment where he is. Otherwise, for her sake, I know he would have done all he could to get out."

"He is still in the same place?"

"They've moved him several more times through the years."

"But you know his whereabouts?"

Sabina nodded. "Presently they are holding him in an old boarding school that was converted to a facility to house religious and political prisoners, as well as some Jews judged too important to execute. He's there with firebrand poets and former aristocrats like himself, as well as political malcontents."

"At least he's still near Berlin. The Russians have always been rather fond of Siberia as permanent lodgings for people they wanted out of sight."

"Gustav wants him nearby and accessible."

"You think he's still trying to find you after all this time?"

"There's no doubt of it. He's continued to rise in the DDR establishment. I've kept track of him even though I made sure I stayed out of his sight. He's now attached to what amounts to the East German KGB, the *Stasi.*"

"The perfect career move for a former Gestapo agent," commented Matthew wryly.

"Gustav's a dangerous man. I have friends who are watching him on my behalf. Spies for the *Stasi* are constantly of concern, and I have to watch my every movement closely."

"Listening to you is like catching up on my own family after a long absence."

"And when are you going to tell me what has happened to *you* during all these years?"

"*My* long story, huh?"

"Yes. I'm as eager to hear about you."

"When the time is right," said Matthew. His reluctance was born out of no motive of secrecy, only that he didn't want to interrupt the mood of having heard Sabina's story by beginning his own.

"How about a walk after dining?" asked Matthew, jumping to his feet. Sabina joined him.

Slowly their talk drifted into other avenues as they ambled off along the trail through the woods.

When they parted at day's end, after several more hours of good, earnest, and worthwhile conversation and fun, Sabina declared that she had not enjoyed a day so much in years.

"Oh, it feels so good to laugh again," she sighed as they drove up to her house. "I actually laughed today, Matthew—did you hear me?"

"I did indeed."

23

Lonely Prayer of Exile

· · ·

THE CELL WAS DARK IN SPITE OF THE HOUR. THOUGH the midday sun shone overhead outside, very little of its warmth penetrated these stones.

The onetime school had been effectively converted to accommodate its present purpose of confinement, which it did without hint of anything resembling luxury.

Inside, an aging man sat on a rickety chair, stooped over a crude wood table, apparently writing. The chair and table were the only pieces of what could be called furniture in the room, besides a bed behind him and an open commode in the corner several feet away. The floor was concrete, the walls of grey plaster. A high, dirty pane let in some light, though it was too high for him to see out of. A dim bulb hung from overhead, barely adding to the thin shafts of the sun's rays angling down from the window.

The tables in this particular prison had been furnished as a concession to moderation and to appease the British, French, and Americans, who still kept what watch they could on events in the sector of their former Russian ally. The writing desks, paper, use of a few books, and mingling of the prisoners qualified this as a minimum security "detention center" rather than an actual prison. Here were kept, according to the records, only nonthreatening political and religious zealots, traitors to be sure, but not so dangerous as to require permanent incarceration in Siberia. They were fed and treated well, it was said, and could hardly expect better.

The exposed cheekbones and gaunt frame of the man gave evidence to the contrary, however, as did the old scar across his jaw and recent welt below the left eye. One look told that this was no pleasure camp. That he was alive at all after so long was testimony to his hearty constitution and rugged determination, more than to the quality of his care.

His hair, still plentiful beyond a forehead that went high toward the top of his head, was as grey as the wall behind him. The once-ruddy complexion of his face now shone with ghostly pallor in the dimly lit cell. The sight of his pale cheeks would have shocked those who had once worked beside him in the harvest fields of this land from dawn to dusk, during a happier era, and who, though younger by a decade, had marveled at his stamina and vigor. Now, at sixty-seven, he remained in tolerable health considering the circumstances, though a first glance might have taken him for at least ten years older than he actually was.

Only one feature of his countenance remained unchanged by the years. The eyes that shone down upon the paper before him bore an almost preternatural clarity of visage.

Indeed, had one been capable of gaining a clear view, the illumination from those silent piercing orbs outshone both bulb and window overhead. For the light within them originated from no earthly source and could not be extinguished by night, by beatings, by imprisonment, nor even by death itself.

He leaned forward, wrote a few more words on the paper before him, then set down the pen from between his fingers, sat back upright, and let out a long sigh. He had been writing steadily for more than two hours. Hand, back, and eyes were all fatigued from the effort.

He closed his eyes and sighed again, from mental exhaustion this time more than physical. He had been awakened early, with thoughts and prayers suddenly going in many new directions, a keen sense of anticipation gradually coming over him. He had been, on and off throughout the day, attempting to bring his mental activity to focus through the pen his cramped hand had been holding, though thus far with a limited sense of satisfaction.

"Lord, Lord," he whispered softly, *"make clear your words. . . . What have you been trying to say to me . . . ? What is your plan and will for this nation . . . and for your people in it?"*

His lips fell silent. Again a long breath of exhaled question left his lungs. The next moment he slipped from the chair, bent to his knees on the floor, and bowed his head low between them.

"Oh, heavenly Father," he murmured in a barely audible voice, "you have been so good to me. Daily you reveal more of yourself to me. Daily you sustain me and fill me with your presence and your love and your care. I do not deserve such kindness as you shower so abundantly upon me. Oh, but, Father! What of them who do not know the goodness of your nature? What of them! What will you do to reveal yourself to them? They need you so desperately!

"Do I dare, Father—is that what you have been saying?—do I dare pray so boldly as to take upon myself the burden for this nation, for these people of mine, kinsmen of blood, who seem to have forgotten their Father? Give me boldness and courage to pray, and to believe that with the urge to pray you are already going before to make straight the pathway to answer."

He paused momentarily, then continued, his voice rising slightly as he realized the import of his words.

"I do pray for this country," he said, "broken and crushed and torn apart as it is. I pray for the burden of guilt it must bear for abominations it has done. Let this people come to face their guilt, and turn to you in repentance in their hearts. Humble this proud land—not merely as the world sees such humbling, for indeed, such has already been done. Humble their **spirits** before you.

"Recall to them their ancient heritage of spiritual fiber and vigor. Restore to this people the faith of our father Martin Luther and his brother Bonhoeffer. Let them see that this recent and terrible waywardness for which they must atone has come, not from **following** a dictator, but rather from **forgetting** you. Let them see that the greatest evil was not even done against your people . . . but against **you**.

"Oh, loving Father, in your time and in your own chosen way, restore and heal this land and her people—not to their former prominence in the world's eyes, but restore their roots of dignity and integrity, and the submission of their hearts to you.

"Draw together this bruised and sundered nation. Bring together hearts and families. Restore the unity for which your Son Jesus prayed. Heal the separation in this land by healing the separation that exists between you, the Father, and these people, your children, whose love for you has grown cold from their great sin—from the sin of turning away from you.

"Enliven their hearts to turn again to you. Prick the hearts of faithful ones to pray likewise. Raise up a silent corps of your sons and daughters to pray for *their brothers and sisters, to pray for healing, to pray for restoration, to pray for unity once again to come to this place.*

"There is nothing I can do but pray. I am an impotent man, Lord, of no more significance in the world's eyes. But I ask that you deepen within me this burden to pray for this land that I love. Do not let me weary of it, nor of the other work you have given me to do in this place. Keep my spirits up, sustain my mind and heart and body, that I may faithfully serve you. Whatever your will is, carry it out in me, my Lord. Accomplish your purposes and your perfect will in and through me. Give me an obedient heart to serve you. I thank you for your care for me, and for your great love. Oh, Father, increase my gratefulness, and add to the small portion of my faith."

Again silence fell in the small lonely cell. Slowly the old man rocked back and forth upon his knees, inaudible prayers now escaping from his heart rather than his lips.

After a few moments he spoke again.

"And, Father, as always I pray for our mutual daughter. Make provision for her perfect sustenance. Care for her, guide her, love her. I pray not that she enjoy a happy life, but that you fashion her into the image of womanhood you destine for her. Let her walk with strength the pathway you give her to follow.

"As always, I pray for my fellows here. Give me opportunity to speak with them, and to tell them of the goodness of your fatherhood. For our guards I pray too. Increase my devotion to love them as Jesus loved. Bless them, and reveal yourself to them."

After another minute or two, he rose wearily, walked slowly to the bed, lay down, and in five minutes was sleeping soundly.

2 4

Call from Moscow

• • •

THE RING OF HIS TELEPHONE SNAPPED GUSTAV OUT OF his reverie.

Unconsciously he glanced down at his watch. *Well, not quite an hour,* he thought to himself. He'd ordered the call fifty-two minutes earlier.

"Yes . . . yes, I'm still waiting for the call," he growled. "Good, yes, I'll hold."

He sat another minute in silence. Then suddenly the features of his face gave indication that the voice he had been waiting for had at last come to the other end of the line.

"Yes . . . yes, it has been a long time indeed . . . yes, always busy, you know."

He was silent a moment or two, listening.

"Developments? Ah . . . no, not exactly," said Gustav. "Unfortunately that is not the reason for my call."

He cleared his throat, not entirely from need, though it had suddenly gone uncharacteristically dry, then continued. "I, ah, was wondering if anything had turned up on your end," he said, trying to give his voice a businesslike optimism.

He waited, though by the expression on his face, he did not appear to be listening to an altogether pleasant response.

"No, I am not expecting you to do my work for me, but I—"

An interruption silenced him.

"Of course . . . yes, I know you have your own people on the Jew, but—"

Another silence, this time lengthier.

"No, nothing more on the girl. That is why I called. There were reports of a woman matching her description connected with Zionist activities here. I had one of my best men on it—actually, one of your men assigned to my office here. The young Galanov fellow."

A reply on the other end broke in.

"Yes, an enterprising young agent. I didn't realize you knew him personally. In any event, the trail we were on dried up completely. Not even the KGB's methods could find out anything, though Galanov assures me he tried everything. Then I found myself wondering if perhaps these Zionists might be linked with your rabbi. If you had uncovered anything new, I hoped there might be connections that would lead us both toward our respective goals."

He paused to listen again.

"I understand. . . . Yes, I know that you wanted the woman to find out where the rabbi had gone after leaving Switzerland. But as I said, all my efforts to locate her have been unsuccessful. . . .

". . . No, of course not," he said, his annoyance rising. "I have not been lax in my efforts. My only thought was—"

The angry voice came through the receiver almost as loudly as if its owner were right in the same room. Gustav was angry himself at the insinuation, but he tried to calm himself. The KGB could be so unpleasant, but it was not wise to irritate them.

"Forgive me," Gustav said after a moment, "such was by no means my intent. But it is clear there *is* a connection. There *must* be, as we have suspected all along. What difference in which direction we follow the thread, from him to her, or her to him . . . ?

". . . I understand. . . . Yes, you have made it clear that the rabbi's thread is still dangling loose. . . .

". . . I will continue to do what I can. Certainly I will notify you the moment I get my hands on either her or the Zionists. We will have them both in our hands eventually."

The other spoke again.

"No, I was aware of no new information network. . . . Yes, we received a communiqué regarding material that was said to be being smuggled out of your country. . . . Hmm . . . we are looking into a recent occurence in Warsaw . . . is there a connection?

". . . The Jewish underground, you say . . . I thought you said you had nothing on the old fellow," said Gustav with suddenly profound conjecture. He bolted upright in his chair.

Could the potential connection he had just mentioned be the very connection they had been seeking all this time? Something about the Warsaw incident and description had alerted him from the beginning.

If it was true—unbelievable thought!—it would mean that Sabina herself was right here in Berlin!

Perhaps his plan had worked better than he'd realized, and her father's presence had kept her close by. Another change might be just the thing to bring her out of hiding!

". . . Yes, I see . . . unconfirmed . . . I will make it top priority," he mumbled, then fell to listening again.

"As to the reason for my call," he went on when the phone went silent, trying to clear his brain, "I have been considering moving the father—"

Again he was interrupted.

"Yes, I'm afraid he is still alive. A feisty old man, but I'm tiring of him. I'm wondering if his presence so close by isn't proving an inhibition to her activities. With him gone, perhaps things would loosen up and enable me to nab her. Using him as bait hasn't worked. Might there be a location there where we could transfer him and get him out of our hair for good?"

The answer was brief.

"There is always the danger of the Western authorities getting wind of something. They have their agents always snooping around too. They watch our prisons. I've exercised extreme care. This is one fish I don't want someone in the American State Department taking an interest in. With things as tense as they are around Berlin, and with Khrushchev and Kennedy at each other's throats, I would prefer getting him away. . . ."

" . . . I see, not far outside Moscow?"

He listened to the answer, thoughtfully nodding his head.

"Good," he replied at length. "That sounds like the perfect place. . . .

" . . . Then make arrangements, and I'll look for a suitable opportunity to move him, probably in a month or two."

PART II

Interlude of Happiness

June/July 1961

2 5

Midnight Transfer

. . .

THE NIGHT WAS BLACK.

Indeed, it had been chosen in advance because of the thin moon, and the weather had cooperated still further by enshrouding what little light there may otherwise have been with the thick clouds of a summer storm.

The hour was not particularly late. But in these regions, behind the iron curtain of communism, as Winston Churchill had called it, the night had become permanent for those who cherished freedom.

The blackness of nazism had been replaced by the darkness of Marxism. The language of its bourgeois class had changed. The faces of the ruling elite of its monocracy had changed. The map indicating the geography of its globular stranglehold had changed. The high temple of its tyranny was no longer called the Reichstag but the Kremlin. The monogram given to those carrying out its cruelty was now KGB, not SS.

Everything had changed.

Nothing had changed.

Fear still gripped those held in the clutches of its grasp.

Thinking people, and those who loved freedom, still sought escape from the blackness.

Now, however, the darkness of autocratic empire did not cover the entire European continent, but only its eastern half. The light of freedom had come again to the west and was visible, as a crack of sunlight at the horizon's edge, serving as a stimulus to those living under the cloud and a hopeful reminder that freedom in some parts of the world still shone brightly.

The light at the western horizon was also a goal, toward which a one-time stream of emigrants had now become a river. Across the invisible curtain they poured in hordes, especially to that island of light called West Berlin—refugees from Poland, Czechoslovakia, Yugoslavia, Romania, and that eastern so-called nation of Germany, the DDR, all new puppet states of Mother Russia, offspring of the Revolution of 1917.

Even from Russia itself they came, though in smaller numbers by virtue of the rigors of escape and the clandestine passage required. The journey was long and arduous, money and barriers of language were constant problems, and the KGB was everywhere on the alert to round up those attempting flight from the motherland.

For some the difficulties posed were more modest. But those of Abraham's lineage had not been destined to an easy time of it, not since Egypt, Assyria, and Babylonia had risen up against the people of Moses, David, and Daniel. The purge of Joseph Stalin against them, though quieter and kept from the world's eyes, continued what his archenemy Adolf Hitler had begun and proved equally horrific in its result.

Jews, therefore, were all the more desperate to escape, yet had to measure their moves with the greatest care and caution. Identities still were kept close track of. Danger still lurked in unseen corners. A new generation of spies had raised itself up, willing to do anything to line its own pockets with accumulated favors to the state.

Spiritual famine continued to enslave the land, and the sons of Jacob sought refuge, both in the West and in their own newly created homeland of Israel.

●   ●   ●

The small band—comprised of a bearded older man, a younger man, two women, and a child—stealing furtively through the deserted streets on this night was not large. But in the quiet of this hour, each of the four adult hearts pounded with fear of discovery. The child already slept, carried to freedom in her father's arms.

Nothing else in the city moved.

The only sounds belonged to the night. Their shuffling footsteps seemed to echo their presence. They felt numerous as an army and sensed somehow that a thousand invisible eyes of the night must be watching their every move.

A sixth walked briskly in front of the tiny caravan to freedom. Before the night was over, he would again be asleep in his own bed while the five rested in preparation for the final stage of their long trek toward their own personal dawn.

They had but another several blocks to go. In wooded country it would not have taken long. But cities were unfriendly to travelers on foot, especially this city, and they had to keep to deserted streets and unpeopled commercial districts. The route the leader took them on, therefore, was circuitous, and the tedious walk lasted another hour and a half. He had done this many times, but each time never retraced his steps the same way. He had a family of his own, and though he had compassion for these people, he would not take foolish risks.

He paused and lifted his hand to signal those behind him to stop. He listened intently.

He'd thought he heard something, but now the bark of a dog in the next block relieved him that they were not being followed.

Still, it wouldn't do if the hound persisted in alerting its canine friends to strangers in the neighborhood. A chorus of barks would be sure to attract curiosity of a more worrisome kind than he knew would be healthy.

"*Schnell!*" he whispered behind him. "We must make haste."

He led the way out from behind the overhanging roof where they had stopped, breaking into a jog now, across the street, along its far side for half a block, then turned into an alley even more black than the rest. Behind him shuffling footsteps and labored breathing were the only sounds to indicate the exhaustion of his troops.

"Keep close behind me," he said, then walked quickly into the alley, straight some seventy meters to what appeared to be a high, solid, wooden wall. No door through it revealed itself. The way appeared impassible.

The man stopped, made sure everyone had made it through the alley and was close behind the first. He reached up and pushed at some concealed portion of the wood with his fingers.

Several minutes passed.

Several large connected beams of the wall now opened into a slit. The invisible gate had been cunningly fabricated and gave no certainty of passage even in bright daylight. Wherever its hidden hinge was located, it was obviously well oiled and made not the slightest sound.

No light nor voice betrayed human presence on the other side, only the faint disturbance of air indicating the breathing of lungs.

The leader of the small band leaned forward and spoke into the black crack where the door stood ajar.

"Haben Sie vielleicht Rosen?" he whispered to the figure shrouded in the invisible darkness.

But the briefest hesitation followed.

"Nein, das ist nicht die Jahreszeit für Blüten," came a soft voice in reply.

"Ja," said the man, behind whom three bodies huddled waiting in fear, *"jedoch für jene die lieben, sogar die Blumenblätter duften, und sind erfüllt mit Wohlgeruch."*

"Aha, ich sehe Ihr versteht die Wege des Vaters," said the voice. *"Wieviele Blüten braucht Ihr?"*

"Fünf."

"Dann kommt doch herein. Ich glaube, wir können schon einige für Euch finden."

26

Lebenshaus Revisited

• • •

SABINA ESCORTED HER GUESTS THROUGH THE BLACKNESS, past the cellar door under the house, and up through a concealed trapdoor into her own apartment.

It was then with extreme effort that she kept her voice low, once, after making certain all the drapes were pulled, she turned on a small lamp.

A gasp of astonishment sounded from her lips. Almost the same instant her hand clapped over her lips.

"Gisela . . . Helga—*oh, my friends!*" she whispered. "But what . . . oh, I had no idea it was *you*—whatever are you doing here?"

Any answer that might have been forthcoming was inundated by an overwhelming rush of hugs and kisses and whispered greetings. Sabina's were not the only eyes filled with tears.

"I am sorry for the abrupt call," said the leader of the pilgrimage, "but we had no time to get word to you."

"Rabbi, I still cannot believe it is really you! Why didn't you just say out there that you were friends, and tell me to open the gate!"

The rabbi chuckled lightly.

"Because for the hour before, as we wandered through the streets behind our intrepid guide . . . the whole way I could not help but be reminded of the night we and the dear Kropf family sojourned to *Lebenshaus.*"

"I will never forget the night of your arrival."

"I wanted to hear your voice saying all the same words of arrival as we heard on that night so long ago. Never had I heard anything that sounded so much like an angel as those words that night. And yours were equally wonderful a few moments ago."

"Thank you, Rabbi. You are a dear man!"

"But now you must meet my little granddaughter, Billa—though she is still asleep—and my son-in-law, Gisela's husband, Karl."

"Karl—oh, Gisela, I'm so happy to meet your little family!"

She shook Karl's free hand.

"You must all sit down," said Sabina, still whispering. "I wish I had something for you, but food here is so scarce. What would you like—I do have some milk and bread and potatoes."

"Anything, dear Sabina," said the rabbi's wife. "We are not in great need."

"Tomorrow, or whenever you can arrange it for us," said the rabbi, "we will be in West Berlin. Then we will eat!"

Suddenly Sabina's face lit.

"Does Ursula know?"

"No. Our departure was so hasty, there was no time."

"She will positively die of happiness!"

"We will try to prevent that, but we are anxious to see her too!"

• • •

An hour later the small ensemble huddled together in Sabina's tiny kitchen, voices low, whispering as they partook of plain boiled potatoes and bread, food for which they were as thankful as ever in their lives.

"Tomorrow would not be best," Sabina was saying. "I would rather put you on the subway on Monday morning."

"The borders are still open in the city, are they not?" said the rabbi.

"Yes, but the *Volkspolizei* are checking papers with more and more vigilance. Entry is not as automatic as it once was. *Torschlusspanik* grows daily, the fear that soon the door of escape will be shut. Occasionally there are detentions. With your names, and Russian identity cards . . . it would be too dangerous. But the subway is still safe."

Rabbi Wissen sighed.

"You are probably right," he whispered. "It is possible they are looking for us as well. The border guards could even have my name. I am being sought at the highest levels."

"Is that why you had to leave Russia so hurriedly?"

The rabbi nodded.

"The KGB has been seeking me for years. I have been blessed to remain out of their clutches. But suddenly, last week, I found myself in grave danger. We had to get out immediately. Otherwise, it is likely we would all have been killed. We are not even safe here. The KGB has fingers everywhere, even perhaps in Israel."

"Why do they want you—because of your work with the underground networks?"

"That is part of it. However, I am certain someone in the KGB has another motive, though I have no idea what it could be."

"The box and stones?" suggested Sabina.

"Perhaps. Though how could anyone in the Soviet Union know of it after all this time? If that is it, they are wasting their efforts."

Sabina nodded.

"I have the feeling it has to do more with the photographs than the stones . . . although perhaps both are involved."

"And your role in the network."

"That too. It is just as well that we relocate," the rabbi went on. "Perhaps I will be able to better use the information regarding Russia's complicity in the holocaust. World opinion must be swayed somehow. The West must know. Are the photographs in hands that can use them to our advantage?"

Sabina was silent. She had known the question would be raised eventually.

"I'm afraid not," she said slowly and softly.

"Nothing happened to them?" asked the rabbi in alarm.

"No, no . . . they are safe. They are still in my possession."

"You did not give them to Ursula?"

Sabina shook her head.

"Then perhaps I should—"

"It is too risky, Rabbi. Surely you know that."

Rabbi Wissen nodded. "You are right. If something was to befall me . . ."

He sighed as his voice trailed away.

"When you and I agreed upon what we would do in the beginning," he went on, "we said that the cause was more important than either of us. I pose too great a risk. But I remain curious—what are your plans with them?"

"I don't know yet. I have renewed an old acquaintance—an American who is high up in the government."

The rabbi smiled. "I think I know what you are thinking. That is risky as well, Sabina, my child."

"I know. I have decided nothing. But if he were to ally himself with our cause, he would have more prestige to make the photographs public than any of our other contacts."

"Perhaps, but Israel also presents a viable platform for world influence these days."

"I will be cautious," said Sabina, "and through Ursula will keep in constant contact with you. I will do nothing without seeking your counsel."

The rabbi nodded his assent.

"Will you not come with us, dear Sabina?" asked Helga Wissen.

"It is not yet my time."

"You said yourself that there is growing fear the way to freedom will not last," persisted Gisela.

"Yes, Sabina," added the rabbi's wife. "Perhaps your work here is nearly done, as ours must be in Russia."

"I cannot go knowing my father remains. Even if there is little I am able to do for him, I must remain near."

"Is there any word on him?" asked the rabbi.

Sabina shook her head.

"Have you changed your mind about the network?"

"You mean, asking our people to somehow mount an effort to free him . . . no, I have not changed my mind. I do not want to endanger other lives. Freeing my father is not the mission to which they have committed themselves. My father himself would forbid it."

"If I know our people, they would be only too glad to help. We have all committed ourselves to freedom."

Sabina nodded.

"That is true," she said. "There are some who have gone so far as to ask me to let them try to help him."

"You have said no?"

"Until now. Our dear friend Erich is so eager to mount some rescue attempt, though his wife is so fearful of their involvement. But

I will think further about what you say. It may be that the time will come when I will have to accept Erich's help and that of some of his colleagues."

A silence fell.

They all seemed suddenly to realize how late it was. At this hour, even whispers might be heard.

"Poor Gisela!" said Sabina, looking across at her friend. "You look so tired! Come, you and Karl shall have my bed tonight."

Sabina rose.

"I'm sorry not to have the quality of accommodations we did at *Lebenshaus*," she said. "I have a mattress rolled up in my closet, and abundant blankets for the couch and floor."

"We consider ourselves richly blessed by your friendship," said Helga. "We need no luxury."

"I will be going out in the morning—actually for most of the day," said Sabina, "with the old friend I mentioned. But my home is yours. Keep all the windows covered and speak only in whispers. The walls are thin. Rest well. I will be back in the afternoon, and we will make plans for your passage to freedom on Monday."

27

Happy and Momentous Times

• • •

THE NEXT DAY WAS SUNDAY. MATTHEW CAME FOR
Sabina again. They attended church together in the morning and
spent several hours of the afternoon in the city.

Sabina's countenance was noticeably lighter than during their
previous meetings. Some of the gaiety of her former self returned,
though always balanced, even in laughter, with faint strains of a
melancholy that would never again be far from her.

After leaving the service, shortly after noon, they sat down at a
sidewalk cafe to have lunch. Sabina sighed and sank wearily into the
chair with a yawn.

"Was the sermon that exhausting," said Matthew, "or is it just that
you find my company boring?"

"I'm sorry," said Sabina, attempting a merry laugh. "I didn't realize
how tired I was."

"From all that driving and picnicking and talking yesterday?"

"That must account for it."

"I was trying to give you a break from your routine, not wear you
out," laughed Matthew.

"It has been wonderful. You'll just have to forgive my yawns,"
Sabina said, smiling.

"And I had our afternoon all planned—the zoo, a walk in the
Grunewald, maybe even a swim in the Havel."

"That sounds better than I can tell you," said Sabina. "Even
though West Berlin has been accessible, somehow when one lives in
the East there is a reluctance to participate in the West's pleasures.
Tired as I might be, I will love every minute of it."

"Are you certain? You look like you need a nap already."

"I probably do. I . . . didn't sleep well. I'm sorry," said Sabina hesitantly.

An expression of concern crossed Matthew's face.

"Think nothing of it," she added, trying to laugh away his concern. "I couldn't help thinking of the ride we had, and about Papa and Mama and all that has happened. I must have lain awake longer than I realized. Seeing you and talking about it all has stirred everything up again."

Trying to divert the conversation, Sabina asked about Matthew's job. "Tell me more about why you're in Berlin," she said. "You said you're working for your president."

"I was sent here as part of the negotiating team for the Vienna conference on the future of Berlin," replied Matthew.

"You mentioned that before. I'm afraid I know very little about it."

"Berlin's whole future is at stake. I thought every German was following the events keenly."

"I don't know if you realize how different the two Germanys have become. I have taken probably even less interest than most."

"Why?"

"I don't know—perhaps because I have other activities to keep me busy."

"You mean your job?" asked Matthew.

"Uh . . . yes, my work," replied Sabina, hesitating slightly. "So then, tell me about what you're doing?" she asked, eagerly bringing the conversation back to Matthew's present assignment.

"You know of the debate over Berlin between Khrushchev and us—first President Eisenhower and now JFK?"

"I'm afraid I know hardly anything," replied Sabina. "News does not exactly come easily our way in the eastern side of the city."

"You do know what Soviet Premier Khrushchev is trying to do?"

"It is said in the news that he is working for the reunification of Germany but that the West, especially the Americans, are resisting all his efforts so that they can maintain their hold on Germany and Berlin."

Matthew laughed ironically.

"That is, in fact, exactly true," he replied, "though not in the way your friend Mr. Khrushchev would have people believe. He is working for German unification all right, but on his *own* terms."

"What are his terms?"

"A united Germany without any ties to the West, without any Western military presence—completely neutral and demilitarized."

"Would that be so bad?" asked Sabina.

"He wants us out of West Berlin and the entirety of central Europe altogether."

"Would that not be a fair price to pay to make Germany one nation again?"

"Not when you know the likes of Lenin, Stalin, and the most recent of their modern-day czars, Nikita Khrushchev. Don't you know what the goal of the Communist party is?"

"We are told they are working for peace in Europe, but that the Americans thwart their every attempt by bringing in more soldiers, weapons, and missiles. I know what they say is slanted to their own advantage, but that is what they say."

"The Soviets have probably a three-to-one missile advantage even as we speak," rejoined Matthew. "They have six hundred ICBMs targeted at the United States right now, and probably half that many aimed at the key cities and installations throughout Western Europe. *Russia* is the one exacerbating the arms race, not us. But back to what I asked—the avowed goal of the Communists ever since 1917 is nothing less than the takeover of the world. Peace is fine with them, as long as *they* are in control. If they can take over peacefully, so much the better. They have no qualms about using military force if need be, as they did in Hungary and Poland five years ago, not to mention the uprising right here in East Germany back in '53. If you were here, surely you remember the tanks they sent in."

Sabina nodded. She did remember.

"They will use force if they have to," Matthew went on, "though if they can take over peacefully, they will try to do that first."

"You think that is what they are trying to do in Germany, take over all of it?"

"I *know* that's what they are trying to do. Khrushchev has proposed a neutral belt of states stretching from the Baltic south to the Mediterranean, and involving both Germanys."

"What's wrong with that?"

"On the surface of it, nothing," replied Matthew. "We want to see Germany unified even more than the Soviets. Disarmament in Central Europe is one of our key goals too. What's wrong with the scheme is that it's nothing but a ploy by Khrushchev to gain control of even more of Europe than he has now."

"How would he do that?"

"It's a well-known political fact that every weak, neutral state, and especially every demilitarized no-man's-land zone ever established in history, has eventually fallen under the authority and domination of its strongest neighbor. Khrushchev knows this as well as John Kennedy. He doesn't just want a united Germany free from Western interference, he *wants* it—period—for himself and the motherland. He's more cunning than he lets on. He plays this diplomatic game on the world stage about what is best for the peace and harmony of Europe. But his plan is takeover pure and simple. Jack doesn't trust him for a second."

"How do you know all that?"

"Because we know the Soviets. We know their objectives, their motives. We know how they think."

"What if you are wrong?"

"We're not. A Communist infiltration in West Germany is Khrushchev's precondition to unification. His ultimate goal is a socialist Germany, not a capitalist one."

"You are certain?"

"Do you want to know something he said?"

Sabina nodded, thinking how much Matthew sounded like a diplomat. Though his arguments were convincing, some of her former doubts about what his response might be to her work again began to surface.

"Listen to this. I won't get it word for word, but I've read it over so many times, it's close: 'What does the reunification of Germany mean under present conditions of existence of the two German states? On what basis could it be accomplished? The advocates of working-class interests cannot even think of making the workers and peasants of the DDR, the German Democratic Republic, who have set up a workers' and peasants' state and are successfully building up socialism, lose all their gains through reunification and agree to live as before in capitalist bondage.'"

"Those are Khrushchev's words?"

"Right from his mouth. Do you see what I mean? Even the name Moscow chose for East Germany, the German *Democratic* Republic, is full of deceit. The Communists are bent on control. Once you realize it, it's visible in everything they do and say."

"I've never heard you speak so passionately about politics," said Sabina.

Now it was Matthew's turn to laugh.

"Sorry. I didn't mean to get on a soapbox. But I'm John Kennedy's aide, and Jack knows Khrushchev like the back of his hand. I suppose I do get passionate when I realize what the Russian dictator is up to and that half the world believes his smooth words about peace."

"You don't think he wants peace?"

"I'm sure he would prefer peace, but as I said, on *his* terms. He wants to control Europe. That's the bottom line. The goal is no different than Hitler's, it's only the method that has changed. Why, the Soviet ambassador said to a group of West German leaders in Bonn recently that among Khrushchev's conditions for unification was that major industry would have to be nationalized, and that what he called the power of 'monopoly capital' would have to be broken and the working class would have to assume political dominance. And you know what he means by the *working class?*"

"Communism?"

Matthew nodded.

"Khrushchev is subtly, diplomatically, and yes, peacefully, trying to eliminate U.S. influence in Europe—first by neutralizing West Germany, then getting the DDR and the BRD unified, and then slowly bringing the neutral, demilitarized new single Germany gradually within the Soviet orbit. If he succeeds, you can mark my words, within ten years of reunification, the Communist Party will be growing in power just like the Nazis did in the late 1920s. Within twenty years, the new united Germany would be taking all its signals from Moscow."

"That's frightening," said Sabina. "Things are not good in the DDR now. I would hate to see it happen to the BRD too. But, Matthew, you still haven't told me what your job in all this is."

"Very simple," replied Matthew. "To *keep* all that from happening."

"All by yourself! You are the one who will decide the future of Germany?" said Sabina in awed astonishment. "You *have* become an important man!"

Matthew laughed.

"Hardly me alone. I am only one of many on both sides. Actually, I'm working directly under the secretary of state, a man by the name of Dean Rusk."

"What do you do?"

"When Khrushchev realized that none of the Allies were going to buy his neutral reunification scheme, he turned his attention specifically toward Berlin. If somehow he could eliminate the island of freedom within the middle of the DDR and turn Berlin into a full Soviet capital, then the DDR would gain enormous prestige and would be a great triumph for Khrushchev. So that's what he's been trying to do ever since—coerce the Allies to give up their hold on West Berlin."

"You're not agreeing to?"

"Not for a second. But when Khrushchev started issuing ultimatums in November of '58, things began getting tense. Everybody was afraid of what he might do. He threw out plan after plan, following them with ultimatums. *Saber rattling* it's called, and Khrushchev is a master at it. Eisenhower and Macmillan in Britain and Adenauer in Bonn all responded to various of the proposals differently, and it seemed one of Khrushchev's aims, at least, was being realized."

"What was that?"

"Causing splits and divisions within NATO. But as soon as Jack was elected, everything changed."

"How?"

"He wasn't about to agree to any of the Soviets' plans."

"Wasn't he afraid of what they might do?"

"More afraid than he let on in public. He feared Khrushchev, but at the same time John Kennedy was bold and confident, and wasn't reluctant to go up to him eyeball to eyeball and stare him down. Khrushchev underestimated Jack from the outset, which is going to be his undoing. John Kennedy is not a man you take lightly. Anyway, the week after the election, Jack called me in and told me he wanted me to pack my bags for Germany."

"You've been here in Berlin ever since?" asked Sabina.

"No, but on and off quite a bit. I've flown back and forth from here to Washington a dozen times, to London nearly as many, and twice to Moscow. I've been living from hotel to hotel."

"Just think, we might have run into each other so much sooner. I wish we had," said Sabina. "But go on with what you were telling me."

"It was very touchy all through the election—that was last year. Talk of war with the Soviets escalated. Then they caught one of our spy planes flying over Russia and brought it down. Khrushchev was full of threats and continued his insistence that the German question be resolved or the West would have to suffer the consequences of what he might be forced to do. So Jack was elected in the middle of a very tense situation. He sent me here, and we've been negotiating with the Russians ever since."

"What happened?"

"Nothing yet. Jack was here just days before I ran into you, on June 7."

"Here in Berlin?"

"In Vienna, for a summit with Khrushchev. It was the first meeting between the two men."

"I knew nothing of it. Did they resolve their differences?"

"Not hardly," answered Matthew. "Khrushchev is a tough, wily cookie. He reiterated all his same demands even more forcefully. Jack has made the comment since that the whole so-called Berlin crisis is Soviet-manufactured. It was a very somber two days. Khrushchev certainly got the best of it. Jack left noticeably shaken. Privately, he said afterward that war never seemed more likely than right now. Khrushchev frightened him."

"How long has the crisis been going on?" asked Sabina.

"On and off for several years. Ever since Khrushchev began trying to force us out of Berlin and get the Germanys united and West Germany out of NATO. There's no reason for a 'crisis' except that Khrushchev doesn't like us being here."

"Why doesn't he?"

"We're too close. We pose a threat. Freedom threatens the Communists. They hate the very idea of a free-enterprise, capitalistic, NATO-allied Berlin right in the middle of their little puppet state. More than anything, I think it's the flow of refugees fleeing from the DDR into

West Berlin. Khrushchev is telling the world that capitalism is dying and that communism is the wave of the world's future. Yet thousands are fleeing from Poland and East Germany—and even Russia—right under his nose. Freedom is a priceless commodity that the Communists cannot understand. People will pay any price to be free."

As she listened, Sabina had grown very quiet, paying attention to what Matthew said with keen interest. This part of it she certainly understood, and very personally.

"They hate this constant reminder that in spite of their words, the people who live under communism want freedom instead and will sacrifice nearly anything to achieve it. I'm sure *you* probably know people who have left and begun new lives in West Germany."

"Uh . . . yes, I have heard about some," said Sabina, caught off guard by Matthew's comment.

"That's the most galling thing for Khrushchev, I think," Matthew continued. "He's watching the youngest and brightest and best, the very lifeblood of East Germany, drain out to the West. The only solution for him is a totally Soviet-controlled Germany, or a completely neutral Germany which he could get his hooks into more slowly. Otherwise, I'm afraid war is inevitable sooner or later. Khrushchev is a proud man. I can't see him allowing his prestige to continue to suffer in the world's eyes indefinitely. Right now, that is exactly what is happening. Every month the flow of refugees seems to double."

Matthew sighed.

"That's why we had the summit in Vienna and why Jack sent me here, to find *some* solution. But Khrushchev is as stubborn as he is proud. So far, we've struck out."

"Struck out?" repeated Sabina, with question in her voice.

"A baseball term—you do know about baseball?" laughed Matthew.

"I've heard of it, and seen pictures."

"When you strike out, that means you've failed, which is precisely what we've done with our Mr. Khrushchev."

• • •

Both were sorrier to see the weekend end than they dared show each other. Berlin's zoo, the Berliner Forst, the Havel River, and several other spontaneous diversions as well, had all been part of the afternoon's activities.

The pleasant memories of the fateful days since they had met outside the consulate building would sustain them through the working week, though it would take two of those days for Sabina to recover from her fatigue of Sunday.

Short nights she was well accustomed to. They were part of what she did. But not when they were followed by such a flurry of activity as Matthew had given her.

"Promise me," he said as they parted, "that next Saturday, your whole day will be mine."

Sabina's smiling acquiescence to his request lasted only until Matthew was out of sight.

The instant her door was closed behind him, a quiet flood of tears began slowly to pour forth from the depths of her being—tears of disbelief, tears of joy, tears of emotional release, tears of happiness for the two days she had just had, tears of grief for the years that had been so cruelly lost, tears of uncertainty about what it all meant and how far she should allow herself to feel things she had never thought she would have the opportunity to feel.

"What it is, dear Sabina?" asked a soft voice behind her.

Sabina turned to see Gisela standing close by, a look of worry and concern on her face.

"Oh, Gisela, I don't know!"

"It was not a good day with your American friend?"

"No, it was a wonderful day."

"Yet you cry because of it."

Sabina attempted a laugh.

"Haven't you ever felt two things at once—excited but tenuous . . . anticipating what might lie ahead, but afraid at the same time?"

Gisela smiled.

"Yes, I think I have."

"Everything *seems* better than I ever imagined it could be."

"But you do not know whether to trust that it is?"

"Yes, how did you know? I do not know how much to trust him. Our lives have gone such different directions. Yet . . . perhaps it is more that I do not know how much to trust myself, and what it is that I fear I feel."

"Right now I think you need to rest," said Gisela, smiling. "Come, lie down on your bed and let your mind think about it no more."

Putting her arm around her, as if she were the hostess and Sabina the guest, Gisela led Sabina into her own bedroom.

Sabina flopped upon the bed, still fully clothed, and wept again, until at length a restless though contented sleep overtook her. When she awoke, the evening was well begun. She rose and talked for an hour or two with the rabbi and his small family. They prepared a simple meal to share together, after which the small household settled down for their second night under Sabina's roof.

The following morning, praying none of her neighbors were awake, Sabina took her guests out through the cellar and alley as shortly after the early dawn as could be managed without arousing suspicion on the streets. She saw them onto the first subway of the morning into the western sector, then went home, dressed for work, and left on her walk to the agency. By the time the day was over, she was exhausted and was in bed by seven.

Matthew and Sabina saw one another briefly again on Tuesday. On Wednesday Matthew flew to Bonn for two days of meetings, promising to be at Sabina's doorstep bright and early Saturday morning.

28

Far Away in a New Land

• • •

A SEARING SUN SHONE DOWN UPON THE DESERT.

Why they called this the land of promise was the first question coming to the mind of many visitors to this place, long forgotten but now suddenly thrust to the center of the world's stage.

A long-bearded man, clad in black as if to defy the sun's intensity, strode purposefully forward toward the small village in the valley below him. Dust kicked up from his sandals, punctuating the arid pathway behind him with a peppering of tiny pebbles.

Despite the heat, he must make haste.

The sun was almost to the horizon. The Sabbath was nearly at hand. He must reach the house of Shalecham before the quickly moving shadow disappeared from the ground in front of him.

Under his left arm he carried a small parcel, his hand clutched tightly around it. His right hand jabbed the ground with a walking staff, more from habit than need, although snakes and scorpions were not uncommon in this region.

The Führer, who had attempted every method his twisted mind could conceive to eradicate from the earth those who now inhabited this place, would be turning over in his grave had not a worse place of torment been devised for him. His own holocaust had so sickened the community of the world's peoples that out of the ashes of his incineration chambers had arisen the sprout of a newly created nation.

The sprout had become a tree, as wide branching as the olive and mustard that grew so abundantly here. The people of this land were indeed as hearty as the wide variety of species that grew and thrived in this dust and heat, and as capable of finding nourishment here for their souls as the roots were for their plants. Where they had come from, where they had been for the better part of two millennia, only the Father of Moses and the prophets could know. That two of their twelve tribes had survived as a recognizable people among the world's races for all that time was a miracle of clear supernatural intent.

In A.D. 70 Titus had razed their holy city.

But no one, save Jehovah, the Lord of hosts, he called I AM who had raised them up from out of the ancient desert city of Ur to become a people as numberless as the stars in the sky, could destroy them.

Their persecutors numbered legion. Yet the children of the ancient Hebrew God survived, flourished, and outlived them all.

Titus was dead. Hitler was dead. Stalin was dead.

But the people of Judah and the Levites *lived,* in the land now known as Palestine. The four-thousand-year-old covenant given to Abraham once more had visual substance and reality in a place called *Israel.*

The round globe in the heavens had now caught the edge of the earth with the outer line of its fire. The traveler had reached the village by now and quickened his pace.

Everyone else in this small collection of homes was by now safely inside in preparation for the Sabbath meal. His was the only footfall to be heard.

He rounded a building, crossed the dusty street, approached a humble, square-framed dwelling, set his staff against the wall, and knocked softly on the door.

It opened.

"Welcome, Rabbi," said the occupant, bearded like his visitor. "We have been expecting you."

The rabbi entered, and the door closed behind him. He had completed the second phase of his arduous journey. His wife, two daughters, son-in-law, and granddaughter had remained safely behind in the western sector of that great divided city to the north. He would get them here as soon as was feasible. But his mission, on behalf of his people, could not wait.

The last rays from the sun emblazoned themselves upon the wood slabs of the door a few final seconds, then disappeared.

Dusk swallowed the valley.

Sabbath had come.

2 9

A Fairy-Tale Ride

• • •

MATTHEW KEPT HIS PROMISE, APPEARING AT SABINA'S DOOR
the following Saturday morning, the twenty-fourth of June, before
the sun was twenty degrees into the sky, only a handful of hours
after his arrival back from Bonn.

"Are you ready?" he asked when she appeared at the door.

"Ready for what?"

"An adventure! I cleared my whole day's schedule."

"What kind of an adventure?" laughed Sabina.

"Don't ask so many questions," said Matthew with mock seriousness. "You'll need to wear pants."

"Why?"

"No questions. Just trust me and come."

There was that word again—*trust*. But she would not fret about it
anymore just now, Sabina said to herself. She was determined to put
the questions behind her for the day and have fun.

She ran back inside long enough to change, then rejoined Matthew. They climbed into his car, and Matthew sped away along the
quickest route out of Berlin toward the south.

"Where are we going?" asked Sabina brightly.

Matthew did not reply. His face, wearing a wily smile, continued
to stare straight ahead as his hands clutched the wheel.

"You're not going to deprive me of the fun of anticipation, are
you?" she said.

Still Matthew did not reply.

"Are you teasing me, Matthew?" she asked, trying to sound
serious, but unable to remove the enthusiasm from her voice.

"Never," he replied, glancing over with a deadpan expression.

"Then where are we going?"

"Have you ever been to the Spreewald south of the city?"

"No," replied Sabina. "I've only heard that the woods and trails are wonderful."

"Well, then, here's your answer—I thought we might explore them together."

"Oh, how marvelous!" exclaimed Sabina, settling in to enjoy the drive.

Within an hour the terrain began to change, and they were climbing gradually. Suddenly without saying a word, Matthew slowed and pulled off the paved road. Within seconds they were inching along a dirt path scarcely wider than the automobile itself, through thick pines that crowded them on each side. When the way grew too narrow to continue and the branches began to scratch against the car, Matthew stopped, turned off the engine, and removed the key.

"I guess we'll have to walk the rest of the way," he said.

"Walk . . . to where?"

"I don't know, through the woods," replied Matthew innocently. "Come on!"

He jumped out of the car, hurried around to Sabina's side, and pulled her out to join him.

Matthew quickly struck out through the wood, Sabina doing her best to keep up, laughing and calling after him.

"Matthew, where are we going?" she giggled.

"Who knows—just to see what we can see," he replied, slowing as she drew alongside him.

"I don't believe you for a minute, Matthew McCallum. You know very well where we are going! You make a poor liar."

"What! Are you saying I have something up my sleeve?" exclaimed Matthew, pretending shock.

"Up your sleeve . . . what does that mean?"

Matthew laughed. "It's an expression from the game of poker, out of the Wild West period of our country. It means you think I know more than I'm telling."

"I do indeed," said Sabina, glancing up at him with a smile.

Matthew saw the expression and returned it. It was so good to see Sabina having fun again!

Their eyes met briefly. There was in the mutual exchange a deep river of friendship that far transcended what they had known before in their youth. It was a result not only of finding that the same magic existed between them after all the intervening years, but also of the added years of maturity that had deepened and strengthened both their characters.

There were in the glance as well stirrings of the seeds of love, dormant so long within the hearts of each, but rousing to life once exposed to the sunlight of the other's presence.

There was so much to say, yet no words could utter what each felt with mingled happiness and longing. The innocent fun of their youthful friendship was passing into something deeper and more profound, and they each felt sensations arising within them that they had stopped hoping ever to feel years ago.

Whatever had been her doubts, in that moment Sabina decided that without trust, life could be no good thing. If she held back now, and kept her innermost self shielded from the intimacy she could feel sprouting between them, she might never have the opportunity to know intimacy again.

What might be its implications, she would think through another time. For now, however, she *would* trust! Something was happening that she did not want to lose.

Quietly Sabina slipped her hand through Matthew's arm and nudged close to him. A peaceful joy surged through Matthew's frame. Unconsciously they slowed their pace, though Matthew continued to lead along the deserted path through the wood.

"How can a forty-year-old woman whose mother is dead and whose father is in prison and who has lost everything she once held dear—how can such a one as me be so happy?" sighed Sabina at length, her voice almost sounding like a purr. "I don't feel I deserve it."

Matthew said nothing, and they walked some time in silence. Each could have gone on thus contented for hours.

"Does it feel to you, as it does to me," she went on, "that no time has passed?"

Matthew nodded. "I've thought that too. Yet we are so much older. Looking back, it seems we were just children then."

Again silence came to the warm and fragrant pinewood.

"Matthew, where *are* we going?" asked Sabina all at once, her voice now sounding as Matthew remembered her at sixteen, playfully insistent and still containing the delightful laughter of an unfolding surprise. Talk of the past seemed to have injected her with the hot impulsive blood of her youth.

"Perhaps we shall find some high lookout where we can sit and look out over the Spreewald."

"Oh, that would be perfect!" exclaimed Sabina. "I can't think of anything I would enjoy more."

"High places, remember?"

"Like hunting towers in woods—of course I remember."

"Exactly. I thought if we looked hard enough we just might be able to discover a new special high place to share new sights together."

"There you are again with that cunning sound in your voice," said Sabina, giving his arm a squeeze of her hand, "with—what did you call it?—something up your sleeve!"

Matthew smiled, walking on without a reply.

"I say—what's this!" he suddenly exclaimed, turning a sharp bend. They suddenly entered a clearing in the wood.

Not fifteen meters in front of them stood two fine-looking riding horses, saddled, tied to the branch of a tree, and waiting patiently.

"Matthew . . . they're beautiful!" exclaimed Sabina. "Whose do you suppose they are?"

"Why ours, of course," answered Matthew. "Care to join me for a ride?"

"Matthew . . . do you mean it?"

"Certainly I mean it. Let's explore the forest!"

Matthew untied one of the animals, handed the reins to Sabina, who still stood gaping in delighted wonder at the astonishing turn of events, then untied the other and bounded up into the saddle. A clear horse path led out from the clearing in the opposite direction from that by which they had entered. It took Sabina only a moment or two to gain her seat and cover the ground between them.

The path was wide enough to allow two horses, and Sabina pulled alongside Matthew.

"Matthew, do you really mean it?" she said. "Did you bring these horses up here just for us?"

"No, I can honestly say I did not," he replied, smiling over at her.

"But you arranged for it?"

"You have me. . . . I must confess, my lady."

"But how?"

"I am a diplomat, remember? I have my ways."

"I can't imagine—"

"Then don't try. Just enjoy the ride."

"It's just too wonderful, like a fairy tale. . . . I haven't been on a saddle in years!"

"Then see if you're still horsewoman enough to catch me!"

Matthew dug in his heels and urged his mount into a gallop. Within an instant he was tearing up the ground at a reckless pace and had disappeared among the trees.

Immediately Sabina gave chase, caught sight of him again in a few seconds, but as fast as she tried to go, she could not lessen the gap between them.

Turning in his saddle, one hand clutching the reins, Matthew saw her chasing after him, let out a whoop of challenge, then turned forward again and leaned forward over his horse's neck.

The race was on!

All the pent-up years of restless inactivity suddenly fell away from Sabina's being. She was a girl again in the fields and woods surrounding *Lebenshaus!*

Laughing with abandoned ecstasy, she lashed and kicked and called to the steed whose name she did not know, determined not to be outdone.

Equally determined not to be overtaken, Matthew, laughing now too, called and urged his mount,.

The course he pursued rose steadily upward along the slope of the wooded hill. A mountain it could not truthfully be called, though its peak, which rose some three hundred meters above the plain to the north through which they had come, was the highest point for fifty kilometers in any direction. Its trails and footpaths lower down were a favorite spot for walkers and hikers, and higher up a great deal of riding was done, though on this particular day they seemed to have this one trail to themselves.

For some eight hundred or a thousand meters Matthew pushed the pace, around the winding way through the trees, until he emerged into a wide, expansive field. Without hesitating an instant, he continued his gallop. The trail led straight as an arrow through the middle of it, climbing now in earnest through the grassy heath.

Halfway, he reined in his laboring mount and turned in the saddle to await the arrival of his vanquished foe.

"Had enough?" he called out as she rode up.

Pulling even with him again, Sabina said, her voice breathless: "Matthew, where did you learn to ride like that! You handled that animal like one of your cowboys, I believe you call them."

Matthew threw back his head and laughed with delight.

"I told myself after the fall and broken leg at *Lebenshaus* that I would never allow myself to be so embarrassed again. So I set out to learn to ride. It took me quite a few years, but I have to say I've never been outraced by a woman since."

"Just what is that supposed to mean?"

"Only a harmless comment."

"I insist on knowing what you meant by it," replied Sabina with a grin.

"Nothing more than that I haven't been outraced by a woman since that day when I broke my leg trying to catch you and jump across that stream."

"You've ridden with *many* women, I suppose?" said Sabina coyly.

Matthew's silence caught her off guard.

"Actually, no," he said. "I've ridden with no one else since that day."

"Why not? Have you had no women friends?"

"To answer your first question, I suppose because I didn't want to spoil the memory of that first ride with you."

"The memory of breaking your leg!"

"I was thinking about the week that followed," said Matthew. "But enough about the past—come on, let's see if we can find the top of this hill!"

Again he was off like a flash, leaving Sabina once more to do her best to catch up. This time she was more successful, though whether Matthew was pushing his horse to the full extent could have been questioned. Within five minutes they crested what appeared to be the summit.

Both slowed.

Ahead stood a huge granite boulder, which invited any serious explorer to climb to its top for a view of the valley spreading out below them.

Slowly now, allowing the two horses to walk leisurely, they continued toward it.

"I say," said Matthew in astonishment as they approached. "What can that be?"

He jumped from his horse and began walking toward the rock. Sabina dismounted likewise and hurried after him.

"Matthew," she exclaimed. "It's a picnic basket. There must be some people nearby."

"There's no sign of anyone," said Matthew, glancing all about. "It doesn't look like it's been touched. Come on—let's see what's inside."

He ran ahead and stopped at the base of the rock, where the basket sat on the ground.

"Matthew, we can't do that. It's someone else's."

"There's nobody around."

"But you can't disturb it. It's not ours."

"Possession is nine-tenths of the law," rejoined Matthew. "Besides, I'm hungry. I wouldn't mind something to eat."

Before Sabina could protest further, Matthew had lifted the lid and, to Sabina's mortification, was proceeding to blithely examine the contents.

"A white linen cloth . . . hmm . . ."

He turned to her, holding an egg and a loaf of bread aloft with both hands. "Just look, Sabina," he exclaimed. "Two eggs, two fresh little loaves, a tin of butter, knives, salt, cheese, meat—already sliced—and jam. It seems prepared just for two people. . . . Why not us!"

"Matthew! What if they come back . . . ? What will they think!"

"Who?"

"Whoever's it is."

"It has to be for us—didn't you say this was a fairy tale?"

"Matthew!" The exasperation was beginning to reveal itself in Sabina's tone.

"Come, help me explore this treasure chest."

Reluctantly Sabina approached and peered inside.

"There's a note. . . . Look at that piece of paper!"

"Why, I do believe you're right. I can't imagine how I missed it—what does it say?"

At last overcoming her timidity, Sabina bent to one knee, reached inside the basket, and pulled out the paper.

"Can you read it?" asked Matthew.

"It's typed. *Welcome, weary travelers, to provisions prepared just for you,*" Sabina read slowly. *"Enjoy the food, but enjoy one another's company even more. Be in no haste to leave this place. Enjoy the fairy tale. Bon appétit!"*

"What can it mean, Matthew?" she exclaimed, looking up from the paper, her face flushed and cheeks glowing with positive delight.

"It must mean that we are to eat and be thankful."

"But how . . . how can it *be?*"

"We have landed in the midst of a fairy tale, Sabina!" laughed Matthew. "And we have been told to enjoy it!"

He replaced the few items under the lid, leapt to his feet, caught up the mysterious picnic basket by its two handles, and bounded up the great rocky incline.

She followed, still glowing but bewildered.

By the time she reached the top, Matthew had unfolded the linen and was unloading the basketful of contents onto it.

"Matthew," she said slowly, sitting down beside him, "this is *your* doing, isn't it—just like the horses?"

"Would you break the spell of *das Märchen?*"

"Knowing you did all this for me makes it all the more a fairy tale," replied Sabina softly. "Thank you, Matthew—I don't know what else to say. You make me feel so special, so alive, so young again."

Matthew smiled. "That's how I want to make you feel."

"Matthew, you are such a romantic at heart!"

"Now will you be able to enjoy everything that's in the basket?"

"Yes," answered Sabina sheepishly. "I should have known I could trust you."

"Come over here—what do you think of the view?"

"I hardly noticed," said Sabina, following him a little higher and to the edge of the giant rock they had climbed. "Oh!" she exclaimed. "It's breathtaking—I had no idea we were so high!"

Together they stood looking out over the opposite slope from which they had ascended and the plain toward Berlin stretching out northward.

"Almost as good a view as a hunting tower?" suggested Matthew.

"Oh, better! Though any view of *Lebenshaus* would be more wonderful than I can imagine."

"Perhaps someday we can gaze upon it again together."

"I'm afraid the fairy tale won't go that far, Matthew," sighed Sabina.

"Let's not worry about that today. Are you hungry after our walk and ride?"

"Yes, I believe I am," laughed Sabina, "though I had hardly noticed."

They sat, eating and chatting leisurely, enjoying the view and the fresh air, but, as the note had said, enjoying one another more, for another hour or two. They continued to talk freely long after having eaten their fill.

At length Matthew rose, walked a few paces along the top of the rock, and stretched. Unconsciously Sabina began to repack the basket.

"Matthew, there's an envelope at the bottom of it," she said.

"Oh?" said Matthew, feigning disinterest.

"Now, you know better than that—you had to have put it there!" chided Sabina.

"Then it must not be for me."

"Who then?"

"I can think of only one person. There's no one here but the two of us."

Sabina understood the meaning of his tone well enough. She reached down and took out the envelope, opened it, and withdrew the single sheet of stationery inside.

"This one *isn't* typed," she said, "and I recognize the handwriting."

"You have caught me red-handed again," confessed Matthew.

Silently Sabina read the lines of poetry, tears rising to her eyes as she did.

> *Es heisst, Liebe soll gleich einer Rose sein,*
> *Die in meinem Herz wächst, so süss und rein.*
> *Doch wird sie auch einen Dorn geheissen,*
> *Der wütend mir will das Herze zerreissen.*

Schöne Zeit einst mit Dir, die mich glücklich gemacht,
Hat die Rose in mir zum blühen gebracht.
Die Jahre der Trennung gebären den Schmerz,
Gleich Dornen zerstach er mein blutendes Herz.

Warum wohl die Liebe, sobald sie verwirkt,
So vieles an Tränen und Schmerz in sich birgt?
Doch ich weiss, mit der Zahl ihrer Dornen da steigt
Jeder Rose Ausstrahlung und Lieblichkeit.

"It's beautiful," she said, blinking back the dam. "Who wrote it?"

Matthew glanced down but said nothing.

"They're yours, aren't they, Matthew?"

"Writing them was a way to remember a very special person," answered Matthew quietly and seriously, the playful fun gone from his voice for the present. "Ever after when I read them over, I thought of my old friend from long ago, Sabina von Dortmann."

"Matthew McCallum," she said, attempting a laugh, but her voice husky and her countenance visibly shaken, "you are indeed a romantic!"

30

A Rose Remembered

• • •

THE WONDERFULLY WEARY AND HAPPY SATURDAY BEHIND
them, Matthew and Sabina walked slowly toward Sabina's apartment.

"I have something for you," said Sabina as they reached the
landing. "Wait here."

She unlocked her door and disappeared inside. Matthew saw a
light go on, then she returned after less than a minute.

"What is it?" asked Matthew, watching as Sabina rejoined him,
one hand held behind her back.

"It's my turn to surprise you," said Sabina.

Slowly she drew her hand out, clutching a small fabric bag six or
seven centimeters square. She handed it to Matthew.

He took it, untied the ribbon on top, and peered inside. The
questioning expression on his face indicated that he did not grasp the
significance of the contents.

"Smell it!" said Sabina excitedly.

Matthew put his nose to the bag and sniffed.

"Dried flowers of some kind?" said Matthew.

"Of some kind?" chided Sabina. "Matthew, it's a *rose*—can't you tell?"

"They smell different when they're dry," said Matthew, laughing
sheepishly.

"Look," insisted Sabina. "Don't you recognize it?"

"Should I?" asked Matthew, looking inside the bag.

"Yes you should! It's the dried bud of the yellow rose you gave me
at *Lebenshaus* that last day we saw each other in 1939, just after the war
broke out."

"You saved it all this time!"

"Of course. You didn't think I'd throw it away, did you?"

"I don't know. After all you've been through, I guess I'm surprised it survived."

"This yellow rose was one of the only things I took with me when we left *Lebenshaus.*"

"You've kept it with you ever since?"

"Wherever I go."

Sabina hesitated, then added, "Matthew, you've got to realize— that little rose has given me some of my most precious memories."

Now it was Matthew's turn to grow pensive.

"I do understand," he said at length. "I have memories of my own, though I don't have a rose to go with them, only the hope of someday seeing the little china box you gave me again. I don't suppose it survived the war?"

"I don't know. I left it behind at the house."

"Why did you bring this rose but not the box?"

"I suppose I left it in hopes I would be back soon. I've regretted leaving it many times since. It's probably been destroyed by now, along with everything else from that era. This dried yellow rose is all I have left of that happy time."

"Well then, I shall add to your memories," said Matthew, his face lighting with inspiration. "I will bring you a new rose every day I see you!"

"Oh, Matthew!" laughed Sabina.

"I promise. You shall have rose leaves of every color!"

"Then I shall make a potpourri of them!" said Sabina. "It will be great fun. We'll start a new collection of roses to take the place of the two we left behind."

"By the way," said Matthew with a grin, "what color *was* the rose from your father's garden that you put in the box?"

Sabina returned his smile.

"I'm not ready to divulge that yet," she answered.

Both grew silent.

As one, they each seemed suddenly aware of the deepening significance of having found one another again. The memory of their first exchange of roses brought to the surface with it many unnamed emotions each had held quietly in the secret chambers of their hearts for many years.

"I . . . I guess it's kind of late . . . ," faltered Matthew, clumsily breaking the heavy, pleasant silence.

"Yes," laughed Sabina lightly, feeling the awkwardness too. Suddenly her neck was very warm.

"I suppose . . . I, uh, ought to be, you know, getting back. Church again tomorrow?"

"I'd like that."

"Come by for you at nine-thirty?"

Sabina nodded, then glanced down in the near darkness.

"With the first new rose," he added with an attempted laugh.

"Oh, Matthew!"

"I mean it."

"Wherever will you get one . . . on Sunday morning?"

"I'll be up before dawn scouring the streets of the city. A promise is a promise. I'll be here on your doorstep with a rose . . . even if I have to steal it from some *Hausfrau's* yard."

Again silence stole over the landing where they stood.

They broke it together, interrupting each other.

Both laughed.

"Excuse me!" said Matthew. "What were you going to say?"

"No . . . go ahead," replied Sabina. "You spoke first."

Matthew shifted on his feet, uncharacteristically nervous for one who walked in his circles.

"I . . . was just going to say . . . that, today—all these days, these last two weeks. There hasn't been a time I remember enjoying so much. Not since *Lebenshaus,* that is. I want you to know how glad I am that . . . you know, that we . . ."

He hesitated, discovering the right words very difficult to find.

"I know what you are trying to say," said Sabina. "I feel the same way. I am more grateful than you can know. These have been the happiest days I've had since the war. You just can't know what it means."

"I think I have some idea. I've waited just as long."

"Waited . . . waited for what?" asked Sabina.

"Sabina," said Matthew in scarcely more than a whisper. "Don't you know?"

What could she say? There were no words. She could not even dare hope to think she comprehended his meaning.

Sabina flushed in the darkness, his meaning suddenly dawning on her.

"Waited . . . *to see you again, Sabina,"* added Matthew after a moment.

Still she looked down, unable to lift her eyes.

Slowly Matthew took one of the two hands hanging at her side, grasped it for a moment in his, feeling only the pounding in his own heart, scarcely aware of the trembling of the fingers he held. Then slowly he lifted them to his lips and kissed the soft back of the hand lightly.

With heart racing, Matthew released Sabina's hand with a final soft squeeze.

"Good night, Sabina," he whispered, then turned and quickly disappeared into the darkness of the evening.

Sabina stood where she was, watching him in her mind's eye long after he had disappeared from sight, for a full ten minutes more.

As the quietness of night settled around her, still she stood on her unlit porch. The questions that had plagued her about Matthew remained. The Communist-conditioned side told her to be cautious. She could have fun with him, it said, but she must guard and protect against his finding out too much. He was a diplomat in high places, who rubbed shoulders with the enemy every day. Who could tell what his deepest loyalties really were? He might take the photographs and turn them directly over to the Soviets in order to gain negotiating favor for his president's agenda. To do so would probably win points for him at the bargaining table. Why should he care about the cause to which she had given—

Sabina forced herself to stop.

She would not think such things of Matthew! She *did* trust him; she could not help it!

He was a good and honorable man! Oh, if only she believed it enough to give him the photos and be done with it!

She sighed deeply. She would not think of this anymore, not now. The day had been too wonderful to mar it with lingering confusion. She turned and went inside, thinking of the ride through the woods.

She locked up, undressed, and readied herself for the night. Before extinguishing the light beside her bed, she sat down and gently unfolded the paper containing the verses from Matthew's hand.

She read them over slowly, her eyes gradually filling as she did. It was too much to imagine that he felt this way, but the words before her could not lie. How could she not trust him when he had so openly bared his soul before her?

When she crept into her bed, the tears that finally came to her eyes this time were not those of confusion, but rather of quiet, joyous contentment and a feeling that all would be well.

31

Pink Roses and Promises

· · ·

"GOOD MORNING!" SAID MATTHEW BRIGHTLY, THE MOMENT Sabina's face appeared the following day. It was about nine-thirty.

"I don't see your car," said Sabina.

"I came by the most ancient of man's transportation devices—my feet! It's a beautiful morning and we have time. . . . I thought we could walk over."

Sabina nodded her assent, disappeared back inside for a moment, then rejoined Matthew outside.

As they began to walk, Matthew pulled his hand out from behind his back and thrust it toward her.

"It's beautiful."

"Didn't I promise?"

"Yes, but . . ." Instead of finishing the sentence, Sabina stopped and lifted the pink rose to her nose and breathed in deeply. "A fragrant one too," she added.

Matthew stood watching with a smile. His hour earlier in the morning had already been amply rewarded.

Sabina lowered the rose and looked into Matthew's face for a long moment. "Thank you, Matthew," she said softly. "You make me so happy. I . . . I don't know what to say."

"Say that after church you'll spend the rest of the day with me!" rejoined Matthew, as they began walking again.

Sabina half laughed with embarrassment. An expression came over her face that puzzled Matthew. "I'm so afraid you'll get tired of me," she said.

"Sabina, Sabina," implored Matthew, "don't you understand?

What's become of the Sabina von Dortmann I used to know, full of optimism, ready to take the world by the tail? We've got to do something about that downcast spirit that keeps trying to take away your spunk and confidence!" he added, as if trying to cheer her up. "You sound like the other East Germans I've met, as if everything good about life is over."

A tear rose in Sabina's eye.

"Matthew, I *am* an East German," she said, and the sadness in her tone was clearly evident. "Prussia, Pomerania, *Lebenshaus* . . . they're all from another time, an era that is gone forever. You asked me if I understood. But don't you understand? I'm a citizen of the DDR, not your United States, not even the German Federal Republic."

"I'm sorry," fumbled Matthew. "I meant nothing by it."

"There have been so *many* disappointments, Matthew. There is no happiness here. To survive here you learn to kill your hope and optimism. You *have* to, Matthew. Otherwise, you open yourself for one shattering letdown after another. You begin thinking that life might be good again, that the sun will come out, that maybe such a thing as love is real after all, and then without warning—"

Sabina stopped and turned her face the other direction. Her face was flushed, and suddenly she did not want Matthew to see the tears streaming down her cheeks. She began walking along the rutted sidewalk briskly.

Matthew hurried after her, doing his best to keep pace, then spoke to her earnestly. "I'm sorry for what I said."

They walked on for some time in silence, crossing over the border and into the western sector of the divided city.

"Matthew," said Sabina at length. "I'm sorry too. I know you were only trying to help. All of a sudden I was just filled with a great fear that—"

Again she looked away and struggled to maintain her composure.

"Fear? Sabina, what are you afraid of?" asked Matthew.

"The disappointments . . . you force yourself not to hope, not to look forward to anything better."

"But what are you afraid of?" insisted Matthew, the deep concern evident in his tone.

Again silence fell, and they continued to walk.

"I wish you would tell me," said Matthew at length. "You know you can trust me."

"It's not that."

"What, then?"

Sabina stopped, faced him, took a deep breath, then glanced down at the rose she was carrying in her hand. "Oh, Matthew," she said, "I feel so foolish. But the instant I smelled the perfume of this lovely rose, I couldn't help thinking of Papa and the garden at *Lebenshaus*. The memories were so painful all at once. Then a sudden wave of fear came over me that . . . that this time with you will be the same . . . and that this happiness will be ripped away from me too . . . and that one day I'll wake up and—"

She began to cry softly.

"You'll wake up and what?" he implored.

"Promise you won't think I'm silly."

"I would never think that," he said tenderly.

Sabina sniffed and tried to stop her tears, wiping at eyes and cheeks with her bare palm.

"I was afraid that one day I'd wake up and find you gone . . . and that I'd never see you again, just like before, and that . . . I'd find all this to have been nothing but a dream . . . !"

She burst into tears once more.

Matthew stood gazing at her forlorn countenance but a moment, then took a step forward and gently embraced her.

Sabina stood immobile and sobbing a second or two, as if debating within herself whether to believe that the dream was real, whether to resist its pull or to yield to it.

Slowly her heaving frame melted into his and began to relax. Matthew stretched his arms about her shoulders and drew her close. She leaned her face against his chest, still weeping. Neither noticed the rose falling to the ground at their feet.

"It is no dream, Sabina," he softly whispered.

"I want to believe it."

"Then do. Is this not real? Are we not together?"

"If only I could know it will not happen again. Hurt is part of life here. We learn not to trust our hopes. It is one of the many curses of living in the East."

"Then can you trust me?"

"I can try."

"Then—give me back the rose," he said, stepping back and releasing her.

"Oh, I'm afraid I dropped it!" said Sabina.

They both looked down and saw the rose lying between them.

"At least we didn't trample it!" said Matthew.

Stooping down to pick it up, he took it by the stem and again handed it to Sabina.

"It seems like whenever we exchange roses we're making promises," he said. "So I want this pink rose always to remind you of today and this promise I am about to make. I promise you that nothing will come between us ever again. We both had to wait too long to find each other, and I will never let anything separate us again, not even another war. I *promise,* Sabina."

A second time she took the rose from his hand.

"I will believe you," she said, smiling through her glistening eyes.

"You can," rejoined Matthew. "I don't make promises I don't intend to keep. This pink rose will join the yellow as the first of many—not memories of times past, but reminding us of happy moments of *now.* Agreed?"

"Agreed!" said Sabina, smiling in earnest now.

They began walking again, Sabina holding the rose carefully with one hand, her other through his arm as she leaned contentedly against him.

"So . . . what do you say to my original proposition?" Matthew asked after some time.

"I've already forgotten."

"That you spend the rest of the day with me?"

"How can I refuse? As long as you promise you won't tire of me."

"Never!"

"Then may I make a request too?" asked Sabina shyly.

"Certainly."

"Would you come back to my apartment and let me fix dinner for you?"

"That sounds wonderful. But are you sure you want to go to all that work? Wouldn't you rather go to a restaurant?"

"I would enjoy it. I don't have much to offer, but I am tired of always being out in some strange place. I don't mean I'm *tired* of going places with you. But it's not the same as being at *home."*

"I understand," said Matthew. "There is an awkward unreality to it, always going from one place to another. I haven't known what else for us to do together. I'm living in a hotel, and that's certainly not like home. But I didn't want to burden you with having to entertain me."

"How I wish we could just spend a week at *Lebenshaus* again!" sighed Sabina.

"That would be the fairy tale of fairy tales come true!"

"But now is now, as you reminded me. So I would love for you to spend the afternoon in my apartment, humble though it is."

"Agreed."

"I will cook us the best potatoes and bratwurst in all of East Berlin! I just three days ago received a new ration card."

"Your food is rationed?" asked Matthew in amazement.

"Not all foods, but many things. I bought my allotment of potatoes and have a good supply."

"Then we shall *pretend* we are at *Lebenshaus!* For this one day at least, we will forget about Nazis and Communists altogether. In all the world there will be just the two of us!"

32

Closer

• • •

NEITHER THE SOVIETS, THE EAST GERMANS, NOR ONE
Gustav von Schmundt were respecters of the Sabbath. The very
word, indeed the very notion of an almighty power to whom one
might owe the allegiance of one's daily activity, was odious to their
Communist sensibilities.

The first day of the week should have been just as well suited for
the carrying out of their designs as any other day—except for the fact
that most of the civilized world shut down so much of its activity.

On this particular day, however, *Stasi* Section Chief Schmundt
intended to make good use of his position.

Earlier in the week he had sent Galanov to Warsaw personally
with the direct and irrevocable order to get to the bottom of the
newsstand incident. After what seemed hopeful leads in the matter of
the two so-called eyewitnesses, their Polish connection had allowed
the trail to grow cold.

"You get out there personally," he had said, "and tell the numbskull
that if he ever wants to see the color of our money again, he'd better
tighten his fingers so that traitors don't slip through them so easily!"

Galanov nodded.

"Then you accompany him to pay another visit on those two that
supposedly had contact with the woman. Remember your aspira-
tions, Galanov. If you have the mettle to make a high-ranking KGB
agent someday, now is the time to prove it. Don't disappoint me. I
want hard evidence. I want the make, color, year, and license of the
automobile. If the man was close enough to have helped her start it,
then I'll wager his life that he knows more than he's told us."

Galanov had returned late last evening with the information they needed. He had had to beat the last pieces of it out of them, but in the end the man and his accomplice had relented.

He handed Gustav the sheet of paper. Gustav smiled. This should be all he needed.

He had spent the morning dragging an irritated bureaucratic colleague out of bed to open his office. It had taken an hour to locate the name and address that went with the license in question.

Now Gustav was on his way to that very address, located in Buchholz in the north of East Berlin.

Driving up, Gustav stopped in the parking lot below the apartment complex, parked his own car, then proceeded to conduct an examination of the two or three dozen cars at the site. In the third row, fourth from the end, he spied the license he sought.

Good, they were home, he thought to himself with a smile. Curious, though, the color and make did not correspond with Galanov's information. He glanced at the paper he held in his hand. No, there was no mistaking the license, though the description of the car itself was certainly different.

He would get to the bottom of it soon enough. He turned, pocketed the paper, and strode briskly toward the doors of the building adjacent to the lot, then up the stairs two at a time.

An hour later he exited the building by the same route, frustrated and angry, his pressed *Stasi* uniform showing signs of the dishevelment caused by the coarse information-gathering techniques of his section.

He stormed to his car and sped away, furious that so promising a lead had led him nowhere.

Deep inside, from the moment he walked in, he knew the woman in the apartment he had just left was innocent. Neither she nor her husband had known a thing and probably wouldn't have even been able to find their way to Warsaw if they'd wanted to. Besides which, the dumpy hag could scarcely have been the beautiful woman described as having been seen leaving the newsstand.

None of that had stopped his venting his wrath upon them, however. He was highly annoyed and didn't much care who happened to be the object of his vexation.

There could be no mistaking the license.

The only explanation must be that Galanov had been duped by the so-called witnesses in Warsaw. If they had helped a beautiful woman in an automobile with Berlin plates, it had certainly been neither this car nor that woman upstairs!

He began to suspect their whole story, yet it was all he had.

He should have gone to Warsaw himself. Galanov was young and untried. He had probably applied too much pressure, forcing them to lie. There had been a partial number earlier—that was probably still valid. They had no doubt made up the last numbers merely to save their skin from Galanov's fist.

It would take some time, Gustav thought, cooling down and allowing his reason once more to gain the upper hand, but he would go through all the Berlin registrations with license numbers that began with the numbers the two witnesses had remembered initially.

He would be able to narrow it to the automobiles of matching color and make. Then he would begin a door-to-door search—himself!

Whoever this mysterious newsstand lady was who lived in Berlin—he would find her eventually!

33

Matthew's Story

• • •

FORTY MINUTES AFTER LEAVING CHURCH, MATTHEW accompanied Sabina into her small apartment.

"I am embarrassed for you to see where I live," said Sabina as they walked in.

"I've been here before," he laughed, surprised at her words.

"Just for a moment or two . . . not to come in to sit and stay."

"Why would you be embarrassed? You don't think it makes any difference to me where you live?" said Matthew, taking off his coat and flopping down on one of the two chairs in the small living room.

"It's so different than *Lebenshaus.*"

"I don't need anything fancy to be happy."

Sabina thought a moment.

"Perhaps it isn't so much embarrassment I feel," she said, looking away and knitting her forehead in thought, trying to focus what she felt. "Maybe more a sadness."

"Sadness . . . about what? My seeing your apartment?"

"No," she mused, "I guess I'd begun reflecting on what it all means. Here I am from a well-to-do family, I grew up on the most wonderful estate imaginable, with even more wonderful parents. It was an ideal life. Yet, look at me now."

She glanced around the small plain room where they sat. The threadbare sofa and two chairs were clearly old and had probably had many owners in their time. One of the windows possessed the barest of covering; on the other hung the remnants of some cloth that had once been green but now had yellowed to something more like a sick grey. No carpet was to be found anywhere in the place, only bare wood, and that well worn.

The aging brick structure itself had probably once been an elegant city home, the residence no doubt of someone of means equal to Baron von Dortmann's. In the "new order" of things, however, it had been crudely partitioned into six smaller units. The single redeeming feature of the arrangement was the fact that each had a separate door to the outside. In that respect, Sabina was far better off than most apartment dwellers in the city, many of whom had to climb or descend several flights of dark stairways every time they walked out their front door. An alleyway at the back of the house separated it from any other buildings adjacent to it.

"Don't you see how deplorable it is?" Sabina went on. "I'm sad, I'm embarrassed for my country, for my people. It's not that I miss the luxury of *Lebenshaus*. I miss the *life*. *Lebenshaus* was special because of what it stood for. It was a House of Life because of the people who inhabited it. I'm saddened that the life has been taken from our land and our people."

"I think I understand," said Matthew.

"This dingy apartment is just like the whole country, of everything proud that once we called a heritage in this land, the land of Prussia and Pomerania and Otto von Bismarck. Now look what we've come to. We cannot even call the country ours any longer. Old Bismarck is probably turning over in his grave."

"No doubt so is old Eppie."

"Thank God she didn't live through the war," sighed Sabina. "Well, I didn't mean to turn melancholy on you," she said, jumping up. "I have a dinner to prepare for an honored and special guest. If I don't have anything fancy, then I'll make the best of what I do have!"

"That's the spirit!"

Matthew rose and followed her into the kitchen. Ten minutes later he was peeling potatoes at the sink, while Sabina whacked away at a head of lettuce for salad, then set the wurst into a black iron frying pan on the stove.

"Is this the right time?" Sabina asked as they worked.

"Time for what?"

"You know," said Sabina. "It's your turn to catch me up on *your* life."

"You mean tell *my* story of the last twenty years?" rejoined Matthew with a smile.

"Yes. I want to know how you got from prewar Berlin to be one of the president's top advisers."

"I never said I was one of his *top* advisers," laughed Matthew.

"I suppose I was adding my own interpretation to it."

"Well, the long and the short of it is that my father is responsible for the doors opening to me as they have. When we went back to the States when the war broke out in '39, we settled in Washington, D.C. My father was, of course, involved at many levels with people high up in the government. When the war was over, he worked with Secretary of State George Marshall on the European Recovery Plan. So he was back in Europe, Germany especially, quite a bit."

"Did you come with him?"

"Some of the time. I was twenty-five when the war ended. I spent a good portion of the next six years in school, though I worked both for my father and at other things during that time as well."

"What did you study?"

"Politics, world diplomacy, and history."

"I didn't know you were interested in history," said Sabina.

"I didn't use to be. It crept up on me slowly, through my other studies. I think your father may have had something to do with it too."

"My father, how so?"

"I can't put my finger on it exactly," replied Matthew. "My visits with your family, my talks with your father, and just being with you all—it reached into places inside me that I kept discovering through the years. As much as anything, I would say, knowing your father broadened my way of looking at things, taught me to begin thinking more widely and deeply. About spiritual things, of course, but about everything else too—relationships, world events, politics . . . and history."

"I am still curious—why history?"

"I've wondered that too," replied Matthew thoughtfully. "Perhaps when you think more broadly, an inevitable result is that you begin pondering causes and effects. Why are things the way they are? What made them this way? How did such and such a thing come to be? I eventually concluded that *thinking* in and of itself breeds an affinity for history. The very questions *why* and *how* are rooted in the past, in the progression of people and events and ideas and nations through time as they all relate and intermix with each other."

"I've never considered that before."

"I suppose that's a bit of a philosophical slant to give it," laughed Matthew. "In any case, your father got my mind pointed in whole new directions, one of which happened to lead me, as I pursued my political studies, toward history. I've been studying and reading it ever since."

"What did you do when you finished school?"

"It took me six years to graduate. I'd mixed in travel and some work. That's when I met Jack."

"Jack?"

"Kennedy. His father, Joe, and my dad were pretty good friends from the diplomatic corps. Jack was elected to the House in '46 and then the Senate in '52. I worked part-time for him when he was a congressman. I graduated with my degree in '52 while he was campaigning, and went to work for him on his senatorial staff the year after that."

"You and he are good friends?" asked Sabina.

"Let's say we are good colleagues," replied Matthew. "Jack's a few years older than I am, and of course his star rose quickly through the fifties. So in one sense I'm nowhere near his league. Nobody like me is *really* a close friend to the president of the United States. But he's treated me well and I have no complaints. I've risen in the ranks too, so to speak, and I'm doing exactly what I always wanted to. I have both my father and Jack to thank for that."

"How is your father?" asked Sabina.

"Doing very well. He speaks of your father every so often, always fondly. I've already written him about you, though I haven't heard back from him. Learning your father's plight will, I'm sure, bring him out of retirement if anything will. I can see him embarking on a crusade to get your father released."

"He is retired?"

"In a manner of speaking, though not officially. He's only sixty-seven, still young for a diplomat. He accepted the ambassadorship to Iceland earlier this year. Jack asked him where he'd like to go, and my father said someplace quiet and out of the way where he could write a book about his years on the diplomatic front. Iceland was available, and my father took it."

"And you," said Sabina, "did your new president give you the same offer?"

"You mean, did he ask me what I'd like to do in his new administration?" said Matthew with a smile.

Sabina nodded.

Matthew chuckled. "That isn't exactly the way John Kennedy has a habit of doing things," he said. "With old ambassadors and assistant ambassadors like my father, a president can afford quite a bit of leeway. When it comes to the gutsy nuts and bolts of running a government, however, and maneuvering through the landmine-strewn regions of everyday cold-war diplomatic life with the Russians, John Kennedy calls the shots. No, he gave me a job and said he wanted me to do it."

"Well, that should about take care of the wurst," said Sabina as she gave the three thick sausages in the pan a final sizzling stir. "I think we're finally ready."

The smell of potatoes and bratwurst filled the tiny room.

"I'm ready for it!" rejoined Matthew.

3 4

Does Truth Matter?

• • •

"DO YOU REMEMBER WHEN WE WERE TOGETHER WITH your father in the garden, and he told me about the *pathway of discovery?*" asked Matthew, slicing off a piece of the hot German bratwurst, dabbing it into the mustard on the side of his plate, then popping it into his mouth with satisfaction.

Sabina smiled.

"I remember," she said.

"That's how I would chronicle my life since I last saw you, as footsteps along that pathway your father spoke of. The most important things I have done and places I have gone have been internal, not political or career related."

"I'm sure my father would be intrigued."

"I owe him a debt I could never repay no matter how long I lived."

"What debt?"

"The debt of challenging me to think, to look at what I thought and believed . . . the challenge to find out what truth was. Of course, the most significant part of that was the challenge to find out what the character of God was like."

Matthew paused. His face filled with the memories of years of internal journeys that were fond to recall.

"I've thought of you hundreds of times over the years," said Matthew, "wishing, praying for the opportunity to tell you. My reluctance is just self-consciousness. Deep down I want to tell you everything."

"I'm happy to hear it."

"It really began with you, you know."

"Me?" said Sabina.

"That day we met at the garden party at your uncle's. You spoke so openly and enthusiastically about God—that's when my pathway of 'discovery' began."

"Hmm," mused Sabina. "I suppose you never know who's paying attention, and what kind of an impact you might be having on someone without even realizing it. I certainly wouldn't have known you noticed anything out of the ordinary."

"Your father added a great deal to it," continued Matthew. "After what you began, talking with him further turned my eyes toward God as a personal and loving and caring Father. When he threw the challenge to my father and me to seek and find the truth, I suppose after that I realized I *was* on a pathway, as he'd said, from which there was no turning back."

As he spoke, Sabina found herself taking in Matthew's countenance anew, almost as if beholding him in his maturity for the first time.

At forty-one, Matthew McCallum's face now gave full evidence to the promise it had shown in his youth. His frame had filled out considerably as his stature had grown to just a shade in excess of six feet. The 175 pounds he carried spread themselves evenly about his musculature, though his shoulders seemed just a hint too small for the expansive chest. His cheekbones and jaw showed no trace of fat nor the sagging so common to the onset of life's fifth decade. Their leanness gave an added expressiveness to his facial features when speaking.

It was his eyes, however, which revealed the extent of his inward development during the two decades since Sabina had last seen him. They had always been lively eyes. Sabina's father had seen it almost immediately and recognized the potential lying beneath them. The young man's countenance of hidden passion had led the baron in the attempt to probe and push at Matthew's internal doors in a more forceful way than he might have done with another.

As he had matured, his dawning determination and intellect Matthew had made his own, and they had brought fully awake the deep fiber of character that his father had implanted and trained into him. A first look drew one's attention and told the observer that there was a man here worthy of consideration. A second, combined with speech from his mouth, confirmed that not only did integrity and mettle of manhood dwell here, so too did purpose, focus, and integration of personhood.

"I'm sure that's what Papa hoped might happen," said Sabina after a moment or two.

"Well, it did. I don't know if it comes of being the son of a diplomat or what, but I've always had an inquisitive mind. I suppose it's one of my personality quirks that I always want to get to the bottom of things."

"A personality strength, I would say," commented Sabina. "So what did you do to get to the bottom of things, as you say?"

"I began reading . . . ," answered Matthew, "a lot."

"Books?"

"The New Testament at first. You knew that. I told you of it and asked you a lot of questions in the letters we wrote. It continued on for years afterward too, throughout the war and my college years. Reading Christian books followed."

"What kinds of books?"

"You might have heard of the Englishman named Lewis, a professor at Oxford. He did a series of talks on the BBC that I heard snatches of when my father and I were in England one time. Afterward I got hold of a couple of his books that addressed the intellectual reasonableness of the Christian faith. Through his writings he put me onto the man he considered his mentor—Lewis himself used to be an atheist until he ran into this fellow, a Scotsman called MacDonald."

Sabina smiled to herself, thinking of her father's old bookselling friend in Berlin, Herr Asher. But she said nothing.

"MacDonald is the best-kept secret in Christian thought. Lewis is pretty well known by now, however. His picture was on the cover of *Time* magazine in 1947."

"These two convinced you that the Christian faith was real?" asked Sabina.

"Not by themselves. I wanted to understand things from as many different angles as I could. I read a lot, from a wide assortment of Christian writers. It was not that I was skeptical, only that I wanted to be sure. I wanted to look at all sides of the thing. The most formidable book of all that helped me sort through it from top to bottom was simply called *Does Truth Matter?*"

"A provocative title," mused Sabina.

"A provocative book, believe me. The way I saw it, there could be only one reason to be a Christian—because Christianity was *true*. If it was, truth itself compelled you to adhere to it and to follow Jesus Christ to the limit in all aspects of life. If, on the other hand, it wasn't true, then nothing else about it really mattered."

"That makes sense."

"I'm not the kind of person who jumps into every new thing that comes along. But when I *do* make a commitment, I make it for keeps. I take loyalty with as much seriousness as anything in life. I told Jack that same thing before I signed on with his campaign in '52, although the conversation had spiritual implications at the time for me too. Jack said that was the kind of people he was looking for. I've been with him ever since."

Matthew paused a moment.

"You felt the same way about loyalty to God?" said Sabina at length.

Matthew nodded slowly. "I think so," he said. "I wasn't putting those words on it at the time. I was still young, and thinking through matters of faith, what some people would call *religion*—it was still relatively new to me. But yes, I gradually began to realize the stakes to be pretty high."

"How do you mean? I don't understand you saying the stakes were high."

Matthew laughed. "Sorry. Another Old West poker expression."

"What does it mean?"

"That everything's at stake, that your whole future, life itself, depends on the choice you make. That's what I came to realize about commitment to God. It wasn't a cavalier decision to be made lightly or hurriedly. Once you made it—*if* you made that commitment—everything would change, because your foundational loyalty in life had changed."

Matthew paused momentarily.

"Your father challenged me to discover what God was like," he then said. "Do you remember?"

"Of course," Sabina said, smiling. "I have never forgotten that conversation between the two of you."

"I never forgot either. I remembered everything he told me. I mulled his words over for years. Every time I did it seemed they peeled off another layer in my capacity to grasp truth. When I finally got to the bottom of it, the two facts that stood out from all the rest were that God was a *good Father,* just like your father had said, and that he was *true.* Those two facts, I suppose you would say, was where my own path of discovery led me.

"It was *truth* and God's *fatherhood,* as I saw it, that demanded a response, and ultimately demanded obedience. Your father spoke to Dad and me about not trying to 'persuade' us to believe the Christian faith. Yet I realized the incumbency upon me to *find out* if it was true. And if it was, then to *respond* to that truth."

"What did your father think of it all?" asked Sabina.

"Dad and I talked about it a lot. In fact, for the whole voyage on the ship back to New York after we left you it seemed like we talked of nothing else. Dad was so intrigued by your father's lack of pushiness that he couldn't help, like me, wanting to know more. I remember him saying once during that time, 'But I don't feel I *need* God in the same way some people do.'

"I answered him, 'But, Dad, what difference does that make? If Christianity is true, and if God is what the baron says he is, how can we do other than ally ourselves with the Christian faith and try to live by it, to try to be men of a different kind . . . even if we don't think we need him?"

"'Maybe you're right, Matt,' he said. 'Besides,' he added, 'maybe we need him more than we think.'

"There was one memorable night. We were out in the middle of the Atlantic. Dad had been in discussions all day long, and we'd received a radio message about the Soviet invasion of Poland's eastern borders. The future did not look bright. Already it was clear enough to Dad that the whole world was eventually going to be dragged into the conflict.

"In the midst of all the turmoil and uncertainty—and fear couldn't help being part of the equation too—we found ourselves standing at the railing of the ship. I think it was our fourth or fifth night out. It was late, probably eleven or eleven-thirty, the sea incredibly calm, the moon shining in a long reflection across the water all the way to the night horizon. We stood there a long time in silence. We were both thinking about your father and the conversation we'd all had that last night at your house a week, week-and-a-half before. Neither of us said anything, but we both had similar thoughts on our mind.

"Finally, as we began talking and sharing, we got into what must be one of the most unique conversations ever recorded between a father and son. We found ourselves making what amounted to a pact with each other."

"A pact?"

"A pledge that no matter where we were, no matter where or how our paths of life and career and responsibility might diverge through the years, that we would write or call one another with any new thought or insight into the meaning of things. We determined, then and there, to share the search together. We called it our quest-for-truth pact."

"How wonderful."

"Yeah, it really was."

"And you've honored it?"

"Ever since—both of us."

"How special that must be," said Sabina, not able to keep from thinking how much she missed her own father.

"Anyway, about that night," Matthew went on, "as I've looked back and reflected on it through the years, I think it was *then* I knew Christianity was true. Even though, as I said, I kept reading and studying and thinking for a long time afterward, I think I knew the truth of it without much doubt after that. But I had to keep investigating thoroughly just so that I would have a solid foundation to base my conclusions on."

"I can understand that."

"I had known Christians—and you meet this kind at college frequently, as I did—who base what they call their faith on such-and-such an *experience* they had, or on some *revelation* from God. The most difficult for me to sympathize with were those whose Christianity seemed to center around what God *does* for them—answered prayers, feelings of joy and elation. All along I decided that, if I was going to count myself as among God's children, I intended to base my belief on something more substantial than any of those by-products of faith.

"But there I am jumping around again! It's not easy to tell this in a linear way when it didn't just come to me one event or thought at a time, but over several years."

"I think I understand, though," said Sabina. "I'm getting the gist of your mental progression."

"So much of what you'd told me, and your father, came back to me as I stood looking out over the quiet Atlantic. After we'd talked, Dad finally left and went to bed. I stayed there alone for I don't know how long, just gazing out to sea. The next time I looked at my watch it was after 2:00 A.M."

"A long time," remarked Sabina.

"I don't want to make it sound overly mystical, because it was very quiet and personal. But as I stood at the railing, the sensation grew upon me that I was not alone, that God himself was *there*. It was somehow exciting, though with a unique kind of fear with it too.

"Yet even as I felt his coming closer to me that night than ever before, a part of me held back too, not wanting to be, if I can say it like this, 'taken in' by just one experience. It was a multileveled process of growth for me. Experiencing the power, even the presence of God, wasn't enough. An experience can never carry through. What would happen when there was no moonlit ocean to look out over? What would happen when it wasn't peaceful and serene and quiet? Thinking that I *felt* God in that moment—which I truly believe I did—wouldn't be enough in and of itself to sustain a lifetime's journey, as your father called it.

"So, as I said, though my heart had touched a reality of God's presence, and though I knew it was true, I continued to read and think and pray for several more years. Something in my *heart* knew the truth of the Christian faith that night, but my *mind,* my brain still had to be sure. So I continued for some time, not feeling like an insider *or* an outsider, but very much like a beginner in the life of faith."

"Did you ever stop feeling like a beginner?" asked Sabina.

Matthew smiled.

"You know the answer, don't you?"

"Yes. I saw the difference in you almost immediately, but I want to hear it from your mouth."

"I told you I graduated in '52. Right afterward, that summer, I returned to Montana. Dad was in D.C., and I was planning to return for the last of Jack's campaign, the election, and what I hoped would be his victory. But I wanted to take a couple months off, to enjoy the wilderness, to see some old friends, and to hike and camp in the Bighorn Mountains."

"The Bighorn Mountains, that's an odd name."

"Yeah," smiled Matthew, "I suppose it is. It's one of my favorite places—northern Wyoming, just south of the Montana border. I took only my Bible and two books with me, the one on truth I mentioned, and another. When I was hiking there, that's when God took it a step further with me—several steps further, actually. That's when I finally realized I was his son for keeps."

"You are going to tell me about it?"

"You're not bored with my story yet?"

"Not at all. I told you, there's no greater story in the world than the story of a man's or woman's life. I want to hear every word."

They had long since finished eating, and the food remaining on the table was now cold.

"Do you feel like some coffee?" Sabina asked.

Matthew nodded.

"Good, so would I. I'll make a pot, then we'll go back into the *Stube,* sit down, and you'll tell me everything—even if it takes us till midnight!"

They rose from the table. Sabina readied the coffee, while Matthew absently cleared away some of the plates and dishes from the table, his mind obviously far away.

35

Arms of Love

• • •

IN A FEW MINUTES THEY WERE SEATED COMFORTABLY IN the other room, cups of coffee in their hands.

Before Matthew began speaking again, however, he was quiet a long time. A reflectiveness passed across his face, changing its expression several times as Sabina watched, a look that spoke of mingled joy and pain at the memory of what he had experienced.

"When I said a little bit ago," he began again at length, "that I went to Montana and Wyoming after graduation, in preparation to return and join Jack's campaign, I was making it sound more definite than it really was. In fact, there has hardly ever been such an *indefinite* time that I ever remember in my life."

"Indefinite—how do you mean?" asked Sabina.

"I was at a crossroads. I didn't really have a specific direction in mind for my future. Working for Jack was just one of many possibilities. I'd been offered a job in the State Department in addition to Jack's offer, and Dad was trying to talk me into joining his staff. I was considering going on with school too, toward an M.A. or even a doctorate. There were many possibilities, but I just couldn't get a focus on where I was *supposed* to go. I'd prayed about all the options, of course, but even there it seemed like God was silent."

Matthew grew pensive again, though this time the pain was even more clear in his countenance.

"There's more you're not telling me, isn't there?" said Sabina.

Matthew nodded.

"It wasn't just a vocational crossroads, but an emotional one too," he said slowly. "I came face to face with my first crisis of faith since

I'd begun to think of myself as a Christian. All the years since being in Germany I'd been steadily growing and deepening in my understanding of the things of God. Now suddenly I found myself up against something I didn't know if I could handle. Whatever faith I may have had at that point became in a single instant of time suddenly very, very shaky."

"What happened to cause it?"

"I had a friend in school, not a roommate or best friend, but a very good friend. We used to spend many hours, sometimes late into the night, talking about spiritual things. He was a minister's son, raised as an evangelical Christian from infancy, but was now questioning many of the tenets of the faith he'd been raised in. We discussed everything, inside and out, backwards and forwards. Of course we were coming at it from diametrically opposite sides. He was, I suppose you'd say, in the process of *rejecting* a Christianity he had had his fill of. I, on the other hand, was in the process of coming *into* a Christianity I was hungry to know more of. But when we met, on that continuum of personal growth, it was as if we were at the same place, though moving in opposite directions. We were asking the same questions, wondering the same things, though I from a perspective of *wanting to know it was true,* he from a perspective of *wanting to prove it false.*

"I suppose the friendship was good for the development of my faith, in giving me something very different from the Christianity of your father's to have to bump up against. My friend forced me to think things through all over again, from the other side of the fence. It was a sharpening, though sometimes frustrating and painful, experience. But his doubts only served in the end to make my belief all the stronger."

Matthew stopped, then sighed and looked away. Sabina waited.

"He was a very moody person, a dark personality, very serious. Almost morose at times. Nevertheless, it was a good friendship. We had fun together too. When the right mood struck us both, oh but could we laugh together! I can remember laughing so hard I couldn't breathe! Anyway, we parted on graduation day, each of us promising to write, to continue our quest for truth together, and to see each other again in the fall when I returned to the east."

"*Did* you write to each other?" asked Sabina.

Matthew smiled, though it was a smile that contained no joy, only a poignant memory.

"Only once. That is, there was but one letter that passed between us," he replied, and his voice was soft and faraway.

"I'd been out walking in the hills of Wyoming all day. It was one of the most extraordinary days of my life. I was facing so much uncertainty, especially regarding my future, which job to take, what to do, whether to pursue my education—I had so much on my mind.

"As I walked, it was like God slowly descended and began to walk with me. More than that, I almost felt like he was uplifting me somehow, almost like my feet were on another path than the one I was walking, like I was moving in two planes at once. It probably sounds a bit weird, like a surreal experience. Maybe in a way it was. The Bible talks about the Holy Spirit praying for you when you don't know what to pray. There was that aspect of it too. I was uncertain about so many things that I didn't even feel that I had the capacity to pray. Yet I found welling up from inside me a continuous string of prayers, about *everything* that was burdening down my mind. I felt almost like an observer.

"As I prayed and walked, feeling the whole time like God was prompting the prayers rather than me, I found myself bringing to the surface each of my concerns, and then one by one handing them over to him.

"*Should I take this job or that?* I put all the options into his hands.

"*Should I continue on with school?* I gave it to him and turned it loose.

"*Should I get involved in the upcoming election?* Again, I prayed, then placed the decision in God's hands.

"I prayed for all the people I knew. I prayed for my father. I prayed for my own spiritual life and growth and asked God to continue to make me more and more his son, more and more of the man he wanted me to be. I prayed for my future wife, whoever she might be, though I had no one specific in mind at the time. I prayed for you and your father and mother, though I had no way of knowing at the time that your mother was dead. And, of course, I prayed for my searching friend.

"I don't know how to describe it. It was just an extraordinary day. I'd gone high up into the Bighorns, to a vantage point on a huge mountainlike crag of rock where you could look down and see in all directions, including the valley off to the east. I stayed there several hours. It was like being in another world, all alone with the Creator who had made it all. Then slowly, toward the middle of the afternoon, I made my way back down to the hotel where I was staying.

"As I descended, gradually the time of prayer came to a close. Such a tremendous sense of emptiness came over me—a good emptiness, a clean emptiness. I felt as though I'd gotten up and out of me all the weights and concerns that had been burdening me down. I felt light, happy, carefree. I skipped and ran part of the way, feeling such an abandonment and joy from having released all the pressures I'd been carrying during my last year of school. I don't know how to describe it but to say I felt so *good,* so alive, so jubilant. I couldn't help but thank God as I went. I knew it was all his doing. I felt closer to him than at any time since the night on board the ship back in '39.

"When I got back to the hotel, several letters were waiting for me that had arrived by mail about noon. Eagerly I tore into them while still in the lobby . . . and suddenly it was as if everything I'd given to God suddenly turned sour.

"One was from the State Department saying the job offer had been withdrawn. There was a letter from my father telling me of a crisis in his life that had come up unexpectedly.

"And there was a letter from my friend. . . . I'd saved it till the last because I knew it would require thought to read it. I went back to my room, sat down, and opened it.

"Just the look of the letter was dark. In a heavy black scrawl he poured out his despondent thoughts. I'd never heard such darkness from him. I could tell he was in a bad way, and as I read suddenly a fear seized me to think what hints I might be hearing between the lines.

"I broke into a cold sweat, threw the letter down without finishing it, and ran back downstairs to the phone. Already my fingers were shaking as I did my best to hold the receiver. Finally the connection to his apartment in Washington came through. But it was a strange voice that answered.

"I asked for my friend.

"There was a long pause. The voice on the other end asked me who I was. I said I was a friend and identified myself.

"Another long pause.

"Then the voice returned. He was afraid he had some dreadful news for me. My friend . . . had killed himself the day before."

Matthew choked on the words, then looked at Sabina with a look of such mute helplessness as she had never seen on his face, his eyes flooding with tears.

"Matthew!" she said, her eyes filling too as she stretched out her hand and placed it lightly on his arm. "I'm so sorry."

"I was stunned," said Matthew, beginning to weep even through his words. "Suddenly everything went black. A huge wave of utter despair crashed over me, as great in its heaviness as had been the sense of lightness and joy only twenty minutes before.

"I lost track of the next hour. I can hardly remember anything except stumbling outside, down the stairs, out of the hotel, and off again along the path I had just come from. My feet were heavy and plodded aimlessly along, my brain in a daze.

"'God . . . O God . . .' was all I could say. "I couldn't even pray, though less than an hour earlier prayers had been pouring from out of me like an unending stream.

"All had grown black. Everything seemed crumbling around me. Suddenly there was no meaning, no purpose, no reason even to go on. Very life itself was gone. It was as though I had come under the cloud of my dead friend's despondency and spiritual despair.

"The prayers of earlier in the day, the sense of God's presence, it was gone so far from me now. Everything had shaken and twisted upside down. My feet were swept out from under me.

"I had given everything in my life to God . . . and he had *taken* them.

"Taken *everything!*

"Left me with nothing, with not so much as an atom worth living for.

"On I stumbled, unconscious of my way. 'God . . . God, why . . . O God, why . . . ,' I continued to groan."

Sabina listened, expressionless, her eyes wide, feeling Matthew's anguish with him.

"I reached a point probably two hundred yards from the hotel, where a tiny stream flowed under a stone bridge. The path took me to the bridge. Without thinking why, I stopped, and there stood staring blankly down into the trickling water, leaning against my hands and arms on the rough stone baluster.

"Five or ten seconds passed. My spirit slowly calmed.

"I took in a deep breath, then another. The next words out of my mouth were different. They were a cry from the depths of my heart.

"*'God . . . God, help me,'* I said, and never had a prayer from my mouth contained more urgency or desperation.

"The sense of calm deepened. Again I took in a deep breath.

"Then very slowly a remarkable thing began to happen. The sense of God's presence again returned and stole in upon me. But this time it was not jubilant or full of the kind of happiness that would make me skip down a hill. It was quiet and full of what I can only call an indescribable love.

"I *knew* the Father was with me, that he loved me and would take care of me. More than that—I knew *my* Father was with me, that he truly was a Father to call *Father,* and that now was the moment for me to look up, to utter that precious word to him, and to let him be all a *Father* should be to me in that moment of my pain and aloneness. It was time to melt into his arms.

"Somehow the sense returned that all was well, and that he was still God. I literally felt his arms of love wrap themselves about my shoulders and encircle me with his tenderness.

"I'm not ashamed to say that I wept as I stood there," and as Matthew spoke, tears continued to flow freely down both his face, as well as Sabina's.

"It's difficult to describe because I'm not really an emotional person. I mean, I *am* emotional . . . but inside, not where people can see. I *feel* things deeply, but I don't express them in the way that people ordinarily associate with emotionalism.

"Anyway, in those few minutes as I stood there on that bridge, all alone in the world, feeling a loneliness like I'd never felt in my life, literally like I was the only human being left alive, from inside me welled up huge reservoirs of feeling and emotion more than ever in my life before. At the core of it—in spite of the pain, in spite of the loneliness, in spite of the anguish over my friend—a great joy of quiet contentment surged through me, contentment just to be in my Father's arms, and to know that I was loved by him, and to know that the only thing that mattered was that I was his son.

"The marvelous thing is . . . that was all I wanted to be right then—his son. Suddenly nothing else mattered.

"In that moment, my whole life changed. It was the watershed experience. Everything till then led up to that moment, everything thereafter in my life has its roots in that moment."

36

The Moment Comes to All

• • •

MATTHEW STOPPED, THEN LAUGHED LIGHTLY.

"It's funny," he said. "I said earlier that as I read and thought and prayed, I didn't want my faith to be based on an emotional experience. Yet what I'm describing as the most important single event in my life was as emotional as an experience can be. I wonder if there's a contradiction in that."

"Maybe not contradiction," suggested Sabina, "but balance."

"I hope you're right."

"Perhaps, too, the emotional experience has validity and made such an impact upon you because it was rooted in a sound intellectual foundation. But don't analyze it just now, Matthew," Sabina added. "I want to hear the rest of the story!"

Matthew sighed, thought a moment, then continued.

"It's difficult to put words to. This is hard to do, you know, even though I've longed for so long to be able to tell you. So many emotions surged through me, most of all the great love I felt. The empty loneliness was still there. It didn't just suddenly disappear. But my feelings were transformed from the despondency of earlier to an astringent kind of pain, cleansing, purifying, healing. I felt that I was being sliced open and then stripped bare of anything left I could call myself, to call my own. I don't mean to be crude, but it felt like when you rip the guts out of a fish. Everything that I had previously called *myself*—all the things I had prayed about earlier and had given over to God—everything was utterly gone.

"Nothing was left.

"The pain had seared it out of me, burned it up. All that remained

161

was an empty hole. And into that hole, that vacuum, that emptiness, God now poured the only thing he had to give me—*himself.* As I stood there, I could literally feel his love filling me."

Again Matthew stopped, glanced away, and let out a deep sigh.

"It always takes such an effort to relive it," he said. "All the emotions come back. It's like being there again."

"What did you do then?" asked Sabina.

"Eventually I turned around and walked slowly back to the hotel. I don't suppose it was all that long a time I stood there at the bridge. Five, ten minutes maybe. But an eternity at the same time.

"When I turned around to walk *back,* I was on an altogether different road than I'd been on walking *to* the bridge. The former me had walked out there and had died.

"There on that tiny little bridge, I left the innards, the guts, of everything I thought comprised what I would have called *myself.* In a sense I had released them all earlier when I'd prayed about all those specifics and given them to God. But maybe, without knowing it, I still held onto them. So God reached down and took them, laid them aside, and put them to death. When I turned to walk back, the inside of me was an empty shell, so to speak, with nothing in it but God the Father, and his love."

"What did you do?"

"You mean for the rest of the day?"

Sabina nodded.

"I don't even know. All I can remember was a sense of the love and joy I felt starting to spread out. Things began to look different. Even as I walked those two hundred yards, it was like a dark cloud lifted up from the earth and the sun came out. In my memory—"

Matthew stopped and smiled to himself.

"Obviously it can't have really been this way, though I can't recall anything of what the weather was like," he said in a musing tone. "But as I think back, there is even almost a sensation of *squinting* from the excess light. My hotel room looked brighter. The other people who were around became suddenly so vivid. Everywhere I looked I felt things and people tinged with an undefined holiness. All I wanted to do was reach out and give away this great love I felt. I couldn't help smiling.

"Oh, the love I felt even for strangers I would see in the halls or the lobby! A few times I caught some odd looks coming my way, and I know it was because I was just so exuberantly happy."

Matthew chuckled.

"It rings so humorous in my ears to hear myself tell it. It doesn't sound like me."

"And the rest of the day was joyful like that?"

"Yes, though I don't recall the specifics of how I spent the rest of the day, nor the next. I read, I wrote a few letters, I walked in the Bighorns for miles and miles, talking to God.

"Everything had suddenly changed. The concern over my future was gone. A great carelessness came upon me during the following weeks for what was to become of me. I wrote to friends, trying to tell them what had happened. I read tremendously."

He paused for a second or two, then continued.

"I told you I had two books with me. The second was called *Life in the Center*. There is no describing how that book got into places inside me that had never been opened before. How the hand of God had been directing events such that *that* book was awaiting me in my room when I walked back from my encounter on the little foot-bridge! There could not have been a more fit way for God to follow up the experience than with what he revealed to me through the words on those pages.

"Over the next two weeks I devoured that book. I think I read it five or six times. That, along with the New Testament, and walking and talking with God—it took up nearly all my time.

"When I returned to D.C., I wasn't the same young man who had left for the Bighorns. I tried to tell Jack about it, but the idea of a personal God was just too big a stretch for him to comprehend. He still wanted me for his campaign, though, and eventually I felt that God would have me work for him. But my motives and directions in life weren't the same as they had been before. None of the old things mattered. Only one thing *did* matter to me then, and it's really the only thing I've cared seriously about ever since."

"What was that?" asked Sabina.

"I'm sure you remember when your father was talking to my dad and me and he told us that in every man or woman's life a moment of decision always comes."

Sabina nodded.

"The Spirit of God sets the time and circumstances, he said. I remember his words almost exactly. He said that whenever and by whatever circumstances the challenge comes, all of life hangs in the balance in that moment. There can be no avoiding it. The moment of decision has come. Jesus looks us in the eye, and though he uses ten million different sets of circumstances to utter it, the words are always the same—*Follow me.*"

As Sabina sat listening, it was eerily like hearing her own father speak. The words indeed were his. She remembered the night almost as vividly as did Matthew.

"When those words sound in our hearts, your father said, there are only two paths to take—forward into life with him, or to turn your back and walk away.

"It took some time before I was fully aware of the implications of what had happened. But I came to realize that the moment your father had predicted had come for me that day between the hotel and the bridge, after I had received my friend's letter and then learned of his suicide.

"I had emptied myself completely before God. He had, like with Job, peeled away my flesh and soul to the bone, going even deeper than I had been able to go into my own self. Then he had allowed me to see my friend's black despondency, and to feel the weight of horror at what becomes of a man who makes the latter of those two choices, who turns his back, rejects God, and says to himself that life is no longer worth living.

"Then it was as if God said to me, *I have shown you all this. I have let you feel the anguish and pain of death. I have stripped you bare. I have heard your prayers and I have taken all that you offered me, taken it forever, never to place it back in your hands. I have emptied you. I have slain you from your former ambitions and hopes and goals. I have let you face the loneliness of having nowhere and no one to turn to. Now I put before you the choice—can you, in the midst of all that, trust me? Do you trust me? Do you still believe that I am a good Father to all my children, that I am a God to call Father? Can you believe it and trust me . . . will you trust me? Even more . . . will you now follow me wherever I may lead you? I beckon you to come, my son. I command you to come. But the choice is yours.*

"Between the hotel and the bridge the two choices presented themselves, exactly as your father had said. Two roads opened before me. My friend had chosen his way. Could I trust God in spite of the fact that some did not? It was a Rubicon, a moment of decision, as I spoke about earlier.

"I reached the bridge, and there made my choice. That's why I call it the watershed moment of my life.

"So to answer your question, Sabina," Matthew said, "after that the only thing that mattered was to do what God had commanded me to do: *Follow him.* That's the path I chose—to follow him, to be his disciple. I wanted nothing but to be completely, entirely, utterly God's person—his man, his son—and to do what he wanted me to . . . to give him my absolute all, to obey him in every phase of life."

A long silence followed. When Matthew next glanced over at Sabina, she was crying softly.

It was several minutes before either of them spoke.

"It was always one of my father's strongest convictions," said Sabina, "that great spiritual damage is done by trying to rush an individual's response to God. He felt the inner dialog between a man or woman's spirit and the voice of God's Spirit was a holy one into which he was loathe to intrude. He trusted God so much that he would rather wait and pray for a person for twenty years than push him prematurely toward a moment of decision that may not be of God's initiation."

"I owe my very faith to his trusting in God that way for me," said Matthew. "I left your father hungry to find God, probably hungrier than if he'd rushed me. So God continued to probe deeper and deeper into me, until, thirteen years later, he was at last ready to look me in the eye and command me to follow. By that time I was ready to give him my all."

"My father always had great wisdom when it came to trusting God for other people."

"He had wisdom in many things," said Matthew.

"And great patience to await God's working," added Sabina.

"The patience of the Father," rejoined Matthew. "How grateful I am for it. He waited a long time for me."

"Did you call your father to tell him about what had happened to you on the bridge?" asked Sabina.

"I called him that very night. We talked for over an hour."

37

A Box for Memories

• • •

IT WAS SEVERAL DAYS LATER.

Matthew and Sabina sauntered slowly arm in arm along the sidewalk of Kurfürstenstrasse in West Berlin. On every side hurried men and women bustled in and out of shops and along the sidewalk in both directions. Matthew and Sabina were oblivious to the frenetic pace about them.

Hardly thinking of what she was saying, Sabina suddenly asked, "Why did you never marry?" The words had escaped her lips before she considered the implications. Once out, she could not retrieve them.

A long silence followed. Sabina began to grow both concerned and embarrassed over her words.

"I'm sorry, Matthew," she said at length, "I didn't mean to—"

"No, no, it's all right," he interrupted her. "I don't mind telling you."

"You don't have to say anything."

"I *want* to tell you. Your question made me realize, I think for the first time, that I have wanted to tell you without even knowing it. But I didn't know what to say."

He stopped. Sabina waited.

"Before . . . you know, when Dad and I visited you before the war, we were so young, and I suppose what you'd call innocent. It was pure, unencumbered. We just had such fun together, without having to be anxious over all the . . . you know, the kinds of things young boys and girls usually fret over. I'm sure you've thought about it too."

"Many times," Sabina said, nodding. "You were like no one I'd ever met."

"As you were for me," rejoined Matthew. "Yet part of the chemistry of that special time didn't have to do with either one of us, but what we were *together,* if that makes any sense."

"It does."

"At least so I have come to think about it since," added Matthew. "There was such a delightful freedom and carefree quality to it. If I can say it without hurting your feelings, you were not so much a girl, a young woman to me, as a friend, a comrade. Can . . . do you understand?"

"Of course I do. It was exactly the same for me."

"Yet I would not deny that I was aware of something more at the same time. When you walked in at the Schmundt place, after I hadn't seen you for—what was it, a year or year-and-a-half?—I thought I had never laid eyes on someone so beautiful. When we danced later, I confess that my heart was pounding inside me."

"I remember the first dance that day too. I had been so looking forward to seeing you again."

"Do you remember the next night, after Eppie's tale of ghosts and the dungeon, up on the balcony?"

"I will never forget," said Sabina.

"When your hand slipped into mine, I could have grabbed you and hugged you so hard I might have squeezed the life out of you! I was so happy to be there with you. Yet I was shaking in fear at the same time, so happy I was terrified."

"Afraid—not of me!"

"No . . . I don't know why. I was feeling so many things that were new and strange and wonderful. Surely you understand."

"Of course I do," laughed Sabina. "Why do you think I suddenly ran off and started yelling at the sky? I didn't know what to say or do either!"

"I thought I was so grown up then. But when you look back from forty, nineteen seems awfully young."

"We *were* young, Matthew. That was the wonder of it."

"There we were standing in the rain together," Matthew went on. "We'd been working in the fields earlier, exploring the house, running, laughing, doing everything that friends do, yet at the same time standing there alone, both our hearts probably racing faster than they ever had, in the middle of a thunderstorm, wanting to be nowhere else. . . . All I can say was that it was extraordinary."

"I've relived that day a hundred times in my memory, Matthew."

"It was such a special *friendship,* that's all I can say. We not only had fun together, there was a bond developing somewhere deeper too, spiritually . . . on many levels."

"Such talks we had!"

"Yes, and about so many things! Don't you see what I'm getting at, Sabina? After all that . . . there just could never have been anyone else."

"I do understand," said Sabina in scarcely more than a whisper. In truth, she understood perfectly. She had lived the perfectly correspondent other half of their mutual story.

They walked on, some of the pedestrian traffic thinning.

"Do you remember your asking me a few days back," Matthew said, "or was it a week or two ago, about whether I'd ridden horses with no one else, and then whether I'd had any women friends?"

"You only answered the first of my questions."

"You noticed, huh?" said Matthew with a smile.

"Of course. But I didn't want to press my luck."

Matthew laughed. "Well now I'll answer the second. Yes, I've known quite a few women. In my line of work you can't help it. There have even been some who have shown, shall we say, an 'interest' in a deeper level of acquaintance and have made it clearly enough known."

"Did anything come of any of them?"

Matthew shook his head slowly.

"I just wasn't all that interested," he said. "I dated a few times, but it was artificial and lifeless. There was such a camaraderie between you and me, right from the beginning, that all other relationships since couldn't help but pale in comparison. Once you've tasted the real thing, anything less doesn't hold much attraction. I stopped thinking about marriage years ago and resigned myself very happily to the life of a bachelor. I've been very content."

There was a long silence, full of unspoken pondering memories.

"Now it's your turn," said Matthew. "Why did *you* never marry?"

"Don't you know by now?"

"Maybe, but I want to hear it from you," Matthew said, grinning.

"There's no point in my repeating it," said Sabina. "You've already told my story down to the last detail."

As they walked along the sidewalk, a shop with an array of glassware, china, and porcelain gifts in its window caught Sabina's eye. They wandered inside, looking around at the items on display with half-interested nonchalance.

"Oh look, Matthew!" exclaimed Sabina. "What a beautiful tiny container! It's covered with miniature roses. It reminds me of the box we put our roses in back at *Lebenshaus.*"

The small box Sabina had picked up from the shelf was slightly smaller than that she had given Matthew on the morning they had parted at *Lebenshaus.* Fashioned from creamy alabaster, it measured only some nine centimeters by six and about three high with a lid fashioned of the same. All about were small clusters of tiny multicolored raised roses, with leaves and stems wandering about the box in green and gold, the blossoms themselves hand-painted in lavender, red, white, and pink. In the very center of the lid sat a cluster of twenty blooms, some so tiny as to hardly be visible, one or two measuring seven or eight millimeters across.

"I'll buy it for you," announced Matthew. "You gave me the other, now I shall make *you* a gift of this one, to serve as a reminder of the roses we gather together."

"I shall save every petal from every bloom!" said Sabina excitedly.

"Until the day we see *Lebenshaus* again . . . together," added Matthew. "Then we shall take off the lid and sprinkle the dried leaves all about *Der Frühlingsgarten,* as the perfume to bring it all to life again!"

Matthew took it to the counter, paid for it, and they walked outside together.

Sabina was pensive as they came back out into the fresh air.

"Do you really think we shall see it again?"

"Yes . . . yes, we will. I promise."

"Another promise?"

"One which I shall seal with—let me see, how about a light yellow-orange rose whose petals are tinged with a fiery red?"

Sabina laughed.

"A rose for every occasion, is that it?"

"Indeed, my lady, you have stumbled precisely upon the truth," said Matthew in a courtly tone.

"Oh, Matthew, I *want* to believe it. But my hopes have been disappointed so many times."

"Now you have me to share your hope," said Matthew.

Sabina looked into his eyes. She was reminded again, as she was so often, of the moment they were introduced at her uncle Otto's.

"You cannot possibly know how much that means," she said, "or how deep your words go."

Matthew returned her smile.

"I will do all I can," he said, "to make sure your hopes are never disappointed again. We will not only hope, we will *pray* to see *Lebenshaus* again . . . together."

38

That Ancient Brotherhood

• • •

HE HAD READ THE WHOLE THING OVER FROM WORN cover to worn cover no less than a dozen times through the years, this book by his friend that by some mercy he had been allowed to keep all this time, *Widerstand und Ergebung: Briefe und Aufzeichnungen aus der Haft.*

He never tired of the papers and letters from Bonhoeffer's hand during his imprisonment at Tegel. What kinship he felt with Dietrich, what inspiration to go on . . . and to write himself. Truly the martyr lived on through his writing and his thoughts, especially for one whose own imprisonment had by this time lasted so much longer.

It was as though the Lord had been preparing them, each in their own way, during their brief time together prior to the war, for the imprisonments both would face as a result of their faith. Though they had walked out those faiths according to different roads, they had been led to remarkably similar ends.

Slowly, with a sense of reverence, he folded back the worn coverboard. Even though nearly twenty years had passed and fascism was long dead, the words still possessed a timeless capacity to move him and cause beneficial self-evaluation within his own soul.

He first began reading again the familiar words of reflection on the Nazi years, written as the year 1943 opened, just months before his imprisonment.

> *Ten years is a long time in anyone's life. As time is the most valuable thing that we have, because it is the most irrevocable,*

*the thought of any lost time troubles us whenever we look
back. Time lost is time in which we have failed to live a full
human life, gain experience, learn, create, enjoy, and suffer; it
is time that has not been filled up. . . .*

O God, he thought, closing his eyes, *thank you for making my life full,
as you did Dietrich's. Even in this place, Father, I have so much to thank you
for. I have learned, I have enjoyed, I have suffered. You have been good to me
. . . and I thank you.*

He opened his eyes again and continued reading.

*I believe that God can and will bring good out of evil, even
out of the greatest evil. For that purpose he needs men who
will make the best use of everything. I believe that God will
give us all the strength we need to help us in all times of distress. But he never gives it in advance, lest we should rely on
ourselves and not on him alone. A faith such as this should
allay all our fears for the future. I believe that even our mistakes
and shortcomings are turned to good account, and that it is no
harder for God to deal with them than with our supposedly
good deeds. I believe that God is no timeless fate, but that he
waits for and answers sincere prayers and responsible actions.*

He turned and now read Dietrich's first letter from Tegel to his
parents. How similar he remembered feeling himself!

*I do want you to be quite sure that I am all right. . . .
Strangely enough, the discomforts that one generally associates
with prison life, the physical hardships, hardly bother me at
all. One can even have enough to eat in the morning with
dry bread. The hard prison bed does not worry me a bit, and
one can get plenty of sleep. . . .
    A violent mental upheaval such as is produced by a sudden
arrest brings with it the need to take one's mental bearings and
come to terms with an entirely new situation—all this means
that physical things take a backseat and lose their importance,
and it is something that I find to be a real enrichment of my experience. I am not so unused to being alone as other people are,*

*and it is certainly a good spiritual Turkish bath. . . . Besides
that, I have my Bible and some reading matter from the library
here, and enough writing paper. . . .*

He read for an hour, pausing many times to ponder the words of
his friend, to reflect on his own years . . . and often to weep and pray.

After some time, he closed the thin volume of letters that had
been accumulated by family and friends and set it aside. He reached
across his table and pulled his Bible toward him, a volume whose
covers were even more worn, and opened to the great prison epistle
to the ancient church at Philippi and began to drink in the words of
another brother he considered a dear friend in the Spirit.

*My friends, I want you to understand that the work of the
Gospel has been helped on, rather than hindered, by what has
happened to me. My imprisonment . . . has given encouragement to many of our fellow-Christians to speak the work of
God with more courage. . . .*

*I will continue to rejoice, knowing that through your prayers
and the help given me by the Spirit, all that has happened will
turn out for my deliverance. I eagerly hope that I will not be
ashamed, so that . . . through my life or my death, the glory of
Christ will shine out clearly in my person. For me to live is
Christ and to die is gain. . . .*

Reading the familiar words forced the aged eyes closed. With the
book still open before him, his hands covered his face as scarcely
audible prayers sounded from his murmuring lips.

"God, O God, make me worthy to pray the apostle's prayer with him!"

No more could be heard, though the lips continued to move for
some time longer in silent entreaty to the Father of that ancient
prison brotherhood, of which he had now for seventeen years been a
member.

39

An Invitation

• • •

MATTHEW AND SABINA CONTINUED TO SEE ONE ANOTHER as often as possible, though trips to London and Paris kept Matthew away longer than he would have liked.

The pace of his schedule remained hectic upon his return early in July, but he caught Sabina during lunch the day after he had arrived back in Berlin.

They greeted one another warmly.

"I only have a few minutes," said Matthew, "but I wanted to ask you an important question. I just found out about it this morning."

"About what?" asked Sabina.

"Do you remember my saying a few weeks ago that I didn't go in for the gala festivities of the diplomatic life?"

Sabina nodded.

"There's an exception I want to make."

"You have my permission," laughed Sabina gaily.

"Do I?"

"Of course. But since when do you need to ask me what you do?"

"For this particular occasion you are precisely the one whose permission I need."

"I'm afraid I don't understand."

"The French are hosting a summer ball at their consulate. I want to attend, and . . . I'd like you to go with me."

"Me!"

"Whom else would I go with?"

"But . . . Matthew. I couldn't go to a fancy ball. I'm just a poor working lady."

"And the most beautiful one in all Berlin."

"Matthew, please—don't tease me."

"I would never make light of anything about you, Sabina. I mean it. You are the most beautiful lady in all the world to these eyes of mine."

"Matthew, stop!" Sabina protested, trying to laugh, but unsuccessfully.

"I mean every word. And I *am* serious about the ball. I would be honored to have you at my side. Besides, we'll have such fun!"

"It sounds wonderful, but . . . I could never . . . I don't have anything that would begin to be suitable to wear."

"I've thought of that already. We'll get you a new dress, just for the occasion."

"You are too good to me! Will this fairy tale never end?"

"Not if I can help it."

"But I wouldn't even know what to look for. I don't know what's in style. I don't know any stores."

"I'll take care of everything."

"It's been so long since I even thought about clothes. Why, I didn't even buy what I have on now. Those of us in the—"

She stopped abruptly, but then went on hurriedly before Matthew had a chance to question her.

"I mean, there is a group of us who pass along second-hand clothes. Our money has other places to go."

Her voice trailed off, as she once again realized that there were still things she was keeping from Matthew. She consoled herself that it was for his safety, as well as for the safety of others. She was glad he did not press her just now.

"Well then," said Matthew, "try to remember what you and your mother did when planning for a party or a celebration. We'll do the same."

Sabina laughed with the mirth that wives and daughters and sisters often feel at how simple men consider the details taken more seriously by women.

"Mother was so practical and clever when it came to styles," she said, brightening at the memory of herself and her mother making plans for new dresses. "She would look through magazines to see what was popular and then select fabrics and colors that would be in keeping with a country estate. Papa would often comment on how she would stand out at any social occasion because of the old-world loveliness that hung about her, in contrast to the modern glamour of so many of the other women."

As she spoke, Matthew was delighted to see the enthusiasm in Sabina's eyes as she enjoyed the memory of her parents.

"Your father was right," he said. "Now that you actually put words to it, I remember noticing that very thing when I saw you at the Schmundt affair. Your cousin looked like a painted doll out of a fashion magazine—not attractive to my eye in the least. You, on the other hand, looked like you had just stepped out of a storybook, with the flower in your hair and that beautiful, long, pale green gown."

"You remember?"

"Of course, every detail."

"Will you never stop being full of surprises!"

"I hope not! So that's what we will do. We'll go to the biggest store in Berlin and see what is in style. Then you shall make it even better."

"*Mutti* always told the dressmaker what she wanted. You can't buy that sort of thing."

"We can and we will, if we have to go to twenty shops! I shall enlist the services of a dressmaker myself, and you shall tell her exactly what modifications to make, just as your mother did."

"Are you sure you want to go to all that trouble just for me?"

"Absolutely positive. I will be your fairy godmother."

"What is that?"

"We have a fairy tale where a poor little girl who worked among the cinders and ashes wanted to go to a great ball. But she had no dress. Her fairy godmother came and waved her magic wand and suddenly an exquisite gown appeared. Then she went to the ball, but nobody recognized the girl who had always before been dressed in rags. Her name was Cinderella."

"Cinderella! We have a fairy story in Germany like that too. She is called Aschenputtel. It has always been one of my favorites. But the birds made Aschenputtel's dress, not a fairy godmother."

"Well, you have neither birds nor fairies—I shall buy you a new dress myself! Next Saturday morning we shall scour the streets and shops of Berlin and not stop until we find just the dress that you and your mother would have chosen."

Matthew glanced down at his watch with a grimace. "I've got to go," he said. "I'm already late. Meetings, meetings, meetings," he added, hurrying off down the sidewalk toward his car.

"Bye!" Sabina called out after him.

"I'll see you Saturday!"

40
Stratagems High and Low

• • •

IN THE EASTERN SECTOR OF THE CITY, AN AMBITIOUS young Soviet officer sat quietly pondering the information that had come into his hands that very morning.

This could be, he thought, his opportunity to move up at least one of the ladders upon which he found himself perched. It might mean nothing, a meaningless coincidence. Even if it was the same man, it might lead nowhere.

But in this precarious business, taking risks, and following thin leads, and having eyes to see what would not have been visible to an ordinary glance—these were the separating factors between those who rose to prominence and those who spent their lives on the insignificant lower rungs of the bureaucracy. This might be his ticket out of the trenches and could establish him as a full KGB operative in his own right. It would stand him in good stead in the eyes of both his uncle and his father, though the information more immediately concerned his German superior Schmundt here in Berlin.

He glanced down at the list of names again.

He couldn't believe his good fortune at having obtained it. That was another thing you needed if you hoped to enter the exclusive KGB club and rise in it—you needed contacts. Lots of them, in high and low places.

Finally one of his had paid off.

A drinking chum who worked for the French in their sector, and who had high-up contacts in the French consulate. He was certain he was the only one on the eastern side to have a copy of the invitation list.

The only question was how to use the information to the best advantage. Should he contact his uncle in Moscow or keep his activity confined to Berlin for now? Whom would it most immediately benefit him to please? That was always the question these days—how to weigh the two loyalties inherent in his position.

It was his uncle in Moscow who had gotten him this assignment. Loyal Party member though his father was, his older brother had more clout in the ways that counted. Besides, his uncle was KGB through and through. And his uncle had made clear enough that one of the reasons he was being sent to Berlin was to "keep an eye on things," as he'd called it, within the office of his German so-called comrade. It was not difficult for Andrassy to see that in spite of the many years the two men had worked together, the level of trust between them did not swell to particularly high levels.

At the same time, however, there was a loyalty he had to show to the German section chief too, for in the DDR he was powerful in his own right. To please him would mean advancement, higher contacts, and being drawn into wider spheres of activity here and now. He could not mortgage the present in hopes of some future assignment.

His uncle had made promises, to be sure. But Andrassy was no fool. He knew his uncle's character well enough and what kinds of stories circulated about him. He and his father had hardly known one another when he was young, and Andrassy knew his present assignment had come from no filial loyalty between the two men. He didn't trust his uncle any more than he trusted the German.

There could be no denying the fact that the KGB was as active in Berlin as in Moscow. So playing his cards right here could prove his entrée into a bright future with the agency as well. He had to keep his file clean and his reputation sound in both Moscow *and* Berlin.

His identity, of course, had to remain unknown to the section chief, which kept him always walking a fine line, as did his ongoing contact with his uncle. How much to tell either of them was always the quandary. And in truth, neither the Russian uncle nor the German chief had any idea what motives and ambitions swirled in the brain of Andrassy Papovich Galanov, nephew to the one and protégé to the other.

Again his eyes fell on the one name on the list that had given rise to all this speculation.

He was well-enough acquainted with the background of his German superior to know its significance. The name of the American appeared in no file. There was no *official* connection between the two men. But he had spoken sufficiently with his boss regarding the girl and their attempts to locate her that the name had come up between them.

His eyes drifted away from the page as his brain tried to sort through all the options.

Slowly he nodded his head, signifying having arrived at what would be the best course of action.

He would tell them both, he thought to himself.

Separately, of course. He had to tell the German, that much was clear. But at the same time he wanted his uncle to know that he was being diligent in keeping his eyes open. If he should find out that he'd told the German and kept the information from him . . . well, his uncle's wrath was not something he had the desire to incur.

That was to be avoided at all costs.

He rose and left his small flat. The phone he always used to contact Moscow was a twenty-minute walk, a minor annoyance to make sure the chief learned nothing of his identity. That his personal phone line was tapped he had little doubt. Mistrust was one of the few commodities in good supply around here.

He made the call, then waited.

Thirty or forty minutes later the public phone jangled loudly. He picked up the receiver instantly.

"Uncle Korskayev . . . it is Andrassy. . . . Yes, greetings to you too. . . . I have obtained some information that might prove useful to us. . . ."

41

The Search Begins

• • •

THE SATURDAY FOLLOWING THE INVITATION, SABINA AND
Matthew searched for the dress Sabina would wear to the ball.

"How do you know where to go?" Sabina asked as they entered
the first dress shop of many they would explore that day.

"Ah," replied Matthew with a sly grin, "diplomats as well as spies,
you know, depend heavily on their informants!"

This and several others comprised their initial stops, though after
two hours they had succeeded in finding nothing suitable.

To his satisfaction, however, Matthew *had* succeeded in bringing
Sabina fully into the magic of the occasion. Whether they found a
dress or not, they were both having so much fun it hardly mattered.
Matthew was not a little proud of his success and to no small degree
filled with the magic himself.

Sabina emerged from one of the dressing rooms and approached
him in the latest of her attempts. Matthew grimaced.

"It isn't right, is it?" said Sabina.

"Not in the least."

"I knew it the moment I slipped it on. But I had to see what the
silk felt like, just for fun."

"How about the green one we picked out with it?"

"I'll try that next," said Sabina, turning and disappearing again.

Three or four minutes later she emerged once more.

"Aha, now *that* has possibilities!" intoned Matthew, nodding his
head carefully. "What do *you* think?"

"It feels good," replied Sabina. "But somehow it doesn't have a
look that reminds me of Mama."

"Turn around."

Sabina did so.

"I like it, but I see what you mean. Perhaps a bit sophisticated."

"It's too low cut in the back. I don't think I would be comfortable in it."

A sudden playful urge struck Matthew. He grabbed up a dress from one of the nearby racks, held it up in front of himself with feigned seriousness, then spun slowly around, holding out one of its sleeves at arm's length as if dancing with the empty gown.

"What do you think, my dear?" he said with a pretended stuffy British accent. "Does it do anything for me?"

Sabina was already laughing too hard to reply.

"Please, my dear," Matthew went on seriously. "You simply must get control of yourself. It won't do to make a scene like this in public."

"Matthew—you are so silly!" said Sabina, still laughing.

"I insist you tell me what you think."

"All right then, if you must know," said Sabina, forcing herself to swallow the laughter. "I think it looks positively becoming. It highlights your features to perfection, and I think you would be the talk of the whole ball."

"No doubt," said Matthew, cracking a smile at Sabina's humor.

"Certainly the prettiest man there," Sabina added.

Both of them burst into laughter. Matthew spun around in one final pirouette with the lifeless gown, then with a flourish tossed it flopping back onto the top of the rack.

He continued to laugh, suddenly realizing the ludicrous display he had made of himself. If only his straight-laced and serious diplomatic colleagues could see him now!

What if John Kennedy were to get wind of this!

The world in crisis? Not for Matthew McCallum on this day!

He continued to chuckle to himself.

"What is it?" said Sabina.

"Oh, I was just trying to imagine the gossip in Washington or Moscow if either of the negotiating teams managed to obtain pictures of me dancing with a dress."

Again they both burst into laughter.

"I think we had better get out of here," said Matthew.

"I'll change out of this," said Sabina, disappearing again into the dressing room.

Five minutes later they made their way toward the elevator. As they approached it, the doors opened, and a man and woman stepped out.

"Oh no . . . I can't believe it!" murmured Matthew, quickly doing an about-face and slinking off down an adjacent aisle between lingerie and a tall rack of women's coats. Clinging to his arm, Sabina followed.

"What is it?" she said.

Matthew said nothing, scurrying behind the coats and crouching down.

"What *is* it, Matthew?" giggled Sabina. "You are acting *very* strange today."

"Did you see that man getting off the elevator?"

"Yes. Who is he?"

"What I said about being spotted by the negotiating teams must have been prophetic. That is Bonn's representative to the talks we had in Vienna last month."

"Why don't you want to see him? You weren't still wearing the dress." Sabina couldn't help from continuing to giggle as she said it.

"Be serious," said Matthew, unable to keep a straight face. "They wanted to have meetings this morning about a new problem that came up with the Russians. *I'm* the one who kiboshed it."

"What did you say?"

"That I had a prior commitment, a 'pressing engagement' I believe I called it."

Matthew began to chuckle himself.

"None of them were too pleased with me," he said. "In fact, some of them, including Herr Schultz over there, were downright upset."

He was now laughing in earnest.

"How would it look," he said, struggling to get the words out, "for him to see me now . . . with you . . . and my prior commitment to be revealed as a morning's shopping in Berlin!"

They were both giggling uncontrollably by now.

Still crouching, Matthew led the way around the other way behind the coats until he could see the elevator door from the next space through the display racks.

"You've got to run interference for me," he whispered.

"What does that mean?" whispered Sabina.

"Never mind. Just go spy out the elevator. Push the button, and when the coast is clear, give me a signal. Keep your eye on him, though."

"Are you sure Berlin will be safe if the president's friend is discovered hiding beneath the women's lingerie?"

"You're no help!" laughed Matthew.

Sabina let go of his arm and, standing up to her height, walked toward the elevator, giggling softly as she glanced about the store.

A minute or two later Sabina had successfully reconnoitered the approach to the elevator. Holding the door open, she now signaled Matthew. Crouching low, he bolted from behind the safety of the coats, nearly knocking over a small stand of women's unmentionable items, into the open aisle, and made for the elevator. Ten seconds later the doors had closed behind them.

"Whew!" he sighed. "That was a close one!"

Breaking into laughter once again, they were glad nobody else was in the confined quarters with them. Their giggles continued all the way out of the building, attracting more than one stare from a stoic clerk on the ground floor as they walked toward the front door and out once again to the street.

"That store definitely does not have what we're looking for!" said Matthew. "I think it's time to try some smaller shops."

Sabina clutched Matthew's arm and snuggled tightly to his side. Whether they found a dress could not have been further from her mind. If this could go on indefinitely, even if she could only see Matthew on weekends, she would be happy forever.

42

The New Dress

• • •

AFTER SEVERAL MORE SHOPS, BOTH MATTHEW AND Sabina had begun to weary of the task.

"I am about ready for lunch," said Matthew, "but not until we look in at least one more shop."

"I don't think I can try on another single dress," sighed Sabina.

"You can, and you shall, my dear," said Matthew confidently. "Take heart. I feel assured that our search is nearly at an end. And," he added brightly, seeing a small sidewalk vending stand up ahead, "I think I see just the thing that will seal the good fortune that is about to come our way."

He suddenly dashed off, leaving Sabina standing in the middle of the sidewalk alone. Two minutes later he returned, handing her the single long-stemmed rose he had just purchased.

"Lavender . . . oh, thank you, Matthew—it's beautiful." She lifted it to her nose and breathed in deeply.

They walked on, growing quiet and pensively content.

Ahead a small shop across the street caught Matthew's eye. The old script–lettered sign read Boutique for Occasions Formal and Simple.

"Let's try over there," he said.

The minute they walked into the shop, both knew that the very dress they had been looking for all morning was hanging right before their eyes.

The search was over.

"Matthew . . . it's perfect!" exclaimed Sabina, looking over the light blue silk intermingled with floral shades of pink. "I must try it on!"

She ran back to the dressing room full of anticipation. All morning she had completely forgotten the austere and practical life she lived on the other side of the city, on the other side of the world. Still the dream persisted, for another twenty or thirty minutes, while they selected all the needful accoutrements to accompany the dress, including a pair of elegant white shoes.

The moment Matthew stepped forward to pay for the accumulated purchases, however, suddenly the reality of the moment came to her. A thousand emotions rushed forward unbidden. A cloud passed over Sabina's face.

• • •

Matthew found Sabina waiting for him outside. "Is something wrong?" he asked.

"Oh, Matthew, the dress suddenly reminded me of a dress my mother wore. And I thought of her, and then my father—dear Papa! Please understand—finding you again, being with you, finding the perfect dress—it's all made me so very happy. But how can I be happy when Papa . . . and others . . . ? There is so much misery in the world."

Matthew drew his arm around her, but remained silent as Sabina's thoughts tumbled out.

Sabina looked up into his face, her eyes moist and shining.

He thought she was the most beautiful woman in all the world.

"Matthew," she sighed, "are you sure it is not wrong for me to be so happy? So many people have so little. How is it possible to fully delight in having you do so much for me, in laughing with abandon, in enjoying myself . . . in allowing you to buy me that expensive dress? Something feels I ought to hold back, to keep a little piece of myself miserable and sad for the sake of the rest of the world that is miserable and sad *all* the time. How can I not feel almost guilty to be so blessed?"

"Come," said Matthew, releasing her and leading the way back toward the shop. "Let's get our things. Then we shall talk."

• • •

"You asked how it is possible to fully delight in receiving happiness," said Matthew as they walked away from the shop, carrying the parcels that had prompted Sabina's pensiveness. "Would you really like to know what I think?"

"Do you have an answer?"

"I don't know if I have *an* answer," laughed Matthew, "but I have thought about it a good deal."

"Then I want to hear everything you have to say, because it often troubles me. I honestly do feel that I have to be a little bit miserable, perhaps for Papa's sake, and for the sake of everyone else who knows God so little it doesn't seem like there's anything in their lives worthy of being called a blessing at all. Do you know what I'm trying to say?"

Matthew nodded. "There are millions of miserable people in the world," he sighed.

"My life has been bleak enough these last fifteen years," Sabina went on, "so this is not something I've had to face. I suppose you could say there was a part of me that felt comfortable with my lot because I didn't have to feel out of step with all the misery around me. Growing up on Papa's estate, I was no doubt out of step with most of the world too. Being young, however, I just accepted our life, and the blessings that went along with it, as a matter of course. There are so many things you don't stop to think about when you're sixteen or twenty, or even twenty-five."

"How true!"

"Now it's all changed, Matthew. *You've* changed it for me!"

"The feeling is mutual," he added with a smile.

"Suddenly I feel like the most wondrously blessed woman alive. You've made me so happy. You give me so much! I'm deliriously happy, Matthew—tears and all!"

Sabina laughed, still with a look of sheepishness at being full of so many contrary feelings.

"But then, as I said, I find that happiness bringing with it a thorn of its own—the feeling that I *shouldn't* be so happy, that the rest of the world is depending on me being miserable with them . . . and especially, that I don't *deserve* such happiness and such blessing."

"Do you think God always gives us what we deserve?"

"No, I don't suppose he does."

"Does your father *deserve* prison?"

Sabina's eyes filled with tears again at the memory. She shook her head.

"He's one of the most Christlike men that ever lived," she answered softly.

"Do you *deserve* this happiness you feel?"

Again Sabina shook her head.

"Did I deserve the tremendous outpouring of God's love that came to me when I was in the Bighorns?"

"I see what you're saying. . . . I don't suppose so."

"Our deserving or undeserving has very little to do, it seems to me, with the equation of how the blessings and gifts and joy of God fall in our lives. God is engaged in purposes so much higher and larger than ordinary eyesight can see. I think that when we fall in with those purposes, and flow with the intent God has in mind for us, then gifts and blessing will very naturally flow from his hand into our lives, notwithstanding *every* human's undeservedness."

"Then why are so many people miserable?"

"Because they have not entered into the flow of God's purposes."

"That's a hard thing to say about most of the people in the world. Life is difficult for them, Matthew. Life is much different under the Communist cloud than you might realize."

"True. But except in cases of extreme poverty and destitution, life is difficult, not from outwardly unpleasant circumstances, but because people are trying to please *themselves* rather than falling in with *God's* design for their lives. Rich people *and* poor people, West Germans *and* East Germans are all engaged in the same attempt to live for themselves and gratify their *own* wishes and desires rather than asking their Creator what kind of people he would have them be. For that reason, they are all miserable together. Believe me, Sabina, the rich West Germans are just as poverty-stricken of soul as the poor East Germans. Free Americans are just as self-possessed as captive Russians."

Matthew paused thoughtfully.

"Tell me," he said after a moment, "what do you suppose was your father's deepest heart's desire in all the world?"

"That's not hard," replied Sabina with a thoughtful smile that came from her depths. "To be like his Master."

"What did he most often pray?"

"That the Father would accomplish that in him."

"What was his Master's chief aim in coming to the world?"

"To show us the Father."

"And?"

"To give his life for us."

"Exactly. To sacrifice himself so that we might live. Do you see what I'm getting at, Sabina? God has *granted* your father the deepest desire of his heart. He has *answered* his prayer. What more fitting way for the life of your father to culminate than literally being allowed to walk in the sacrificial footsteps of Jesus, to be imprisoned for his faith? Do you think your father is saddened by his lot?"

Sabina shook her head.

"You told me so yourself that he was content just where he was. You see, he is so at one with God's purposes and thus so capable of praying according to what God's will is that God is able to pour out blessing after blessing upon him, which I have no doubt he has been doing all these years, *before* prison and now *in* prison. Your father was blessed materially before the war, it is true. Outward and visible blessing came to him. But the greatest gift God gave him, even back then, was integrity of character—the kind of *man* your father was. That is why my father and I are Christians today, and why your spiritual roots go so deep into the bedrock of sound training and example—because of the man your father was.

"I am confident to say that *that* flow of blessing has continued to pour into your father, perhaps even more, during his years of imprisonment—the blessing of character and Christlikeness. Some of his present comrades no doubt are angry and bitter at their lot. If I know your father, however, he is full of joy."

"I am sure you are right," Sabina said with a smile. "Though they are sparse, every communication that does manage to come to me from him conveys exactly what you speak of."

"Well then, the same truth applies to accepting outwardly *pleasant* circumstances when God chooses *that* method for transmitting his blessings. Does God want everyone to spend years in prison? Of course not. It's all a question of falling in with what God ordains for *you* . . . and then rejoicing in it. For your father, it was material abundance before the war, but today prison. For you, it's being happy with me."

"Don't you think, though, that it is easier to fall in with God's purposes, as you say, during times of want?"

Matthew thought for a moment.

"No . . . no, I don't really think so," he replied. "Just look at the difficulty you are having coming to terms with the blessings you suddenly find coming to you, feeling almost guilty in light of other people's misfortune. As Christians I believe we ought to be doing what we can to alleviate the misery of those less fortunate than ourselves, and help them. But in the matter of each individual's *own* personal response to God's work in their *own* heart, I don't know that the rest of the world's misery has much to do with it. The Bible says that he *delights* to give good gifts to his children."

"Then why is it so hard to accept those gifts?"

"Perhaps it is only difficult for sensitive natures. A young child is so self-absorbed that he takes a gift that is offered and accepts it as his own without thought of sharing it. The more mature individual, especially a thoroughly others-centered individual, will by his very maturity of character immediately think of sharing whatever comes his way. Thus when God lavishes plenty upon him, as the Father sometimes chooses to do, it can cause great strain of conscience to accept it from God's hand without feeling guilt that everybody else in the world is not likewise blessed.

"Yet the gift has come, not from deservedness as we talked about before, though, notwithstanding, from a degree of faithfulness in living according to God's principles. That faithfulness is not transmittable from one person to the other as easily as are material things. There are reasons why some persons are blessed and others are not, though most of the time they remain invisible to human sight."

"I had never thought of that before."

"And, if I can add to your question, I think perhaps it is even harder sometimes for people to accept *good* gifts than unpleasant ones. I'm talking now about people who are trying to fall in with God's designs. Some Christians, I think, almost expect misfortune from God's hand. That's why you find this new happiness more incongruous to your soul than your previous humdrum life."

"That's it, and I can't figure out why."

"Don't you think it goes back to exactly what your father said to me in *Der Frühlingsgarten* that very first time we talked about God's Fatherhood?"

"What exactly?"

"When he said that God was a *good* Father, whose delight is in revealing himself and who is anxious to give his goodness to his creatures, anxious to smile with them."

"Those are Papa's very words. I remember them."

"I'm sure you are familiar with Psalm 37:3-4. It's become one of my favorite biblical passages. *Trust in the Lord, and do good. . . . Take delight in the Lord, and he will give you the desires of your heart.* Those words always reminded me of you and your father and mother—of all of *Lebenshaus,* actually."

"Why?"

"Because that's what you all did—you *delighted* in God. You were not dour-faced Christians. From our very first conversation you so enthusiastically talked about God. That's how it always was. Religion is such a boring abstraction to many people. With you and your father and mother, however, it was completely different. You all were so full of zest and life. Working in the fields and laughing and having fun, entertaining, growing roses . . . *life* was so evident there!"

Sabina could not help laughing, though feeling a melancholy grip her too from the poignant reminders of the past.

"I have spent years pondering and praying about that Scripture," Matthew went on. "I have come to the conviction that God does indeed want to give *every* man and woman the desires of their heart. He *wants* to bless them, *wants* to make them happy, *wants* to shower them with such goodness and love that they could scarcely comprehend it. But he cannot do so until those hearts' desires line up with his purposes.

"When someone *delights* in God, it reveals that they want *what God wants* more than what they might otherwise want themselves. Such a man was your father. He delighted in God so thoroughly that he knew God's purposes were the *best* purposes. So he ordered his life in harmony with that. His own heart's desires lined up with it. Thus God was able to fulfill his purpose by giving your father what he wanted—*Christlikeness of character.* That has become my heart's prayer in recent years too."

"Tell me what exactly."

"I pray, not that God would give me the desires of *my* heart, but that he would deepen my delight in *his* ways, and make my heart to desire exactly what are *his purposes.* Then I know that whatever comes from his hand is exactly what he purposes for me, and I can rejoice in it—be it poverty or plenty . . . *whatever* it be."

"I don't see what that has to do with me and being happy," said Sabina.

"It's exactly the same," rejoined Matthew enthusiastically. "You delighted in God too. It was watching the three of you trust God and delight in him that intrigued me enough to begin my own walk of faith. You, like your father and mother, have lived the first part of that passage too. It says that when we *trust in the Lord and do good . . . and* when we *delight* in the Lord, then he will give us the desires of our heart. Are you going to complain to God that he has fulfilled this truth by giving happiness and blessing in your life, and tell him he ought not to have given you quite so *much* happiness?"

Sabina laughed.

"That would be foolish of me, wouldn't it?"

"When the blessing comes from God's hand, not to take it is the same as not trusting him."

"Then I will trust him and be happy," Sabina said, smiling.

"You may. It is all a gift from him. I believe we have been given to one another, as gifts from the hand of God. How can we not delight and rejoice in the happiness that is part of it?"

"My, but you have come a long way as a Christian, Matthew. If I didn't know better I would think I was talking to Papa."

Matthew laughed.

"I told you, when I make commitments, I make them for keeps. Besides," Matthew added, "I had a couple of pretty wise teachers early on who tilled the ground and planted the seeds of my faith in good, fertile soil. With the start I had, and the perspective of the Father I received at *Lebenshaus,* how could I do less than give myself to him lock, stock, and barrel?"

43

Section Chief and Lieutenant

• • •

YOUNG ANDRASSY GALANOV STRODE INTO HIS SECTION chief's office with more than his usual tempo of youthful assertiveness.

"Good morning, sir."

"If I didn't know better, from your walk I would say you are a German," replied Gustav, adding cynically, "and a *West* German at that."

"Do I take that as a compliment?"

"Russians have not been in the habit of considering affiliation with us Germans complimentary," remarked Gustav wryly.

"These are new times, *mein Herr*," said Galanov. "We are friends now. Before long the races throughout Eastern Europe will be indistinguishable."

"I doubt the times are quite *that* new, my young Russian friend."

"You know what *Pravda* says, that Russia will one day dominate the globe."

"If anyone believes that, then Moscow does not know the German mind as well as it thinks."

"You would not want Moscow to hear you say such a thing."

Gustav eyed his assistant shrewdly. There was no mistaking the subtle tone. For only twenty-one, the young Russian officer had more cheek than was healthy. Schmundt had half a mind to send him back east where he belonged. Still, the fellow was capable and did have his uses.

"No, and you wouldn't dare tell them either," Gustav said after a moment, "if you know what's good for you. The Russians and

Germans may hate each other, but at present we are in the *German* Democratic Republic, not Moscow, and I happen to be your superior. I am not without a great deal of influence in Berlin, you know. So keep your veiled threats to yourself. In any event, you may take my comment however you well choose, though the reference to West Berliners was certainly no compliment."

Galanov smiled, amused at the exchange. Normally he kept his thoughts to himself, but every once in a while he allowed himself the luxury of expression, and the resulting responses from the droll Herr von Schmundt were usually worth the modest tongue-lashing he received in consequence.

"What are those papers you are holding?" asked Gustav pointedly.

"Something which I believe may be of interest to you, sir," replied Galanov, resuming his submissive and obedient air.

"Which is?"

"One of my contacts on the western side obtained for me an invitation list for an event being held next week at the French consulate."

"What kind of event?"

"A ball."

"What interest would we have in such a thing?"

"One of the names on the list caught my eye, sir. I thought I should bring it to your attention."

"Give it to me," snapped Gustav, stretching out his hand. "What name?"

"It's there on the third page, sir," replied Galanov, handing the sheets to Schmundt. "The name is McCallum, sir."

Slowly Gustav scanned down the list. There it was. There could be no mistaking it: *Matthew McCallum, U.S. State Department.*

A stab of unsought jealousy shot through him, and he simultaneously chastised himself and cursed the American for it. A dozen other demons equally self-serving, following in jealousy's wake, rose quickly within him. He struggled to suppress them, but, having spent a lifetime cultivating friendship with the Enemy who governed those hordes and fraternizing with the bondslaves of his ranks, the attempt was altogether unsuccessful.

"What is . . . what use did you surmise I might make of this?" he asked, clearing his throat in midsentence.

"You have mentioned the fellow in connection with the girl," answered Galanov.

"Yes, I have often wondered if they might somehow have maintained contact," rejoined Schmundt with forced self-possession. It would not do to allow an inferior to detect emotional disquiet. Besides, it went against everything in his creed. "Though it has been so many years," he went on in a musing tone, "I doubt such is possible."

"It never hurts to investigate. All our other leads have been unsuccessful."

"Yes . . . yes of course, you are right. Good work, Galanov," said Schmundt, gaining full control of his composure once again.

The fellow may be onto something after all, he thought to himself. Perhaps this was just the stroke of fortune he had been waiting for! All it would take was a minute or two with McCallum. Their past hostilities were long behind them. They had been mere boys fighting over a girl. Hardly uncommon. McCallum would have no idea of his present position. For all he might know, Gustav could be a loyal West German working for the same goals he was. He would attend the affair in a plain business suit, greet him like an old friend, invite him to have a drink or two, and then casually ask if he'd seen Sabina recently. One look in McCallum's face and Gustav would know whether he was lying. It was his business to know a lie in less than a second.

Yes, thought Gustav to himself, this was a most propitious turn of events!

"Tell me," said Gustav, still affecting mere casual interest, "how much clout does your friend have?"

"Not a great deal."

"How high up is he?"

"Mid-level."

"What do you suppose his chances would be of getting me an invitation to this event?"

Galanov screwed his face into the look of serious question.

"I can't say. Perhaps if we made it worth his while."

"Then make it worth his while, Galanov!" rejoined Gustav, immediately regretting his tone. "I'm sorry," he added. "I only meant that it might possibly prove beneficial for me to be in attendance. See what you can do."

"I shall, *mein Herr*," answered Galanov.

"That will be all," rejoined Schmundt with finality.

Galanov turned on his heels and left the room, a faint grin playing around the edges of his lips.

44

Unwelcome Intrusion

• • •

SABINA HAD BEEN FEVERISH WITH AN ANTICIPATION more resembling delirium all day.

Everything had suddenly become a fairy tale, and *she* was living right in the middle of it! She was *Aschenputtel* herself, and tonight was the *Maskenball* when *Der schöne Prinz* would dance the night away . . . with her!

And she had no wicked stepsisters to worry about.

Oh, how could such happiness have come to her!

All day long she was so distracted at work. How thankful she was that the ball was on Friday and she would not have to worry about this place again all weekend. She had nothing to think about for almost three days but her prince!

How would she make it through the day? Several times already she had been asked what she was smiling about, and in the women's room she had found herself singing out loud.

How long had it been since she had done *that!*

What had come over Karin Duftblatt? She knew that's what everyone in the Agency for the Aged was wondering.

She didn't care. Let them think what they would!

For tonight at least, she would be Cinderella. Nothing could remove the smile from her face!

At last five o'clock came.

Sabina bolted for the door and down to the street, and then fairly skipped her way home.

Her steps were light not merely from having another day's work behind her.

Love throbbed in her breast.

Once again life was a good and happy thing. She would throw off these rags and this scarf on her head. She would bathe slowly and then take all the time she wanted to put on the new dress Matthew had bought.

Then she would take time for each shoe, in memory of Cinderella herself. Hers would be no glass slippers, but her very own to keep . . . to remember this night forever!

Then her hair. After washing it, she would brush it until it glistened.

She would make herself beautiful tonight . . . for Matthew!

She owed everything to him—life . . . love . . . joy . . . the skip in her step . . . the song in her heart . . . the smile on her lips.

Most of all she owed him the fresh hope springing alive within her—that the future held a promise of happiness.

Caught up in her real-life fairy-tale daydreams, Sabina approached the intersection beyond which stood the large house where she lived.

All at once her countenance fell. With it all the daydreams crumbled to the ground like a breaking glass slipper.

Oh no, she said to herself, *not tonight . . . please not tonight!*

She approached the street corner slowly.

A bulky man stood leaning against a deserted building across the street, looking down at the sidewalk, casually smoking a cigarette. To all appearances he was on his way home from a tiring day in one of the East Berlin factories. His clothes were dirty and his hands and face splotched with grime.

Sabina approached slowly, but he paid her no heed.

"Hermann," she said, "why are you here?"

"Why am I ever here, Duftblatt?" he replied, not looking up.

"Please, Hermann, I am not available tonight."

"An odd objection, coming from you."

"I have plans."

"Don't we all."

"Get someone else."

"There is no one else."

"Please . . . I will be busy, till very late. There must be somebody—"

"I do not set the timetables," interrupted the man called Hermann. "You know that better than I."

Sabina sighed. Of course he was right. It was not his fault. They came when they came. Those who helped agreed that they *would* help, whenever the summons came, no matter how inconvenient. She had wanted it that way. She had forced such a commitment from others. Now she was caught in cross-purposes of her own design.

"Can't it be put off a night?"

"Impossible."

Sabina sighed with resignation.

"What time?"

"Midnight."

"Midnight! Hermann, can't you delay it? I can't possibly be home by then."

"They arrive at eleven. It's too late to change that."

"Then keep them somewhere. I won't be home until at least one or two."

"I'll be there at midnight. They can't wait."

"It is too dangerous to leave them alone."

"What else can I do?"

"I will *not* be home by then," said Sabina with finality. "Postpone it, I tell you, Hermann. Figure something out. I've given my blood all these years. Tonight is mine, and nothing will make me give it up!"

Without another word she strode briskly across the street, her quick pace no longer the result of the joy she had felt only moments before.

Still the man called Hermann had not once looked up into her face. He took another puff or two on his cigarette, then tossed it to the ground, crushed it with his heavy boot, and sauntered slowly away along the sidewalk.

45

Dreamy Ride Back in Time

• • •

SABINA DID HER BEST TO FORCE HERMANN'S UNWEL-
come visit from her mind.

Nothing, as she had said to him, was going to take the joy of this
night from her. Summoning the strength of her ancient Celtic
bloodline, and not a little of her mother's fiber of servanthood and her
father's example of sacrifice, by the time her body sank into the
bubbly, fragrant water of her bath, she was able to close her eyes, lie
back in the warm water, and calmly remind herself of the spiritual
focus by which she had long ago chosen to align her life.

O God, she prayed silently as she lay there, *I am sorry for losing my
patience with my brother Hermann. I know that you order all things. My
footsteps are in your hands, not my own.*

She stopped and let out a long contented sigh. What right did she
have to be upset? She had been blessed these past weeks beyond
measure. If the Father still required her service in the midst of this
new bliss, it was hardly a heavy price. She was the King's daughter,
after all, a princess in fact, not merely in fairy tale. It was *he* to whom
she owed her allegiance and her obedience, not to her own fancies
and dreams.

"*Forgive me, Father,*" she whispered. "*Let me serve you and your
people with faithful hands and loving heart. Thank you for Matthew, thank
you for tonight. But do not let me take my eyes off you for anything, not even
Matthew. Oh, Father, transform this small heart of mine, transform my whole
self and being into the image of Jesus. You know the desire of my heart. But
nevertheless, I ask that you accomplish your full purpose within me, Lord. Do
your will with Matthew and with me, and let me be content to receive your will*

thankfully, knowing that you do only what is good and best for your children. Let me, like Matthew reminded me, receive all the gifts that come from your hand with delight and rejoicing."

By the time she stepped out of the tub to dry twenty minutes later, Sabina was humming and singing cheerfully and proceeded to enjoy the evening's preparatory toilette as much as she had anticipated earlier.

Her appearance, her hair, what she wore—it had all ceased to carry any meaning for her years before. Suddenly, now everything mattered again! Matthew had made it matter.

She had even discovered, in a shop several days before, some of the old perfume she used to wear. She'd completely forgotten how much she had loved the fragrance when she was young. Her father once commented, laughing, that everything in her room bore the aroma of her perfume bottle!

How the sight of it in the shop had taken her back to those wonderful days before the war! She was surprised the same brand was still being manufactured. She purchased a small bottle, all she could afford, had scented her bathwater with it, and now splashed on a few extra drops before slipping into the new dress.

When Matthew appeared at the door a few minutes before seven, a radiant princess indeed appeared at the door.

"Oh my!" he exclaimed, unable to keep his jaw from falling slightly. "Sabina . . . you look magnificent!"

She dropped her eyes, blushing but pleased.

Indeed, though she had tried on the dress days before in the shop, never, Matthew thought, had he beheld such loveliness. Her blonde hair hung bouncily down, not nearly so long as it had been when he had known her before, yet nevertheless almost to her shoulders. Even as she stood in her doorway, the sun, angling in its descent from low in the sky to the right, shone against her, giving a brilliant whiteness to the topmost strands of her head, bathing the image upon which Matthew gazed in a half halo of light. He scarcely knew whether he was standing before a princess or an angel. In that moment, to Matthew McCallum, indeed, she was both.

Her skin was soft and creamy, cheekbones still flushed with the faint pink that had rushed up from her neck the moment she had seen Matthew, and her lips a light hue of red. The blue of her eyes, without necessity of makeup, gave resplendent exclamation to her whole face, accented further by the light blue of the dress. Even the sun could not match the dazzling luminance reflected back to Matthew's eyes as he took in the bewitching sight before him.

He had not seen the dress since Sabina had received it back from the tailor he had enlisted, with all the needful alterations in place to make it exactly as she wanted.

The fabric was raw silk, cut into a princess style with an empire waist. A small cap sleeve served to broaden the shoulders. In style the dress perfectly complemented Sabina's tall, thin frame, though these days she had become almost too thin. She had replaced the glamorous sequined drape from the shoulders with a flowing pink fabric bow at the high waist that also served to fill out her slender form. Her mother had taught her well, and the tailor's work made every centimeter fit to perfection.

The whole outcome was a simple, yet stately and stunning, picture of nothing less than royalty itself. The tiara of baby rosebuds that Matthew had had sent to her office earlier in the day, pinned up now in her hair, completed the picture. She had removed one of them from the hairpiece and added it to the bow at her side.

Sabina smiled. The sun now sent a flash against the whiteness of her teeth, framed to a perfection any artist would covet by the soft red lines of her lips.

"Thank you, Matthew," said Sabina, almost shyly. "You look quite dashing yourself in that tuxedo."

"Standard fare for these diplomatic affairs," he replied, shifting somewhat nervously on his feet. "You, on the other hand, will be the talk of the ball!"

"Oh, Matthew, I will not!"

"You'll see. I see you got the roses I sent."

"Matthew . . . thank you. You are always so thoughtful."

"I told you . . . every time I see you. So, here is another to go with it."

"What shall I do with it?"

"Whatever you like. Leave it here, or . . . carry it with you all evening and word will circulate around the ballroom about the *rose princess.*"

"Oh, Matthew!"

"Are you ready . . . ? As you can see, our transportation awaits us impatiently."

With the words Matthew turned slightly and gestured out toward the street.

Sabina turned to the amazing sight. At the curb sat a nineteenth-century, two-seat carriage, fully outfitted in black leather, a tuxedo-clad groom in stovepipe hat holding the reins of two jet black horses of obvious exquisite heritage.

"Matthew!" she exclaimed. "I can't believe it. But where did you get them?"

"Ah, too many questions spoil the fairy tale, my lady," he replied, again assuming the accent of the Fair Isle across the Channel. "Remember," he added, "you must rejoice and delight in the good gifts and blessings that come your way, not question them."

He tipped his head in slight indication of a bow, punctuating his words with chivalrous nod, then offered his arm. She took it.

Slowly they descended the steps to the ground, then glided wordlessly toward the carriage, Sabina stepping softly, as if tiptoeing gently through a dream so as not to break the heavenly spell, Matthew exuberant inside and feeling not a little pleased with himself for pulling off his surprise with such flamboyance and panache.

The only reminder of reality to intrude upon their senses as they approached the street was an occasional equine snort of wide nostril or stamp of thick hoof, for even the most expensive of breeds had yet to be true to their genus.

Gathering the lower regions of her dress about her as best she could, Sabina took Matthew's offered hand as he helped her up to the step and finally into the rear of the two carriage seats. He leapt up in one bound and landed beside her, jostling the chassis from side to side.

"Let's be off!" he cried with boyish enthusiasm.

Displaying no movement of his body other than a nearly imperceptible flick of the wrist, which was accompanied by that most mysterious of humanly created sounds understood by horses in every land, a *click* of tongue and cheek, the groom urged his royally black team into motion.

A slight lurch followed, amid the pleasurable sounds of twisting and stretching leather, more hooves and nostrils, and creaking wooden frame, and within seconds the antique ensemble was moving steadily along the city street.

In spite of Matthew's obvious ebullience, neither passenger spoke a word, and true to his station, the groom sat still as a silent museum statue. The occasional movement of his forearms and wrists as he deftly manipulated the reins between skilled fingers remained invisible to the two sitting behind.

As the carriage rolled bumpily along, the sounds of the steel rails of its wooden wheels, the dreamy jostling of the seat on its coiled springs, the rhythmic *clop, clop, clop* of the old-fashioned hooves on the street, and the constant creaking of parts and places and joints unseen, mesmerized Sabina's senses still further, until at length she rode truly as one wakeful but dulled to all reality about her.

By the time they reached the western sector, and the groom found the difficulty of his assignment exacerbated by a steady increase of automobiles, pedestrians, and traffic signals, Sabina had become altogether desensitized to everything in the world about her. No sound reached her brain. She had been transported back in time, not merely to the youth of her prewar years, but whole decades earlier—a whole century, to another era altogether.

The fantasy had invaded every atom of her being. She was not merely living out a dream, she had *become* the dream.

Sensing her mood, and reluctant to intrude upon it, Matthew said nothing, though he was unable to keep a smile from sneaking across his lips every minute or two.

46

Aschenputtel's Maskenball

• • •

THE COMMOTION OCCASIONED BY THE ARRIVAL AT THE
French consulate of a horse-drawn carriage, led by a tuxedoed
groom maneuvering his way between a steady stream of black
Mercedes, was altogether lost on Sabina.

As one in a daze, she allowed Matthew to help her to the street,
surrounded by an approaching crowd from amongst the other de-
barking guests, which, as it drew near, began to buzz with as much
whispered curiosity and fascination over the beauty of the unknown
princess on the arm of the American presidential attaché as it did over
the novel manner of their arrival.

Altogether sensitive to her condition, after a few words of instruc-
tion to the groom, Matthew led Sabina through the two ceiling-high
doors in the midst of the white stone building, offering but few
rejoinders to the string of comments, questions, and expressions that
met them along the way. He paused but momentarily to take in the
scene before making the social plunge, then continued into the
ballroom. Once within the hall, the mass diffused and they were
quickly absorbed into the great multitude.

The room was huge, an obvious necessity with a crowd this
large, and decorated fully and lavishly as befit their French hosts.
The ceiling suspended about twenty crystal chandeliers, which
perhaps even overlighted the room slightly. In one corner of the
great chamber sat an eighteen-piece string orchestra, though not
more than a quarter of those present were dancing to its music.
Most, whether in pairs or groups of fives and tens, were either
discussing the current world tension that all in Berlin found

themselves in the middle of or else gossiping about who was being seen with whom.

Not much had changed, only the details, from the party at the Schmundt villa so long ago. Let the world and all her business change, thought Matthew, the gossip of the diplomat, and his wife, will not. But how exceedingly different was the world in 1939. Back then, he thought ironically, Russia had been a friend!

He led Sabina purposefully toward one side of the ballroom, away from the few lingering stares following them, then stopped, turned, and faced her.

"Well . . . here we are!" he said, smiling cheerfully.

"I . . . I don't know what to say," stammered Sabina, glancing about slowly as if trying to clear her head.

"Say that you'll have a dance with me."

"I never imagined I would see such sights again," she continued, oblivious to his request. The sounds of the strings seemed to revive her, and she glanced around to locate it.

Even as she did so, out of the corner of his eye Matthew noted one of his American colleagues heading their way. The expression on his face and the glass he held in his hand confirmed what Matthew might well have expected without evidence of either—that he had arrived a good while earlier and had already enjoyed more liquor than was good for him. The comment that would likely leave his lips the moment he made winking contact with Matthew was sure to contain more color than the amber Scotch in his hand, and Matthew wanted no part of his unrefined wit tonight.

Without further hesitation, he took Sabina's right hand in his left, placed his other about her waist, and wheeled her off into the center of the dance floor to the strains of the waltz in progress. Though she had not danced formally since the affair at the Schmundt villa some eighteen years earlier, within seconds she felt as comfortable as if it had been the week before.

The years had added a maturity not only in the eyes of both, but to their carriage as well. A poised, suave sophistication was evident in Matthew's bearing, and the unmistakable elegance of nobility followed Sabina's every movement. They swept across the oak floor in effortless circular motion to the rhythm of the music, she matching his every step as though their feet were connected by invisible cords.

Frustrated, the undersecretary turned to seek a refill for his glass, while Matthew and Sabina were soon lost to sight in the swirling crowd.

Two minutes later the music stopped, though not for Sabina: notwithstanding that she and Matthew had eased to a gentle standstill, the dying strains of Strauss continued to eddy about in her brain, as waters agitated by unseen piscine movement below the edges of a still pool.

Subdued applause, buzzing comments, and a general rustling ensued, followed within sixty seconds by the rousing opening stanzas of yet another Strauss waltz, this time *Morgenblätter.*

Sabina soon found herself being swept along once more by Matthew's gentle yet confident lead into the middle of the dance floor.

The two dancers' words were few, they spoke softly and but occasionally, relishing the moments close to one another in a way whose mood words almost seemed to interrupt. *Wo die Zitronen blühn* came next, followed finally by the *Kaiserwalzer,* which closed the medley by the younger Strauss.

A round of applause went up throughout the ballroom as the orchestra rose and disassembled for a break. A violinist, violist, and cellist sat down to occupy the orchestral intermission with a string trio of Haydn and Handel country dances.

The waltzers slowly dispersed and waiters made their way through the room, bearing silver trays laden with drinks and hors d'oeuvres while the three or four hundred guests from West Berlin's international diplomatic circles congregated into groups large and small, gradually slipping into the sort of generally purposeless confabulation for which such soirees were noted.

Flushed and glowing, perfume emanating from her body, smiles lighting every inch of her countenance, Sabina was able to contain her exhilaration no longer.

"Are we really here?" she exclaimed. "Tell me I'm not dreaming, Matthew!"

He laughed, delighted to see her coming to herself again.

"You're not dreaming, Sabina," he said. "I guarantee it."

"I can't help but think it's not real. I feel like Aschenputtel herself!—what do you call her?"

"Cinderella," replied Matthew.

"I say, Matthew," sounded a voice from behind them, "isn't it about time you introduced me to your lady friend?"

If Matthew felt chagrin at finding himself unwittingly cornered by the inebriated fellow American he had been attempting to avoid, he did a masterful job of hiding it. "Hey there, what do you say, Wahlen?"

"I say that's one mighty fine looking br—"

"May I present the rose princess!" interrupted Matthew hastily, cutting him off.

Sabina nodded courteously.

"This, my dear," Matthew went on, "is the esteemed Frank Wahlen, undersecretary on the staff of Bill Tyler's European bureau, and all-around American ne'er-do-well—right, Frank?"

"That's me!" he replied, then turned toward Sabina. "Charmed," he said, scanning her hastily then glancing back at Matthew with a wink and smile whose intent could not be mistaken. "Now come on, McCallum, where'd you find her?" he added, sidling toward Matthew and speaking with a confidential sideways tilt of his head. "And that's not her name—"

"She's a princess," rejoined Matthew, "and I'm telling you the truth. You'll have to find out from where on your own."

"Come on, you can tell your old buddy Frank," insisted Wahlen.

"Old buddy or not, in your condition that's all you're getting out of me, Frank," laughed Matthew, attempting to make light of the exchange, adding a poke with his elbow and a wink of his own to hopefully diffuse the other's crude intent.

He turned back toward Sabina, stepping away from the undersecretary's unsteady lean.

"Come, Miss . . . ah, Miss Duftblatt," he said, attempting to lead Sabina off through the crowd.

"Not so fast, Matt," said Wahlen, following with clumsy step. "You haven't given me the chance to ask your . . . your *princess* for a dance." As he said the word, he again flashed Matthew a suggestive wink.

"Sorry, Frank, she'll be with me the entire evening."

At last Matthew and Sabina were successful in breaking away and quickly widened the distance between themselves and the nonplussed undersecretary, who stood watching another moment, glanced down long enough to see there was still a half-empty glass to be taken care of, lifted the contents to his lips, emptied the other half, then looked up again to find that his quarry had disappeared from sight.

"I'm sorry," said Matthew sincerely. "I had hoped we wouldn't run into him."

"Is he a friend of yours?" asked Sabina.

"I wouldn't say that. One of the members of our State Department. Actually not a bad sort of fellow when he's sober. And he knows his Russian history inside out. But when he's like this, another side of him surfaces that's not very pleasant."

"Is he a typical American?"

"I hope not!" laughed Matthew.

"But why did you tell him I was a princess?" asked Sabina.

"Because you are."

"No I'm not!"

"To me you are. To your father and mother you are. And in the kingdom of God what else would you be called?"

"Oh, Matthew, you are so . . ."

The word died away and the sentence went uncompleted.

"So what?"

"So . . . often saying such nice things about me."

"Well, they're true—every one! Besides, in Frank's condition I thought we ought to add an enigmatic twist to your identity, just to give him something to think about. It'll keep him out of trouble!"

Sabina smiled.

"I do appreciate your not telling him my name," she added.

"Are you kidding? One false word around him when he's been drinking and everybody here would know you. I'm enough of a diplomat to know when to hold my tongue, which is more than I can say of Frank."

With Sabina on Matthew's arm, they moved slowly through the hall, continuing to talk between themselves, even while Matthew greeted and shook hands with many diplomatic acquaintances, exchanging pleasantries and small talk, though conspicuously avoiding introducing Sabina to anyone. She remained content to follow, smiling as they went, leaning close between interviews and whispering in his ear, which brought smiles and subdued laughter and quiet rejoinders from Matthew in response.

Thus conversing in the seclusion of their private world, even as Matthew carried out his diplomatic duty, the two shuffled through the ballroom, leaving more curious stares and inquiring comments circulating behind them than either was aware.

"No . . . no, I've never seen her before," said one, an Englishwoman, in low tones to the wife of a U.S. State Department assistant.

"I have no idea who she is," rejoined the American lady. "Goodness knows I've been to enough of these things, but I've never seen Matthew with anyone like *that!*"

"I've never seen Matthew with anyone at all," added the woman's husband, walking up to join the women with two drinks in his hand. "Here you are, my dear," he added, handing his wife one of them.

"Can't you find out who it is?"

The American shrugged. Before he could reply, the three were joined by the Englishwoman's husband.

"I say, Jenkins, quite some dame your McCallum has on his arm," he said, nodding off in the general direction where he had last seen Matthew and Sabina.

"The women here were just talking about her."

"Do you know who she is, William?" implored the man's wife.

"No, haven't an idea. McCallum's keeping tight-lipped himself, though his lady's all anyone's talking about over by the bar."

"We've simply got to find out!"

"What on earth for?"

"Why . . . why, just to know. Isn't that enough reason?"

"All I heard was that she's related to a throne in one of the capitals," interposed the American wife.

"Only distantly, my dear," added Jenkins.

"You might as well say she's European and leave it at that," put in the Englishman. "Every noble family in Britain or the continent is related to every other if you go back far enough. Our own queen's family came from right here in Germany."

"You think she's royalty, William?" asked the man's wife.

"I didn't say that. I only said that all the noble families of Europe were related."

"She's of ancient aristocracy, then?"

"One look will tell you that, and make no mistake," rejoined the Englishman with finality. The other three pondered his words with nods and knowing looks, unconsciously all sending their eyes roving the ballroom for yet another glimpse of the dazzlingly beautiful mysterious lady on the arm of the American presidential envoy, with conspicuous but as yet unidentified nobility in her veins.

Oblivious to the rippling crosscurrents of inquisitive interest Sabina's presence had elicited, Matthew and Sabina continued to passively meander through the ballroom.

Before long the string trio ended their musical interlude, and the eighteen-piece orchestra again resumed their seats, this time for a tribute to the great master of Salzburg, Wolfgang Amadeus Mozart.

"Listen, Matthew!" said Sabina as they began, "do you recognize it?"

"Uh, yes . . . but *why* do I recognize it?" he added, laughing with embarrassed bewilderment.

"It's the minuet from *Eine Kleine Nachtmusik.*"

"And . . ."

"It's what the string quartet was playing the day we met . . . you remember—at my Uncle Otto's!"

"I'll never forget the day, though you'll have to forgive me if I better remember what you looked like to my young eyes than what the music sounded like."

"Matthew, you sometimes say the funniest things," said Sabina.

"I wasn't saying it to be funny. I remember every inch of your face that day."

"I remember the music too. There are many ways for a happy day to lodge in your mind."

"How right you are."

"Look, there are some people lining up for the minuet. Let's join them!"

Sabina began instantly walking toward them, pulling Matthew's hand behind her.

"The minuet! Sabina, I don't know the first thing how to do it," laughed Matthew. "How about a nice easy two-step with the others over there?"

"I'll teach you," said Sabina, still urging him on with a determined pull.

"I've never done anything like it. They don't teach us old-fashioned dances in the States. You might get me into a bop, a Charleston, or a swing maybe . . . but not a minuet."

"I'll show you everything!" replied Sabina.

Already they were lining up with the others.

"Take my hand," said Sabina, giving it to Matthew. "Now, watch the other men . . . keep in line with them. . . ."

Before Matthew could object further, he was stumbling and fumbling to the ancient dance of the French court, much to Sabina's delight.

As the movement progressed, Sabina did her best to direct Matthew, though with limited success.

"Keep hold of my hand . . . now turn left . . . small, dainty steps . . ."

She could not keep from laughing to see his gallant efforts to follow along in what was obviously an utter mystery to him.

By the time it was over, he had mastered, if not the grace of the unfamiliar movements, at least most of the footwork, and was plodding through the steps with a diligent and wooden clumsiness. Some of the others watched out of the corner of their eyes with humor, though a few seemed offended by the obvious butchery of such a cultural heritage.

"You were wonderful!" laughed Sabina.

"Don't fib!" said Matthew, trying to move quickly away from the eyes now following him as much as Sabina.

"You were! I haven't had such fun in years!"

"Didn't you see how they were all staring?" added Matthew, trying to walk inconspicuously toward the edge of the crowd as the music began for the next dance. "Let's get away from here for a while!"

Still laughing, but now taking his arm and squeezing close to his side, Sabina followed.

"I don't know which is worse, making a fool of myself on a dance floor . . . or stumbling into a goldfish pond!" Matthew added, laughing now himself.

47

Subtle Inquiries

• • •

MATTHEW'S TIPSY COLLEAGUE HAD BEEN BUSY, GAINING more attention than was healthy for the ego of anyone in his condition.

He had sought to soothe his annoyance at being, as he considered it, snubbed by his fellow American and rejected in his dance invitation by the snooty lady who was too good to speak to him, by loosening his thickened tongue with partial truths of which he was aware about the latter, blowing upon the sparks of general curiosity as he stumbled his way bumptiously about the ballroom. As he did, the alcohol found its way farther and farther into his brain, until the minor annoyance over his interview with Matthew grew disproportionately large in relation to what had actually occurred.

As the minuet came to an end, and altogether unaware that the subjects of his thoughts were in the public eye as a result, he was engaged at the far end of the giant hall in conversation with a low-level diplomat from Bonn, likewise fond of the amber brew from the north of Britain, whose acquaintance he had made in Vienna. They were speaking in German, though Wahlen's brain was having more and more difficulty responding coherently to the language in which he was ordinarily fluent.

At the moment they were discussing recent developments, notably Khrushchev's heightened threat to sign a separate peace treaty with the German Democratic Republic.

"It will be the end of any hope of unification for the two Germanys, Frank," the German was saying. "You must make sure your president Kennedy knows how serious it is."

"He knows, all right," said Wahlen absently.

"I mean really knows, Frank," repeated the other, grasping the American's arm in a plea of great seriousness, betraying his declining sobriety with a physical gesture of emotion. "If Khrushchev legitimizes the DDR, Berlin will be divided forever. Besides that, there could be war. You've got to tell him."

"Next time I'm in Washington, I'll tell him myself," asserted the American, pursing his lips in an expression of absolute conclusive reliability. In point of fact, Frank Wahlen had only met JFK once, and then by a mere handshake. It gave rise to another of the silent irritations he carried around with Matthew's name attached to it, that the young upstart was such a good friend of the president, and had been given a status throughout the negotiations almost on a level equal to the secretary of state.

A third man now joined them from behind. The fluidity of his German tongue and the clarity of focus in his eyes manifested that the clear liquid in the glass he held was neither bourbon nor vodka, but club soda. He had been listening intently, as he moved slowly throughout this end of the room, for just such a connection to the American president that he might be able to make use of.

Easing his way into the conversation, he nodded to the German but spoke first to Wahlen.

"So, you are a friend of the new American president," he said smoothly, "if you will pardon my eavesdropping."

Wahlen nodded.

"I am impressed," added the other. "You must be an important man."

Wahlen shrugged, smiling unconsciously from the puffery, hardly immune to the other man's ploy. The new arrival now turned back toward the West German, with whom he apparently was acquainted.

"*Guten Abend,* Herr Kreutz. How are things in Bonn?"

"Touchy, as you I'm certain are aware," returned the West German. "Your Mr. Khrushchev is making life difficult for us all."

"He is hardly *my* Mr. Khrushchev. I am but a bureaucrat who happens to find himself on the other side of the line, trying just like you to make the best of the situation."

"As you seem always to do. But tell me, how do you come to be here? I did not think invitations were circulating . . . uh, on *your* side."

"There you go again, Kreutz, making it sound as though we are two countries. There is only one Germany."

"Not if the bear Khrushchev has his way!"

"Mr. Khrushchev is attempting to reunite Germany into one. It is the Americans and the British, and, if you will forgive me, those of you in Bonn, who are standing in his way."

"Reunite! He would have all of Germany, the West included, brought into his Russian domain, and we will have no part of it."

"Tut, tut, Kreutz. Perhaps I will be able to talk more reasonably to your American friend here—you still have not introduced us."

Calming, the West German proceeded to introduce the two men.

"Frank Wahlen, meet Herr von Schmundt, from the *DDR,*" he added with obvious expressiveness.

"Gustav von Schmundt, at your service, Herr Wahlen," said Gustav, shaking the limp hand that was offered him. "I am intrigued, Herr Wahlen," he went on, turning now fully toward the American to begin the subtle interrogation for which he had intruded himself into the conversation. "I take it you are here as part of the American negotiating team?"

"That's right, Herr von Schmundt," he replied listlessly.

"You were in Vienna?"

Wahlen nodded, failing to add that he had been sent back to Berlin before the most intensive talks had begun and had never once even laid eyes on either JFK or the Soviet Premier.

"Do *you* see a breakthrough at hand?" asked Gustav graciously, with feigned humble interest.

"No time soon," replied Wahlen.

Gustav took a slow drink of the sparkling water in his glass, appearing deep in thought.

"Tell me, Herr Wahlen," he said after a moment, "do you know most of the Americans here in Berlin?"

"As many as anyone, I would say."

"There is a man, also one of your president's advisors, that I have been trying to make contact with. You would certainly know him if you are both on Mr. Kennedy's staff."

"I might know him. What is his name?"

"Ah . . . McCallum," replied the East German casually.

At the word, Wahlen's eyes opened wider and his brain cleared temporarily from its stupor.

"Why do you want to find *him?*" he asked.

"There is . . . ah, a matter of some delicacy we must take up. Are you acquainted with him?"

"I may be," replied Wahlen cryptically.

"Come now, Herr Wahlen," rejoined Gustav sharply, a flash erupting from his eyes. The fire lasted but an instant. Recovering his poise, he calmed. The American had not noticed the quick ruffling of feathers, which now settled gradually back down into place. "You do not strike me as one to play verbal games."

Wahlen smiled drunkenly, then slowly nodded.

"Yes . . . I am familiar with the name you speak of," he replied, keeping the reminder of his own anger as well concealed as Gustav had his.

"McCallum?"

"Yes . . . Matthew McCallum."

"It is most urgent I speak with him—is he here?"

"You mean *here* . . . tonight?"

"Yes, that is what I mean. Is he in attendance?"

Hazily perceiving a way to get back at Matthew for his snobbish conceit, Wahlen skirted the question.

"Whatever you have to say to the American delegation, Herr von Schmidt—"

"The name is *Schmundt,*" flashed Gustav.

"Whatever you have to say, you may say to me. Just between us, McCallum's on the outs around here these days. I can take care of you."

"I must speak to McCallum personally."

"Why, Smudt?" rejoined Wahlen, his speech steadily slurring.

"For reasons that are between him and myself," Gustav replied, with effort holding in his mounting irritation at this blundering fool. "I must insist that you tell me where I can find him."

"Really important, eh, Schmidt?"

"Extremely urgent."

"Well, you won't find him tonight," retorted Wahlen, giving both Matthew and this pompous German their due in one fell swoop. He would tell this arrogant fellow nothing!

"He's not here?"

Wahlen shook his head, then took an unceremonious swallow from his glass. "Nope," he repeated. "Nowhere around! Haven't seen him in days."

Without further ceremony, Schmundt turned and disappeared, vouchsafing no word nor even gesture of departure to either the idiotic American or his West German acquaintance.

48

Old Memories . . . and New

. . .

ANOTHER WALTZ HAD BEGUN. ONCE MORE SABINA AND Matthew moved graciously to the dance floor.

"Let's hope I can keep from stumbling all over you," said Matthew as they began.

"There is hardly any worry of that," said Sabina.

"Only if I'm waltzing," rejoined Matthew with a grin.

She slipped into his arms, and within seconds they were moving in perfect time to the music.

"You are an excellent dancer," Sabina went on. "I knew it from the very first time we danced at Gustav's."

The reminder of that earlier time caused both to grow pensive. They danced awhile in silence.

"What were you thinking that day?" Sabina asked at length.

"About what . . . you mean about *you?*"

"I don't know, about anything."

"Well, I *was* thinking about you," said Matthew. "Almost immediately after I walked in, your cousin Brigitte approached me and turned her wiles on to full strength. But the whole time we were talking I was looking about trying to find you."

Sabina glanced down shyly.

"By the way, what ever became of her?"

"Brigitte?"

Matthew nodded.

Sabina smiled sadly. "It's sad . . . at least to my eyes."

"How so?"

"I suppose she has everything she always wanted. But the last time I saw her, which was years ago, I was so grieved for her."

"She was . . . not doing well?" said Matthew.

"In the world's eyes I'm sure she was the envy of many. She had carried on the family tradition, marrying a banker just like her father. Uncle Otto came out of the war landing on his feet, not exactly with his fortune intact, but far less ruined than many in his position. I don't know exactly how he did it—he seemed to have connections somehow. He's still in East Berlin, and quite high up in the DDR banking system. I haven't even seen him since the war."

"Living in the same city . . . your own uncle? He hasn't been of any help in the matter of your father?"

Sabina shook her head.

"The Communists are just like the Nazis in this," she said. "They alter loyalties, and they leave no room for sentimentality. I doubt my uncle would even know me if we met on the street, or would acknowledge it if he did recognize me."

"What about Brigitte?"

"She married well, moved to West Berlin with her husband, and is now at the center of a very wealthy and elite social circle. I saw her several years ago, quite by accident. I wept afterward. She had gained weight, and it seemed she was trying to hide the fact with expensive French gowns and makeup and jewelry. She looked—I don't know how else to say it—pathetic to me. Her hair glistened, her eyes and eyelashes and lips were painted so thick that she didn't even look like a real person. She reminded me of a doll—just like what you said—or perhaps someone pretending to be a movie star. Gold hung about her everywhere—from her ears, on her wrists, rings on every finger. I felt sorry for her. In the midst of all the riches and glamour, she looked so lonely and unhappy."

"What did you say to her?"

"I couldn't bring myself to approach her," replied Sabina sadly. "I let the moment pass, just staring at the sight. She never even saw me."

They both reflected on Sabina's poignant words.

"And," she went on after a moment, "there was the matter of my father's safety to think of. I was no longer Sabina von Dortmann by then, remember. I'm certain Gustav has made contact with both

Brigitte and Uncle Otto. I couldn't afford for them to know either my new identity or my whereabouts."

Sabina sighed from the memory.

"I can't say I'm altogether surprised," said Matthew. "Your cousin was always very different from you—at least from when I first met you both."

"The differences were there even in childhood," remarked Sabina thoughtfully.

"I remember when she approached me when we walked into the Schmundt place. But I wanted to see *you*. And wearing that long, light green dress, you were even more beautiful than I remembered. Everything about you was so full of life and expression. You were both a grown woman and a young teenager, all at the same time."

"You were more than a little handsome yourself," she replied, glancing up with a smile. "That is one of your features that the years have treated well."

"Aw, get out of here!" said Matthew with light derision.

"I mean it. You are still the most handsome man I have ever met."

"You shouldn't say things like that."

"Ah, but you are allowed to, is that it?" queried Sabina, teasingly.

"What I said about you was true," laughed Matthew.

"No more than what I said about you. Women see things in a man that men aren't able to see themselves. They know what to look for. It's more than just facial characteristics themselves. It's the way a man carries himself, how he behaves, the way he treats people, the way he speaks, whether his eyes have a fire of purpose in them or are vacant, how he walks—and especially how he treats women. Everything mingles together. A woman responds to the whole man, not merely his face. When I say that you are handsome, it's everything about the man you are. And now, with all that's happened to you since, all you've become, how can I not think it all the more?"

Now it was Matthew's turn to grow silent.

Thoughts and emotions swirled within their hearts and minds, just as they swirled about the dance floor in a silence that spoke volumes. Flushed from both the activity and one another's presence, never could a man and woman have been more in love than Matthew McCallum and Sabina von Dortmann were at that moment.

Around the floor they danced, oblivious to everyone in the world but one another, drawing closer and closer each into the other's embrace. Presently their bodies moved to the music as one, while Sabina's head rested contentedly between Matthew's neck and shoulder.

"I now know that from the very beginning God was the one drawing us together," he whispered into her ear. "There was no way I could have known it then, but now it is so clear. I see how he has been at work ever since, saving each of us for this present time . . . for this moment."

He felt Sabina's head nod in silent agreement.

"Can't you see the hand of the Lord in all that has happened, in our meeting again, in our both still carrying the same feelings for each other . . . and even more that neither of us ever married?"

Again he felt the nodding of her head.

"I'm even coming to sense a deep gratitude to him for the years apart. How could this special time now ever have been without them? I wouldn't trade these weeks I've had with you . . . *for anything!* The Father, as your father would have said, really does work all things for good. Do you see what I'm trying to say, Sabina—I truly feel the Lord *meant* us for one another."

Several seconds passed. Gradually he became aware that she was quietly weeping.

His feet came to a stop and he pulled away several inches to face her, an expression of grave concern filling his countenance.

Sabina's head lifted. Their eyes met. Hers were large and full and swimming in the liquid of love.

Divining his anxiety, all she could do was shake her head slowly from side to side, attempting to find the words to dispel his concern, struggling to give expression to the pounding sensations deep in her breast, unable even to form her lips into the smile that would reassure him.

They stood, as an island in the midst of dozens of waltzers, for several seconds, gazing fathomlessly into one another's eyes, expressing with the light dancing from black-pupiled depths what ten thousand books could never proclaim.

"Oh, Matthew!" Sabina murmured at length. "How *can* you have made this woman so very, very happy!"

Her eyes filled with tears, even more than before.

Gently he took her again in his arms, drawing her near, their heads side by side, eyes now closed.

"Because it's a fairy tale, remember?" he purred in her ear, " . . . *our* fairy tale."

The Sting of Wealth

• • •

AS GUSTAV MADE HIS WAY SILENTLY FUMING THROUGH the crowd, he more than half suspected that the imbecile he had been talking to had been lying. Everyone knew you could trust the Americans even less these days than ever.

But he didn't need him. He didn't need any of them. He would find McCallum somehow, with or without the other fool's help!

He began moving toward the far end of the ballroom, from where the sounds of the orchestra came. He had not been there yet tonight. Perhaps he could pick up some threads of conversation that would be more useful than the one he had just left!

An unconscious sense of being ill at ease began to creep over him. He would never have confessed it, but in truth he felt out of place here.

It was too happy, too festive, too gay. He would not have wanted to stoop to the realization that he resented the West Germans and Americans and snobbish British and idiot French and all the rest their happiness.

What did he need with happiness!

Admit it or not, however, he felt uneasy and nervous among the tuxedos and gowns, the smiles and music. The stupid waltzers with equally stupid smiles plastered on their dreamy faces. The whole atmosphere of the place stung, and he found it unpleasant and annoying.

The demon of frustration entered his soul to an even greater extent than usual, bringing along anger, its best friend, that powerful enemy to human betterment with whom Gustav had cultivated a lifelong friendship.

Glancing around, trying to listen to pieces of conversation, his senses grew steadily more callous and unresponsive.

His anger increased.

He could not have identified its root had he tried. He knew himself too little to bother with inward sources. He felt what he felt, thought what he thought, and never bothered to ask why either might be so.

Gustav von Schmundt had made choices long ago that had set the development of his character in motion, and from that course he had never once turned back. Those choices, and the direction of that development, had blinded his eyes to that most important region of growth within the human frame—the ripening of his own being and personhood. His character—inevitably where motives of self are the foundation—was in the process not of ripening at all, but of going slowly to seed.

He was angry at them for their happiness, for their naiveté in the face of Soviet dominance and influence. He was angry at them for looking down on East Germany as the lesser of the two Germanys, though such a fact he would never have acknowledged. He was angry with the universal anger shared by all those who feel unequal and powerless to change the oppression that burdens them. He was angry with the determination to disprove the inequality he felt but would never admit, by the exercise of his own might and superiority and strength.

He was angry with the cur McCallum, angry for the affection Sabina had shown him at his own birthday party, despising him for his success and influence, angry with him for not being here so he could lay his hands on his mollycoddling throat and have it out with him once and for all and beat him into telling him where Sabina was!

At root, he was angry at Sabina above all the rest, for rejecting him, for hiding from him, for managing to elude him all this time.

He would make her pay!

He had long ceased caring if she ever loved him. Revenge had become equal motive to what he still deluded himself by calling love. He would make love to her and laugh at the bitterness it would cause her to know that he, Gustav von Schmundt, whom she had always thought herself too good for, had complete power over her!

And he was still angry with her fool of a father for making a fool of him, angry at him for the idiotic peace on his face. He and his holier-than-thou pronouncements about God and religion and all the claptrap that went with it!

He would show them. . . . He would show them all that their happiness was ill-founded! They were morons to pretend to be so happy! Stupid idiots every one of them!

He would find them! He would get rid of the baron altogether—send him to Moscow or Siberia, what did it matter—arrange to throw McCallum into prison with him, and take Sabina for himself!

He would find her! He was getting closer. Something told him it would not be long now!

Gustav's cognition of his own innermost self was so meager that he possessed not the faintest inkling of the power the baron's Christ-like character still exerted upon him. Indeed, the demon friends of anger and frustration were not the only spiritual influences blinding his *Stasi* eyes.

Stretching across time, the baron's sacrificial prayer from seventeen years before—whispered on a lonely road outside the village called Fürstensdorf, its words heard by no mortal—was still being heeded and answered on this evening, within the timeless eternity of the Father's ear:

Lord God, our Father, blind his eyes, and bind his power to harm your people.

Without paying attention to his steps, he found himself wandering distractedly amidst the dancers. A French couple, spinning with exaggerated flourish, backed his way, bumping against him rather soundly. Several oaths the frolicsome couple did not understand were all that met their profuse apologies.

Swearing further under his breath, Gustav did his best to muscle his way unceremoniously out from the middle of the dancers, not without several more minor collisions as he did.

"Why can't these fools watch where they're going!" he muttered angrily.

50
Scents of the Past

· · ·

THE DANCE ENDED. ANOTHER BEGAN.

Still Matthew and Sabina stood unmoving and content in the middle of the dance floor in one another's arms.

Those among the guests inclined to allow room for gossip-mongering demons to do their evil work now had more than ample fuel wherewith to feed their insatiable thirst, and the tongues began to wag in earnest.

Slowly at length, as in one accord, the two began to move in subconscious rhythm to the music of the strings. The conscious gradually came to replace the subconscious, and before long they found themselves dancing again, though more sedately than any of those around them.

Halfway through the piece, a minor commotion seemed to erupt two or three meters behind them. Neither turned to see its cause, though a moment later Sabina felt her shoulder jarred, and she stumbled toward Matthew.

He felt a shudder course through her entire frame, paused, pulled his head back to look in her face.

Her eyes were wide and filled with an unexpected expression of terror. For an instant she did not even seem to see him.

"Sabina—what is it?" he asked in alarm, his voice low and unheard by any other.

His voice brought back her senses.

She shivered again and drew her shoulders up.

"I . . . I don't know," she said. "Suddenly I was overcome with the strangest sense of fear, and all at once I felt icy cold."

•   •   •

Jostling his way through the crowd, Gustav's senses jolted his brain into mad, almost deranged agitation.

He froze, glancing all about, as if attempting to force into his mind something undefined upon which he could not focus.

Breathing deeply, he sent himself into a paroxysm of wild memory.

It was the smell of Sabina's room. It was the smell of Sabina herself!

In an instant he was back at his own birthday party many years earlier, dancing with her, feeling her body so near, the aroma of her perfume engulfing his head with its heavenly aroma, making him insane with desire for her. And then another memory: later, at *Lebenshaus* on the night they had ransacked the place, the very pillow where she had laid her head.

He stood like a pillar of marble yet a moment more, closing his eyes, relishing the aroma yet inwardly cursing whatever woman it was who had chosen to wear it this night.

Suddenly he turned and tore off toward the doors through which he had entered, in a demented passion of confused wrath, jealousy, and lust.

He had to get out of this place!

If McCallum wasn't here, there was no point in staying. He needed no more reminders of Sabina! He didn't want to smell her perfume again until he could splash it all over her himself!

•   •   •

Sabina shook herself, as if to cast aside the last lingering effects of the peculiar sensation, then drifted into Matthew's arms once more.

"I can't imagine what I could possibly have been afraid of, especially with you so close to protect me," she said. "It's . . . it's gone now. . . . I'm fine."

They danced a few more circles to the music, then Matthew spoke. "What you need is some fresh air," he said. "How about we take a break, have some punch, and see what the moon is up to out on the balcony?"

Sabina nodded, smiling her assent.

51

Moonlit Gardens

• • •

THE NIGHT AIR REVIVED BOTH, AND SOON THEY WERE talking and laughing with a joyous and expressive freedom reminiscent of their days together as teenagers at *Lebenshaus*.

The sun had set, and the long summer dusk had settled the warm, quiet serenity of its pale azure blanket over the city. Fading imperceptibly toward night, the blue overhead and the reds and oranges at the western horizon all thinned, stretching downward and upward to meet halfway up the July sky, where here and there the first twinkles of the night heavens could be seen. In the east, the bright glowing lunar orb rose, seven-eighths full, as if in defiance of the sun's approaching slumber.

"There's something mesmerizing about the moon," remarked Matthew as he looked up toward it.

Sabina nodded. The mood between them gradually stilled.

"Jack is determined to land men there before the decade is out."

"What?" said Sabina, glancing over at Matthew. "Where?"

"On the moon."

"Land men on the moon!"

"Yes," laughed Matthew. "That's our plan."

"I've never heard of such a thing. It's impossible!"

"Nothing is impossible for Jack Kennedy, believe me . . . or for the United States either, for that matter . . . unless Russia with its fleet of cosmonauts gets there first!"

Again silence fell. The mystery of the bright heavenly face staring down upon them penetrated their souls, and neither felt inclined to disturb its spell.

"There are extensive gardens here at the consulate," commented Matthew casually.

A murmured acknowledgement of interest was Sabina's only reply.

"Too bad it's not the middle of the afternoon. We could explore them," Matthew added absently.

Several minutes passed in comfortable silence.

"Well . . . perhaps we ought to go back inside," said Matthew at length. Smiling, Sabina nodded.

They turned and walked back into the ballroom.

The evening's musical backdrop had changed again. It took several seconds, then suddenly Matthew picked up the orchestra's tune. It was the *Serenade for Strings* by Tchaikovsky. Even in the smallest ways, he thought, Russia was making its influence felt throughout the West.

They attempted to reenter the spirit of the ball, but without success.

Both became uncomfortably aware of glances and stares pointed more than occasionally in their direction. Out of the corner of his ear Matthew detected here and there questioning comments of inquiry. Chastising himself, he suddenly realized how foolish it had been to make such obscure remarks about Sabina to such a one as Frank Wahlen.

This fairy tale he had promised Sabina would quickly turn into a nightmare if he didn't do something. Besides, he had things to say to her that he wasn't going to get said here.

"You want to know something?" he said, laughing lightly and trying to sound casual. "Suddenly I don't feel the least bit in the mood for a formal ball and all these people and the music and the din of conversation. What do you say we go have a look at those gardens right now?"

"You must have read my mind," replied Sabina. "I was just thinking how much I would enjoy that very thing."

"Come on, then," Matthew said, turning quickly around. "Let's get out of here!"

• • •

Ten minutes later they were walking softly and slowly along a hedge-lined path into the formal gardens of the consulate. Their pace was slow, for their steps had no goal. Sabina had slipped her hand through Matthew's arm and leaned close to him, dreamily thinking how her own *Märchen* had indeed come true. Was Matthew not twice the man of any fairy tale Prince Charming?

On his part, Matthew was pondering how Sabina had so radiantly come into her own as God's woman, the bud of her former self now flowering to perfection.

Dusk had enshrouded the city, the full blackness of night kept at bay by the receding greater light of day and the climbing lesser light of night. Lingering memories of the sunset were nearly gone, glowing but faintly in the west, while the rising moon in the east cast her eerie shadows about their footsteps as they walked.

The gardens were spacious, easily equal in size to the baron's former plot at *Lebenshaus* if not larger. Of a more formal design, however, with square and rectangular hedges, evenly spaced trees, and wide predictable walkways, bordered on one edge by the River Spree flowing through the city, the whole appeared to have been plotted out by diagram rather than to have grown naturally more expansive by degrees through the years, as the best gardens always do. Had their visit come in broad daylight, neither Sabina nor Matthew would have found them so interesting, having cut their horticultural teeth on the baron's unique and creative way of interacting with living things. As it was, however, they made their way easily along, enjoying the occasional reminders of *Lebenshaus* without having to pay close attention to the direction of their steps.

Other things than gardens were on their minds.

"Do you find such places difficult?" asked Matthew softly as they went.

"How do you mean?" said Sabina.

"Gardens, hedges, paths . . . reminders of your father?"

She thought a moment. "In many ways, I suppose there will always be a sadness that pierces my heart when my eyes behold a well-tended garden. Yes, they cannot help but remind me of him, and of Mama, of the happy past, of our garden which is now no more."

"But you don't mind being here?"

"Oh no. I still enjoy gardens. I have walked many of Berlin's for that very reason through the years."

"What reason?"

"For the reminder."

"I don't understand."

"There is a melancholy pleasure that accompanies such nostalgic reminders at the same time. I am more able to pray for my father surrounded by the kind of growing things I know he would enjoy. Though there is pain, the reminder makes me feel close to him . . . and close to my heavenly Father at the same time."

"Do you realize how much like your father you are?"

"Hmm . . . I don't suppose I do."

"Obviously you have your own personality, but so much of how you express yourself, how you look at things, how you think, all reflects him so clearly . . . at least to me."

"It makes me happy to hear you say so."

"You are very much the daughter of Baron von Dortmann, and yet . . ."

Matthew's voice trailed away.

"And yet what?" she asked after a moment.

"I was going to say that you have also become very much a mature woman on your own . . . a woman—I don't think it is any secret— that I have become more than a little fond of."

They continued, the shadows from the moon casting phantasmic shapes on the ground all about them.

"Sabina . . . ," said Matthew in a faltering voice, "I didn't want us to come out here to talk about your father or gardens, but I . . . I don't know how . . . oh, good grief!"

"What, Matthew?"

"This is so frustrating!"

"You can say anything you want to me."

"I know . . . but getting it out is another thing. I talk to people all day long, but then with the person I care about most in the whole world, my tongue ties up like I'm a little kid again!"

Again an awkward silence fell.

"Don't you see," Matthew blurted out suddenly, "we can't just keep going on like this forever. We're too old. We're not just carefree teenagers having a good time. We're forty years old, for heaven's sake . . . we're . . ."

Matthew let out a great sigh.

"I don't *feel* old, Matthew. In fact, I feel younger than I have in years, almost like I *am* a teenager again—a teenager in—"

Suddenly it was Sabina's turn to break off in the middle of a word. She glanced down, feeling suddenly very warm.

"That's exactly it," Matthew blurted out. "We don't feel any different. But things *are* different. We *are* older. We have responsibilities. The world has changed. You're in the East, I'm an American. I could be sent back to the States anytime. . . ."

"Don't speak like that, Matthew. The thought of your leaving—"

"But don't you see, we *have* to think about these things. We don't have as many years left as before. We . . . we can't afford—"

Again he paused, breathing in deeply.

"We've got . . . we need to think about the future," he added quickly after a few seconds.

"The *future,* Matthew?" said Sabina, her voice quivering.

"Yes . . . the future. We've . . . we've got to make plans. I made up my mind after we met again that nothing would come between us again."

He stopped and glanced sharply away, drawing in a deep breath.

"Sabina . . . this is harder to get out than I thought it would be. What I'm trying to say is that I want . . . that is, I would like to ask you . . . if you would be my wife."

Even before he was through, Sabina stopped walking and faced him.

"I think the Lord wants us together," Matthew went on. "I don't want us ever to be apart again, no matter what happens in the world situation. I think God brought us together . . . and I want to ask you to marry me. There!" he added with a great exhaling sigh. "I said it!"

Now Sabina's eyes, full of tears again, sought his in the moonlight. She could do nothing but murmur his name before she broke into quiet sobs of joy. *"Oh, Matthew . . ."*

She fell against him, her head on his chest, weeping freely.

He wrapped his arms gently around her shoulders. They stood once more, as they had on the dance floor, saying nothing, content to remain in each other's presence forever. All around the dark quiet peacefulness of the expansive garden seemed to close around them like a protective covering of the Father's care. They each sensed, in their own way, that he was with them too and had ordained and made possible this great love that had grown up so unexpectedly between them.

It was Sabina who at length broke the wondrous silence.

"There are no sweeter words I can think of in all the world," she said, "than *Sabina McCallum.*"

"Does that mean . . . ?"

"Of course, Matthew. You only had to ask."

"How long . . . when did you—"

"I've been yours since you gave me the yellow rose at *Lebenshaus* . . . and I will be yours forever!"

Matthew placed his hands on her two shoulders, moved her back from him, again gazed deeply into her eyes for several long seconds, then bent forward and gently kissed her, then put his lips to her ear.

"I too will be yours . . . forever," he whispered.

52

Blind Observer

• • •

EVEN AS THE TWO NOW STROLLED TOGETHER HAND IN hand, less than three hundred meters away in the middle of a stone bridge bordering the consulate grounds, a solitary figure stood staring off in the opposite direction, his mood as chilly as the silent waters of the river flowing beneath him.

In the light of the moon it was not altogether dark. Had Gustav turned and fixed his gaze toward them, he would have seen the very object of his lifelong obsession, and his search, for good or ill, would have been over.

But he had not trained himself to look in the right directions for anything; neither did he do so on this night. As Sabina and Matthew built their own dreamy castles for the future, so likewise did Gustav von Schmundt. While theirs were castles resting upon the clouds in which to live out their fairy tale of the future, however, his more resembled gloomy stone enclosures where dungeons predominated for the carrying out of his grim and morbid fantasies.

He sucked in a long drag on the cigarette his fingers held between them, letting the smoke exhale slowly, enveloping his cheeks and shoulders, eyes and hair, as it drifted lazily upward into the breezeless night.

His mood had calmed since leaving the ballroom, and as he stood leaning over the waist-high stone parapet, he found his thoughts drifting more in the direction of Sabina's father and his own and the houses of the two men, than toward Sabina herself.

Everything had changed under the new regime. Both estates had been confiscated by the new government. In that sense, he was little better off than his nemesis the baron. But he had been careful to keep possession of all papers and documents of ownership, of his own status as the count's son, and of all ancient rights that accompanied the heritage. The day would come, he had little doubt, when the Schmundt estate would be restored to him. If not by a change in Communist policy, then by his own resources and cunning. It was well enough known that, even in this era of so-called communal equality, there were those individuals of stature and importance who were granted rights of possession more equal than their lesser peers. He was on the rise. He had connections in Moscow. He was gradually lining his own pockets as he had been well taught. And in due course he would submit his bid to reacquire his father's estate, where he had spent his boyhood years. He had no doubt it would be granted. Hard cash would always be in demand in the DDR, and when he had accumulated sufficient reserves, and had bolstered his reputation both in Berlin and Moscow, then he would make his move.

As he reflected upon it further, a wider strategy began to present itself to his calculating brain.

Perhaps he had been going about this all wrong.

What if he could get his hands on the baron's former estate as well? An outright purchase would never be authorized. Since he had last been there shortly after the war, it had been turned into a government-run asylum, and they were unlikely to relinquish it to an individual no matter how important.

But what if he could prove what his father had always told him, that the Dortmann estate rightfully belonged in Schmundt hands? What if, furthermore, the connections to the ancient cache of Prussian gold *were* true? As a boy he'd been wide-eyed to hear the tales. As he'd grown he'd come to assume it no more than legendary humbug.

But what if . . . ? Gustav found himself wondering.

If he could secure the estates under his control . . . and *if* the gold was really there . . . might he not be able to induce Sabina to live out her days with him, not with threats against her father, but with promises to restore her father to his former position?

Threats didn't work with either Sabina or her fool of a father. Both of them were content to let the old man live out his dying days in a prison cell.

But how could either of them resist the thought of living once again at *Lebenshaus,* with the old place restored to its former glory, with wealth and status to go along with it? He could even promise the baron to restore his old garden! It would be a powerful inducement.

He would gain Sabina's hand by promising to do the old man good!

He would move him, just as planned, to add to the inducement a return to *Lebenshaus* would provide. He would shake them both up a bit before laying the plum before them.

If they were in touch, as he suspected, all he needed to do was let the baron know he had *Lebenshaus* in his possession, and that it would all be his again, with only the stipulation that Sabina consent to see him, and talk to him about the possibility of marriage. He would play his hand slowly and carefully, not even making marriage a requirement at first.

For his plan to have any chance of success, he would have to acquire the documentation to prove his ancient right both to his father's place and the baron's.

It would help immeasurably, he thought, if he could lay his hands on the original deeds of the Dortmann estate. His father had always told him of some hidden room where reports said the gold was hidden. If there were papers, no doubt they would be in the same location. His great-granduncle, or had it been even further back than that, had snuck into the place in the dead of night back in Bismarck's time, so the story went, and had never been heard from again. He had never believed the story any more than he had believed in the gold. Now he found himself wondering if there hadn't been more truth in both accounts than he'd suspected.

The Prussian gold . . . papers linking ownership between the two estates . . . they might have brought doom to the old Schmundt spy for the Austrians, but for him they were the keys to the carrying out of his plan!

The secrets of both were hidden away in the secret room. If only he'd paid more attention to the layout of the place when he and Sabina had played there as children!

No matter. He could find it, if only he could gain access again now.

In the meantime, he had plenty of work to do.

He threw the end of his cigarette down into the waters of the Spree, then walked on across the bridge with renewed vigor and purpose in his stride.

53

Castles in the Air

• • •

HOW LONG THEY HAD BEEN WALKING THE GARDEN PATHS hand in hand, neither Matthew nor Sabina knew. Both had lost all track of time. An hour, maybe two, had passed since they had left the ball, whose music still filtered through the night air behind them.

Dusk was past, night had come, though still the moon lit their steps and they could see their way without difficulty.

Their dialog was sporadic, quixotic, blissful, and scarcely above a whisper, as they dreamed and planned and added many a room to their airy castles of romantic happiness.

Now at length the conversation had begun to move in the direction of certain practicalities inherent in their mutual plight.

"What do you think about living in the United States?" Matthew asked after they had been walking awhile in silence.

Sabina did not answer. After a minute or so had passed and she had still said nothing, he glanced over toward her, concerned.

She felt his eyes upon her and turned her gaze up to meet them.

"I . . . I feel so foolish," she said. "All this time we've been talking about what it would be like to be married, about having a home and children and my cooking breakfast for you and all the things we would do . . . yet the reality of what it would all *mean* somehow never dawned on me."

"You mean moving to the West? To America?"

"It sounds so funny to say, but I suppose I forgot that . . . that you are an *American* . . . and an adviser to your president . . . that your life is more involved than just how it affects me."

"None of the rest is as important to me as a future with you," said Matthew sincerely.

Sabina nodded. "I see now so clearly—it would be the only possibility. America is where your life, your work is. I . . . just hadn't stopped to consider all the implications."

"Does moving to the States frighten you?"

"Frighten . . . no. As long as I was with you."

"What then?"

"You must see how difficult it would be. Germany is my homeland."

Matthew nodded. "I would never ask such a thing if I weren't so determined not to lose you again. Besides, wouldn't getting out from under Communism and living in freedom again . . . wouldn't that more than make up for it?" he asked.

"Perhaps if it was only a move here, to West Berlin. But all the way to the United States . . ." Her voice trailed off, and she grew pensive.

"I could probably get a European assignment," he mused.

Sabina said nothing. Matthew could tell she had hardly heard him. He sensed that the sudden change in her mood had to do with more than simply the thought of relocating in the West.

"Who knows," Matthew added optimistically, "we could probably spend six or eight months of the year right here!"

"Yes . . . yes, that might be nice," she said at length, though her voice sounded hesitant and distracted. It was clear Sabina was weighing factors in her mind that she did not want to talk about. Were the same reservations coming over her that had clouded their relationship earlier?

They continued to stroll casually through the moonlight. Matthew's thoughts now turned themselves toward the chief concern, as he saw it, amid their plans. As if his mind were pulling hers into the same channel, Sabina now suddenly realized there was a much greater and more personal obstacle in the way of their future than the one she had been pondering.

"And . . . ," she said, as if speaking out the thought that had just occurred to her, "I couldn't possibly leave Papa."

Matthew sighed.

"I was just thinking of your father too," he said.

"I'm sorry, Matthew!" exclaimed Sabina, shaking off the melancholy rumination that had come over her a few minutes earlier. "I want nothing more than to spend the rest of my life with you! Please don't misunderstand me! There is just so much to consider."

"I know."

"Even though I haven't been able to see Papa, simply knowing that I am nearby gives me some consolation. I keep hoping that somehow, someday, there will be a change and I *will* be able to see him. How could that happen if I lost contact with . . . that is, if I was far away from him?"

"There is also Gustav to consider," said Matthew. "At least you wouldn't have to worry about him anymore, either here or in the States."

"Though what might he do to Papa once he knew I was married to you?"

The silence that followed was brief. They both knew Gustav well enough to realize the likely answer to their question.

"There's only one thing for us to do," said Matthew, in a voice filled with more resolve than the almost overconfident manner in which the words came out.

"What?"

"We'll just have to get your father released!"

"Oh, Matthew, do you mean it?"

"Of course I mean it. I've never been more serious in all my life. I tell you, I will not lose you again, no matter what I may have to do. Remember the promise of the pink rose."

"I remember," Sabina said quietly, smiling.

They walked on, each in their own way considering the many factors and implications of this new road their love seemed to be leading them on.

Where it would lead, neither could possibly know. There were inevitable risks and uncertainties. Turning back, however, presented itself as an option to neither.

Matthew recognized that the baron's predicament had to be dealt with. Since giving his life to his Lord and Father, everything had changed for Matthew. He saw life from a much different perspective than his colleagues and friends in the world. An order existed in all things that had to be observed. There were priorities that regulated a life lived in submission to the overarching precept that others came before self. The highest truth of all was that God's will existed as the supreme guiding principle of life, *not* one's own wishes, desires, or motives.

Old-fashioned as some might have considered it, had the baron not been in prison, Matthew would have gone first of all to him to ask for Sabina's hand. Under the circumstances, he knew he would have the baron's full blessing. Yet he could not ignore that the baron was part of their lives. There remained an order to be heeded. He had to be brought into their plans, and Matthew saw that it would not be right to marry Sabina without dealing first with the baron's plight. To do otherwise would place her in an awkward conflict of loyalties. He could not ask her to begin a new life while leaving her father's situation unresolved.

In proposing marriage to Sabina, and then by marrying her, he would be being adopted into Baron von Dortmann's family. He would become the baron's son and would thus be taking onto his own shoulders a responsibility for him. Whatever marriage plans they made must necessarily be contingent upon getting the baron released.

"At least," said Matthew at length, "let me make arrangements immediately for you to emigrate here to West Berlin."

"I . . . I don't know if I'm ready for that, Matthew," replied Sabina, with a hesitancy he thought odd.

Suddenly all Sabina's former doubts swept over her, including the ongoing dilemma of what to do in the matter of the photographs. What would become of her work, her contacts, and all the people who depended upon her? The wider implications of Matthew's proposal sent her into a renewed quandary of confusion.

Why shouldn't she just tell him everything? she thought. Did she still not trust him entirely? If so, what was the source of her hesitation?

"There's no reason for you to stay where you are. Thousands of refugees are leaving the East. Why shouldn't you be one of them? We'll be able to work on your father's situation just as well with you here—perhaps better."

"It's . . . it's just not time for that yet."

"What better time could there be? Things aren't going to get any better in the East."

"There are . . . some things I need to be sure of first," Sabina replied vaguely.

"What kind of things? Something to do with me . . . with all we've talked about?"

"No . . . oh, no, Matthew—nothing like that!"

"Why can't you tell me then?"

"I'm sorry . . . I just can't. Trust me, Matthew . . . please."

Even as the unplanned word left her lips, Sabina cringed inwardly, hating herself for saying it. How could she ask Matthew to trust her when she was unwilling to trust him?

"I do trust you. I only want what's best for you, and remaining in East Berlin longer than you have to doesn't seem to qualify in my thinking."

"I want nothing more than to be with you—you have to believe that," said Sabina earnestly. "But I just can't leave. Not yet."

"If we could get your father released, that would change things, wouldn't it?"

"It would change everything," replied Sabina.

A Hasty Pumpkin Ride

. . .

AGAIN THE QUIET MOOD DESCENDED UPON THEM.

They walked for ten long minutes without another word, putting aside for the moment all thoughts other than that they were with one another. Matthew stretched his right arm around Sabina's shoulder and drew her toward him, and she shrunk into his embrace with a sigh of contentment, trying her best to forget the doubt and questions occasioned by her awkwardly diverse involvements and loyalties.

"I wish I could find the rose garden around here," said Matthew at length, "that is, if there is one."

"Why?" murmured Sabina coyly.

"If you have to ask, then you haven't been paying attention to anything I've said all evening!"

Sabina laughed lightly.

"I confess . . . I think I do know the reason."

"Has the time come when I could be so bold as to venture giving you a *red* rose?" asked Matthew.

Sabina turned her head and glanced up into his face with a smile well visible in the moonlight.

"I would take no offense should such an occasion present itself," she said.

"I am delighted to hear it. I shall look forward to a suitable opportunity."

"As shall I. But you know, Matthew," she added with great expression of vague and hidden meaning, "it's not only what the red rose signifies that is important."

"*Oh?*" he said, drawing out the tone.

"The setting must be just right as well."

"I see," replied Matthew, as if a great puzzle had just been revealed to him. "So . . . more secrets to the German mystique of which I must beware, so as not to commit romantic suicide, is that it?"

Sabina laughed with delight.

"You are funny!"

"Now you have me worried. I shall be afraid to ever give you a red rose—even after we are married!"

Sabina's merry laugh was the only reply Matthew received.

They had been wandering in a great unconscious circle for the past twenty minutes, drawing nearer the consulate buildings without realizing it. All at once, Matthew became aware of the orchestra's music intruding its way into his ears.

"I wonder how long we've been out here," he remarked without thought.

A purr of disinterest sounded faintly at his side.

Unconsciously he glanced down at his watch, whose hands were but barely discernible in the light of the moon.

"Hmm . . . ten to twelve—we *have* been out here awhile."

They walked on.

Suddenly he felt Sabina's body jolt to attention beside him.

"What did you just say?" she asked with an urgent tone.

"I said that we'd been out here a long while," answered Matthew casually.

"No, the time!" she rejoined importunately.

"I said it was ten to twelve."

"Before *midnight!*" exclaimed Sabina.

"Yes," laughed Matthew, "why?"

"Oh, Matthew, I have to go!" she said, breaking out of his hug and beginning instantly to walk rapidly back toward the consulate building.

"What's the sudden rush?" he asked, following her but clearly confused.

"There's no time to explain. . . . I just have to get home."

"Is there some curfew I haven't heard about?" he said, still finding her sudden change humorous. "I've got it!" he added. "We're playing out the fairy-tale thing all the way. Great—let's go!" He broke into a run, caught her quickly, and now did his part to hurry *her* along, grinning widely. "Make sure you don't lose your slipper!"

"Matthew, I'm not pretending. I must get home—and quickly!"

Within a minute they were hastening up the broad stone steps out of the gardens into the ballroom.

"How about one last dance with the prince?" said Matthew, slowing his pace and trying to catch her eye with a wink.

Sabina continued forward through the guests who still remained at that hour. "I'm sorry, Matthew, I wish I could," she said. "There's just no time."

They exited the tall front doors to the ballroom.

"Maybe we ought to take a taxicab," said Sabina.

"Please, after all I went through to rent the carriage," said Matthew, frustration beginning to show in his tone.

"I'm sorry," said Sabina, pausing briefly to face him. "It was thoughtless of me to suggest it. It can't take that much longer."

Matthew smiled. "Besides," he said, "I made the driver promise when I hired him that the carriage would *not* turn into a pumpkin after the stroke of twelve."

Sabina's humor returned. She smiled reassuringly. "You will tell him to get me there as quickly as he can, won't you?"

"Though I am reluctant to leave you when the night is so young," Matthew replied, "I will bow to your wish, my lady."

With the words, Matthew ran off to fetch groom, carriage, and black team of two.

It was not exactly how he had envisioned an end to the evening in which he had proposed marriage to Sabina.

But he had told her earlier that he trusted her. Now, he thought to himself as they jostled bumpily along back to East Berlin, he had been given an opportunity to prove it, though he hadn't a clue what could possibly account for the sudden change in Sabina's demeanor.

They reached her apartment at twenty-five minutes past midnight.

After but a few final words of parting, Sabina hastened inside, leaving Matthew staring after her, at a loss to know what to think.

Finally he turned and, with a few words to the groom, began the leisurely ride back to West Berlin in the carriage alone, wondering if there was more to this fairy tale than he realized.

Behind him, in the darkness of her apartment, Sabina's eyes were wet with tears at the way she had been forced to end the most wonderful evening of her life.

Maybe she was *Aschenputtel* after all, she thought ironically, as she quickly took off the beautiful gown Matthew had bought her, and replaced it with the rags and scarf of her former life.

Already it seemed like a distant dream.

Had he *really* asked her to be his wife . . . Sabina McCallum!

She didn't even have time to think about that now! Duties pressed.

Still without turning on a single light, she went to her back door, opened it as quietly as she could, then stole out into the small yard behind the building and toward the fence at its far end.

PART III

Dangerous Mission

July/August 1961

55

In the Oval Office

• • •

IT WAS NOT THE FIRST TIME MATTHEW HAD BEEN IN THE Oval Office of the White House. But it was the first time *he* had been the one to request the meeting.

Matthew walked through the great double doors, shook hands with the president, then sat in the chair offered him.

"I appreciate your seeing me, Mr. President," he said.

"The least I can do for an old friend and faithful ally," replied the president. "Especially after all you've done for me in Vienna and Berlin. What is the mood like there since I left?"

"Pretty much the same. Bonn is nervous. They appreciate your commitment to the German people, but your formal response to the Soviet aide-mémoire on the seventeenth didn't help allay their fear of war."

Kennedy smiled humorlessly.

"I didn't think it would," he said. "But there's no use pretending the consequences of this standoff aren't serious. I won't do any good to anyone by downplaying it. If I don't stand tough, Khrushchev will think me weak—which I understand he *already* thinks. The *boy president*, someone said he called me. That's why I worded the reply as I did, warning the Soviets of the serious and grave dangers in their present course."

"There's no doubt you did the right thing, Mr. President," said Matthew. "But public opinion over there is tricky. The West Germans may be our allies now, but they're still independent thinkers, and sometimes difficult to figure out."

"You'll be around long enough to hear my speech on the twenty-fifth?"

"That depends on what I have to discuss with you."

"I'm going to tell the American people of the rising stakes in Berlin, and ask Congress for an immediate increase in defense spending, as well as putting B-52 and B-47 bombers on ground alert. I'm even considering calling up reserve units."

"Strong measures."

"After the drubbing he gave me last month in Vienna, I'm not sure Khrushchev will understand anything less."

"You don't mean you're trying to bluff him?"

"Let me put it this way—I hope he'll realize that it would be foolhardy for him to continue as he's going. On the other hand, if he doesn't . . . no, I'm not bluffing. I'm prepared to risk war to preserve Berlin's freedom, though I hope to God it never comes to that."

Silence fell briefly. Both knew these were historic and serious times.

"Well, you didn't ask to see me, and fly all the way back to Washington from Berlin, to get a sneak preview of my July twenty-fifth speech," said Kennedy after a moment. "So tell me, what's on your mind?"

"You must promise you won't laugh."

"I'll do my best," said Kennedy, flashing the smile that won him the presidency.

"What's on my mind, then, Mr. President . . . is a woman—"

Kennedy appeared about to chuckle, but held it in, and instead only widened his smile.

"—A woman I hope soon to marry."

"I see," the president intoned significantly. "And how does that affect me? I hope you're not here to hand me your resignation. I'm not sure I could accept it."

"No, nothing like that," laughed Matthew. "But there are some problems related to the engagement which you might be able to help me with."

"I am intrigued."

Matthew took a deep breath, then spoke again. It was evident from his tone and manner that he had given careful thought ahead of time to every word.

"It actually concerns my fiancée's father, sir," began Matthew. "We don't consider ourselves at liberty to proceed with our plans without securing his freedom—he's an East German . . . so is my fiancée."

Kennedy nodded thoughtfully.

"I see the dilemma," he said, "though it's not so insurmountable as to require my assistance. Getting them to West Berlin ought to be rather a simple matter. Clearly you don't need me for that."

"I haven't told you the worst of it yet," Matthew went on. "The man's in prison, somewhere in East Germany."

"I see. So the plot thickens. What's the crime?"

"There is none."

"Ah . . . one of those. The Communists love their crimeless offenses *against the state,* I believe they call them."

"Baron von Dortmann, my future father-in-law, has been in prison since the war."

"A war criminal . . . . was he a Nazi?"

"More a religious criminal, imprisoned by the Nazis during the war. You've heard of Dietrich Bonhoeffer?"

"I believe so," Kennedy said, nodding.

"The two men were friends. Bonhoeffer was hanged in '45. For reasons unknown to me they kept the baron alive."

"Why wasn't he released, then, after the war?"

"That's where it gets complicated. Officially there was no reason to hold him, but a young Gestapo agent, who became influential in the new Communist regime, had a personal vendetta against him . . . besides which, he was in love with my fiancée."

"An old-fashioned European melodrama!" laughed Kennedy.

"It turned out the fellow had enough clout to keep the baron behind bars, where he's been all this time."

"Did his daughter go to the authorities?"

"She tried every avenue she could, went to all the occupational powers. You know the red tape with such things. The Russians weren't being too cooperative between '46 and '48."

"Nor ever since."

"Exactly. He is one of the casualties of an inhuman regime, got lost in the system, and has been there ever since."

"I'm afraid there are thousands like him," sighed the president.

"So that's our dilemma. We've got to get him released before Sabina will come west with me."

"I understand her feelings . . . though I'm not sure I see the connection. What does his release have to do with your getting married?"

"I suppose you'd say I feel an obligation to him equal to the love I have for his daughter," replied Matthew. "He has been very influential in my life, to say the least. It's something I *have* to do."

"I see you have strong feelings about the matter, which, knowing you as I do, doesn't surprise me."

"You're right," Matthew said, smiling. "Very strong. I would make just about any sacrifice I had to for either of them."

"What do you think I might be able to do for you?"

"I hoped there might be some leverage we could apply on the East German government, going over the head of the fellow I mentioned who has a vendetta against the baron."

"These are touchy times for me to be asking the Communists for favors. It could backfire. I'm not exactly a hero on the other side of the curtain. My asking to have your baron released could actually make things worse for him."

"I considered that," replied Matthew.

"I doubt going through State, or any of our normal diplomatic channels, would be perceived any better."

"On the other hand," Matthew said, "if we worked through the Bonn government, keeping out of sight ourselves—"

"I don't know that Bonn would carry any more weight with the East Germans than we do. The friction between the two governments is growing over this ridiculous treaty proposal of Khrushchev's."

"You could be right."

"Do you think this official who is keeping the man in prison has contacts in Moscow?"

"He well could . . . I don't know."

"If Moscow is involved too, that muddies it up all the more. Understand, Matthew, it isn't that I'm unwilling to help. But right now I've got to walk a tight line."

"I understand, Mr. President."

A brief silence fell, both men pondering the possibilities.

"What would you say to a small clandestine operation?" suggested Matthew at length.

The president paused. "I know by the sound of your voice that it's a thought you've considered seriously."

Matthew nodded.

"You're not really suggesting I involve the CIA in this? With all the problems I've got shaping up in Cuba, not to mention Berlin, Russia, Laos, and the rest of southeast Asia—where Ike left me a snootful of land mines this country doesn't even know about yet. . . . I tell you, this world could blow up in our faces. There are a half-dozen fuses lit and burning already all over the globe. You know I can't approve that . . . officially."

Matthew paused, considering the wording of the president's last comment. "Yes sir, I realize that."

"What else did you have in mind?"

"Could you authorize me at least a mid-level entrée with the CIA, just enough to enable me to find out a little more about where the baron is being held?"

"You don't even have a handle on his whereabouts?"

Matthew shook his head. "We're pretty certain we know where he is. But they're in the habit of moving him around, and I need to confirm it before going any further. Then we need to see what the place is like, if anyone can be bought, that kind of thing."

"I'll call Langley," replied the president. "Deputy Director Smith will put you in touch with his people. We've got more agents circulating through the two Germanys per square mile than in all the rest of the world!" Kennedy added, laughing.

"I appreciate that, Mr. President."

"But I can't ask the State Department to make formal inquiry about this baron of yours. If something happened later, Khrushchev would know we were involved. He'll seize on any excuse. We *cannot* get caught with our pants down in the Soviet sector. I'm sorry, I just don't see that there's anything I can do other than try to help you locate him."

"That will be a big help."

"And if you get into any, shall we say, *difficulties,*" Kennedy added, "you never worked for me . . . and this conversation never took place—clear enough?"

Matthew nodded. "I'm very grateful, Mr. President," he said.

"Just help me keep that tinderbox over there from blowing sky-high," said Kennedy with a smile. "You're still part of my team, and we're far from out of the woods in Berlin."

56

Momentous Communiqués

• • •

MATTHEW EASED HIS WAY INTO THE SEAT OF THE BOEING 727, then let out a long sigh. He leaned back and closed his eyes. He could not help but have mixed feelings about what lay ahead. Though it had only been five days, he was as anxious to see Sabina again as if it had been months.

Such pleasant anxieties were not his only concerns, however.

Accompanying them were forebodings over the course upon which he was about to embark. He was experienced enough to know the hazards involved . . . and the potential consequences.

He opened the morning's edition of the *Washington Post* while the stewardesses made their last-minute inspections up and down the aisle before takeoff. The headlines and whole front page were devoted to the president's speech last evening. He had watched it from his hotel room, and now he read the words of it over again:

> *We do not want to fight, but we have fought before. And others in earlier times have made the same dangerous mistake of assuming that the West was too selfish and too soft and too divided to resist invasions of freedom in other lands. . . . We cannot and will not permit the Communists to drive us out of Berlin, either gradually or by force. . . . The solemn vow each of us gave to West Berlin in time of peace will not be broken in time of danger. If we do not meet our commitments to Berlin, where will we stand later? . . . If there is one path above all others to war, it is the path of weakness and disunity.*

"Excuse me, sir," the stewardess said beside him, interrupting Matthew's thoughts, "would you like some coffee?"

"Oh . . . uh, yes . . . thank you. Yes, please," he replied. He'd been so engrossed in the article he had scarcely noticed the takeoff and that they were already well airborne.

Not only had the president called up the reserve units, as he had hinted to Matthew during their meeting, he had placed half the Pentagon's arsenal of bombers on ground alert. There could be no mistaking either action.

What had been vaguely alluded to previously as the "Berlin crisis" had escalated to a new level. A genuine *crisis* it had indeed become. There were actually tanks and armored trucks entering Berlin on both sides. The place was taking on more and more the appearance of a war zone.

The president had even used the dreaded word, Matthew thought, glancing down again at the paper. There it was, for all the world to see:

*We have fought before . . . will not permit the Communists
to drive us out of Berlin . . . vow will not be broken . . . war.*

Matthew could not have picked a worse time, given the tense world situation, to try to work toward the release of Sabina's father.

After being served his coffee, Matthew folded the *Post,* then sat back to reflect upon what had transpired since his visit with Jack Kennedy two days earlier.

He had spent the afternoon at CIA headquarters in Langley, Virginia, discussing the baron's situation with several of their German and Russian experts. By day's end, after several phone calls to Europe, steps were under way to pinpoint the baron's exact location, hopefully perhaps even by the time Matthew touched down in Berlin.

"There are enough double and triple and quadruple agents over there to staff an entire secret intelligence army," Smith had told him. "The kind of information we're after isn't usually that difficult to come by. Especially when our people begin flashing hard cash and American-made cigarettes. Spies on the Communist side will turn in their own mother for cigarettes!"

"What about getting somebody out?" Matthew asked.

"That's more difficult to come by than information. We can pull off almost anything, *if* you're not worried about the consequences. But on this one I've been told there can't be any consequences at all. We can't so much as set off a firecracker. There must not be the slightest hint that the CIA's been snooping around."

"Right. I understand," said Matthew.

Matthew left Langley with arrangements to meet the CIA's man in West Berlin day after tomorrow with whatever information his people had been able to obtain.

He had then gone back to his hotel to draft a letter of resignation, which he had sent to the White House this morning on his way to the airport. He hoped it wouldn't have to be used, but he had to leave the president the option of exercising it.

The cover letter read:

Mr. President:

I appreciate the time you took with me the other day. The people at Langley were most helpful. I am optimistic that we will find the baron quickly; then I will see what might be able to be done. Hopefully no danger will come to anyone. Be assured that I will do nothing that will in any way compromise your reputation or U.S. interests.

It is always impossible, however, to anticipate how such matters will turn out. In the unlikely event that something should happen to me, I would not want my position to bring a shadow upon your administration or future negotiations with the Soviets.

Therefore, I am enclosing a letter of resignation from your staff, dated as of the date of our meeting. Be assured that my desire is to continue in service to your administration. However, if it becomes necessary for you to use the enclosed, my return to Washington can be easily explained as being for the purpose of my delivering it to you in person. You may cite stress over the crisis and over the Vienna meetings as my reason. That should distance the two of us well enough, so that my questionable actions cannot in any way be traced to you.

If you are agreeable, I will take the next two or three weeks off, so as to validate the resignation later if its use becomes imperative. I will let you notify the State Department in whatever manner you feel most protects your own position.

I assume you will destroy this cover letter.

Appreciatively,
Matthew McCallum

• • •

Sabina had never before received a telegram.

Its arrival at her place of employment caused no little stir, though she did her best not to show the fluttering of her heart.

She would open it later, she said, after she was home.

How could she wait? her fellow workers clamored. What if it was urgent?

It would have to wait, she replied. She was not going to open it until she was alone.

Two hours later, with fingers trembling, she carefully tore open the edge of the thin yellow envelope and pulled out the single sheet of paper inside.

The message was brief, though she understood its implications perfectly.

HELP FROM WH UNAVAILABLE STOP WE'RE ON OUR OWN STOP MATTHEW, was all it said.

Initial Contact

• • •

"ALL RIGHT, MCCALLUM, HERE'S WHAT I COULD DIG UP for you since Langley called."

The agent handed Matthew the sheet of paper.

"It's not much. If I had another week I could get you more."

Matthew scanned the page.

"He's still down in Potsdam, I see," remarked Matthew. "That's good . . . not much else here—description of the layout, converted to a prison in '51 . . . pretty much confirms what we had."

"I couldn't get much on the staff of the place," the agent added apologetically. "Our top guy in East Berlin cased the facility out. He said he might be able to help, but you'd have to move fast."

"Move fast . . . why?" asked Matthew.

"He said there was a lot of activity around the place. He couldn't get close and wasn't about to start asking questions of the wrong people. It had the look to him that they might be getting ready to move some of the prisoners."

"Moving them . . . where?"

"Don't know. Our orders were explicit: help get you what information we could, but keep our distance. My advice to you, McCallum, if you're serious about this thing, is to get into East Berlin and find out for yourself. We can't help you beyond this. I can put you in touch with our man there, but after that—"

"All right, fair enough," said Matthew. "So, how do I find him?"

"I'm going to write down a name, two password phrases, and a telephone number. You memorize them all. You get into East Berlin, find a safe public phone, call this number, and identify yourself by this name. You'll get a response naming someplace in Scotland. Doesn't matter where. But if you don't hear a town or city or region, hang up. If you do, remember what you hear. Paddy may want you to repeat it later. Then give the first phrase, and the rest will be clear soon enough. That will put you in touch with our head man over there, Paddy Red. 'Course that's not his real name. Paddy'll tell you what to do."

"I'll get in touch with him."

"Don't say another word. I don't want to know a thing about your plans."

"I appreciate all your help, Clatchen."

"Just understand, McCallum," the man said as Matthew turned to leave, "that if asked I will disavow all knowledge, both concerning you and your situation. The CIA's out of it—that's orders from high up. This is the last you and I ever see each other . . . and this conversation never took place."

Paddy Red

• • •

MATTHEW DISLIKED THE PHONES IN EAST GERMANY AS much as the toilets. There were more advantages of a free and progressive society than made the newspapers.

He had taken extreme measures to be sure he wasn't followed. Yet making secretive contact with the CIA, first in Virginia, then in West Berlin, and now behind the Iron Curtain, couldn't help but make him nervous.

These were *spies* he was talking to!

He was a diplomat, not an undercover sleuth! Yet . . . here he was sneaking about, glancing around behind every block, making sure no one was trailing him. He felt like a character in some old Humphrey Bogart movie!

Again he surveyed the sleazy hotel. Satisfied, he picked up the public telephone. Two or three minutes later he heard a ring at the other end of the line.

A click indicated that it had been picked up, though no voice spoke a greeting.

"Prince Charlie calling," said Matthew nervously.

"Cold in Banff in February. Too much snow for the bonny young man," replied a thick British accent.

"Red is the color of my true love's hair," said Matthew.

"Burns never wrote that."

"Burns was mistranslated. He meant red, not black."

A short silence followed.

"Liebermannstrasse 4. Three-ten this afternoon. Go to the door, knock twice, then turn, go across the street, and walk immediately east."

Instantly the phone was dead.

Matthew hung up, then left the hotel. The cryptic message didn't put him any more at ease. These people even talked likes spies!

• • •

That same afternoon, in a remote section of East Berlin, Matthew found himself walking along a deserted sidewalk among run-down brick buildings that hadn't appeared to contain life for years.

He glanced down at his watch. It was five after three.

He'd located the street named after Liebermann. There was the building just ahead with the old and badly chipping paint on its stairs indicating number 4. All he had to do was wait.

Matthew strode up and down the sidewalk slowly a time or two, took another look at his watch, then slowly climbed the stairs to the door. He knocked once, then again.

There was no answer.

Matthew turned and descended to the sidewalk, crossed the street, and began walking to his right. He had seen no car nor other human presence in the last ten minutes.

Ahead a figure came into view, walking slowly his way. Matthew continued forward.

The man approached, looking down at the ground, apparently oblivious to Matthew's presence.

They began to pass. The man stumbled and knocked into Matthew. Both stopped.

"I say, mate," the man said apologetically, "dreadful clumsy of me." He spoke in English. He turned and looked into Matthew's face. "What would you think of a trip to Scotland in February?" he asked.

"Uh . . . too cold," hesitated Matthew, "especially in . . . uh . . . *in Banff,*" he added, more questioningly than decisively.

"You'll do, Charlie," said the man, turning and falling in beside Matthew as they continued walking. "The name's Paddy Red, and from here on we use German."

"But what's with the building back there?" asked Matthew.

"Nothing. This whole street's vacant. I just had to be sure it was you."

"And the English accent . . . I thought you were—"

"Don't say it, Charlie. Them's three letters you want to forget you ever heard. I try to make them believe I'm a German, but they're a shrewd lot. So when they see through it, I want them seeing the Union Jack, not the Stars and Stripes. As far as anyone here knows who *thinks* they've discovered my 'real' identity, I'm an Englishman through and through. I keep the ruse going with accent, passwords, even my code name. I even let slip now and then an English twist to my German accent, though I know the language well enough to make them think I'm from anywhere in Europe. So . . . I understand you need info on the Neustädt Schule in Potsdam."

"Whatever help you can give me."

"I gave most of it this morning."

"What section of Potsdam is it?"

"Southeast, on the edge of the Babelsberg Forest, right next to the Nuthe River."

"It's not actually in the city, then?"

"Technically no. There's a large government preserve—what we'd call a national forest—south of the city. It's called the Staatforst— pretty good-sized, hilly, wooded region. It comes right up to the outskirts of Potsdam itself. Anyway, this school was built south of the river on the edges of the forest."

"There was mention made of a fellow who might be able to help me?"

"Schlaukopf—a mean customer."

"Are you serious," laughed Matthew, *"Sly old fox!"*

"If ever there was an artful dodger worthy of the name, Schlaukopf's it."

"That can't really be his name?"

"Naw, he's got a dozen aliases and probably forgotten his own himself. But it's what everyone knows him by."

"What's his allegiance?"

"Himself and no other. He's a Lithuanian by birth, came into Germany with the invading Soviet army in '45—unless he's lying about that too—and stayed in the DDR. Speaks about every language there is to be found in the Warsaw Pact."

"He can be bought?"

The CIA agent nodded. "Whenever I look SK up, I take three cartons of Camels with me just in case. SK knows everything and everybody in and around East Berlin, and how the system works. Everybody uses him. But if you want to stay alive in his game, you'd better figure a way to keep them from finding out who you are. Don't *ever* let on you're an American—can you pass for a German?"

"I think so," answered Matthew.

"He thinks he's penetrated my cover. To him I'm a Brit; that's the only reason he talks to me. He hates Yanks. He's killed more'n one of our guys. The Commies use him for low-level hits, so watch your step."

"If the guy's so dangerous, why do you use him?"

"He knows more than any twenty trench coats fresh out of Langley. And he's got no loyalties except to himself. His kind comes in handy from time to time, when you need their particular kinds of services—which, the way this looks to me, you do. And you'll have to up the ante beyond cigarettes if you actually want his help. Take cigarettes *and* money."

"Can you put me in touch with him?"

"That I can. But you'll be in over your head. He's a lowlife without even a hint of a conscience. He finds out a Yank's been using him and you'll feel the cold blade of his deadly dirk between your shoulder blades. He's ruthless. I'd go with you myself except that we've got orders to make sure there's no link between us and you in this thing. I don't like sending you out unguarded. The KGB and the independents over here, they play by different rules. But if you're determined, I can tell you where to find him and that's it."

"All right," said Matthew with a sigh. "I'm in this deep enough already. You better tell me how to find him."

Der Schlaukopf

• • •

MATTHEW STEPPED INTO THE DIMLY LIT *GASTHAUS*.

A tavern such as this in West Berlin would be lively and full at this time of day, with activity and polka music and conversation flowing as freely as the dark beer from its huge oak kegs.

Here, however, the mood was subdued.

No music came from inside. The man behind the bar seemed bored. Three or four patrons scattered throughout the room were his only customers. Two sat at a table engaged in low conversation. A thin haze of tobacco smoke hung lazily in the air, suspended about one quarter of the way down from the ceiling to the floor.

Matthew walked to the bar.

"Zwei Bier," he said.

The man eyed him suspiciously. *Everyone* was suspicious about *everything* in the East, Matthew thought to himself, struggling to keep from looking nervous. Already he didn't like this, but it was too late to turn back now!

"Warum zwei?" growled the innkeeper.

"One for myself, and one for my friend," replied Matthew coolly, in the best colloquial German he could muster.

"I see no friend," said the man in a tone Matthew didn't altogether like.

"My friend is a sly one," rejoined Matthew. "He appears when least expected."

Still the man perused him, as if trying to detect something slightly affected in the accent from Matthew's tongue. At length he set two beers on the counter in front of him, then turned and walked to the phone hanging on the wall behind him. Matthew picked up the beers and took them to a vacant table.

He sat down and waited.

Ten minutes later a man walked in the door. The man behind the bar motioned with his head toward Matthew. The newcomer approached, sat down opposite Matthew, laid hold of one of the two glasses of beer still on the table, downed it nearly in one swallow, motioned the innkeeper to bring another, then first settled his gaze upon Matthew where he sat across the table.

"I understand you need my services," he said.

"If you can help me," replied Matthew, shivering unconsciously.

"What do you require?"

"Information first, perhaps more later."

The innkeeper arrived, setting a full pitcher of dark beer on the table in front of them.

Schlaukopf poured himself another glass and sent it down his throat after the first.

"What kind of information?"

"There is a certain man being held I need released."

"Held . . . where?"

"At the Neustädt Technische Hochschule in Potsdam," replied Matthew.

The man's face took in the information with a knowing nod. Paddy Red had told him to act confident and hard-boiled, even a little brash if possible, and Matthew was doing his best. Though he passionately hated Americans, the agent had told him, SK wanted his accomplices to boast the very characteristics for which American GIs had been known during the war. If he sensed timidity or weakness, he would know he was not dealing with a professional and would break off the contact immediately. Matthew hoped his diplomatic experience would enable him to pass the scrutiny he knew was even now being leveled upon him.

The man known as the fox certainly possessed the physical features and expression to match the name. Whether the correlation was factual, or but a figment of his own active imagination, Matthew had no way of knowing.

Matthew fancied the man's hair bore traces of red, though in this darkened and hazy light it was impossible to tell for certain.

The hair he did own was thin and utterly uncombed, beginning some ten centimeters above his eyebrows, which were also thin, allowing for a wide and unbecoming forehead. His complexion was pale, another indication of foxlike mien. The face was tall and angular, accentuated by the forehead, though very narrow, highlighted by a narrow, pointed nose, which may have been attributable to the images of Matthew's excitability, but which also seemed to be subtly sniffing the air for clues with which to outwit his prey. The eyes were but thin slits and altogether too closely spaced, showing no sign of human emotion. Likewise, the lips contained little flesh and were much too thin to give normal Germanic expression to the thickly consonantal tongue. Two ears extended out from the side of his head, slightly pointed at the top like two hairy fox-ears. A scratchy, high-pitched voice fit the rest of the unplenteous carriage to perfect effect.

At first appearance, pity would be a more likely emotion to be generated from an encounter with the Sly Head, as his name literally indicated, than fear. Of only average height and certainly unextraordinary bodily strength, Matthew had to remind himself of the several injunctions that had been given him as caution.

Once he set eyes on the man in the full light of day, however, he needed never remind himself again. The shiver he had felt at first glance thereafter became permanently implanted while in this man's presence. The eyes were not merely dispassionate, but cold, calculating, and cruel. The injunction to be wise as serpents yet innocent as doves went through Matthew's brain, and he could not help thinking that "the serpent" would be a more suitable appellation than "the fox."

"What man?" said Schlaukopf.

"His name is Dortmann . . . Baron Heinrich von Dortmann," replied Matthew.

"Why is he being held?"

"He has been imprisoned since the war."

"That does not answer my question," said the fox, his eye slits narrowing.

"The Nazis did not find it compulsory to divulge their reasons for incarceration," said the diplomat evasively.

As close to a smile as ever escaped the thin lips now played about their edges momentarily, but quickly disappeared.

"Why do you seek this man's freedom?" asked the fox.

"I was told you would ask no questions as to motive."

"Told by whom?"

"I was also assured my own history would be of no interest to you," snapped Matthew, beginning to rise. "If you do not want the job I offer without keeping your curiosity to yourself, I will take my request elsewhere."

The fox eyed him with humorless interest, then motioned him back to his seat.

"Perhaps I can help, perhaps not. It is sometimes useful for me to know the nature of the business, but not required."

"I will disclose nothing more than what I have said," said Matthew. "Do you want to earn my marks or not?"

"West German marks?"

"Of course."

"Cash?"

"Upon receipt of the baron into my hands."

"I take it he is an aristocrat from the old era?"

Matthew said nothing.

"He must be very valuable. . . . My assistance will cost you."

"I am able to pay."

"Has he a fortune stashed away that the Nazis were not able to find?"

"Many questions, sly one. I was warned about you," said Matthew, stretching his bravado to the limit. His heart was pounding wildly inside his chest. "But you'll get nothing beyond your fee. Find out for me the baron's status and anything else I should know. I will meet you here in exactly forty-eight hours. If you have something for me then, I will decide whether to proceed with you."

Matthew rose and left the inn quickly without another word.

As he stepped into the street he could hardly keep his knees from trembling, afraid he might feel in his back that knife blade Paddy had told him about. He kept walking briskly. If a little audacious cheek was what it took to secure Schlaukopf's confidence, then he had just given it his best shot!

60

Hesitations and Decisions

• • •

THE MOOD BETWEEN THEM WAS MORE SUBDUED THAN ever before. The grave realities of what Matthew was proposing had begun to sink in more deeply.

"I . . . I just don't know, Matthew," said Sabina. "I can't help feeling frightened."

"If we want to get your father out, I don't see any other way," replied Matthew. "I'll admit, it's scary. But it's a risk I'm willing to take given that there don't seem any more reasonable diplomatic options open to us."

"I . . . I don't want anything to happen to you." As she spoke, Sabina's eyes filled with tears.

Matthew took her in his arms.

"Nothing will happen," he said. "I'll be very, very careful. But if we don't follow this through now—let's face it—in all likelihood you will never see your father again."

"I know," said Sabina softly. "I'm just so worried about losing you again. I suppose I'm having second thoughts about what I said the night of the ball. Maybe it's time for me to accept Papa's own words more than I have before, accept that he is at peace, and resign myself to his fate."

"Could you really could do that? And be happy and at peace *yourself?*" asked Matthew.

Sabina smiled weakly.

"How well you know me," she said. "No, I doubt I could. I cannot rest knowing Papa is where he is. The thought of one day seeing him again is the main thing that has kept me hopeful all these years."

"We could marry, but you would never be at peace with yourself in the West, separated as that would make you, even more, from your father. As far as my forsaking my past to begin a new life with you in East Germany, I don't think that is something I could ever do."

"I would never ask it of you, Matthew. I know *you* well enough to know you could never be happy under such circumstances."

A brief silence fell between them. Sabina eased herself away from Matthew's embrace and leaned back against the couch.

"There is something else on my mind," she said.

Matthew raised his eyebrows, encouraging her to continue.

"Papa told me not to try to contact him or attempt to get him released," Sabina went on.

"His hesitation was based on the danger from Gustav to you," said Matthew, "not because he didn't want to be free."

Sabina nodded.

"Still," she said, "to proceed without his knowledge or approval would be to go against his wishes . . . though I suppose I could get word to him through the network," she mused.

"No, no," said Matthew pointedly. "The fewer people who know about this, the better."

He paused, then added, "What network?"

"The, uh . . . the people I . . . uh, told you about who had contacts inside the prison," faltered Sabina, realizing she'd said more than she intended.

"What *people?*"

"Friends . . . contacts I've made. It's different here than in the West, Matthew. To survive you've got to know people in all sorts of walks of life. Please . . . don't ask me more. I promise I will tell you everything . . . soon."

Matthew kept his peace, thinking back to the strange end to the evening when he had proposed to Sabina. He knew there were aspects of her life she was keeping from him. But he trusted her and could wait.

"In any case," he said after a moment, "not even your father must know there is anything in the wind. It will be safer that way. I will assume full responsibility for the decision myself. Gustav will no longer be a danger to you, which was his chief reluctance as I see it. I have asked you to be my wife. That makes me your protector and places responsibility for your father in my hands as well. I will take upon myself the right to make the decision, for both you and him. I hope you can be comfortable with that."

"Yes . . . yes, I can," agreed Sabina. "I am frightened, but I see the wisdom in what you say."

"So there we are—without any option left but attempting to get your father released, through bribery and whatever else is necessary, as dangerous as it might be. It is the only way we will be able to begin a new life together in the West . . . with your father coming with us."

The quiet that descended between them this time lasted several minutes. Both were absorbed in their own thoughts.

When Sabina spoke, her words were the last Matthew had expected to hear.

"Then I'm going with you," she announced at length.

"What!"

"You heard me—I'm going with you."

"You can't," objected Matthew. "You said yourself it may be dangerous."

"Those are the only terms on which I'll agree to it," rejoined Sabina firmly. "I'm an East German. As flawless as your German is, Matthew, it isn't perfect. There are occasional words that give you away. When you get in a hurry and start talking rapidly, your German remains too polished, without the slurs and dropped endings of a native's unconscious speech. It's not something you learn; it's part of growing up as a German. I know the language, I have contacts. . . . I know people all around Berlin—"

"In Potsdam?" interrupted Matthew.

"Near there."

"How near?"

"Eighteen kilometers . . . a small village called Grossbeeren."

"That might not be near enough to do us any good," said Matthew, thinking aloud.

"No matter, I'm still accompanying you," said Sabina. "If anything should go wrong, you'll be better off with me there."

"I will *not* put you in danger."

"I will *not* let you go without me."

Matthew eyed her, then smiled and let out a sigh.

"I said to myself from the very first that you were a spunky young lady," he said.

"If your plan *should* fail," said Sabina, "I'm not about to pass up the opportunity to see my father again, even if it's only for a moment. To be able to look in his face and tell him I love him will be worth almost any danger."

Matthew realized nothing he could say would dissuade her. He slowly nodded his head in acknowledgment.

"You've got to understand, Matthew, to see you and my father again—it's what I've lived for for over fifteen years. Now that I'm so close, don't ask me to turn my back on a chance I may never have again. Even the risk of imprisonment will be worth it for me. I *have* to be part of it."

Matthew sighed, then nodded his head. She would have to be part of it, he saw that now. He and she would have to work out every detail . . . together.

"There's one more thing," Sabina added, suddenly coming to the resolve she had wrestled with so long. "Before we begin this, I want to give you a small package—for safekeeping. Will you put it in your hotel in West Berlin, just in case something should go wrong—but without asking me any questions?"

Matthew thought a moment.

"I'm curious," he said with a smile. "But, yes—of course I'll do it."

61

The Fox Again

• • •

MATTHEW'S SECOND VISIT TO THE DREARY BERLIN *GAST-haus* did nothing to heighten his original estimation of the place.

He walked straight to the counter and asked the same man to call Herr Schlaukopf. In return he received nothing but a bewildered stare.

"There is no one here by that name."

"The man I spoke with two days ago," said Matthew. "Surely you cannot have forgotten."

"I do not remember you," said the man, with a blank expression.

"Perhaps if I purchased two beers, neither of which I intend to drink, it might help your memory," said Matthew, annoyed.

"Perhaps."

"All right then, I'll play your little game—*zwei Bier,*" said Matthew, placing a handful of coins on the counter.

"Warum zwei?" said the man.

"One for myself, and one for my friend," replied Matthew with an imperceptible roll of his eyes.

"I see no friend," said the man.

"My friend is a sly one. He appears when least expected."

Still without cracking a hint of recognition, the man poured out the two glasses of beer, then made the call.

Matthew took the glasses to the same table as before.

Charging SK's customers their perfunctory two-beer fee for the use of his table was probably the man's main form of income, Matthew thought wryly. There certainly wasn't much else going on around this place!

The warm beers still remained untouched when Schlaukopf entered ten or twelve minutes later, nodding to the bartender, then sitting down across from Matthew. He glanced at the two glasses, but, seeing no foam remaining, waited for the pitcher and new glass, which arrived a moment later. He did not speak until he had emptied his first glass of the dark brew.

"You still owe my friend over there for the pitchers and two beers from last time," he said, wiping his lips with his sleeve. "He is not pleased when my associates walk out without paying. And I am not pleased when I must pay myself."

"Put it on my tab," said Matthew.

"Better yet," rejoined the other, "why don't you go over there and pay the man right now—for today's as well. He will want forty marks for the two days."

"Forty marks!"

"He must stay in business too. That is what he charges me to use this table here."

Matthew rose, walked to the counter, took out two DM20 bills, slapped them on the counter without a word, then returned to the table.

"What do you have for me?" he said.

"That depends on whether you brought cash," replied the fox's unpleasant raspy voice.

"I told you payment would be upon the baron's release," snapped Matthew, speaking too hastily.

Schlaukopf eyed him carefully.

"What I have cannot wait. It is valuable information, and if you want it, it will cost you . . . now. Otherwise, I will let you take your request *elsewhere,* as you said."

"Our bargain was payment upon receipt."

"I made no bargain. I have information. If you want it, you pay. Otherwise . . ."

This time it was Schlaukopf who made as if to leave.

"Sit down, Schlaukopf," said Matthew, digging out his wallet again. "What's your price?"

"One hundred marks."

"For a lousy piece of information!"

SK nodded his thin foxlike head.

Eyeing him with an expression he hoped passed for belligerent anger, Matthew took out a single DM100 and placed it on the table. Schlaukopf's thin arm immediately stretched toward it.

"Not so fast, Herr Fox," said Matthew, covering the bill. "Give me what you have, and then your fingers can lay hold of the green stuff."

Schlaukopf's hand paused. His thin, beady eyes bored into Matthew a moment, then he spoke.

"Your friend the baron is about to be moved," he said, "transferred elsewhere to another facility."

"Where?" asked Matthew.

"That is not known. All that is certain is that he is to be moved out of Potsdam and further east, perhaps to Moscow."

Matthew did his best to hide his reaction.

"When?"

"About a week, perhaps ten days from now."

"That doesn't give us much time, then," said Matthew, glancing down as he hastily pondered this development. Slowly he drew back his hand. With marvelous speed, SK's hand now completed the motion it had earlier begun, his fingers shooting out and laying hold of the bill like the tongue of an anteater, then withdrawing and stealthily depositing it within the invisible folds of his garments.

"It may provide the perfect opportunity," the fox added after a moment.

"How do you mean?" asked Matthew, raising his eyes again across the table.

"If they are planning to take him out of the prison already, it will give us many potential ways to exploit that fact—that is, if you are still in a position to request my services."

"How much?" asked Matthew.

"Four thousand deutsche marks."

"Four thousand!" exclaimed Matthew. "That's a lot of *rehbock*—it's an outrage!"

"There will be many to pay off. I will be fortunate to clear one thousand myself. Do not forget, my friend, should this opportunity slip by you, your baron will be in Moscow and you will *never* get your hands on whatever it is of his you want. Time is short, I have been to the prison already, and I can deliver him into your hands. The cost may be an outrage, as you say. However, I am your only hope for success."

Matthew thought within himself. The man was right. This was not an opportunity that could be passed by . . . at any price. Four thousand marks was not really so bad, only a thousand dollars. He had that much in the bank. He would pay ten times that to free Sabina's father.

"All right, Schlaukopf," he said, with feigned reluctant resignation. "I will pay your price. But you won't get another pfennig until I see Baron von Dortmann with my own eyes and he is safely in my custody. What the baron has that I want, as you say, *may* be worth four thousand marks, but not much more. So don't try to double-cross me, or that hundred in your jacket is all you'll get from me. Nothing more until the job is completed. Understood?"

Schlaukopf nodded.

"All right, then—what now?" said Matthew.

"Meet me here in four days, at noon," said the fox. "By then I should know the exact time of the transfer. I will make arrangements to get you safely inside the prison and to insure your exit. While I am thus occupied, you will have to devise a plan to get to the man's cell and then back to me with him. I will have a floor plan of the place to give you, which you must memorize. If you are discovered while inside, I will not be able to help you. Until that day, make sure you get the money. If there is any slipup on payment, neither you nor the baron will see the leaves turn yellow next month."

62

Hidden Shadow

• • •

FOR A YOUNG MAN OF TWENTY-ONE, ON ASSIGNMENT more than fifteen hundred kilometers from home, he possessed uncanny pluck and even brash daring.

But no one had ever accused Andrassy Galanov of being timid. Now that he saw his opportunity, he wasn't about to let it pass by without making what use of it he could.

He came from a line of climbers and opportunists, his uncle supreme among them. But young Galanov's ambition matched even his uncle's. Before he was through—though none of them could divine the future course his zeal was destined to mark out for him—he would likely surpass them all. His influence for the Communist cause was yet to be felt, and the directions of his still-forming loyalties, objectives, and hatreds were yet fluid, seeking the deeper currents into which they would ultimately flow.

He had—whether by inheritance, training, or natural predisposition—acquired his uncle's antipathy for all sorts of religious persons and their humbug, Jews and Christians supreme among them. He did not, however, share his hatred for Germans and Americans.

His father and uncle were of the old school. But these were the sixties. It was a new global era. There was no reason to hate the adversary. The Soviet Union now reigned supreme. The people of the motherland could afford a little tolerance toward her lesser foes. By cultivating a more liberal attitude, one could use the Americans and Germans more skillfully to his own end.

He would *hate* Christians and Jews, but he would *use* Americans and Germans.

His present assignment as *Stasi* Section Chief Schmundt's assistant afforded him just such a position. He could line his own upward path here in the DDR, as well as enhance his potential KGB future at the same time.

If the good Herr von Schmundt knew that his assistant was operating on his own, he would make life none too pleasant. But then, Galanov smiled to himself, the section chief would not find out until such time as the benefit from whatever information he acquired proved more useful than the annoyance over the independence by which his assistant had obtained it. He would tell him he had merely been attempting to keep him from having to involve himself in the details until he had more concrete evidence to present him with. Herr von Schmundt would accept it, he thought to himself, smiling again. The German was not the world's most clever man, and his passions blinded his good sense.

Speaking of the man's passions, if the section chief had any idea that the car Andrassy was at this moment tailing might contain the woman he had been searching for all these years, he would fly into a towering rage to learn he had not been informed of the surveillance.

But, thought Galanov, he could not be certain it was she. He would know more before playing his trump card. His uncle would want to be informed as well. He had to find out more and then consider his options carefully.

After giving the section chief the information about the ball at the French consulate, he had reflected upon the matter himself. What if the American had *already* made contact with the girl? What if, despite all their efforts to locate her, she was somewhere nearby, even right under their noses? If the American had been interested long ago, why not still? There existed every likelihood he might have been more successful in locating the girl than his boss.

He had, therefore, enlisted the further help of his friend the Frenchman, this time even more secretly than the first. It had cost him. He would owe the Parisian several favors after this.

But it would be worth it!

For he had learned that the American had in fact attended the ball with a woman answering the general description in age and build of the one they had been looking for.

Schmundt had returned the following morning full of plans of an entirely different nature—talking about getting into the old Dortmann place, some nonsense about ancient deeds and bribing the officials who were presently in charge of the asylum there, and stepping up the arrangements for moving the old man from the prison at Neustädt.

Whatever it was all about, Galanov had realized, he had *not* seen the American at the ball.

His Frenchman, on the other hand, had apparently been more shrewd, coming to him that same day with his costly findings.

If only he knew what the woman looked like, thought Galanov.

Nobody at the ball had known the identity of the lady on the American's arm. Rumor had it that she was royalty of some kind—a princess, the Frenchman had said. That would seem to preclude her being the woman his section chief was in love with. But Andrassy had determined to play it out just in case.

With the information the Frenchman had given him—the enterprising fellow had been alert enough to tail them at the end of the evening, by foot, slinking through the streets after a horse-led carriage, no less!—he had been able to get the lady's address, and from that her name.

Duftblatt, she was called.

The name meant nothing. No investigation revealed a scrap of information on her. She held a meaningless job, seemed to have no friends or relatives or activities of the slightest significance. This was clearly not the woman his boss had been seeking.

It would seem he had arrived at a dead end.

But to be sure, Galanov had placed one of his own lackeys nearby to keep his eye on the house. You could never tell what might turn up. Even if it wasn't the right woman, she *was* a link to the American. In the meantime, he would say nothing to the section chief until he knew more.

By a stroke of luck he had been present himself when the lady had gone out to meet the big hulking fellow on the sidewalk and then had driven off herself.

Suspicious, he followed. Now, leaving the city toward the south, he wondered if this peculiar journey of hers had anything to do with the American, or if all he'd managed to do was put himself on the wrong end of a wild-goose chase.

He wouldn't give up just yet, however.

It wasn't until halfway out of the city that suddenly the realization struck him—he was following the same color and make of car that had been identified in Warsaw.

Could this woman be *one and the same* as she whom they had been unsuccessfully seeking?

What a stroke of luck if it was true! This might change every-thing—though he would have to think through the implications of what it all might mean.

If only he could get close enough to confirm the entire license plate!

His instincts told him something untoward was in the air.

63

Unscheduled Network Business

• • •

SABINA HOPED MATTHEW WOULD FORGIVE HER THIS ONE time.

She would get on with the business of being a properly obedient wife the moment they were married. But she had to make sure they lived long enough to see their wedding day. Right now the first priority was to get her father safely out of prison, and out of the DDR altogether.

If that meant going behind his back, well, it would have to be.

It wasn't that she didn't believe in Matthew's plan.

But from all he'd told her about this fellow called *Der Fuchs,* she had formed a clear picture of the kind of man they were dealing with. She had run into his type frequently in her work. They abounded in the postwar Communist countries. Indeed, Communism seemed to breed them. Gustav was one, now this Schlaukopf—there were thousands—all working the corrupt system however they could for their own ends.

As genteel and guileless as her mother and father had raised her to be, she had learned not to trust the fox's kind. One look in their eyes, one quick perusal of the hard and calculating expressions in their unfeeling faces, and she *knew.*

There was a time when she had hated herself for thinking such thoughts. She didn't want to judge or think ill of anyone. But the years perhaps had caused a few calluses to grow over her heart as well. She prayed it wasn't so.

There could be no denying she had grown wary. She had seen too much cruelty. If it took a more sober-minded outlook, even a cold mistrust—yes, she would call it that—to prevent these mercenaries of greed from hurting people she cared about and was committed to help, it was a flaw in her Christian character she was willing to put up with. She would talk to the Lord about it in the next life. For now, however, she would do all that lay in her power to guard against their schemes, even if it meant a potential conflict with her husband-to-be.

There was no way Matthew could possess the experience to know what manner of man he was dealing with. His years on the diplomatic front could not have prepared him as had hers in the network. A Westerner could not fully *grasp* what it was like on this side, under the black Communist cloud. As careful as he would be, and as skillfully as he had thought out every aspect of the plan, he could not adequately apprehend the constant danger of treachery.

Betrayal was *always* nearby in the DDR. When dealing with the kind of men whose eyes revealed cunning, avarice, and spiritual emptiness, Sabina had come to expect it.

Better to be disappointed and find out you were wrong than to endanger the lives of innocents.

Thus contemplating the ethics and justification for what she was about to do, Sabina drove into the small village of Grossbeeren south of Berlin.

She had never driven here alone, but had no difficulty finding the place. She parked Hermann's Kelly-green Trabant, got out, and walked the circuitous route to the school. It was late afternoon. The children were all gone.

She walked into the building, went down the deserted corridor, turned left, and went into the classroom she sought. A middle-aged woman glanced up from the desk where she sat.

"Fräulein Duftblatt!" she said in astonishment. "I did not know you . . . why are . . . is something wrong?"

"No, Clara," replied Sabina, approaching with a smile of reassurance. "There is nothing to be anxious about. I must speak to your husband."

"Erich? But what—"

"Have no fear, Clara. I have an important favor to ask of him . . . of you both. When may I see him?"

"He is not home from the factory until eight."

"Would the two of you go for a walk?"

The lady nodded with obvious hesitation.

"I will walk slowly across the bridge at eight-thirty," Sabina went on. "I will allow you to overtake me. We can walk on across together, then I will turn off. That should give us the time we need."

"Won't you join us for *Abendbrot,* Fräulein?" said the lady somewhat falteringly. "I know my husband would consider it a great honor—"

"Thank you, Clara," replied Sabina. "I dare not. The request I have may involve danger. I must not be seen at your house."

She turned to leave the room.

"I will tell Erich," Clara said after her.

The teacher watched the door close behind the unscheduled visitor to her classroom, then closed her eyes to fight back the tears. She could not help it. This business of her husband always made her afraid . . . and she could not say that she altogether understood why he took such risks for people he had never met.

She especially worried for her son Willy. He was too young, she thought, for all this.

Clara was so preoccupied with the anxiety of prayers of half-faith that she could not have been more oblivious when she left the school twenty minutes later to the car parked seventy-five meters from the building. She never suspected that the man who emerged from it and followed on foot as she walked home was watching *her* now with equal interest as she whom he had followed from Berlin.

•　•　•

Driving back into the city in the evening's dusk about nine-thirty, Sabina's heart was full. Not only had Erich agreed to help, he was *eager* to do so.

"For so long we have been praying for just this day," he said. "I and the other men have hoped you would give us leave to do what we might. We owe your father a great deal by his example. I will arrange for what we need. Herr Meier, the baker, will assist me . . . Herr Jung has many buildings on his farm we occasionally make use of. I will speak with Bietmann over in Kehrigkburg. My son is a stout lad with deep convictions. He and I will accompany you all the way to the border. I will speak with Brother Hermann in the city, and he will contact you with details. Worry about nothing, Fräulein."

•   •   •

Sabina's mind was too occupied in its own directions to heed the headlights some three hundred meters behind her on the otherwise little-used road between Grossbeeren and Heinersdorf.

She could not have known what danger she had brought upon herself . . . and others of her secret band. Indeed, treachery was closer at hand than even she herself knew.

64

Suspicions

. . .

EVEN THOUGH THE PLAN WAS SET AND HE STOOD TO
profit handsomely from its successful conclusion, the rapacious man
known as the Sly Fox was experiencing misgivings about the affair.
He had the apprehensive feeling of having been used.

The fellow had been too nervous right from the beginning.

Not that he didn't encounter plenty of agitated characters in this
business. Everyone was looking over his own shoulder about something.

But there was a certain hardness, an unfeeling glint in the eyes, a
chilly callousness you came to expect that confirmed you were
dealing with someone like yourself. It wasn't that you found such
people appealing or even trusted them. But knowing they would
double-cross you just as readily as you would them gave the exchange
a certain predictable foundation, a boundary between individuals that
a man like Schlaukopf knew how to deal with.

The only motives he understood were those that paralleled his
own—greedy, nefarious, cunning, ruthless. As long as his associates
were of like persuasion, he hardly cared whether they were allies or
foes, colleagues or adversaries.

What was the difference anyway? A few extra marks, dollars,
pounds, or rubles turned an ally into an adversary. There were no *real*
loyalties in this game . . . except to oneself.

The man who had met him in the *Gasthaus* a few days ago had
been different.

Something about him didn't feel right. He made all the right
moves, spoke the right words . . . but his eyes contained none of the

coldness Schlaukopf had come to anticipate, the mutual mistrust that kept such interviews honest.

Behind the obdurate appearance, there was something in the man's expression and manner that seemed more apprehensive than the circumstances would account for. His outbursts seemed simulated, his tough exterior a mere camouflage. He was out of place.

The thoughts of his own reflections continued to revolve in the convoluted grey matter of Schlaukopf's brain.

A few extra marks or dollars turned an ally into an adversary . . . ally into an adversary . . . a few extra dollars . . . The words of his own thoughts repeated themselves in his mind.

A few extra . . . *dollars!*

Suddenly his brain exploded in recognition. Of course—how could he not have seen it instantly? *That* was what had been gnawing at him all this time!

It wasn't only the man's manner . . . it was his own *words,* spoken in near-flawless German, that gave him away.

The conversation came back to him in vivid detail.

He'd thought it odd, but had let it pass. What had the fellow meant by *green stuff* when he'd covered up the DM100 bill? The bill was blue, not green.

Suddenly it made sense!

They called *dollars* "green." All denominations of U.S. currency were the same color!

He'd slipped later too, giving himself away with his exclamation about his fee being *a lot of rehbock!* He'd wondered what the fellow had meant comparing money to deer. His idiom had betrayed him! *Buck* was American slang for money . . . or dollars!

He was getting careless. How could two such clues have gone right by him!

He hadn't been talking about deer at all!

He'd noticed a peculiar twist to the fellow's accent when he spoke fast and his words ran together.

Everything suddenly fit.

He had been duped. The man was an *American!*

Schlaukopf rose in wrath, kicking at his vacated chair and knocking it halfway across the room. Pacing across the floor, his hand unconsciously sought the deadly knife in his pocket. Within seconds his fingers were probing the long steel blade, examining every milli-meter to make sure its razor edge was honed to perfection. He had had the lethal weapon custom-made in Prague, and it had served him well. Kills were not noted with notches in this part of the world, but if they had been, the handle Schlaukopf now fondled would not have been sufficient to contain those his knife was entitled to.

Revolving many a morbid plan in his brain for the American's demise, slowly the sly cunning of the fox began to replace the fury of the murderer.

Perhaps there was a way to yet turn this development to his own profit—even more profit than the four thousand marks he would take from the American before he killed him. His informers at the prison had indicated that there was an East German involved around the edges of this thing too. An official, somewhat high up, with interests that had the aroma of hidden motive.

What was to keep him from profiting from the information he possessed and ingratiating himself to this man at the same time?

The contact would prove useful in the future—if he didn't kill them both when the whole thing was over—besides which fact, there was clearly money to be made. East German marks would probably be all he could extort from the official. But he would demand enough to make it worth his while.

He would, of course, make no mention of his *own* involvement in the baron's escape.

He would only require payment for half the information regard-ing the plans. In this business, to divulge everything was suicide.

If the man didn't want to play along, then he would deliver the baron, take the American's money—then kill them both.

It was time to do some homework on his new victim.

His anger subsiding, he replaced the knife, then left the room. There was much to be done and not much time.

65

Machinations

• • •

THE UNLIKELINESS OF THE TEMPORARY CAMARADERIE could not have been more visible had the souls of both men been undressed for all the world to see.

Every expression, every gesture, every tone of voice, and especially every glance of the eyes, gave open and unconcealed testimony to the skeptical mistrust floating thickly in the air between them.

As two experienced and savvy maneuverers in the game of espionage, intrigue, and duplicity, they sparred adroitly back and forth with words and probing looks, each attempting to read more into the other than he divulged about himself.

"Yes, Herr Schlaukopf, I have heard of you."

"You know of, ah . . . my services?"

"I do. You are an information peddler, among other things—any-thing for a price, is that not correct?"

The fox showed a hint of amusement, though nothing resembling a smile.

"You are correct, Herr Section Chief."

"Then what may I do for you?" asked Gustav, pretending an aloof disinterest but actually highly curious what had caused this Russian weasel to seek him out.

"It is what I may do for *you*, Herr von Schmundt," rejoined the high perfidious voice.

"Don't toy with me, Schlaukopf," snapped Gustav. "I am an important man."

"Which is why I have come to you. I too know of your reputa-tion. I am aware that you have connections to a certain man in

prison," said Schlaukopf, giving his voice the inflection of significance.

"What is it to you, little man? I have put many men in prison since
the war. It is my job to protect the state from traitors."

"How many of them do you know *personally?*" The fox gave the
word peculiar emphasis. "How many, for instance, at the old school
prison called Neustädt?"

Gustav's eyes narrowed imperceptibly. He eyed the man a moment, then answered. "There are several at the prison you speak of
with whom I am personally acquainted," he said vaguely.

"I understand there is one whom you plan to move to a facility
farther to the east," said the fox. "Two days from now, if I am not
mistaken."

"How do you know of that?" barked Gustav, his eyes widening
and making no attempt to hide his vexation. "That move is highly
secretive."

"In the business I am in, I am often privy to information at, shall
we say, high levels."

"I insist you tell me how you came by it."

"You may insist, Herr Section Chief, but I will tell you nothing,"
replied Schlaukopf, rising now in annoyance himself. "Do not
threaten me. You said yourself you knew of the wide range of my
activities. It would not be healthy for you to give me grounds for
adding you to my list of prospective projects. As I said, I came here
with information that could possibly be of interest to you in the
matter of the prisoner we have been speaking of."

"What information?" said Gustav calmly, hiding his irritation. He
would jail *this* man in the baron's place! But not until he bled him of
whatever he knew.

"I am in business for myself, Herr von Schmundt. I do not give
away my goods free of charge. Information comes with a price."

"Tell me what you have. If it is worthwhile, you shall be paid."

At last a weak smile of cunning escaped the fox's thin lips.

"Unfortunately, that is not how I conduct my affairs," he said. "If
I was so trusting, I would have starved long ago."

"You are a weasel! Don't you realize I could have you jailed
instantly?"

"You won't. The information I possess is important to you."

Again Gustav forced himself to hold his tongue.

"Go on," he said.

"I also know that you have been looking for a certain American that may have connections to this prisoner."

"How do you know that?" Gustav barked, his demanding tone returning.

"Again, my methods are unimportant."

"They are important to me."

"Nevertheless, they shall remain my own private affair."

A thick shroud of dubious silence fell between the two cynical men.

"I will give you enough to show you I am in earnest," said the fox at length. "If you want the rest, then payment will be required. Agreed?"

"I bargain with no traitors."

Schlaukopf rose as if to leave.

Gustav rose also, blocking the way to the door.

"Tell me what you have, Schlaukopf." From the holster at his side, Gustav drew his pistol, pointing it in the general direction of his visitor. He had never shot anyone, but liked to brandish the weapon for effect.

Hastily surveying his options, during which moment the thought of his concealed knife came to mind, Schlaukopf resumed his chair.

"The American you seek knows the whereabouts of the prisoner at Neustädt," he said coolly.

"Impossible!"

"Forgive me, Herr von Schmundt, but you are in error."

"He could not know, unless . . ."

The incredible thought was too much to take in.

If McCallum does know about Neustädt, it seems likely Sabina knows too!

Gustav's brain spun wildly.

Perhaps my plan has worked after all! Sabina discovered her father's whereabouts, she and McCallum made contact, and . . . but how to locate them!

"He does know," repeated Schlaukopf's voice, intruding into Gustav's gyrating emotions. "For the price we spoke of, I can deliver the American into your hands."

"What price?" said Gustav, distractedly trying to think on two levels at once.

"Eight thousand marks."

"What!" In an instant Gustav was wide awake to his ruthless comrade.

"I will settle for East German marks," added Schlaukopf, as if the concession significantly lowered his request.

"Bah, where do you think I could lay my hands on that kind of money?"

"I know more about you than you may think. What I have asked is reasonable. If you would prefer, I would be willing to take four thousand West German marks . . . or perhaps one thousand U.S. dollars."

"What is to keep me from killing you?" threatened Gustav, waving the pistol he still held.

"That you want the American. It is a risk I am willing to take. Without me, you will never see him."

"I could keep close surveillance on the school. Eventually they would attempt to contact the prisoner."

"I have facts in the case you are not aware of."

"And if I kill you?"

"Then I die. But you will never see the American," bluffed Schlaukopf with his most crafty foxlike expression. In all likelihood, with what he had divulged the section chief probably *could* find the American without him. He might very well guess that the prisoner's move was involved. He hoped he had read the fellow right, and that he would accede to his demand. He would not tell him of the planned escape until it was too late for him to stop it. He would only tell him enough at present to force him to depend on him.

"Does all this involve the move of the prisoner?" asked Gustav, slowly putting away his gun.

"How very astute of you," rasped Schlaukopf.

"Does the American know of it?"

"In all likelihood."

Struggling to contain his anger, Gustav spoke in a measured tone. "Is he planning an attempt to wrest the baron from our custody?"

"Again, I believe it is likely."

"Where?"

"Between Warsaw and Minsk," lied the fox.

"A large area," remarked Gustav, thinking with curiosity of his and Galanov's efforts in that area. "Again it strikes me that I could foil their scheme and capture the American without your assistance."

"As I said, I have facts in the case you are unaware of. Let me say only that to spurn my help, or to attempt to gain my further knowledge without payment in full, could prove fatal."

Gustav eyed his foe with a blank expression.

"What do you want me to do?" he said at length.

"Allow the move to go off as planned. Raise the sum of money we spoke of. Give me a telephone number where I may be certain of reaching you at any time. Be prepared to move your men at an instant's notice. Warsaw is 525 kilometers. You will have to drive quickly. I will notify where you are to meet me. It will not be as you think, Herr Comrade. Do not attempt some alternate plan that does not involve me. Remember my reputation. My memory is long, and my methods unpredictable."

"I will pay your price," said Gustav, still undecided inside about quite what to do. He went to his desk and wrote on a scrap of paper. "Here is the number where I can be reached."

"Stay near," concluded the fox. "I will contact you. The moment the American is in your hands, the money must be in mine."

Rendezvous

* * *

THE LONELY STRETCH OF DIRT ROAD IN THE MIDDLE of the hilly pinewood on the northern slope of the Kleiner Ravensberg, some two kilometers south of Potsdam, would have been pretty and inviting under any other circumstances.

As it was, however, Matthew and Sabina sat on the warm earth, much too jittery to enjoy their surroundings. The warm August sun beat down upon the trees, bringing out fragrances both loved. But the circumstances were too filled with angst to remind either of their romps in similar woods far to the northeast many years before.

The only reminder, of both past and present, was the velvety lavender rose Sabina now held, where her hands rested in her lap, Matthew's promised daily gift that he had given her on this portentous morning. It would be the one whose leaves would not be placed with all the others of the past weeks in the small alabaster box that now rested safely back in Matthew's hotel room.

She had brought it along to give her father.

Matthew had followed Schlaukopf's instructions to the letter, stashing the car before dawn in an abandoned barn about two kilometers east, then walking to their present location. Sometime within the next two hours, SK would retrieve them and take them the rest of the way to Neustädt.

Matthew didn't entirely understand the rationale behind every detail of the plan. He knew the fox was not a man to be trusted, yet he had no choice. It seemed they would waste a great deal of time walking. But Schlaukopf said an extra automobile so near the prison might arouse suspicion. Through the woods, he insisted, was their best chance of a safe escape. By the time they retrieved their car from the barn, if the guards realized what had happened, the search for the escapee would be many kilometers distant. They should have a clear way back through the woods to Drewitz, then again by dirt road across the Parforce Heide to the highway into Güterfelde, then north to Stahnsdorf, and finally to the border crossing into the American sector of West Berlin at Teltow, where he had sufficiently bribed the guards to insure unrestricted passage.

All would go smoothly, the fox promised, as long as they weren't in too great a rush after the actual escape.

There was so much that could go wrong, Matthew didn't even want to think about it. In some respects, Schlaukopf and the prison were the least of their problems. The border itself loomed large in Matthew's thinking. He possessed the forged papers the CIA had prepared for him to get into East Berlin. But what about Sabina and the baron?

If they were successful at the prison, the border crossing at Teltow was bound to be tense. Schlaukopf had guaranteed he would take care of the guards and had secured documents for the baron. But three East Germans seeking passage across the border into the BRD only a kilometer or so from the refugee processing center at Marienfelde were bound to raise eyebrows. The *Vopos* were checking the borders much more tightly these days. If the *Vopos* had indeed been bribed, of course the West's guards would offer no resistance. But the crossing itself still contained too many unanswered questions in Matthew's mind. He would have preferred an escape route into East Berlin first, and then across the intercity zonal border.

Matthew had questioned the final phase of the proposed route in his last meeting with the fox.

"Once I've paid you, how do I know we will find the way safe all the way into Berlin?"

"You can trust me," rejoined Schlaukopf with an expression Matthew didn't in the least care for. Now that he was certain he was dealing with an American, it was with considerable more difficulty that Schlaukopf maintained his composure.

"As you've reminded me several times, this is not a business built on trust," said Matthew.

"How can I set your mind at ease?"

"You accompany us to the border at Teltow," suggested Matthew. "When we are on our way into West Berlin, you will get your money."

"If I accompany you, I will not be able to watch in case the guards come after you when you are gone."

"If I pay you and then leave through the woods with the baron, you could just as well go back to the prison, say I overpowered you and escaped with the prisoner, and send the guards directly after us."

"You may trust me," repeated Schlaukopf.

"You'll forgive me if I would rather trust in something more substantial," said Matthew sarcastically. "I'll tell you what, you meet us at Teltow. You'll receive payment there."

"If I deliver your prisoner and let you go without payment, you can find any way back into Berlin you choose. You don't have to go back through Teltow, and I will be left waiting without payment."

"So," said Matthew, "it would appear our mutual mistrust has brought us to an impasse."

"Half upon delivery of the prisoner, half upon your safe crossing at Teltow. I am willing to risk two thousand marks that you will see the wisdom in crossing where I say."

Matthew nodded. Such an arrangement could not hurt them, he thought. Schlaukopf was only in it for the money, and if he did not receive half his payment until they were to the border, he would not double-cross them. All should go well.

The sound of footsteps approaching interrupted Matthew's thoughts about the day before. He and Sabina rose the moment Schlaukopf came into view.

The narrow eyes of the fox eyed Sabina suspiciously.

"Who is this?" he said, looking at Matthew while tilting his head in the direction of Sabina. If so much money wasn't at stake, he'd kill them both on the spot and let the prisoner rot where he was. But he knew the fellow would have only half the money on him. He hated doing business with Americans!

"She's with me, that's who she is," Matthew replied.

"I don't like changes I don't know about."

"You never asked if I was involved by myself. I'm not. She's with me, and that's it."

"Can she follow orders?"

Matthew nodded.

He now proceeded to look over their attire.

"A doctor and nurse," he remarked. "Not altogether original, but it may work. We'll discuss it on the way. You got the money?" asked the fox.

"I've got it—half, that is—which you'll receive once the baron is in our hands. You'll get the other half at the border."

Schlaukopf glanced back and forth between them another moment, then without another word motioned them to follow. He turned and began walking through the trees the way he had come. Matthew and Sabina followed.

67

Neustädt Technische Hochschule

● ● ●

SCHLAUKOPF'S AUTO RUMBLED AUDACIOUSLY TO THE front gate of the prison, sending scrunching gravel flying from beneath its tires and bringing the guard at the gatehouse to attention.

The fox rolled down his window and nodded with cool belligerence to the guard as he approached, presenting him with several official-looking documents.

"Final check on the prisoner before tomorrow's transfer," he said.

The guard glanced over the papers, then eyed Matthew and Sabina where they sat in the backseat, trying to appear outwardly disinterested but inwardly trembling. He picked up the phone on the wall beside him, spoke briefly into it, then hung it up, took a step back, ordered the barricade opened, and waved them through.

Schlaukopf revved the motor and sped through the tall brick wall, topped with coiled barbed wire, and into the stark compound. Before them the large single building of the former boarding school rose grey, imposing, and deathly still. Glancing back, Sabina saw the iron gate clank shut behind them.

On the third floor, a shadowy figure moved from the desk where he had only a moment before hung up his phone, to the window overlooking the compound. The fifteen hundred marks he had been paid to authorize the so-called KGB agent's entry into the prison was probably too little. But his position did not offer him many such opportunities, and he had to take what he could get when it came along.

He only hoped nothing went wrong. Otherwise, he'd have to pay off his own guards for their silence later, to save his own neck. And if he did, it would come out of his share of whatever monkey business the foxy little man was up to. He didn't want to have to do that, but it was a risk he'd decided to take for the fifteen hundred.

He looked down below him where the automobile was just now driving up to the building.

The car stopped.

The three conspirators climbed out. Schlaukopf walked confidently to the guard at the front entrance, Sabina and Matthew a step behind.

"KGB," he said, flashing identification, then stuffing the same papers he had used previously in the direction of the guard. "We are here for the final medical check on the prisoner before tomorrow's transfer."

"I heard of no check," said the guard, glancing hurriedly over the papers. "We were told there would be a vehicle for him tomorrow morning."

"There is some question about the man's capacity to survive the rigors of the move."

"I shall call my superior for authorization," said the guard, a young East German of no more than twenty-three. "If you would just wait—"

"Those papers are your authorization!" shouted Schlaukopf, the fox suddenly transforming itself into a lion. "Did you hear me, you fool—I am the KGB! Unless you want yourself to occupy the cell vacated by the prisoner, I suggest you allow us immediate access. Neither I nor the doctor have time for your bumbling idiocy!"

"Yes . . . yes, sir," stammered the guard, fumbling for his key.

The moment the door opened, the three walked inside. Schlaukopf paused, then lowered his voice and spoke in confidential tones to the guard.

"There is also a report," he said, "that the prisoner may have contracted a deadly virus. His records have been gone over thoroughly. That is another reason for this examination. It may be necessary to execute him immediately. The doctor has brought along an injection should such become necessary. I suggest you pass the word among the guards on that wing to keep their distance once the doctor and his nurse enter the cell. Notify them that whatever the doctor says, they must do immediately."

Wide-eyed, the guard glanced unconsciously at the doctor's black bag in Sabina's hand, then nodded and hurried to the phone on the wall behind him.

"We will need a stretcher brought to the cell," said Matthew, "in the event the man must be moved."

The guard did not seem to have heard.

"Did you hear me, guard?" shouted Matthew sternly. "Tell them to bring a stretcher and leave it outside the room."

The guard nodded, relaying the request by phone.

Schlaukopf motioned Matthew in the direction of the stairway leading to the wing in question, while he continued on through the main corridor toward the rear of the building.

"Come, nurse," said Matthew, leading the way up the stairs.

Once out of sight from the others, she crept close to him as they walked into the corridor at the top, turning left and moving along it.

"Oh, Matthew!" she whispered as she glanced about, her voice unable to hide her fear, "do you know where you are going?"

"I hope so."

"How do you know what to do?"

"We have an expression where I come from—'faking it.'"

"This is so frightening. Do you realize where we are!"

"I'm trying not to think about it!" Matthew whispered out of the corner of his mouth, continuing his blank stare straight ahead.

"But . . . but what if—"

A guard turning around the corner just ahead and walking toward them broke off her words. Quickly she slowed her step. Allowing Matthew to widen the distance between them, Sabina just heard him whisper under his breath: *"Protect us, Lord . . . in the name of the Father, the Son, and the Holy Spirit, here goes—"*

Suddenly his voice changed and he spoke out loudly. "The Dortmann prisoner is just down the block there to the right, is he not?" he said gruffly as the man approached. "Cell D-14?"

"Ja, Herr Doktor," answered the man.

"Have the guards been notified to withdraw themselves?"

"Ja, they are doing so now."

"Very good," said Matthew, continuing on with brisk step. "Make sure they stay away," he added. "There may be danger."

They rounded the corner, entering the second floor of the east block where the D cells were located. A lone guard stood in front of the door about halfway down. Hearing them approach, he glanced toward them.

"Give us the key, guard," said Matthew with authority, stopping directly in front of the man. "It is for your own safety."

The man fished out a chain, located the key to D-14, and handed it to Matthew.

"When is the last time this man was examined?"

"I do not know, *Herr Doktor.*"

"He is fed twice daily, I believe?"

"Ja, but through the door. He is not seen."

"The food disappears?"

"Ja."

"This morning's?"

"The trays are retrieved each evening, Herr Doktor. I do not know about last night's or this morning's."

"But he has not been seen in several days?"

"Nein, Herr Doktor."

"Then you had better remove yourself with the others," said Matthew. "I fear the worst. The farther away you are the better. A stretcher is to be delivered. When it comes, place it at the end of the hall there, but do not come closer. Is that understood?"

"Ja, Herr Doktor."

"The nurse and I will be going in presently."

Without hesitation the guard hurried down the hall. In less than a minute the corridor was empty.

Matthew sought Sabina's eyes, held her gaze for only a moment, then set the key into the lock and turned it. The heavy iron lock gave way with a dull clank somewhere inside the thick wooden door.

Taking a deep breath, Matthew grasped the handle, then pushed on the door. It ground rustily on its hinges, then slowly swung forward into the cell.

68

Reunion

• • •

BARON HEINRICH VON DORTMANN HAD HARDLY SLEPT
in two days.

A huge sense of anticipation, such as he had never felt before, had
grown to envelop him.

At first it had been a quiet feeling of enormous contentment. He
found himself unable to read, unable to write, unable even to pray for
the very serenity and peace that filled him. All that first night, most of
which he had spent lying awake, had been occupied in the tranquil
intimacy of inaudible holy intercourse with his heavenly Father.

He had dozed now and then throughout the following morning,
feeling remarkably fresh and rested. A great sense of physical well-
being came over him. He felt strong and vital again, his vision clear,
his heart passionate, his limbs vigorous and eager to climb the high
mountains of the Master's kingdom.

Yesterday afternoon the quietude had gradually turned to urgency.

The sense stole over him that a change was at hand.

Oh, Father! he exclaimed sometime midway through the afternoon, *are you preparing to bring me home!*

With feverish and joyful excitement, he continued to pray, earnestly beseeching his Lord and Father to ready his spirit to meet him,
praying again, as he had so often these many years, for every individual
he remembered meeting during his earthly life, for his family, for
Sabina especially and her work, and for his captors and those whom
the world would deem his enemies.

By evening the nature of the urgency itself began to change.

Now the baron felt a tugging upon his spirit that there was something he was to do, work yet undone that must be completed.

What is it, Father? he prayed imperatively. *What would you have me do before my hours here are over?*

He turned to the prison letters of his New Testament, reading them again with fresh purpose, praying fervently for direction.

Suddenly a light broke into his spirit.

What was Paul doing to the very end, even as his execution seemed at hand?

Writing!

Giving instructions to those who followed, reflecting on the course he had run, and always pondering the meaning of faith and the depths of God's nature. There were messages to be conveyed to the Father's children, and no prison bars kept Paul from his appointed task.

His thoughts turned to his friend Dietrich Bonhoeffer. He too had written letters and papers while in prison, many of which had subsequently found a wide audience among believers in Germany. Both Brother Paul's and Brother Dietrich's prison letters had been of great encouragement to him. He had only completed Dietrich's prison book again three or four days before.

He had been writing to himself for years, the baron thought. But suddenly new vision swept through him. He perceived, as with the eyes of eternity, what lay at the core of that which he had been trying to communicate in his papers and journals and notebooks all this time. Suddenly a foundation of new vision burst into a unifying pinpoint of light in his consciousness.

Without hesitating, he grabbed up his pen, the sense fully upon him that he was in his final twenty-four hours of earthly life, and began, with a marvelous mingling of compulsion and calm, to record what suddenly had come so distinctly into view.

He ignored the food that passed for supper. It was uninteresting to him.

Sleep now became the final distraction of the bodily tabernacle he would soon need no more. Into the night he wrote, praying for a continuation both of the inner light that so illuminated his spirit and of the dim bulb burning overhead. Yet if it gave way, he would continue to write even in the dark.

Midnight came . . . three o'clock . . . then morning.

The baron was unconscious of time. Alertness had never pulsed so wakefully through him.

The morning's tray of food passed under the door.

Another distraction. He ignored it. What did this body of his need any longer with food!

He was bound for another land, a higher home, a new chamber where his *new* body would rest and refresh itself—why concern himself any longer over the last-minute necessities of this dying thing he wore called *the flesh?*

Still he wrote, praying as he did that the Father of whom the pages on his table spoke would protect and preserve the words from his pen and enable them to find their way into the hands that would proclaim them among his people.

Another hour passed . . . two . . . then three . . .

Metallic rusty scraping sounded in his ears.

The baron did not look up. What did he care for another tray of earthly manna?

Light shone into the dimly lit cell. He squinted, suddenly confused, still not glancing up from the paper before him.

A voice sounded. What were the guards doing here? He did not need another distraction just now—unless this was the moment he had anticipated. The soldiers had come also for the Lord in the middle of the night, shining the bright lights of their torches in his face.

It did not sound like a guard. Why was the voice so high and so filled with—

He glanced up, trying to focus. The light disoriented his vision. Suddenly fatigue and confusion swept over him.

There were two guards. . . . Why were they whispering . . . ? What was that word he kept hearing over and over . . . ? A memory from out of the distant past . . . a familiar sound . . . it reminded him of happy days . . . and of roses. . . .

His brain slowed in delayed exhaustion. . . . Consciousness tried to leave him. . . .

Roses . . . roses . . . he could even smell them now. . . . What did the word mean that now filled his ears with tearful, whispered animation . . . ?

What was this face now coming so close to his own . . . ?

"*Papa . . . oh, Papa . . .*" The words continued to sound in his sleep-starved ear.

Focus gradually returned.

This was no guard. . . .

A jolt of confused recognition seized him like a bolt of lightning crashing through his skull. His eyes widened, body suddenly trembling . . . it couldn't be. . . .

"*Sabina!*" he murmured, eyes full of mist.

"Oh, Papa . . . yes, it is me . . . it is your Sabina!" she cried softly, bursting into uncontrolled weeping, smothering the poor man with a thousand kisses as she embraced him with what felt to him like at least a dozen arms.

Behind them, Matthew was hastily closing the door to keep the inopportune sounds from escaping, keeping it unlatched, then stood carefully by while father and daughter's reunion gave way to abundant tears, embraces, prayers, and whispered questions and assurances.

"Yes, Papa," Sabina was saying, "it is Matthew over there. . . . He and I have come to take you away!"

By now the baron's earthly vessel, and all the emotions it housed, had again assumed the upper hand. He slumped into his chair, weeping freely and joyously. Sabina kissed again the tear-stained cheeks. Slowly he stretched his thin and aging arms around her shoulders and drew her close.

"*My daughter . . . my little Sabina!*" he whispered through her hair into the ear near his lips. "Our Father is so generous to grant these old eyes the blessing of seeing you again. Oh, my daughter, my daughter . . . how young and beautiful and healthy you look!"

"I am very well, Papa, and I am happy to see that you are too. I brought you this," she added, pulling her hand up in front of him.

She handed him the rose, nearly squashed from being pressed between them.

"A beautiful rose," he murmured, tears flowing afresh from his eyes as he held it gently to his nose.

"For those who love, you know, Papa—," said Sabina, hesitating with a tone of expectant interrogation.

"I remember, my child. . . . The petals, the leaves—"

"And even the *thorns,* as you taught me the last day our eyes saw one another," added Sabina.

"Yes . . . they *all* carry the fragrance of love that their Creator put into them."

Behind them Matthew spoke.

"We must make haste, Papa," said Sabina, standing back from the baron's embrace. "There is still great danger."

"But . . . but I do not understand. . . . Have I not been released?"

"No, Papa. No one knows it is I."

"But . . ."

"It is an *escape,* Papa," said Sabina. "Matthew and I have come to take you away. If they catch us, they may kill us all. You will have to trust me, Papa, and do exactly as I say."

"I will trust you, my child," he replied with the marvelous submission of maturity.

As they were speaking, Matthew opened the door and glanced out into the corridor.

"It has come," he said. "I will be back in a moment."

He left the cell, returning in less than a minute with the folding canvas stretcher. Leaving the door open now, he laid it on the floor to its full length.

"Baron," he whispered. "There is no time to explain. I want you to lie down on the stretcher. You must be absolutely still, and make not a sound until we are safely outside the prison. Will you be able to do that?"

The baron nodded.

"You must not twitch so much as a finger."

"I understand, my son," said the baron affectionately, bending his aging knees and crawling onto the canvas.

"You must bring all my papers," he said, suddenly remembering and glancing up at Sabina. "They are of far more value even than my life."

"Not a one shall be left, Papa," said Sabina.

She set the black bag she had brought on the rickety table, opened it, and pulled out a single thin white sheet of linen. She handed it to Matthew, who proceeded to cover the baron from head to toe.

Sabina then gathered everything she could find in the small room that might be of importance to her father, including all the papers on the table and the several journals and books in a small box on the floor beside the bed, and stuffed them inside the bag in place of the sheet.

Matthew and Sabina now glanced at one another with expressions of readiness.

Sabina stooped down, quietly reassuring her father, while Matthew picked up the two trays of food and once again left the cell and began walking down the corridor.

69

Escape

• • •

TURNING THE CORNER, MATTHEW WALKED BOLDLY straight to the far end, where two guards with rifles stood at attention. They had been joined by the young guard whom Matthew had sent away from the cell a few minutes earlier.

"It is exactly as I had suspected," he said, approaching them, indicating the two full trays of food in his hands. "The virus was faster-acting than we realized. The prisoner is dead."

The guard's expression showed his concern.

"The danger is . . . past, then, *Herr Doktor?*"

"No," replied Matthew gravely. "I'm afraid the danger is even greater."

He paused, then went on in a most serious tone. "As you can see from the undisturbed food, he must have died sometime during the day yesterday. The virus, therefore, is still highly active, and we must destroy the body without delay."

Matthew set down the trays.

"If you will come with me," he said to the guard, "I will need your assistance."

He turned to walk back to the cell. The guard hesitated.

"Come, guard," he ordered. "It is imperative that we take the body out of the prison quickly. My nurse and I will carry the corpse. We have been inoculated. You must lead us by the most direct route out the rear exit to the compound, where we have an ambulance standing by."

"Ja, Herr Doktor," said the young man nervously, now following Matthew down the corridor.

Arriving again at the cell, Matthew motioned the guard to lead the way ahead of them.

"You may keep a safe distance from the infected body," he said. "For their own safety, and the safety of the prison, you must keep all others well away. Clear the corridors of guards and officials as we go, especially where they may be concentrated about the exit. The body is highly infected."

Already the guard was halfway down the corridor ahead of them and more than anxious to do exactly as Matthew had ordered and keep his distance.

Matthew entered the cell, motioned to Sabina, took the bag from her, looped it around his arm and one of the stretcher poles, then both stooped down to pick up their precious and long-awaited burden and followed their apprehensive escort down the corridor.

Ahead as they went, they heard occasional shouts of urgency from their unwitting accomplice, who kept just within sight but as far ahead as he could, to his fellow guards, ordering them to stand back and make the way clear for doctor and nurse.

It took five or six minutes to navigate the corridors, descend back to the ground floor, and finally arrive at the rear exit of the old school building.

Matthew and Sabina emerged into the open light of day without incident. The two guards, as well as their chaperon from the D wing of the second floor, stood well away as they exited.

Matthew walked several strides away from the building, paused, and looked back and forth, then saw Schlaukopf's black car some thirty meters away where he had brought it around from the front, now parked near the high surrounding brick wall toward his right. Matthew glanced back to where the three guards stood watching them.

"I suggest you get back inside," he said, "and notify the front gate that we will be coming through immediately. It is imperative we get the body back to the hospital facility for incineration with all haste."

Turning again, Matthew led the way to the car.

The guard from the second floor followed him with his eyes, wondering if the small automobile toward which they were walking was the ambulance the doctor had spoken of. Thinking better of saying anything, however, he followed his two companions inside, then rang the front gate.

Carrying their cargo around to the far side of the car, where it would not be visible to prying eyes, Matthew opened the rear door, glancing toward Schlaukopf in the front seat with an unspoken expression indicating their successful mission, while Sabina stooped down to the ground.

"Papa," she said, "you may slowly rise now. We are getting in a car."

As she spoke, she removed the cover from the baron's head and body, gently helping him into the backseat. She climbed in beside him. Matthew closed the door behind her, then ran around to the other side and climbed in.

"Get us out of here, Schlaukopf!" ordered Matthew.

"You have your quarry?" said the fox.

"Yes! Now step on it."

"Then there is the matter of payment to be taken care of first."

"Can't it wait until we're outside the gate!"

"I'm afraid it cannot. Otherwise I may have to stop and tell them I have foiled an escape attempt."

Frantically Matthew fumbled in his coat for one of the two envelopes that each contained two thousands marks. Thus far he'd been lucky the fox hadn't searched him and learned that he had brought both halves with him.

"Here you are!" he cried, throwing it into the front seat. "Now get us out of this place!"

Still the suspicious fox hesitated long enough to tear the envelope open and quickly scan its contents to his satisfaction. A moment later the engine roared to life. He pulled the car into gear, then inched forward, not so hasty as to arouse undue concern, slowly increasing speed around the inside perimeter of the compound and to the front gate.

"Scrunch down between us, Baron," said Matthew. "We will try to keep you out of sight. Sabina, put the blanket over his back and head, then lean over as close to me as you can, as if we are talking. I don't think they will see him."

The baron and his daughter did as Matthew said.

Sabina glanced over at Matthew, wondering within herself how she could ever have had any doubts about him at all. Her questions of trust had by now receded so completely into the past that she marveled they had ever existed. Trust him? After this, how could she not trust him with everything in her life! He had arranged every detail of this complicated plot for her and her father's sake, risking his life and future . . . for them. Not only was he trustworthy—he was a brave and courageous man!

She was glad she had waited to place the photographs into his hands until this was all over. She had been right from the first—he was the one to decide how best to use them. As soon as her father was safe, she would talk to him about them.

The car approached the guardhouse. The gate already stood open. Schlaukopf slowed slightly, flashed his phony KGB card through the window, and continued on.

Within seconds they were out of the prison compound, steadily picking up speed. Matthew and Sabina both breathed a collective sigh of relief.

Only some two kilometers did the fox drive along the highway, then he slowed and pulled off toward the right, onto a dirt road, northward into the Staatforst, by the same route they had come along earlier. He stopped where he had parked the auto that morning, then turned off the engine.

"Do you know your way from here?" he said, turning around to face Matthew. "Follow this dirt road up the hill we walked down an hour ago to where I met you. Retrieve your car and make for the border by the route we discussed earlier."

Matthew nodded.

"There will be one slight change of plans," Schlaukopf added.

"What's that?" said Matthew.

"When you come in sight of the crossing gate at Teltow, stop. I will walk out to meet you. You will be some fifty meters away. You will give me the rest of the money then."

"Why?"

"If the guards at the crossing see a large sum of cash passing between us, greed may enter their thieving hearts. They may suddenly not consider what I paid them sufficient."

"That is your problem," said Matthew. "I'll not pay you until we're *on* the border."

"You'll do as I say!" snapped the fox, dangerously close to losing his composure. "Remember, I can still call in the authorities until you are across the border. You will have to believe that no harm will come to you after you give me the rest of the money. I will accompany you the fifty meters into West Berlin if you like."

Reluctantly Matthew consented.

"One more thing, *mein lieber Freund,*" said the fox with cynical sarcasm, narrowing his eyes with intensity, "it would prove very, very dangerous for you to attempt a crossing elsewhere than Teltow." He pulled out his knife, flashing its blade in the sunlight to emphasize his threatening words. "Saving the extra two thousand marks would cost all three of you your lives. . . . Do I make myself understood?"

As he spoke he glanced toward Sabina.

Her eyes returned his gaze, and she held it for several long moments, during which time more intensity of *knowing* passed between them than either had anticipated.

"Yes . . . clear enough," said Matthew, breaking the spell.

"Then be gone, all of you," said Schlaukopf.

Moments later, Matthew, Sabina, and Baron von Dortmann stood alone in a deserted pinewood, Sabina holding a thin white blanket, Matthew holding a black doctor's bag, watching the trailing cloud of dust from Schlaukopf's temporary ambulance disappear down the dirt road in the distance.

70

Betrayal

. . .

THIRTY MINUTES LATER, THE SLY FOX CRADLED A LARGE dark beer in one hand, while the other held the telephone receiver up to his ear.

". . . You must move quickly," he was saying.

"I thought the attempt was set for tomorrow, during the transfer!" barked Gustav on the other end.

"As I said, there were factors involved you did not know about."

"You are a sneaking traitor, Schlaukopf!"

"Tut, tut, Herr Schmundt. All is in order. I will bring the American you want straight into your lair—*if,* that is, you have been successful in raising the money. If not, then you will never see either of us again."

"I have it, you cur."

"Good. I thought you would see the wisdom of my plan in the end."

"My men are ready. If the baron has already been snatched, I take it my trip to Warsaw should be canceled."

"How very astute of you, Herr Schmundt. Meet me at the border crossing at Teltow."

"That's less than two hours from here!" exclaimed Gustav.

"Be there in ninety minutes."

"Will the American be there?"

"As soon as your eight thousand marks is safely in my hands, I will tell you where you may find them."

"Them? The American and the prisoner?"

"The American, the prisoner . . . ," Schlaukopf said, then added with deliberate emphasis, *"and the woman."*

Gustav's brain first flitted to the Warsaw newsstand and the woman they had been looking for. So there *was* a connection, as he had suspected.

But the Polish direction of his thoughts only lasted half a second.

All at once another sensation burst into his consciousness like a detonating atomic bomb.

"The *woman?*" repeated Gustav, his mouth suddenly dry and his voice shaky. "Describe her," he croaked.

"Between thirty-five and forty by my estimation," said Schlaukopf, "fair-skinned, light golden hair, eyes . . . hmm . . . blue, I believe, tending toward hazel, tall slender neck, well-proportioned body, 176 to 178 centimeters in height . . . and *extremely* beautiful. Does that answer your question, Herr Schmundt?"

The telephone was silent a moment.

"I . . . I will be at Teltow in seventy-five minutes," said Gustav, struggling to get the words out of his mouth. "You will have your price."

Schlaukopf hung up the *Gasthaus* phone, then walked back to his table. He was already in east Potsdam, nearly halfway to Stahnsdorf. No hurry. He could enjoy another beer or two in satisfied contemplation of what he would do with 4,000 West and 8,000 East German marks.

· · ·

Gustav von Schmundt hung up his phone at his office in East Berlin, trembling from head to foot, and staggered to his chair.

"*Sabina. . . !*" he gasped in no more than a whisper. His face had gone deathly pale.

The realization that within two hours Sabina von Dortmann would be in his possession, the interfering McCallum dead, and her fool of a father in his clutches for the obtaining of the deeds and gold that were rightfully Schmundt property . . . it was nearly more than his normally placid constitution could tolerate.

He waited but an instant. In a cold sweat, he picked up his phone. "Fräulein Reinhardt, get me Galanov!"

He waited a moment, then shouted orders to his assistant to assemble the force immediately and head for Teltow. Slamming down the receiver, he dashed from the building for his own car.

He stopped suddenly just outside the door.

What was he thinking!

It was midday. Teltow meant either a drive through West Berlin or a circuitous route far out of the way east and south. The traffic would be extraordinary in either case.

This was one appointment he would *not* be late for under any circumstances!

He turned and ran back into his office, grabbed up his telephone again, and ordered up a helicopter.

"Pick me up on the roof in fifteen minutes!"

Setting down the receiver for the last time, he sucked in a deep breath and tried to calm himself. Unconsciously his hand laid itself on his hip. He unsnapped the leather holster, withdrew the pistol, then opened the top drawer of his desk, pulled out a fresh cartridge of bullets, and inserted it into the handle.

It never hurt to be sure.

He wanted nothing going wrong this time.

71

Joyous Journey

• • •

THE TRAMP OF THE THREE PILGRIMS THROUGH THE
Staatforst was as exhilarating as it was exhausting for their elder and
once-again-present spiritual father and head.

That Sabina's father had scarcely slept nor eaten in twenty-four
hours did not help his already dwindled and weakened sixty-seven-
year-old frame cope with even the moderate rigors of the two-kilo-
meter journey to the car Matthew had surreptitiously rented for the
day. More than once he stumbled and nearly collapsed from light-
headedness and sheer physical weariness, and they stopped every three
or four minutes to rest. It was the first exercise he had had of any
strenuous kind for seventeen years.

"I could carry you on my back with ease, Baron," said Matthew.
"I wish you would let me."

"It may come to that before we are through, Matthew, my boy. But
as tired as I am, you must know how wonderful it feels to work this
old body of mine again to the point where I am *able* to make it tired.
Let me enjoy the blisters, the aches, and the exhaustion fully, and
when I crumble, then by all means, hoist me onto your strong young
back!"

"But, Papa," objected Sabina, "I am fearful you will injure yourself."

"What better way to do so than relishing again God's creation! Ah,
Sabina, you cannot imagine what sensations and wonders are flying
through this heart of mine!"

"I have not forgotten who my papa is!" laughed Sabina. "Perhaps
I have some idea."

"Just the smell of this pine forest is making my brain wild with delight."

The baron drew in a long breath, the most contented expression of pleasure on his face. But even before he had time to exhale the sigh to its conclusion, his feet lost their balance from the influx of oxygen to his head.

"Oh, Papa!" cried Sabina, steadying him as he stumbled against her.

On the other side, Matthew quickly grabbed his other arm.

"Perhaps it is time for another brief rest," said the baron. They helped him gently to the ground, then sat down beside him.

"We have food in the car, Papa."

"Yes . . . yes, that will be nice," murmured the baron quietly, breathing in and out with shallow breath.

The wood was deathly still. Not a whisper of a breeze played among the highest needles of the pines.

"It is peaceful here," sighed the baron, his voice extremely quiet. "I would be quite content to lie down and sleep all day and all night, with the canopy of God's trees, and above them his heaven, for our only blanket."

"You will sleep in my own bed tonight, Papa," said Sabina. "But I am afraid to do so we will not be able to lie down and nap just yet."

"There is so much to say, so much to ask. I want to know everything, but somehow I do not think my brain could contain it all just now."

"We will have many years, Papa. I will tell you all. There is no hurry."

"There are times I feel as young and strong as when Marion and I were married. Then I look at my arms and legs and see how thin and white they have become, and I wonder if that same thing has happened to my brain."

"Never to *your* brain, Papa."

"I do wish—forgive my unfaith, Father!—but I cannot help thinking about Marion, and wishing she could be here with us."

"She is, Papa," replied Sabina softly.

"Yes . . . of course. I am forgetful of even the most elementary truths Jesus has taught us. He that believes shall *never* die."

The baron sighed. His heart was full at the thought of his dear wife, though his eyes remained dry.

"I loved her, Sabina, my child—I loved your mother more than I think a man ever loved a woman."

He paused reflectively.

"Yet no doubt," he added with a smile, "every man thinks *his* love is the greatest love ever to flower upon the earth. Ah, such self-centered creatures we are! The Father fills each one with the deep love of his nature—fills men, fills women . . . fills *roses. . . .*"

As he spoke, he again lifted the rose, limp now, that he still carried, to his nose, as if in its fading scent was contained a hidden secret of love that *only* he and his departed Marion—in all the history of the world—could share.

"He fills his whole creation with his love," he went on in a moment, as if thinking aloud, "to the very texture and color and wonderful beauty and mysterious fragrance of the rose, and yet we take that love, considering it our own, and think ourselves uniquely qualified to partake of it, when in truth it has been showered lavishly abroad upon the whole of creation."

"You need have no anxiety about your brain, Papa," said Sabina with a smile. "I think while the outside of you may have diminished, the inside of you has grown larger!"

The baron returned her smile, though weakly.

"Suddenly I am so very, very sleepy."

"It will not be much longer, Papa." As she spoke, Sabina glanced up at Matthew with a sigh and a smile. He returned it with a reassuring nod.

"I knew someone was coming for me today," said the baron, speaking nearly inaudibly.

"You mean about the transfer?" asked Matthew.

"What transfer?"

"You were to be moved."

"No, I knew nothing of it."

"We believe Gustav to be behind it, Papa," said Sabina.

"Gustav . . . the poor boy. Is he still giving you trouble, my child?"

"No, Papa. I am quite safe from him. Who did you think was coming for you, Papa?"

"Our Father, my child. I was certain my day had come to finally meet him! I was so blissfully happy. I could not sleep. I was full of such anticipation! Yet there was much to write . . . for you, and for others. I was up all night with my thoughts and prayers, attempting to record what the Father was showing me, all the while looking forward to going home. Then what should I find, but that the Father had sent *you* for me, instead of coming himself!"

The baron's face and eyes shone with the light of expectancy and jubilation.

"You can have no idea what happy days I had there," he said quietly. "The Father was so close and took such care of me. Yesterday, awaiting, as I thought, the death of my earthly body, I think was the happiest day of my life."

"And yet," he went on after a moment, "to see you, my child, again, to set eyes upon your face, has increased even that happiness tenfold. Were I to die this very moment, I would bless the Father for giving me everything my heart could desire!"

Sabina looked away.

She felt tears, but she could not afford to let them flow.

Their time would come . . . but it was not yet.

72

The Maturing of a Daughter

• • •

THE THREE TRAVELERS REACHED THE CAR.

Taking a lengthy break for food and water, the baron grew weaker and quieter. The food would accomplish its nourishing work in time. But at present his body found that absorbing it required all the little remaining strength he possessed.

At length they loaded inside, Matthew driving, Sabina in the backseat with her arm cradling her father, who laid his head tenderly in her lap.

In less than five minutes he was sleeping as soundly as a baby.

Matthew made his way down the hill, slowly along the dirt road, still through several kilometers of woods and fields, through Drewitz, across the open *Heide,* again by dirt, then onto the highway and into Güterfelde. As they drove, both he and Sabina found themselves lost in their own thoughts.

Sabina's mind was full of her father. Emotions and sensations she had never felt surged through her as she glanced down upon him where he slept against her. Suddenly he was a child and she, now a woman of forty, was taking care of him, as he and his Marion had once cared for her.

A sense of the maturity of her own womanhood came upon her as it never had before.

Whenever the baron had come to her mind over the past years, which was often, if not daily, the image was always of a man in the virile prime of his manhood, her *father*—and she was always his little girl. Suddenly the mortality of his earthly frame was a present and visible reality.

The gradual inversion of generational strength had overtaken this most prized earthly relationship between father and daughter. Feeling the weight of his worn, sleeping frame filled Sabina with a warm, quiet sense of the eternal tide into which all earthly things ultimately flow.

She glanced down at his face.

She had known there would be great changes.

But even the undeniable light that still radiated from his countenance when he spoke could not prevent Sabina, as she looked upon him, from an occasional stab of pity and dismay over his physical appearance. As sternly as she had striven to equip her mind to accept the inevitable changes she knew would be apparent upon him, nothing could have prepared her for the thin figure of a man she had seen that morning hunched over the table in the prison cell.

His hair had thinned, though there was no evidence of balding, and had grown utterly grey. His wide forehead, thin cheeks, and neck and forearms, all showed the wrinkles of age and attrition. No hint of fat could be seen anywhere on his aging body, and his clothes hung as if several sizes too large.

Sabina had yet kept at bay the flood of tears that would one day be released. For now she was too happy in his presence again—to feel his touch, to hear his voice, to put her cheek next to his—too altogether happy to let herself reflect upon what Gustav and the horrible system to which he had given his allegiance had made of this fine and honorable and stalwart man who was her father, a nobleman of the old Germany, a Germany they were all proud of before . . .

She could not even complete the thought.

She shut her eyes tightly against the tears struggling to emerge.

Not now. Not yet.

There was no time to relax, no time for the full rush of emotions. She had to parcel them out a little at a time, otherwise this day and all it signified would overwhelm her.

As they drove, Sabina gradually quieted. In the exultation of being with her father again, for a time she had forgotten the dangers they still had ahead and that they were yet far from any safe haven to call home.

The eyes of the man Matthew called Schlaukopf came back to her from their parting an hour or two ago. She had seen deeply inside him in those few seconds, and the sight was anything but pleasant.

The brief moment had confirmed everything she had earlier suspected from Matthew's descriptions.

From that look, and his changing plans at the last minute with Matthew, she had known nothing about him was to be trusted. She had to rely on her instincts, even should Matthew object. She could *not* allow her father to be at that man's mercy.

She would do as she had planned.

Teltow Crossing

• • •

WHAT HAD ONCE BEEN A SLEEPY FARMING VILLAGE SOME sixteen or eighteen kilometers from the center of the city had, through the course of time and the slow encroachment of progress, been swallowed up in the expanding outskirts of the sprawl known as Berlin.

Teltow was unremarkable except in this: Fate had ordained that it chanced to fall, like another half-dozen or ten villages similarly situated, at precisely that point of demarcation selected by the Allied powers where the city of Berlin would end and the Democratic Republic of East Germany would begin.

That boundary separating the American sector of West Berlin from the Communist so-called democratic nation of the DDR snaked its way through the heart of Teltow. It was a line to the north of which meant freedom, progress, and eyes that looked Westward, to the south of which meant impoverishment, containment, and a focus Eastward . . . toward Moscow.

More than a decade had passed. None would ever forget, but most had learned in their own way to accept the cruel fate that divided their village, divided families, divided neighborhoods—half now prospering and free, the other half living another kind of life altogether.

Indeed, the division that had sliced the heart of the German people into two coexistent halves, breathing and alive but not unified and whole, was reflected to miniature microcosmic perfection in Teltow. The story of its divided people and divided streets was Germany's story as well.

In spite of this notoriety and of the pain silently endured by the division, Teltow yet managed a good deal of the time to maintain its village flavor and atmosphere. On each side of the boundary, whose crossing was patrolled by border guards, the people of Teltow went about their business, trying to ignore, or pretending to ignore, that scar through their village that could never be ignored.

Suddenly, into the midst of a tranquil midday, had come the ominous whirring sounds of a helicopter, first approaching ever closer, then descending and setting down in the middle of the street in front of the crossing, where it had remained now for more than an hour and a half.

The inhabitants of Teltow tried not to notice, but something was in the wind. In this part of the world, helicopters never came bringing good news. They always meant danger . . . to someone.

More traffic had arrived at the tiny border station.

A black automobile from the south had stopped a short distance from the helicopter. The little man driving it had been alone.

About an hour after the helicopter several automobiles rumbled in. A young man had jumped out of the lead car and gone straight to the first arrival. Receiving orders, he returned to deploy the rifle-carrying men now piling out of the three cars. Within several minutes the roadblock throughout the entire region of the crossing was secure. Not even a small army would be capable of breaking across the border here.

Now the three stood, apart from the rest, three faces impatiently scanning the approaching road from the south, anxious for any sign . . . waiting for their prey.

The man from the helicopter, by the mere appearance of his uniform, would have seemed to be in charge.

Gustav stood still, feet apart, hands clasped behind his back, gun firmly in his holster at his side, his gaze fixed down the street into the heart of the village. The waiting had already become interminable. His heart could not stop pounding. What drew Gustav to his task this day was a personal passion that had burned for longer than he could remember. Over and over he told himself that if he had been waiting more than twenty years, he could wait for Sabina another hour. Now that he had opened the door to his desires, however, he was nearly mad with frustration and delirium.

"Where are they, Schlaukopf?" he demanded impatiently.

"Relax, Herr von Schmundt," replied the foxy one. "They will be here."

Two more different men could not have been chosen to carry out the task before them. In truth, they were not chosen at all, but both had willfully come here on their own, each seeing himself as the most capable to do what, in their warped imaginations, needed doing. Each perceived the other inadequate to conduct his part.

Whether or not he had inherited his keen sense of opportunism from his father and his wealthy upbringing hardly mattered to Gustav now. Since the coming of his manhood he had been working only on one side, his own. Communism was no different in that regard from the earlier dictatorship that had trained Gustav in his cunning and devious ways. At first it had been the SS, now it was the *Stasi*. But the duties of all assignments were of the same caliber, thriving upon the corrupt inner motives of their members.

It was ironic, he mused, that McCallum's side had won the war, and that for a period he and his fellow Nazis were made to beg for mercy at the hands of the American tyrants. But now the tables had been turned from the days when Allied troops had stormed Berlin. So much so, in fact, that Gustav, had he wanted, could have brought out half an army to command against the hated American. It was gratifying to know that Matthew McCallum was a fugitive in enemy land. *Yes,* he thought, *ironic indeed.*

Such thoughts gradually calmed his passion, though not his anxiety, as he glanced down to see his Swiss watch ticking away the completion of an hour.

Muttering a curse, he looked over at the man to his right.

I'll endure this fool for now, he thought to himself. *My reward will be having the American at my mercy and Sabina in my hands.*

"You must remember not to be anxious," Schlaukopf said after a few moments of silence. "I will meet them alone, at the end of the street. When they come into sight, they will stop. Then you must give me payment in full. I will then walk out to make initial contact, assuring them all is well."

"If I refuse to pay you?"

"I will wave them off."

"If I pay you and you get in their car and make a run for it?"

"Then you will chase us down with your helicopter and drop an explosive and kill me along with them."

Gustav was silent. The shrewd little man, though he distrusted every centimeter of his sleazy frame, thought of every angle. The eight thousand marks was in his pocket. It was a small price to pay for Sabina. Besides, he might just hunt down this weasel later, kill him, and get the money back.

As they fell silent again, Schlaukopf's malevolent thoughts began to course along similarly low and insidious mental tracks. He trusted the *Stasi* section chief no more than the German trusted him. Twelve thousand marks was a sizable stash of money, even if eight of them would be valueless in the West. He wasn't in the West, and here it was a small fortune.

This was the big opportunity he had been waiting for!

The only problem, he thought, was that his face was known to too many people. The only way for him to insure his own safety would be to kill them all somehow once he had the money securely in hand—the American, who had lied to him, the woman with him, who was prettier than any mortal deserved to be, and the prisoner, who was practically dead anyway. They would be easy. This *Stasi* agent, standing and fidgeting beside him, would be a greater challenge. He should probably wait a week or two . . . but he would have to be killed along with the rest.

The only one saying nothing was the boyish assistant to the section chief, the Russian Andrassy Galanov.

His thoughts were occupied with the secret drive he had made into the countryside only a few kilometers east of here several days earlier.

His boss had not confided in him. But then neither had he confided in his boss about what he had learned concerning the automobile from Warsaw they had been searching for. From listening to the two other men talk, however, and putting two and two together from his own investigations, he was certain who was in the automobile they were waiting for. There was no doubt the two women were one and the same. Whether today's activity had anything to do with the woman's questionable moves of the other afternoon he couldn't be sure.

He would continue to watch, observe, and listen. He had the

feeling something more than met the eye was at hand, and he didn't want to be the one caught looking the wrong way. If he was right, the clue to the photographs his uncle so desperately wanted was coming their way too. He would keep that tidbit of information to himself for now. He would see how this thing played itself out before committing himself.

Still they stood, the German, the Lithuanian, and the Russian—an unlikely and dubious alliance of night—awaiting the arrival of their three unsuspecting counterparts, three whose natures were of the day.

Hiding his own mounting anxiety, the fox stole a hasty glance downward at his watch.

They should have been here by now!

His fingers began to twitch at the thought of losing the ten thousand marks he still had to collect.

With every minute that passed, the clash between the light and the darkness drew ever nearer.

Change of Plans

. . .

MORE THAN AN HOUR HAD PASSED.

Still Matthew drove. The ride had been bumpy and long. Little conversation had passed between him and Sabina.

The baron continued to sleep peacefully, regaining strength internally by invisible degrees.

The dream of freeing Sabina's father, seemingly unattainable a few days before, had been accomplished. Yet both were absorbed in the reality of what perils still lay between them and freedom.

They had emerged from the *Heide* and were now bumping along a stony road. Güterfelde lay just ahead.

Matthew slowed as they entered the village. Passing the lake on their right, the rough cobblestones under them came to an end as they intersected the north-south highway connecting Stahnsdorf and Saarmund.

Matthew stopped, then turned left, easing his way onto the road, also of stones but somewhat smoother, which led through the heart of Güterfelde. Winding through the narrow streets, within five minutes they were leaving the last of its houses behind. Picking up speed once more, their route now lay north through Stahnsdorf and beyond to Teltow, the border, West Berlin . . . and freedom.

It would not be long now, thought Matthew. *They were on the home stretch!*

Behind him, Sabina's thoughts were occupied in a far different vein. They had just passed the turnoff to Grossbeeren. It would have been the most logical route for the carrying out of her plan.

But, she thought, *if* the fox was as cunning as she suspected and *if* he had reason to mistrust Matthew's veracity, that would be precisely the direction he might anticipate a double cross taking.

She could not be certain, therefore, that he would not be watching them, *even now,* to make sure they did as he had instructed.

She would wait until it was positive no invisible eyes were upon them. There were plenty of dirt roads by which they could make their way, either back to the highway or through the woods south of Mühlenberg to Ruhlsdorf, then south to Grossbeeren.

Approximately a third of the distance to Stahnsdorf, after one more glance at the desolate road behind them, suddenly Sabina spoke up from the backseat.

"Matthew, stop the car."

He glanced back with an expression of question on his face.

"Matthew, please," she repeated, "stop the car—immediately!"

He began to slow. "Is something wrong?" he asked.

Freeing her father from her embrace as gently as she could, Sabina readied herself to get out.

"No, nothing is wrong," she said. "But you must stop the car."

Matthew continued to brake. The instant they had come to a standstill, Sabina jumped out, closing the rear door behind her and opening the driver's door almost in the same motion.

"I must drive from here," said Sabina. "My father is still asleep. You may sit over on the other side."

"But . . . I don't—"

"Matthew, please," interrupted Sabina, "there is no time to lose. Just get out."

Confused and half-laughing, Matthew climbed out and walked around to the passenger side. Sabina was already in place by the time he closed the door. She ground the car into gear, accelerated rapidly, but within less than sixty seconds slowed quickly, then turned off onto a farm road to the right.

"What are you doing?" exclaimed Matthew, no longer laughing.

"Now it's my turn, like your fox, to say there has been a change of plans."

"Sabina, Teltow is our only safe way into Berlin, and the road to Teltow is straight ahead . . . back there."

"It may not be as safe as you think."

"You must turn back. It's the road we've got to take."

"There are many routes into Berlin," replied Sabina, pressing the automobile forward across the farmland toward the wooded hills ahead of them, though the way was pitted and rough, with as much speed as she dared. "If I read Herr Schlaukopf right, and believe me, I've met many like him, some trap awaits us at Teltow."

"That's impossible. He has to let us through if he wants the other half of his money."

"Something is wrong. I feel certain of it."

"Please, Sabina, you've got to turn around. Everything's been arranged."

"Matthew, you're going to have to trust me one more time. Now that we have my father, I'm not going to risk putting us into the hands of that man called the fox."

"You just have to know how to deal with him."

"He is evil through and through. I don't want to see him again. We are not going to Teltow. I'm sorry."

"Then how are we going to get back to Berlin? There could be roadblocks at all the other borders looking for us."

"I've made other arrangements for us."

"What! What kind of arrangements?"

"You'll just have to wait and find out. I am certain they will be safer than what is waiting for us back there."

"If we do not appear at Teltow with the rest of his money, Schlaukopf will come after us. He is a ruthless man."

"Exactly my point."

"He must be paid or our lives will be in danger ever after."

"You can drive back to Teltow from the American side," said Sabina. "I have no objection to you finding him and giving him the rest of his money. But I will *not* take my father near that man again while we are in the DDR. I tell you, Matthew, there was duplicity in his eyes. He is planning to betray us."

"It would appear I have a mutiny on my hands," said Matthew, attempting to laugh again.

"Let's just say that for the rest of the time we're in *my* country, I will be in charge," said Sabina. "The moment we cross into the American sector, I will gladly relinquish decision making back to *you*."

Confused and not knowing what to make of it, Matthew sat back and tried to take in the implications of this sudden new twist Sabina had thrown at him.

If he didn't know her so well—and trust her—he would think . . . well, he didn't know what he would think!

Forty-five minutes later the three fleeing pilgrims emerged from the hilly region east of Ruhlsdorf, Sabina still at the wheel, and were soon speeding southeast toward Grossbeeren.

75

Treachery at Teltow

• • •

IT HAD BEEN FAR, FAR TOO LONG.

Schlaukopf had secretly sensed treason on the part of the American some time ago, while outwardly maintaining his confident posture on behalf of the ranting East German section chief. But it had now reached the point where neither was fooled.

"You are a moron, Schlaukopf!" cried Schmundt at length, who had been pacing back and forth for several minutes. "How I let you talk me into this insane scheme—"

"The treachery is not mine," rejoined Schlaukopf, attempting to retain his composure, but with difficulty.

"Perhaps not, but the idiocy is yours!" shouted Gustav.

He had long since ceased trying to maintain his outward poise. It was obvious the plan had turned sour. The thought that Sabina was out there somewhere—and *close!*—with him standing here powerless to snatch her . . . the thought threatened to overpower him with wrath and lusting bitterness. He could hardly keep from exploding in passionate frustration and vile anger.

"And you will pay for your mistake!" he shouted, coming to a sudden decision to end the stalemate.

"Galanov!" he bellowed, turning toward his assistant, who was standing several meters away near the helicopter. "Bring two of your men and have this weasel transported back to Berlin in one of the cars. Keep him under armed guard until we return and I decide what is to be done with him. If he tries anything, instruct them to kill him."

"You cannot arrest me," rasped Schlaukopf in as agitated a voice

330

as his vocal cords were capable of, backing slowly away from the suddenly hostile interview. "I am still the only one who can deliver the American to you."

"You have failed, you miserable wretch!" shrieked Gustav. "It is *you yourself* you have placed into my hands, and I will see you rot in prison. As for the American, I will continue my search without you!"

"You cannot cheat me out of the money you promised!" yelled Schlaukopf. "You'll pay, one way or another."

"You will get nothing, Schlaukopf!"

Still moving away from his briefly temporary comrade, suddenly a great knife was in the fox's grasp, the glint of its lethal blade glistening in the sunlight.

With a menacing movement of the knife waving in the air against any thought of following, Schlaukopf backed hurriedly toward his auto. He would intercept the American on the road and take the money off his body, he was thinking to himself . . . *after* he had plunged his knife through his traitorous heart! Then he would come back and do in this scum of an East German!

"After him, Galanov!" shouted Gustav.

The young Russian came running from the direction of the helicopter.

Schlaukopf bolted for his car.

"Stop!" yelled Schmundt, but the command died in the air unheeded.

"Stop him!" he cried to his assistant. "Galanov, I order you to kill that man!"

Schlaukopf reached his car and threw open the door just as Galanov came running up. The fox turned and lunged toward him, waving his arm wildly. Behind them, Gustav now approached, staying behind his assistant with a cowardly authority.

"Galanov, kill this fool!" he screamed.

The Russian made a dash toward the little man. But his inexperience betrayed him. The next instant he staggered back, crying out in pain and grabbing at the wound flowing with blood from a deep gash in his arm.

The demon of crazed fury entered the fainthearted German.

Gustav tore the pistol from his hip, took several steps forward, and threw aside his young assistant as he wobbled backward, blood dripping down his arm.

The fox's lethal knife was no match for its enemy now.

The air exploded with several deafening shots, fired from a distance of no more than two meters.

The crafty one's body slammed backward into the car he had tried in vain to reach, blood spraying over his chest and onto the car seat behind him.

Even as the huge knife flew into the air, two more shots came in rapid succession.

Gustav stood as one paralyzed, pistol frozen in the mortal grip of his fingers, watching as the broken and bloody body slumped to the ground in front of the open car door, several gaping bullet holes disclosing the flesh ripped from his chest. Red poured over the slain man's clothes and down onto the grass near where the knife now lay stained but still.

Echoes of shouts and gunfire now died away.

A silence of death descended over the treacherous border crossing of Teltow.

Gustav slowly backed away from the murder he had committed, unable to tear his eyes from the grisly sight in front of him.

The pain in his forearm, whose bleeding he now managed to stop by wrapping the sleeve of his shirt tightly around it, sent keen jolts of acuity through young Galanov's brain.

Suddenly he saw the situation for what it was!

The deception had been wider-spread than his murdering boss or their dead colleague had realized.

The automobile they had all been waiting for was not bound for Teltow at all! By now it was many kilometers distant! He was himself the only one who knew where possibly to intercept it!

He turned and ran to his chief, who still stood stupidly numb at the scene before him.

"Come . . . come, Herr von Schmundt!" he urged, trying to wake his boss to the imperative and renewed need for haste. "They will get away if we do not intercept them."

"Get away . . . who . . . ?" mumbled Gustav.

"The American and the escaped prisoner. They are not coming here at all. We must hurry!"

"I do not . . . what do you—"

"I know where to locate them—if it is not already too late! Come—we must take the helicopter!"

By now he was pulling Gustav away and shouting out orders to his men where to follow them by automobile.

Within minutes the huge blades of the helicopter were whirring up a new frenzy of wind about the crossing gate below. The insectlike machine rose quickly off the ground, then slanted steeply at a downward angle as the pilot tilted his controls and sped southeastward, Galanov shouting directions for their search into his ear.

Thoughts of Fear

• • •

CLARA BRUMFELDT, OBEDIENT WIFE AND FAITHFUL
instructionist to the young scholars of Grossbeeren, had wanted
nothing to do with the network when it had formed after the war.

The loose arrangement her husband had found himself part of,
more by accident than design, during the Nazis' closing months of
power, had been acceptable, even necessary. His cousin Hermann's
life had been in danger, and if they had been swept up in more
lives than Hermann's, such involvements and risks were part of
what they called the fortunes of war.

But there had been no war since then. She knew there were
reports about the dictator Stalin's silent and invisible purges, but she
didn't believe it could be as bad as they said. They had taken care of
themselves all these centuries. Now they even had a country to call
their own again. Why couldn't those people take care of themselves?

So many had been through here during the years, the faces and
situations turned into a blur. Her husband and Hermann and gradually so many others came to be involved. Now their own son
Wilhelm, whom she still called Willy but who was capable of a man's
work, was caught up in it all with conviction and enthusiasm. She had
taught Willy his beliefs, but she had not intended for him to take them
so seriously as to risk his life for them!

She had never been able to understand Erich's compulsion to help
anyone in danger—no matter how much danger it also brought to
him and his son. But she was his wife, and she would do her part as
faithfully as she was able, though she had never totally accustomed
herself to it.

There was nothing she could do now but pray for their protection and pray that it would all be over soon and Willy and Erich would come home safe . . . and alone.

Praying at such times was always so hard. Her own anxieties threatened to overwhelm her thoughts of God.

But she would try.

Slowly she slipped from the chair and sank to her knees, bowing her head in the cup of her hands.

Clandestine Flight

• • •

THREE KILOMETERS OUTSIDE GROSSBEEREN, TWO AUTO-
mobiles raced across a wide dirt path between cultivated fields of
oats. Their destination was a brick-and-timber barn with a thatched
roof some half kilometer still ahead.

Had the helicopter of their pursuers begun its pursuit ten
minutes sooner, the dust flying into the air in the midst of the oats
to the east would have given away their position immediately. As
it was, however, the helicopter was six hundred precious seconds
behind them. The two sets of probing eyes in the glass bubble
below the clamoring blades gazed downward over only empty
wooded hills, scanning ahead for the orange roofs in the distance
that would tell them they were approaching their destination.

As had been arranged the evening of their discussion on the
bridge, when Sabina sped into the village, she saw the small green
Trabi with bent rear fender parked beside the road. How long father
and son had had to wait she didn't know, but such a rendezvous was
better than meeting at their house. That was a risk she did not want
to take, for Clara's sake, though she had no idea that the anonymity of
the Brumfeldt home had already been compromised by her visit of
several days ago.

A quick toot of the horn as she passed alerted Erich, who did not
know what kind of automobile to expect, that it was she. He pulled
out to follow some distance back.

Creeping her way through the village, Sabina slowed, allowing the
green Trabi to pass, following him eventually out of town to the east
toward the barn now ahead of them, where they would hide

Matthew's rental car until the network could arrange for its transport back to West Berlin.

Arriving at their destination, Erich stopped in great haste, sending still more dust spewing about from under the tires. Behind him, Sabina braked more slowly. By the time she reached the barn, young Wilhelm had already jumped out to open the two wide wooden doors, now motioning Sabina to continue into the black empty interior. A moment or two later Erich's tiny automobile followed, and in less than two minutes all were safely enclosed in the blackness, while Wilhelm made the doors once again fast behind them.

"The plot thickens!" said Matthew, astonished at the organization that had preceded their arrival, of which he had known nothing.

"I'm sorry, Matthew," said Sabina. "I thought it would be safer for you not to know. I had to devise some other means to get Papa back into Berlin besides whatever the fox might have had planned for us."

"And this, I take it," replied Matthew, "is it."

"Some of the friends I have told you about. Papa," she said, turning toward the back seat, "Papa, you must wake up. It is time for us to change vehicles."

She jumped out, opened the back door, and attempted to arouse him as Erich and his son walked up.

"Fräulein Duftblatt, this is my son Willy," said Erich.

"Ah, Wilhelm, your father says you are one of my great allies." Sabina smiled at the boy. "I cannot tell you how much we all appreciate everything you do—especially me . . . *today!* This is my own father here. I have not seen him before this day for seventeen years."

She stooped and leaned down into the backseat of the car.

"Come, Papa," she said, "if you can just get to your feet for a few moments, we will be on our way again."

Groggily the baron allowed Sabina to help him from the car. Supported by Sabina on one side and Matthew on the other, they led the baron to the white van waiting on the other side of the barn. The smells of straw and animals seemed to revive the baron, reminding him, like the rose earlier, of happy days at *Lebenshaus.* He squinted, glancing about in the thin light, to attempt to make sense of where he found himself, while submitting like a docile child to his daughter's leading and instructions.

Another figure, dressed in white from head to toe, emerged from behind the waiting vehicle and now opened its back door. Matthew leapt up and inside, then stooped down to take hold of the baron's shoulders as best he could. With Sabina steadying him from behind, Matthew pulled the baron up and inside, where he was immediately overwhelmed by yet another familiar smell, the aroma of fresh-baked loaves of dark rye bread.

Sabina jumped up and inside to join them. They helped the baron to lie down as best he could, spreading on the floor the thin linen blanket that had helped their escape with their own outer garments over him. The next instant the door slammed shut and they found themselves in near darkness while Erich jumped into the seat in front on the passenger side of the van.

The engine roared to life.

Again the barn door opened. The van sped through and across the oat field along a well-rutted wagon route to the north, while behind them Willy removed his father's green Trabi, shut and locked all the barn's doors, then began a slow drive back to the village.

Half of the six hundred seconds had been consumed.

78

Cruel Search

• • •

A STRANGE AERIAL SOUND, DISTANT AT FIRST BUT approaching with a chilling whirr of omen, echoed outside, but the brain of brave Erich Brumfeldt's good wife was too full of prayerful angst to absorb the meaning of the sound.

"God," she prayed, "Cause your will to be done this day. Keep your servants in the care of your mighty hand. Let the father of Fräulein Duftblatt find safety, and let no harm come to my—"

Suddenly the stillness of the small room shattered with the crash of a door opening.

Booted feet thundered across the floor.

Glancing up in fright, the barrel of a rifle met Clara's gaze.

"Where are they!" demanded a voice.

"I don't . . . who—," she stammered in dread.

"You know who—the prisoner, the American!"

"I don't know who you—"

Clara never completed her words. The butt of Galanov's rifle thudded against her side, knocking her sideways to the floor. She screamed in pain from two broken ribs. New footsteps approached, and the next instant a fisted grip yanked her to a sitting position.

"We know they were here, woman!" shouted Gustav. "Tell us where they have gone, or we will kill you!"

The young Russian with the knife-wounded arm stepped back and now began to search the room.

Paralyzed in fear and pain, poor Clara was dumb with terror. The front of Gustav's hand slapped across her jaw. Blood immediately flowed from her lip and nose.

"Tell us, you old hag, or breathe your last!" shrieked Gustav, whacking her again and sending the lithe woman's body bouncing cruelly onto the floor. The violent spirit of murder had consumed him at last.

"Herr von Schmundt," called Galanov.

Gustav heard nothing. Already he had bent down to seize the woman again with his left hand. His right had closed in a tight fist and was raised to strike.

"Herr von Schmundt!" repeated his assistant loudly. "Leave her."

Gustav heard this time, glancing back over his shoulder.

"Leave her—it is unnecessary. I know the car from earlier. It was not outside. We can locate it from the air. And there is a name here," he said, holding a scrap of paper.

Gustav stood and ran toward him, snatching up the note.

"*Meier!*" he said. "What does this mean?" he yelled down to the figure on the floor.

A moan was the only sound of reply.

Again Gustav approached her threateningly.

"Look," cried Galanov, still rummaging about. "A bag of *Brötchen—Bäkerei Meier . . . Heinersdorf!*"

Within seconds the accelerating blades of the helicopter sounded outside.

The tiny house was empty again, the crumpled heap of its occupant lying bleeding, broken, and quietly sobbing on the floor.

Thus Willy found his mother when he returned only minutes later.

He bandaged her wounds as best he could, helped her to her bed, and made her as comfortable as possible. Then he left the house again, and in his father's green Trabi sped out of the village northward, on the road to Heinersdorf.

It would probably be too late, he thought. But he had to see if there was anything left he could do to help.

79

Bäkerei Meier

. . .

THE DISTANCE BETWEEN GROSSBEEREN AND HEINERSDORF
was only some six or seven kilometers due north.

Had the helicopter of death been a few minutes sooner, its speed
would have overtaken the van of life en route. It covered the distance,
however, observing nothing, neither of the two passengers scanning
the countryside below with binoculars realizing how warm indeed
was the scent of the trail they sought.

"There is the village—get as low as you can," barked Gustav to
the pilot, moving his magnified eyes back and forth across the
buildings below as rapidly as he could.

"There it is!" he cried. "Set it down!"

The pilot instantly dove the machine skillfully toward the ground.

"Now we will find where the vermin have gone," cried Gustav as
the two jumped to the ground and ran to the storefront whose sign
they had observed.

The bakery door crashed open, breaking several panes of glass.

Seeing the gun waving in the hand of the uniformed official, the
poor young lady behind the counter did her best to stifle the scream
that erupted from her lips at the sound.

Two or three other customers in the shop, one a lady with two
small children, backed terrified toward a corner.

"Where is your owner!" shouted Gustav, still waving the pistol
about.

"Herr . . . Herr . . . ," stammered the young lady.

"Yes, you idiot—Herr Meier! Where is he!"

"He is . . . making deliveries."

"In what kind of vehicle?" demanded Galanov.

"He . . . there is a van. . . ."

"Where are his deliveries!" demanded Galanov.

"I, uh . . . I don't know . . . Grossbeeren, I think."

"You are lying!" growled Gustav, approaching now with look of evil intent.

Unable to contain her fear any longer, a scream escaped from the lady's mouth.

Gustav stepped toward her, but she retreated, and he was unable to strike her across the counter.

"Back to the helicopter!" said Galanov. "There can be no doubt now—they are making for the border. . . . It is only two or three kilometers!"

The two men ran out of the shop.

"North to the border!" Schmundt shouted to the pilot as he and Galanov raced across the ground and jumped into the idling helicopter. "If you see a bakery van, stop it at all costs! If they resist, Galanov," he added to his assistant, "shoot to kill!"

Twenty seconds later they were aloft again, screaming at a height of only twenty or thirty meters above the northward road out of Heinersdorf.

80

Good and Evil

• • •

"HOW MUCH FARTHER IS IT?" SAID MATTHEW THROUGH the tiny opening into the cab from the cargo hold of the van.

"Less than a kilometer," replied Brumfeldt, glancing back.

"How will we get across the border?"

"I make deliveries twice a week to homes just on the other side," replied Herr Meier. "I have been traveling this route for many years. We will not even be stopped."

Matthew leaned back and sat down on the floor beside Sabina. She slipped her hand through his arm and snuggled close. Her father again slept, and at last she allowed herself to relax. They were in the hands of faithful friends now.

The engine of the van reverberated loudly in their ears, though in the midst of it Matthew began to discern the approach of another sound he recognized but at first could not make sure of.

He glanced up.

Suddenly he knew what it was. Panic seized him. There could be no mistake!

He rose to a crouch on his feet, then made his way uneasily to the back of the van. Steadying himself, he pushed down the latch and opened one of the two rear doors a crack to peer out.

Approaching rapidly from behind and at a height only slightly above them, a helicopter screamed toward them.

• • •

"That's it—that's the van!" shouted Galanov, pointing ahead of them, *"Bäkerei Meier* is painted on the side. They're making for the crossing!"

"Get ahead of them!" yelled Gustav to the pilot. "Set down in front of it and cut it off!"

Slanting downward, the pilot flew over the roof of the van, then angled sharply to the right, descended, and set down on the cobblestones directly in front of the approaching van.

Herr Meier yanked the wheel hard, swerving off the road and bumping along rudely in the open field beside it.

In the darkened compartment behind, Sabina let out a scream. Matthew, who had just relocked the door, fell hard from his feet. Loaves toppled over them. The baron was knocked sideways against the side of the interior, awakening with dull groans of confusion.

Jamming the accelerator to the floor, the skillful baker wielded his jostling bakery van around the helicopter, bouncing and tottering back onto the road.

"After them!" screamed Gustav.

Instantly the machine was aloft again, once more screaming overhead and by the speeding white van.

Rapidly the chase bore down upon the border, only some eight hundred meters in front of them.

"This time they will not get around us!" cried Gustav, grabbing a grenade from the helicopter's store of weapons. "Get in front of them but remain airborne!" he said, pulling the pin with his left hand from the grenade he grasped tightly in his right.

Again the pilot angled perpendicular to the road beneath them. Gustav leaned out of the cockpit, took aim, then threw the explosive toward the van, heedless now of the thought that he was attempting to kill the very woman he had tried to convince himself all these years he loved.

The van was coming too fast. The grenade landed on the road behind it, exploding with deafening harmlessness.

A great oath of fury burst from Gustav's mouth.

Within seconds the van had again passed them, rumbling now toward the border only two hundred meters away.

The pilot angled left, passing the vehicle quickly again. Another grenade was already in Gustav's hand. He pulled the pin and this time did not wait until they were ahead of it but dropped it as they swept only a meter or two overhead.

Seeing the foolhardy move that could explode helicopter as well as van, the pilot yanked back and leftward on the control lever, sending his helicopter high and away. His quick reaction kept them from the heart of the blast but was not sufficient to pull them entirely to safety.

Gustav's rash and ill-advised throw this time found its mark.

• • •

The grenade hit the ground about four meters in front of Herr Meier's speeding van, exploding into a fireball of red and orange.

Unable to control it, Herr Meier caught the front of the van directly in the explosion. The front left tire and a portion of the frame blew into the air. It careened dangerously to the right and off the road.

He could see out of the left corner of his eye the helicopter rocking dangerously from the blast beneath it and starting to spin out of control toward the ground.

The van left the road, tilting momentarily on its front and back right tires, then twisted in a grotesque circular motion and finally toppled with a loud banging crash over onto its side, sliding and bumping to a smoky stop.

Inside the cargo compartment, the three passengers were tossed about like the loaves of bread. Aware of Sabina's screams behind him, Brumfeldt saw the more immediate danger to the driver, Herr Meier, whose face and chest were covered with blood from wounds caused by the shattered glass.

Reaching over him from his position where the passenger door lay flat on the ground, Brumfeldt managed to force open the door and shove the semiconscious baker up and out, where he toppled down in a heap onto the earth. He climbed out, quickly surveyed the scene, apprehended the danger from the smoking engine, then dragged the baker across the grass and away from his van.

Running back, now he saw the helicopter spinning toward what seemed a certain crash, its dying blades mingled with the sound of screams and cries for help from the three trapped inside the back of the overturned van.

With difficulty he threw open the latch, releasing the jammed back doors.

"Get out . . . get out quickly!" he cried.

Sabina's father did not move. Matthew, whose own leg was broken, though he knew it not at the time, was struggling to pull the baron to safety.

Matthew jumped out, landing on the foot of his fractured leg. Crying out in pain, he collapsed on the ground. Behind him, Erich had pulled the terrified Sabina out of the van and was now carrying the limp frame of the baron, whether alive or dead he didn't know, in his arms.

"Run . . . get away!" called Erich to Sabina. "The van is about to blow apart!"

Matthew rose on unsteady feet, then took a step toward Sabina. Already she was running as best she could, followed by Brumfeldt with the baron in his arms.

"Matthew . . . Matthew, come!" cried Sabina, glancing back and seeing his difficulty.

He tried to run, crumbling again on his nearly useless leg.

Witnessing his desperation, Sabina stopped, turned, and ran back toward him.

"No—Sabina—run!" cried Matthew. "Don't wait for me. I'll catch you!"

Again he gained his feet, hobbling forward.

Sabina continued toward him.

Matthew was running now, bent over in pain, managing somehow to keep his feet under him.

"*Matthew . . . !*" he heard Sabina's voice call out. But he had no chance to reply.

A blast sounded behind him as the helicopter struck the ground. Its explosion only a few meters away set off the gas tank of the van, which now thundered like a fireball high into the sky.

The blast knocked Matthew to the ground onto his face.

Sabina was thrown backward into the air from the explosion, then fell to the ground motionless.

"*Sabina . . . !*" cried Matthew, looking toward her only a short distance away. She lay on the ground as one dead. He rose to go to her.

An afterblast now sounded from one of the burning vehicles. A searing heat ripped through his back and head, knocking Matthew off his feet again. The next instant he toppled to the ground.

Aware of only confusion, great pain in his skull, and descending darkness, Matthew struggled to raise his head. He tried to look around.

There was Sabina where he had last seen her. Not a muscle of her broken body had moved.

With great effort Matthew attempted to crawl. But he could only manage a short distance before his arms gave way and he collapsed again, his head exploding with violent throbs.

Eyes barely open, he stretched up his neck, seeking to find her.

"Sabina . . . !" was the only word he could whisper before he himself descended into blackness.

PART IV

A Rose
Remembered

August—December 1961

The Fragrance of *Rosen*

• • •

A WHITE-CLAD NURSE WALKED DOWN A LONG COR-
ridor, clipboard in hand, stethoscope hanging from her neck.

She passed three or four closed doors, then stopped, opened one,
and walked in.

"Good morning," she said, greeting her patient where he lay.

No response came from the bed.

Indeed, she expected none. Bandages covered most of his head
and came down over his shoulders, and his left leg was raised in a
heavy cast of plaster. He had scarcely spoken since being brought to
the facility five days earlier, unconscious and as near death as possible
to be while yet breathing.

"Time for your blood pressure and temperature," said the nurse
cheerfully.

A slight movement from the bed to accommodate her wishes was
the only signal of life from the inanimate and prostrate form.

That the eyes were cognizant of their surroundings and that the
mouth surrounded by white gauze linen was capable of movement,
were indicated by the opening of the latter a crack to receive the
thermometer as the nurse's hand approached.

"That's it . . . now just let me slip this under your arm," she said,
"and we'll get your blood pressure."

Setting the stethoscope to her ears and the inside of the patient's
elbow, she listened intently while slowly releasing the air with her
thumb and forefinger.

"One-twenty over ninety-four—very good. Everything is coming along nicely. Did you sleep well?"

A slight nod, all the bandages would allow, was the patient's answer.

"Have you remembered anything since waking?"

The slow movement of the head this time went the opposite direction.

"Ah, well, it will all come back in time. Let's see how that temperature is."

She reached forward, removed the thermometer, read it, picked up her clipboard from the foot of the bed, jotted down the two sets of numbers, then turned to go.

"The doctor will be in to see you presently," she said, then left the room.

She met the doctor halfway down the corridor as he emerged from another room.

"How's the new fellow doing?" he asked.

"Vital signs good," replied the nurse. "No changes otherwise. Have you found out who he is yet?"

"No, but we may have something by tomorrow. We're checking fingerprints through Bonn, Washington, and Interpol, and I turned over the things he had on him to the authorities."

"Are you going to talk to him again?"

"I'll try. Some of the wrapping can come off this afternoon too, which should make it easier, if he's so inclined."

"Will you show him the newspaper?"

"I don't know," replied the doctor hesitantly. "Timing is crucial in cases like this. I've got to make sure I do it at just the right moment, otherwise he could regress even deeper. I've got to get him talking first, and then see if the article and picture bring his memory the rest of the way up."

The nurse continued on down the hall, while the doctor walked in the opposite direction, entering the room she had recently left.

Later that afternoon, the doctor returned, this time accompanied by a nurse and the hospital's burn specialist. They were with the patient an hour, during which time several of the bandages over the most minor wounds were removed and the dressings changed to allow their continued healing exposed to the air.

At length doctor and patient were alone again.

"Does that feel better?" asked the doctor.

The man nodded.

"I'm sorry, but some of the others will have to remain in place another week or so."

"I understand," replied the patient in what amounted to little more than a low whisper.

"How about the leg?"

"All right . . . itches some," came the throaty murmur.

"Yes," chuckled the doctor. "The curse of the cast, as they say. Any other pain I should know about?"

"Only the head."

"Yes, I know. I hope that will be better by tomorrow."

The doctor paused, then asked, "Would you feel more like telling me what happened today?"

"Can't . . . ," said the man.

"Can't?" repeated the doctor.

"Don't remember."

"It would help with the treatment if I know what had caused the explosion."

The head from the bed slowly shook sideways. "Can't remember, Doctor," the man said. "Running . . . yells . . . screams . . . then here . . ."

The doctor listened, pondering his words, revolving in his mind how best to attempt entrance into that most mysterious place in all the universe—the subconscious human mind.

"You had some money in your jacket . . . ," he said at length, then paused.

The patient seemed unresponsive to the information.

". . . A good deal, as a matter of fact," the doctor went on. "Something over two thousand marks. Do you have any recollection why you might have been carrying that kind of money?"

"Sorry, Doctor."

"There was no other identification, so I'm afraid I'm as much at a loss as you are yourself."

Again the doctor paused. He did not want to push too hard. He was far from an expert at these sorts of things. If there wasn't a breakthrough within another day or two, he would call in a psychiatrist.

"There *was* a car rental receipt," he said after a moment. "Do you remember renting a car?"

The bandaged head went slowly back and forth.

"Unfortunately, there was no car such as the slip indicated anywhere around. We went to the agency, showed them the tag, and were given a name. However, some further checking indicated it to be fictitious. No record of any such person exists. So I'm afraid without some information on this mysterious Herr Rosen whose name appears on the rental, we have nothing much to go on . . . and the car still hasn't been found."

"Rosen . . . ," repeated the patient, ". . . sounds like 'rose.'"

"Yes, that's the meaning of it—Mr. Roses. Do you speak German?"

"I . . . I don't know. . . . I think maybe I do."

"Do you think *you* might perhaps be this Herr Rosen?"

"I . . . I don't know. It . . . it sounds familiar to me . . . but . . ."

"But what?"

"The name . . . the word . . ."

"Rosen?"

The man nodded slowly.

"You like roses, I take it?" asked the doctor.

A lengthy pause followed.

"Yes . . . yes, I think I do like roses, Doctor. . . . I'm not sure why."

"Well, I don't want to tax you too greatly this afternoon," said the doctor, rising. A sudden thought had just occurred to him. He was a physician of the body, not the mind, but he knew the power of subtleties to infiltrate the subconscious where more direct tactics sometimes failed.

Outside the room he walked briskly down the corridor. Reaching the nurse's station, he announced his plan.

"Get someone to put a vase or two of roses in that room," he said, indicating the unknown patient with burns and fractured leg. "Get them from the grounds, from some other room that doesn't need them—have some sent in from a florist if you have to . . . aromatic roses."

"What color, Doctor?"

"I don't care . . . perhaps a mixture. Just make sure they have a strong perfume. I want that room reeking with the fragrance of roses."

• • •

The subtle aromas permeating the sick chamber gradually carried out their delicate persuasions.

The night was filled with dreams undefined, of faces whose features would not quite come into focus, of places familiar but distant.

The way before him was steep and difficult. All around were trees whose branches were like long arms reaching to grab at him, preventing him from getting to the top.

Struggling, he labored on, sometimes atop a great, slow-moving equine beast, then again on his own feet trying to run but slowed by the steepness of the way and by the many trees—arms snatching and grabbing and blocking the path.

All around, the forest smelled like spring . . . wonderful aromas of grasses and flowers and sunshine beating upon the forest floor of dying needles. But whenever he glanced down, his feet were mired in the mud of winter. Everywhere were signs of desolation. This was a terrible land, he thought as he trudged ever upward, where the smell of life filled the air, but where spring never came.

Where did the fragrance originate? Surely not from this mud, from these hard and leafless and unfriendly branches.

The way began to ease . . . a thinning of the trees . . . a lessening of the upward slope. He could walk more easily now . . . yes, his feet moved more rapidly. The mud was not so thick . . . and the air seemed warming.

He quickened his pace.

He was running now. Oh, how good it felt!

He looked down. Wonder of wonders—his feet sped along a green, grassy heath!

Glancing about, he suddenly realized the trees were gone. He had emerged from out of the unfriendly forest of winter and was cresting the hill up which he had been toiling so long.

Spring *had* come!

He had outrun the winter behind him. Try though it might, it would not catch him now!

Here was growth and green and loveliness. Bees and birds sounded in his ears. The air was warm with fresh rays from the sun. The springy turf rebounded from each indentation of his step from the great thickness of the grass.

The fragrance was stronger now. He was approaching what appeared the peak.

Suddenly in the distance two faint figures came into view.

He ran toward them, increasing his pace. Some sense told him they were in danger—the mud and trees and branches and cold of winter were after them, seeking to overtake them. It was the two figures ahead it wanted, not him!

He had to help them . . . save them . . . rescue them . . . get them safely away from this place so that the evil forest could not grab and consume them.

Faster he ran.

"Stop!" he cried. "Stop! Let me help you."

They were now running too, fleeing for their lives. With horror he realized that they were running *from him!* They did not know their greatest peril lay elsewhere.

"Stop!" he cried again, "I am a friend." His voice died in the air.

The distance between lessened. He was catching them. He would overtake and make them understand.

Suddenly his brain was filled with the powerful aroma of the place again. It grew mightier the closer he came. Now he realized—it originated from one of the two figures ahead. It was not the smell of springtime, it was the fragrance of . . . of something else . . . of . . . he knew what it was, but he couldn't remember!

It came from just ahead.

It was the *fragrance* the winter was trying to capture!

Winter hated the aroma of the wide velvety petals when they opened to receive the rays of their Creator. The winter sought to destroy that which cannot be destroyed. He had to protect her . . . protect the fragrance . . . protect the petals.

Exhausted, he opened his mouth to call out again.

But his voice was gone. He would have to catch them, though still they ran, as for dear life, from him.

Closer . . . closer . . .

At last he reached them. He would tell them . . . he would explain . . . they were safe now . . . safe from the winter . . . the fragrance would not be destroyed.

He stretched out a hand to touch the shoulder, to let them know he was a friend.

Overtaken at last, they stopped.

With sudden loathing, he saw that the arm he had reached out to them had become the stiff greenless branch of a gnarled woody tree. She whom he had been chasing ceased her flight, not because of a friendly touch, but because she realized the futility of fighting her pursuer any longer.

He glanced down.

The thick lush sward had given way again to oozing brown mud.

A sudden chill swept through him.

What had become of his legs? Where were his feet? Why did he see below him only the thick trunk of a forest tree?

Most hideous horror—*he* had become a tree of winter!

He had not rescued them. . . . He had himself *brought* the winter to overtake, consume . . . and kill them.

The shoulder caught now in the grasp of his branchy grip slowly turned.

The face was coming into view. If he could just look, for an instant, into the eyes of its owner . . . surely then he could make her understand.

But he was now a tree. He had no eyes. Yet—strange to tell—he could yet see.

She turned her face at last toward him.

Aghast, he sought to scream from the ghoulish sight!

The face was blank. . . . There were no eyes . . . no nose . . . no mouth . . . no cheekbones . . . no ears. It was formless and void . . . an unperson whom he could not see and did not know.

Winter had killed the individuality of the face, and it was no more.

Suddenly winter was everywhere. . . . The fragrance of spring had vanished. . . .

Darkness swept over the land.

Attempting to scream, his faceless and voiceless tree trunk could only gnarl itself into twisted silent contortions of wooden futility. . . .

With a dull groan, he sat halfway up in bed just as the door opened and the nurse entered the room. He was breathing heavily, drenched in a cold sweat, struggling to give expression to a panicky voice that was utterly mute.

Sensing his state, the nurse hastened forward to calm her patient.

"Easy," she soothed. "You've been dreaming. It's morning now, you may relax."

Slowly he recovered himself, breathing deeply but gradually more evenly, lying back down under the pressure of the nurse's hand.

"Do you think you might like to try eating some gelatin this morning," she asked, "now that you're feeling better?"

"Yes . . . yes, that would be nice," he replied after a moment, drawing in a heavy lungful of air.

"The doctor says we might try to get you outside in a wheelchair today. He thought you would enjoy the fresh air, and it's been very warm and lovely out."

She proceeded to rearrange him, while attending to the morning duties of checking his temperature, blood pressure, and IV.

"Nurse," came the voice from the bed after a moment or two, "what's that I smell?"

"Oh, it's the roses," she replied. "I brought them in last evening. After your talk yesterday, the doctor thought you would enjoy them."

82

A Rose Called *Peace*

• • •

THE WARM SUN WITHIN THE ENCLOSED GROUNDS OF the hospital's courtyard was especially active this day, lifting from the earth the sweet aromas of the green grass that had been cut only yesterday. The doctor in charge of the case had wheeled the patient outside half an hour earlier, and after some brief dialogue had left him to enjoy the warmth alone. He was hopeful this day would signal a breakthrough.

A few other wheelchaired patients sat nearby, two or three walked about with canes or crutches, and a bevy of nurses were scattered through the spacious garden to accommodate whatever needs any of them might have.

After some forty minutes, the doctor returned, greeted the patient again, then proceeded to wheel him gently about, being especially careful for the cast that hung over the end of the footrest.

"How are you feeling now that you've had the chance to breathe some genuine sunshine?" the doctor asked.

"I feel much better today," said the man, his voice soft but its normal timbre returning rapidly. "Now that I can open my eyes all the way and move my lips, I feel almost alive again."

"Wonderful. The nurse says you ate some breakfast."

"It tasted good—even if it was only gelatin."

"You sound encouraged."

"They tell me I should be grateful to be alive."

"That's not altogether inaccurate. You had some pretty severe burns—explosive burns—and a tremendous concussion. That's the source, I'm sure you are aware, of the temporary amnesia."

"You say *temporary*, Doctor," said the patient, with the first hint of something resembling humor the doctor had yet seen. "Do you use that word for my benefit, or do you truly think such to be the case?"

"Ninety-nine percent of the time it's a matter of but a few days, maybe a week or two, before memory filters back. However, the wound on the back of your head will probably keep you well supplied with headaches for six months . . . but yes, you are alive, and I think we should both be very thankful."

"The better I feel, though, the more I hurt."

The doctor laughed.

"That's normal. The drugs wear off and your body begins coming to itself. Before long it starts to notice all those places where things are wrong. Pain, however, can be a hopeful sign of health. I don't know what to say—you're going to have discomfort for a while—it's part of the recovery process."

The doctor led the way to the edge of the lawn.

"We cultivate several varieties of roses," he said casually, pointing the wheelchair toward the thorny bushes as he spoke. "Do, uh . . . do you have a favorite?"

"Not that I'm aware of," replied the patient. "That's a very pretty yellow one there. . . . Come to think of it, it seems I am partial to yellow."

"Here, let me pick one for you," said the doctor, walking over and clipping a newly opened bud with about ten inches of stem. He handed it to the patient, who, with difficulty, lifted his hand to take hold of it.

"It's called *Peace,* one of the few yellow varieties with a strong perfumy fragrance—*if* it gets plenty of sunshine. It was hybridized in 1945 and named for the war's end. It's always been one of my favorites."

The patient said nothing but sat staring at the perfectly formed rose in his lap as if trying to draw out of it some story it knew but was reluctant to divulge.

As he sat in silence, an aide walked out of the hospital and approached, handing the doctor the two pages of a report that had just come to the hospital by special courier.

He scanned it for several moments, then set it in the pouch at the back of the wheelchair and spoke.

"Tell me," he said, "does the name *McCallum* mean anything to you?"

The patient continued thoughtful, though now with active involvement of crinkled eyebrows and forehead.

"Something does stir inside me at the name," he said after a minute, "though I can't tell what. Do you have some information on whoever it is? Am I supposed to know him?"

"I don't know," answered the doctor. "I was hoping you might tell me."

"Could you . . . perhaps they might come here . . . we could ask if they know who I am . . . how I got here."

"We know how you got here," said the doctor. "We're just not sure what you were doing at the border station, or who the fellow was who got you there. They called us here at Marienfelde immediately, and we sent an ambulance out for you."

"Hmm . . . ," mumbled the patient, slowly shaking his head. "I don't remember a thing of what you're talking about."

"How could you? You were unconscious for the next three days. For the first two we weren't sure you were going to live."

"Who was it that took me to the border station?"

"We don't know. Suddenly he appeared on foot, carrying you, yelled at the guards—ours, you understand: Americans, on our side— that they had to get you to a hospital. He set you down, then ran off, back into the DDR, and disappeared before anyone could ask him a single question. . . . No recollection of how you got into his hands?"

The patient shook his head.

"They'd seen several explosions, of course, off across the way two or three hundred meters from the crossing. It undoubtedly had to do with that."

"Explosions?"

The doctor nodded.

"From what?"

"Why don't I tell you what I know this afternoon. I'm not anxious to tax that aching head of yours *too* much all at once."

The doctor pulled back on the handles and eased the wheelchair around and away from the roses. With the yellow rose in his lap and the name McCallum filtering through his brain, he judged the poor man had plenty to occupy his thoughts for the present.

He would show him the newspaper later.

•   •   •

It was half past three when the doctor again entered the patient's room. He had had the chance to go over the file that had arrived that morning in detail and was pretty certain he would be able to guide their conversation into avenues where he hoped familiarity would be the result.

"Have you had any more luck with the name McCallum?" he asked as he walked in.

"None beyond the sense that it's a name I know . . . or at least ought to know."

"I've brought something for you to look at," said the doctor, opening the file he held and removing a folded section of newspaper from several days earlier. He handed it to the patient lying again in bed with his leg elevated, then sat down beside him and waited.

As he glanced over the page, at first with casual detachment, a gradual heightening of interest began to appear over his facial characteristics. Before long he was reading every word, pausing every so often to scan, then rescan, the photograph and headlines.

As he did, his brain began to reel in a phantasm of frenetic half-recognition, even as words and phrases from out of the doctor's own mouth echoed in his ear:

. . . Explosions . . . concussion . . . McCallum . . . two hundred meters from the crossing . . . unconscious . . . yellow rose . . . McCallum . . . rented car . . .

Suddenly his dream from the previous night came back to him . . . *two figures running . . . trying to help . . . trying to escape . . .*

The newspaper page began to grow hazy, its words and pictures blurring together, now spinning around in his brain.

More words from the doctor's voice bombarded him:

. . . Do you know German . . . ? roses . . . McCallum . . . escape . . . Herr Rosen . . . fictitious name . . . explosions . . . escape . . . McCallum . . .

Over and over came the words—*escape . . . McCallum . . . roses . . . explosions . . . escape . . . McCallum . . . McCallum . . .*

Suddenly the article before him sprang off the page with clarity of recognition. His eyes opened wide in stunned wakefulness, and his mind at last absorbed the scene as it was described by the West Berlin daily headline: FIVE TO EIGHT KILLED IN FIERY BORDER

CHASE. Underneath, a photograph showed wreckage of what was described as an official DDR helicopter attached to the Berlin headquarters of the *Staatssicherheitsdienst,* and a half-exploded overturned white van, on whose charred upturned side could barely be read the words *Bäkerei Meier.*

With face pale, cold, and perspiring, slowly he pulled his gaze away from the paper and glanced over at the doctor.

"It is as you suspected," he said slowly, half shaking his head as if to shake all its scrambled pieces back into place. *"McCallum* is me. . . . I remember now. I am Matthew McCallum. I am an American, and . . . yes, I was here," he added, indicating the picture he held.

He turned back to the paper and again began to read, suddenly with keen and fearful attention to every detail. The report was dated August 11, 1961.

> *In what appears to have been a dramatic but unsuccessful flight to the border of the American sector of West Berlin north of Heinersdorf, officials from the Staatssicherheitsdienst of the DDR pursued an East German delivery truck to the border by helicopter. While American border guards looked on, the helicopter swooped low, discharging explosives from the air, forcing the van from the road, where it overturned, apparently hit, and exploded. Only seconds later, the helicopter, for reasons which are still unclear, also crashed to the ground.*
>
> *The incident intensified growing tension between East and West, revealing the mounting desperation on the part of East Germans to find a way, whatever the danger, into West Berlin. Within the first ten days of this month, nearly 20,000 East Berliners have fled their homes to take up new residence in the western sectors of the city. It appears that the DDR, under orders from the Kremlin, is preparing to take stronger measures to stem this tide, the result of which seems certain from this incident three days ago to mean increased violence and bloodshed.*
>
> *Tensions continue between U.S. President John F. Kennedy and Soviet Premier Nikita S. Khrushchev, though neither the White House nor the Soviet news agency Tass has released a statement concerning this latest border incident. Neither*

Secretary of State Dean Rusk nor presidential envoy to Berlin
Matthew McCallum could be reached for comment.

Officials of the DDR have not made public full details of
the crash and have sealed off the site, though aerial photographs
for this paper were obtained. Investigations indicate that the
pilot of the helicopter and his passenger, an unnamed official,
were both killed. The number of passengers in the van has not
been determined. Officials from the DDR report only that there
were no survivors from the attempt. Estimates range from three
to six deaths among the escapees in all, but no official reports
have been released.

Whether the incident is isolated, or connected in some way with
the events of an hour earlier at Teltow crossing, has also not been
determined. Rumors are circulating concerning the unidentified
body of a man at that location thought to have participated in
an escape attempt at the high-security DDR prison at Neustädt
in Potsdam. Official reports indicate that the attempt was dis-
covered and all the conspirators other than the dead man captured.
Several bodies were reported delivered to the morgue at Potsdam
late in the day, though their origin has not been made public.

Links between the three incidents south of Berlin, if any,
have not been ascertained at this time.

By the time the paper fell from Matthew's hand, his face was white
and his body was trembling.

So, he thought, *there had been danger at Teltow—Sabina had been*
right, though what difference did it make now?

It would have been better to remain unremembering. He had
awakened only to discover his whole world crumbling before his sight!

He glanced away, closing his eyes, which were already filling with
tears.

Sensing what he had uncovered, and that this was no time for
further conversation, the doctor rose and quietly left the room.

•   •   •

The remainder of the afternoon of remembrance Matthew spent
alone. How the time passed he never knew. He lay in his bed as one

dead, with only his memory kept alive, swimming in the deepest sorrow known to mankind—the loss of love.

Thankfully, he slept well that night. He scarcely could have endured the silent lonely hours of blackness had the mercy of God not brought the gift of sleep to temporarily overwhelm his grief. The thought of Sabina's lifeless form lying on the ground a few meters away would surely have broken his spirit unto the very death of his own broken flesh before morning.

The next morning, the merciful grace of the Father remained near his son Matthew McCallum. With first wakefulness, the streams of sunlight pouring down from a high window into his room reminded Matthew that God was still in the heavens, that his love still shone upon the earth, and that rays of it still fell upon him as well.

The revelation came in an instant and was followed the next second by the torturing reminder of his grief. Yet, though reason told him to mourn, still the rays of sun shone through the window as if compelling him to a deeper response—commanding remembrance of the Father's faithfulness and goodness, in spite of earthly appearances to the contrary.

The sunlight seemed to speak of life, not death. Perhaps she had not been killed after all! Perhaps this was God's way of sending him a ray of hope, a message from on high not to give up. How did he know whether the reports were true? The Communists were famous for doctoring the news to reflect their own propagandist purposes.

He would investigate further the moment he was able! He had contacts, resources. He would get in touch with people he knew in the State Department. They would find out. He was certain he would find that Sabina was still alive!

A wave of doubt and gloom suddenly swept away the momentary sunny optimism.

Whom was he trying to fool? He had heard the explosion. It had ripped the skin off half his own back. He had nearly been killed himself!

With a shiver he relived the final moments he could remember. She was running toward him. She had been facing the blast. How could she possibly have survived it!

There was her face, as always full of life . . . running . . . calling his name . . . fear now in her eyes as well, something he had never seen before.

His mind filled with her beautiful face . . . running toward him.

Then suddenly the sound exploded in his memory. The face was gone. He was now on the ground, terrific pain everywhere.

He lifted his head to glance about, to find the face of loveliness again, but the only thing that met his gaze was the still body lying there. He could not see her face, for it had fallen to the earth and now lay unmoving . . . then the darkness.

Tears welled into his eyes. In the misery of confusion, between what the rays of sunlight seemed to say and the reality of his anguished memories of the dreadful day, he allowed himself to weep freely.

There were no pretenses about strength to worry about now. She was dead. Her father had to be dead too. What else could matter? What would ever matter again?

Minutes passed. The storm within his soul vented itself, then slowly quieted by degrees.

As if prompted by his thoughts, suddenly words from Baron von Dortmann's mouth tumbled back upon him from out of the past. The baron had said: *"He wants us to call him Father. He wants us to go to him so he can wrap his arms around us and speak to us tenderly and lovingly as his children. . . . God is a good Father, anxious to give that goodness to his creatures."*

Sabina herself had drawn comfort from her father's faith during the long years of his imprisonment. Surely he could follow her own example. With almost a desperation of the will, he forced his tears to stop.

The baron's words brought Matthew's own experience of nine years before to mind. He knew about those arms of the Father's love. He had felt them!

"Oh, Lord," he whispered, *"I'm sorry to have forgotten. You **are** good, you **are** love—I know it. Help me, Father! I am so weak, and the pain of this moment is so severe. Keep my eyes upon you, otherwise I do not think I can bear it! Wrap your arms about me once again. I need you so badly. . . ."*

Even as he prayed, the words of Scripture came to him: "It is to your advantage that I go away. . . . The Spirit of truth will bring to your remembrance all that I have said to you."

Quickly they were followed—as if fulfilling them with the baron's words rather than those of the Master who spoke them—with more of what Sabina's father had told him:

"*God really is just what the Bible says of him—he is love. . . . People cannot bring themselves to believe that the Father really is good.*"

"God, oh God," burst out Matthew in prayer. "*Help me to believe in your goodness . . . even now! Help me, Lord . . . please help me. Do not let me be as your faithless children who believe in your goodness only when it is showered upon them. Help me to know you are a good and loving Father, even when . . .*"

He could not bring himself to utter the words.

Again the image of Sabina's motionless form lying on the ground filled his brain.

He could pray no more but fell into still another disconsolate agony of weeping.

Though he felt them not in his bodily frame, the loving arms of the Father, in answer to his own prayer, enfolded themselves more tightly about him. Within ten minutes again he slept, comforted in the dreamless care of the one who loved him and Sabina and the baron more by a millionfold, in life *or* death, than the combined earthly love the three shared for one another.

83

Division!

• • •

AN HOUR LATER, MATTHEW'S LIGHT SLUMBER WAS awakened by the sound of the door to his room opening.

Two men entered, one wearing a white robe, the other an expensive business suit.

"How are you feeling, Mr. McCallum?" asked the doctor in German.

"Actually, now that I think of it, pretty well," answered Matthew, attempting to sit up halfway in his bed.

"You slept well?"

"Yes . . . yes, I did."

"After our conversation yesterday," the doctor went on, "I immediately notified your people. I knew they must be concerned. Mr. Clatchen has come by this morning to see you."

"How are you, McCallum?" said the other man, stepping forward and offering his hand, which Matthew shook, not without some awkwardness. "Bob Clatchen, CIA—we met briefly a few weeks back."

"Right," said Matthew, his face suddenly showing recognition. "Sorry, my brain's a little foggy. But why CIA—how are you people involved?"

The doctor interrupted, offered the visitor the one chair that was in the small room, then excused himself.

Clatchen sat down, then proceeded to answer Matthew's question. The two men spoke in English.

"We got wind of the doctor's call to State," he said. "After the talk you and I had earlier, I had the feeling there might be more to the story than you would want to tell anyone but me. Am I correct in assuming you were involved at the helicopter incident at the border?"

"I thought you told me before you didn't want to know anything."

"That was then. Things are heating up fast. I don't suppose you heard about Khrushchev's speech yesterday?"

Matthew shook his head.

"I quote, 'We shall not be the first to press the buttons at our rocket installations, we shall not start a war. But if the imperialists force a war upon us, we shall meet it bravely and deal a devastating blow to the aggressor.'"

Matthew let out a low whistle.

"I tell you, McCallum, every day now there is open talk of war. People are pouring out of East Berlin. Khrushchev is mad as you-know-what and is rattling his sabers to beat the band. Kennedy is calling up reservists and beefing up our military presence in Berlin. Things are more tense than ever. State is anxious to get you back. The president was notified several days ago that you were missing, and of course he was very concerned. I had already been alerted through Langley to get on your trail. You're a hot commodity right now, especially given the situation. You can see why I need to know what you've been up to."

"The, uh . . . the president did not announce my resignation?" asked Matthew.

"No, why? Did you resign?"

"Not exactly. Let's just say I made that an option if my affiliation with the government became untenable."

Clatchen nodded with interest. "No, you're still on the team as far as I know. So . . . you were going to tell me what you were doing."

"Well, I'll tell you that I was at the border—when was it, five, or is it six days ago? That's where this happened to me."

"What was it all about?"

"For your security, and for the president's sake, I don't think I ought to say more right now," replied Matthew. "You're right, things are hot, and I don't want to give Khrushchev any more ammo than he already has to start something."

The agent smiled.

"I've been in this game long enough to know when it's useless to try to coerce information out of someone, so I won't press it," he said.

"You may be right. Everything these days has wide ramifications. Given your relationship to the president and your connection to this incident—it's important that we get you out of here."

"Out of the hospital—I'm glad to hear that!"

"Out of Berlin altogether. There are spies everywhere, and if the KGB knew of your involvement in this escape incident, whatever it was, Khrushchev could throw mud all over Kennedy's face with it. Does anyone here know?"

Suddenly Matthew realized his error.

"Yeah," he said with a nod, "I'm afraid I told the doctor. I wasn't thinking too clearly when I first regained consciousness."

"All the more reason why we've got to get you moved. There could be DDR plants right in this hospital. The *Stasi* has people everywhere, even here in the West."

"But I can't leave Berlin," said Matthew, suddenly realizing what it would mean to do so.

"Why not?"

"I've . . . there are some things I've got to find out first," hesitated Matthew.

"You're in no condition to find out anything, believe me."

"Then maybe you can find out for me."

"I'll do what I can. We've got to move you regardless."

"Where . . . back to the States?"

"No, the president wants you to remain in Germany. We've got a small debriefing center and medical facility down near the base in Garmisch."

"Bavaria?"

"Yep, a compound of several chalets up in the mountains. Nice relaxing place. You'll be able to recover there and ease your way back into things. Away from the prying eyes of Berlin! From the information I have, the president wants you where he can communicate with you more freely."

"How long am I going to be laid up, did the doctor tell you?" asked Matthew.

"Could be several months. Your back and shoulders got singed up pretty bad, besides your leg and the wound in your head."

"Months. I haven't got months to sit around!"

"You may be celebrating Christmas in the Bavarian Alps."

"I can't leave until I find out if the report in the paper about the explosions is accurate."

"Why wouldn't it be?"

"Do *you* trust Communist news?"

"I get your point, McCallum. What is it specifically you want to know?"

"If . . . if the deaths they reported—"

Matthew stopped and glanced away, suddenly overcome again with the emotion of the memory. Even the crusty CIA veteran sensed that this was no moment to tread with heavy foot, and he held his peace.

"I need to know," Matthew went on in a moment, with a soft and tentative voice, "if the deaths reported have been confirmed. In particular, there was . . ." Matthew struggled to continue, "there was mention made . . . of a woman."

"I understand," said Clatchen. "I will put some people on it this afternoon. Paddy Red ought to be able to get to the bottom of it from his end. In any event, we'll plan to transport you out of here in two or three days."

"If I'm going to be isolated for as long as you say, I'd like to get some things from the hotel."

"Not to worry, McCallum. We sealed off your room days ago, the instant you turned up missing. Standard procedure, you understand. Everything will be packed up and shipped down to Garmisch."

"Everything? There's a little china box—full of rose leaves. It's especially important."

"Where is it?"

"On the nightstand next to the bed."

"No problem."

"And a sealed manila packet in the drawer right underneath it."

"Every scrap will be packed."

"My books . . ."

"Everything, McCallum. You'll feel right at home."

• • •

The next day, August 13, shortly after 11:00 A.M., CIA agent Clatchen again walked into Matthew's room at the hospital, this time alone. His face appeared as though he hadn't slept all night, which was not far from the truth. Nearly everyone employed in any official capacity of significance by one of the three Allied governments, or the Federal Republic of Germany, had been up since two hours after midnight monitoring the history-making events as they unfolded.

Before he had a chance to speak, and without even a word of greeting, Matthew's voice met his ear from the bed.

"Did you find out?" he said anxiously.

The look of strain on Clatchen's face increased as he slowly eased into the empty chair beside the bed.

"I'm sorry, McCallum," he said. "I wish I had good news for you. But I'm afraid Paddy Red confirms that from all he can tell the report is true."

"*All* of it?" said Matthew in disbelief.

Clatchen nodded. "No survivors . . . that's what Paddy said. I'm sorry."

A heavy silence fell in the small room.

"I don't believe it," said Matthew at length. "I *won't* believe it . . . it *can't* be true!"

The agent said nothing. Psychology was not his strong suit. If he'd known the president's friend was going to react like this, he'd have let someone else be the bearer of the hard news. The CIA was a tough game, and he was an action man. He was used to death and used to men who knew how to handle it. Grief and emotions made him uncomfortable.

"I'm sorry, McCallum," he repeated awkwardly.

"I'll go to the site myself!" said Matthew. "As soon as I can walk. I'll scour the place. I'll find out what really happened. I'll—"

"You're not going anyplace, McCallum," said Clatchen, his voice carrying an odd tone of resignation.

"I will!" rejoined Matthew, almost ranting now. "I've used crutches before. No broken leg will keep me down for long!"

"McCallum!" broke in Clatchen, with a firm voice now. "Pull yourself together. You work for the president of the United States. We need you thinking clearly. You've got to put this behind you. You knew the risks when you signed on—we all do."

"I knew of no risks like this," snapped Matthew. "I'm no G-man like the rest of you. I have no intention of accepting it so casually."

"You've *got* to accept it. Whoever these people are, whatever they meant to you—they're dead. You understand—dead."

"I don't believe you!"

"There's nothing you can do for them now, McCallum. You've got to face reality. Life goes on. You've got to move forward."

He'd used this same speech, or a variation of it, a dozen times before on his new CIA recruits at their first initiation to death, more often than not either that of an innocent victim or one of their own colleagues. It was an appeal that usually worked.

But Matthew McCallum was not a CIA agent. Nor, as Bob Clatchen was finding out, was he a man who could take death so lightly. This was no recruit from headquarters in Langley. Here was a civilian suddenly caught up in a personal tragedy, a man altogether unprepared for it.

"I'll go there myself," Matthew said. "Not you, not even John Kennedy can stop me! I'll find what really happened, I'll find them, I tell you, I'll—"

"McCallum!" interrupted Clatchen sternly. "You're not going any-place, do you hear me? It's not your broken leg, it's not me, it's not even JFK who will stop you. You *can't* get across that border—not now. Everything's changed. That's what I came to tell you about. Look at that."

He rose and tossed the half-folded front page of that morning's extra edition of the Berlin newspaper on the bed in front of Matthew.

"Khrushchev has finally made his move," he added, punctuating with finality the words he had previously spoken.

In huge bold letters of red, Matthew read the stunning head-line: "DDR SEALS BORDER, WIRE BARRICADE BISECTS BERLIN."

"I . . . I don't understand," said Matthew. "Are you telling me they've cut off the East from the West?"

"Right down the middle of the city," answered Clatchen. "Two days ago—we found out only this morning—the DDR issued a declaration calling for what they termed 'effective control around the whole territory of West Berlin.' Yesterday a decree specified that from now on special permits would be required for all East German citizens who wanted to cross into West Berlin. Security would be increased along all the borders between the BRD and the DDR, and no agents of Western governments would be allowed into either East Berlin or the DDR without careful scrutiny. Then last night, at 2:00 A.M., they brought in troops, sealed off the border, and began stringing barbed wire."

"I still don't see how that affects me," said Matthew.

"Don't you understand, McCallum? They've positioned troops along all the borders. Already they've begun erecting cement blocks. They're putting up a *wall* to keep people from crossing back and forth—a wall, do you hear me, through the heart of this city. West Berlin has become an island."

"I don't care about getting into East Berlin," said Matthew, then paused. "At least not yet, anyway—not until I see if she's—"

"You couldn't get into the DDR now if you tried, either. We're cut off. Security is tight at every border crossing around the other sections of West Berlin too, like where you were brought, as I understand it. There are troops everywhere. It's a dangerous situation."

"I'll break in," said Matthew, still failing to comprehend the magnitude of what had happened during the night.

"Right now, if you tried something like that, you'd start a war."

"I'll be careful. I'm not going to kill somebody, if that's what you're thinking."

"You couldn't penetrate one of the border stations without a tank, I tell you, McCallum. You'd have to kill a *dozen* Communist soldiers to get through. The border guards are holding guns with orders to kill. There have been a couple of incidents of gunfire already."

"I'll find some other way."

"Don't be ridiculous. You can't even walk. Besides the barricade itself, we're closer to war than ever. Troops throughout Europe are on alert."

Slowly Matthew began to digest the implications of what Clatchen said. He turned again to the paper and now read over a portion of the front-page article more carefully.

The only thought upon which his brain could focus was Sabina's laughing face, carefree and happy such a short while ago, moving with freedom back and forth from her apartment to West Berlin.

Why hadn't he insisted she leave the East? It would have been so easy then. They could be living happily in West Berlin . . . right now. If only . . . if only he hadn't . . .

Why had he been so impulsive?

What a fool he had been, trying to break the baron out of prison!

He was no spy, no con man. He had been in over his head from the very beginning. It had probably been the fox Schlaukopf who had turned them in. How could he have been so naive as to think he could pull off something of such daring?

Sabina's voice came back to him—that sweet, musical voice so full of life! *"It's just not time for me to come to the West yet."*

Why had he listened to her? There were other possibilities they could have explored—other options for him and Sabina, other options for her father.

Now it was too late!

Too late for everything.

How long he lay there, staring blankly at the newspaper, his eyes in a tearless blur of apathy and dull shock, reliving the last joyous weeks with Sabina that had suddenly become so bitter to recall, Matthew couldn't have known.

When he next came to himself and glanced up with uncaring expression, Clatchen was gone. He had never seen him rise and had not heard the door close behind him.

The room was silent.

He tried to call Sabina's face again to mind, but as in his dream, suddenly he could not bring her features into view. He tried to remember her voice, but its sound also had faded.

It was silent. Still he stared dumbly into the thick and oppressive air now so void of life.

A voice sounded somewhere in his memory, reviving him.

There was no one else in the room. Yet a voice brought unwelcome words that crashed back and forth against the empty walls inside his skull. The words that suddenly now jarred his brain were not from Sabina's light and melodic voice, but rather echoed somberly in the deep and passionless timbre of the CIA agent who had brought him such evil tidings.

"Whoever these people are, McCallum—they're dead. You understand— dead."

Matthew slowly lay back on his pillow, then turned to bury his face in its softness, weeping in the quiet, lonely anguish of loss.

84

Moscow Interview

• • •

UNDER MORE FAVORABLE CIRCUMSTANCES HE MIGHT have enjoyed the plane ride from Berlin to Moscow. He had not been home in more than a year, and autumn could be a most pleasant time in the Soviet capital.

Unfortunately, he was still too banged up to make the most of it, although there were a couple of young women with whom he hoped to renew his acquaintance.

It would have been more convenient had his uncle's call come three or four weeks later. But he had been insistent. The moment he had learned of the incident he had called his nephew home for a full report the moment he could tolerate the trip, injuries notwithstanding. He would know firsthand what had transpired before deciding what was to be done.

His uncle was not one you refused. Ties of blood counted nothing in his estimation, only obedience.

When he had first been assigned to Berlin he had thought it fate's way of getting rid of him. Not that he believed in fate any more than he believed in God, but at least an impersonal fate offered a less imposing and less superstitious way of looking at the nonexplainable aspects of life that were just as prevalent under atheistic Communist rule as under Jewish or Christian theism.

In any case, perhaps fate—whoever or whatever it was, if it was anything—had smiled on him after all. No sooner had he landed in Berlin than it had become the hottest of the world's hot spots, pushing Kennedy and Khrushchev to the very brink of war. It was a veritable greenhouse for the rapid elevation of an aspiring KGB agent, even if he did have to take a back seat to the German clown of a *Stasi* section chief.

Now, returning to Moscow, he had the sense of being removed from the source of action. His uncle had assured him it was only to discuss these recent developments in a more personal way, but Galanov knew that displeasing him could mean he would never see Berlin, or continue his climb up the KGB ladder, ever again.

The most gnawing part of his malaise stemmed from the awareness that he had not really achieved much in the way of the purpose for which he had been sent to Berlin in the first place.

Who was he trying to fool? He had achieved nothing.

Every lead of Schmundt's had dried up, and he just hadn't been able to turn anything on his own. Just when he had been about to break the case wide open, the imbecile had started tossing grenades, and everything had blown up in both their faces.

His uncle's annoyance was exacerbated by the fact that he had almost laid his hands on the old Jew he had been seeking, only to have the man vanish before his very eyes. He now had some people down in the Mediterranean region following a scent that looked promising. Yet underlying occasional optimism, he knew his uncle was angry and frustrated, and that, given sufficient time, some of that frustration was bound to come his way.

Galanov didn't like to even think about what could be the result!

His thoughts strayed to Schmundt's secretary Lola.

Since his release from the hospital, he and she had found occasion to become more closely acquainted for the remaining week or two of their boss's absence. There was more brainpower and determination to the lady than he had ever given her credit for, he mused. She paid closer attention to the goings-on of their section than the short-sighted Schmundt realized. Galanov found himself wondering if she didn't really hold the section together herself, to the oblivion of Schmundt and even his superiors.

Ah well, it was none of his concern. He was KGB, not *Stasi*. His fortunes rose or fell according to the subtle and invisible barometric pressures inside the Kremlin, not Berlin.

He just hoped, not without some anxiety, that he would still retain the privilege of calling himself a KGB agent after his upcoming interview.

85

Bavarian Retreat

• • •

MATTHEW HAD BEEN AT THE CHALET SUDERSDORF NEAR Garmisch in southern Germany five weeks.

Still he had not found the courage within himself to open the last remaining box that had been crated up from his hotel room. It was labeled Books; Other Personal Effects. He knew the moment he did so, memories would flood him that he would be unable to control.

Notwithstanding the peacefulness of the place and the idyllic alpine setting, the importance of those individuals sent here ensured a great deal of activity, a busy routine, and a steady flow of traffic in and out. A helicopter pad saw daily use ferrying patients, doctors, advisers, and psychologists up and down the mountain between the chalets and the American military base at Garmisch-Partenkirchen.

Some came for merely a day or two's debriefing from hot spots of America's involvement all around the world. Others with medical needs remained longer, occasionally, as in Matthew's case, for extended periods of time.

No one came, however, who wasn't important to Washington in some unique way. This was no mere hospital setting. The CIA had as many operatives on the premises as there were doctors and nurses. Everything here rated a "top secret" security classification.

Matthew had had his own share of visitors, from both the State Department, keeping him abreast of diplomatic developments, and the CIA, who, as time passed and the danger of an adverse Communist reaction lessened, eventually learned the whole story of the escape attempt in which he had been involved. Further investigation, at Matthew's insistence, revealed nothing more than had been divulged by Paddy Red's original report—that no evidence could be unearthed conflicting with the DDR's version of the incident. There had also been two communications from the president, wishing him well and encouraging him back into full diplomatic action, the latter telling him that he had destroyed the letter of resignation.

The Berlin wall was now the world's most glaring reality, spanning in its grey ugliness the entire border between the Russian sector and the American, British, and French sectors. Three Red Army divisions had been deployed, surrounding and sealing off the entirety of West Berlin. JFK had responded by ordering the American garrison in Berlin increased. Several battle groups were sent in from bases in other parts of West Germany. British and French garrisons were also increased.

On August 22, the DDR reduced the crossing stations between East and West Berlin for foreigners to only one, known as "Checkpoint Charlie," and for Germans to six. The next day charges were issued by the Kremlin stating that the air corridors between West Germany and the BRD were being used illegally. The U.S., on the twenty-fourth, responded with a "solemn warning . . . that any interference . . . with free access to West Berlin would be an aggressive act for the consequences of which the Soviet Government would bear full responsibility." The next day Kennedy announced the appointment of General Lucius Clay, hero of the 1948–49 Berlin airlift, as his personal representative in Berlin. The news came as no surprise to Matthew. The president had told him of his decision privately several days before, assuring Matthew that as soon as he was able, he hoped he would be able to join Clay in a resumption of his former duties.

At the end of August, the Kremlin raised the stakes in the dangerous game of world power when Khrushchev announced a series of fifty- and hundred-megaton hydrogen bomb tests. His words could hardly be mistaken: "In order to discourage the aggressor from criminally playing with fire, it is necessary to make sure that he knows and sees that there is a force in the world which is ready to give an armed rebuff to his aggression."

JFK had already ordered the draft increased. Now he ordered more than seventy-five thousand reservists to report for active duty on October 1. War seemed closer than ever.

As time passed, Matthew's despondency gave way to a cheerless resignation. In the midst of his prayers and his desperate attempts to come to terms with the reality of his personal tragedy, the words of Bob Clatchen continued to pound his brain with the practicality for which the CIA was known: *"You work for the president of the United States. We need you thinking clearly. You've got to put this behind you. You knew the risks. . . . You've got to accept it. Whoever these people are—they're dead. You understand—dead. There's nothing you can do for them now, McCallum. You've got to face reality. Life goes on. You've got to move forward."*

How many times had he silently cursed Clatchen's unfeeling, callous words?

Yet as the weeks passed and the air grew gradually crisp with the high-altitude harbingers of the approaching winter, he grew to thank God for Clatchen's no-nonsense pragmatism. How else could he climb out of the rut of this emotional quagmire but by heeding the agent's bracing words? They were stinging to the soul in the same way as the sharp breezes that blew down occasionally from the high altitudes above them woke the body by sending a shiver up and down the spine.

Sometimes that was what you needed. Clatchen was right. What choice was there but to go on . . . to put it behind you . . . to move forward?

The words might not have been pleasant when he first heard them, but he had to admit now—they offered good sound advice.

As much as he was attempting to heed Clatchen's words and get his professional and diplomatic life back on track, there remained, however, a substantial piece of unfinished emotional business he yet had to deal with.

The time for it had not been right. He hadn't been ready. But he could sense the moment approaching. When it came he was going to have to squarely face what had happened—all of it, from start to finish. He would not be able to put it behind him until he could, in a sense, relive it, come to terms with it, give it over to God, and then close those chapters in his life . . . forever.

Some of the reminiscences would be happy, others would be painful, all would be poignant and bittersweet.

But to find the healing his soul required, he knew he was going to have to allow the Spirit of God access to those most private places within himself, so that the restorative touch of the Father's finger could bring wholeness and finality to the memories of his past.

On the twenty-fifth of the month of September, word came that a hundred-meter zone on the DDR's side of the wall had begun to be cleared in order to decrease the attempts to cross over into the West, some of them dangerous and spectacular, which had continued all month. People were being removed, apartment buildings and houses were being destroyed, and still more guard towers were being built.

The news reminded Matthew of Sabina's small home. It should be safe, he thought. It was far enough away from the border. What had become of it, he wondered. What had become of her possessions—of the dress he had bought her for the ball?

More memories began to come, though he still didn't know if he was ready for them.

How glad he was that she had turned over to him the little china box they had bought to keep their roses in. He had wondered at the time why she had given it to him to take to his hotel. Had she possessed some premonition of what was going to happen?

He was thankful for it now, though he had not looked at it since . . . since that terrible day. Neither had he looked into the envelope she had asked him to keep.

Matthew glanced up toward the mountains and drew in a deep breath of the tangy autumn air. The first snows of the season had blown in last week, giving a fresh coat of white to the peaks that towered high to the south. Most of what had fallen here had melted, though some yet lingered amongst the trees.

Winter was coming, he thought.

He found himself looking forward to it. He needed a change. The cold and rain and snow would make it easier to forget the happy times he and Sabina had shared through the balmy summer months.

Again he drew in a deep breath.

Maybe the time had come. He was prepared to remember.

He signaled one of the attendants nearby that he was ready to be wheeled back to his room. He would open the final case. There were some books he had been wanting anyway.

They had taken the cast off his leg three days ago, though he was still confined to a wheelchair. They wanted to watch it for a few days before determining whether to recast it below the knee or to allow him to begin using crutches without a cast. Likewise, most of the largest bandages were gone from his shoulders, though the wound on the back of his head and smaller dressings on his back still had to be changed and repacked every several days.

Back in his room, Matthew asked the attendant to wait. He wheeled himself to the closet, where a cardboard box sat on the floor. The tape with which it had been sealed was already cut, but it had not yet been opened. Matthew asked the attendant to carry it out for him and set it next to his table. The man did so. Matthew now folded back the two lids and began emptying the contents onto the table. When he came to the one item he had been looking for, he picked it up carefully, then asked to be taken back outside to the large deck at the rear of the chalet overlooking the fields and hillsides to the southwest.

"It's rather nippy out, Mr. McCallum. Wouldn't you like a coat or something?"

"I suppose you're right," answered Matthew. "Hand me that sweater there in the closet, would you . . . the red one."

The man got it and brought it to him.

"Just drape it around my shoulders for me . . . good, thanks. I'll be fine."

They left the room and moved down the corridor, into the large central dining room, and through it outside onto the deck.

"Do you suppose you could get me into that rocking chair over there?" said Matthew.

"You're not supposed to put any weight on that leg, Mr. McCallum."

"Just lift me out of this wheelchair, and I'll sit there as composed as a baby."

The attendant agreed and got another of the medical staff to assist him, and in another minute or two Matthew was comfortably seated in the plain oak rocker, moving gently back and forth, gazing out over the peaceful Bavarian landscape.

He drew in a deep breath. At last the moment had come.

He glanced down at the china box he held, almost as if beneath its lid were contained the very memories he had been reluctant to uncover.

Slowly he lifted the lid.

Inside his eyes fell upon the dozens of dried, flaky rose petals he and Sabina had put inside it together. Every one was a memory all its own.

He lifted it to his nose. The fragrance seemed to cast a spell of weariness upon him. He set the box back down in his lap and replaced the lid. His head hung down upon his chest, and even his arms seemed to lose their life, though his fingers continued to fidget imperceptibly with the ornate miniature roses spread across the top of the lid. His legs, too, felt numb, though with an invisible toe or two he managed to keep the runners of the chair creaking in motion across the floor. The aroma from within the china box had intoxicated him with heaviness, as if in anticipation of the task his mind and heart had ahead of them.

He grew oblivious to all the sights and sounds around him—the movement within the chalet, the bells around the thick grey necks of the cows scattered about the hillside, tinkling out their strangely harmonious melodies, the occasional sound of a hiking yodeler in the distance.

He did not hear their sounds, but he felt their influences. *Everything* now reminding him, in its own way, of the sights and sounds of her face and voice, of letters and discussions they had exchanged, and of roses given and roses received with the one he loved but would never see again.

Oh, Sabina . . . Sabina . . . , he thought. *It was so rich a time. . . . Never had I imagined it was possible to feel such happiness.*

Again he opened the small box, fiddling through the dried contents. Could he even distinguish any of the roses from all the others? Two small buds still retained their shape in the midst of the leafy potpourri. Their color had faded, but he knew both roses well—the yellow one he had given Sabina that night at *Lebenshaus* so many years ago, and the pink one of only three months before.

The thought of the latter was nearly more than his heart could stand. The words they had spoken suddenly came to mind as fresh as if it were yesterday.

"I want this pink rose always to remind you of today. I promise you that nothing will come between us ever. . . . I will never let something like that happen again. . . . I promise, Sabina."

"This pink rose will join the yellow as the first of many—not memories of times past, but reminding us of happy moments of now."

"I will believe you," he could still hear her say.

But he *had* let it happen. He had let her down. He had broken the promise of the pink rose!

God . . . O God . . . why?

How hard it was not to revert to former ways of thinking. He thought he had faced trials as a Christian in years past. But it took every atom of belief he had to hang on to his assurance of God's goodness now. He had never imagined that a crisis of faith could bring on doubts of such magnitude. These last five weeks he had had to rethink and struggle through every aspect of a belief that he thought was secure long ago. There were times he had come within a hairbreadth of saying to himself, "I *can't* believe anymore . . . to believe is too painful!"

He had tried to hold on, desperately at times, for *her* sake even more than for his own. What did *his* life matter *now?*

He knew what she would say. Whenever he thought of her, or heard her voice, the image was of smiles, and he found her telling him, *"Matthew, it will all work for good. We can trust our Father! Don't you remember what my father taught us both—that God is good . . . a father to call Father!"*

So he had clung by a slender thread to his belief. To give it up would be to relinquish what they had shared together . . . and *that* he would never lose sight of.

It was all he had left—her memory. The sound of her voice in his ear . . . the musical ringing of her laughter . . . images of her teeth and lips and smile . . .

And these two buds and few dried leaves in the container they had bought together in that shop in Berlin . . . that she had given him for safekeeping . . . almost as if she had known what was about to befall her.

Matthew glanced down at the box.

Even these rose petals, as treasured as had been the moments they had shared gathering them, now seemed lifeless and old, the aroma of their once-cheery perfume now turned stale, pungent, and melancholy.

He could no more keep himself from the bittersweet nostalgia than he could bring her back. Though the smell seared his heart like a hot iron, it was the fragrance . . . of *her.*

He raised the box to his face, lifted the lid, and leaned forward slightly to place his nostrils over the opening of the small container.

He breathed deeply the ancient fragrance of many years. Even in the short time the box had been in his hotel, he smelled of it a hundred times before that fateful day six weeks ago. And he would do so a hundred times again. For in the aroma, every one of the tiny petals held a secret . . . and his was the only heart that knew them.

He set the small box back again on his lap, a lonely tear now falling from his eye, and, continuing to rock, let his mind drift back many years to the first day he had seen the beautiful face of the one with whom he had discovered the mystery of love.

He could still hear the music of the garden party he had attended in Berlin with his father. The sounds were as fresh as yesterday, especially the moment he had first seen Baron von Dortmann approaching, Sabina on his arm, to introduce them to his lovely, happy, beautiful, lively daughter. . . .

•   •   •

How long he was lost in his reflections, Matthew didn't know. Judging from the late afternoon chill, it must have been two or three hours.

Coming to himself, he realized how tired he had become.

Recalling her face, her words, her smiles . . . it was his only pleasure, yet also his deepest agony. Memory of her face was all he had to live for, the one thing he would fain forget.

The recollection was unfinished. But on this day, even thoughts of happiness were fatiguing.

He lifted the small box once more to his nose and drew in another tired breath from the melancholy fragrance of the dried petals, then set it again on his lap.

He closed his eyes and leaned back in the oak rocker.

I will remember more another time, thought Matthew to himself.

In a few moments he was fast asleep.

8 6

Surprise Visit

• • •

BY THE THIRD WEEK OF OCTOBER, MOST OF THE BURNS
were substantially healed, although further plastic surgery would be
required to replace some of the scar tissue. Matthew was walking
well enough to feel comfortable, though for a time would continue
to use a cane. The wound in the back of his head from the
explosion, about which the doctors had been more concerned than
any of the rest—which concern accounted for his protracted stay
for ongoing observation—was healed to the point where they at
last felt comfortable releasing him.

Matthew had taken on those aspects of his job that could be
handled by courier and telephone. Plans were now being made to
transfer him from the facility at Sudersdorf into a situation where he
could resume as many of his former duties as possible.

Matthew was reluctant, however, to return to Berlin. He needed
more time, he thought, before his emotional equilibrium would be
entirely back to normal. The city still held too many memories. The
scars were too fresh. He couldn't go back . . . not quite yet.

Shrewd judge of men that he was, John Kennedy sensed his friend
was not up to par from the moment Matthew had answered his call.
It was not their first conversation during the latter's convalescence, but
as they discussed the Berlin crisis, with an eye to Matthew's resuming
his full role as JFK's personal envoy in the ongoing discussions, the
president knew he was still not at his best.

He hung up the phone in the Oval Office, thought a moment
or two, then picked up the phone again. It was the best way, he
thought, and possibly the only way, to get Matthew all the way up

to the present, and to the point where he could go forward with his life.

It was three days later when Matthew himself learned the results of that second call made by the president of the United States.

He was sitting in his room quietly absorbing a phrase from a devotional book from the pen of his favorite Scotsman. The words he had just read and was struggling to find meaning for in his present dilemma were these:

> *God's means cannot be so great as his ends. God is our*
> *Father, but we are not yet his children. Because we are not yet*
> *his children, we must become his sons and daughters. Nothing*
> *else will satisfy him, or us, until we become one with our*
> *Father. There are good things God must delay giving. God*
> *must first make his child fit to receive and fit to have.*

Praying, without giving specific thought to the fact that it would be called prayer, he was conversing inwardly with his Lord according to the following train of thought: *What, Father, is the "end" here that you have for me? The means are more than painful. Are you trying to make me into a child worthy to be called your son? Are you attempting to make me fit to receive some good thing? What good thing, Father? Oh, Lord, I do want to be fully your son! But sometimes I wonder if I can go on . . . alone. Make me a son, Father . . . help me—*

The sound of the door opening intruded into his brain.

With thoughts of the Father and his own yet-budding sonship filling his entire being, he glanced up at his visitor.

A blank stare was all the expression his face revealed. The world of the spirit and the world of the flesh for an instant could not be intermingled. He could not bring the identification apparent to his eyes into a recognition of heart and brain.

An instant more he stared immobile, knowing but unknowing . . . unbelieving that what he seemed to see could be other than a figment of an overexcited imagination.

A sound met his ears . . . a voice he knew.

"*Matt . . .*"

The spell was broken.

"*Dad!*" cried Matthew, incredulous.

He was on his feet, the book flying from his lap onto the floor. The next moment the two men were in one another's arms weeping for joy.

Standing back after a long and silent embrace, tearful and unashamed, Matthew laughed.

"It *is* really you! But what are you doing here?" he exclaimed.

"I've come to take you out of this place," replied Thaddeus, also tearful, also unashamed, also laughing.

"What!"

"No fooling—that's honestly why I've come."

"But . . . when did you arrive? Oh, but . . . here—sit down," he added.

"Flew into Munich late yesterday, spent the night there. Drove down to Garmisch this morning . . . and here I am—an all-expense-paid trip to Sudersdorf, compliments of the White House."

"The White House!" exclaimed Matthew. "Now I really don't understand! I just spoke with Jack three days ago and he said nothing. Is something up in Iceland, of all places, that they have to bring you here for debriefing?"

"No," laughed Thaddeus. "Nothing so dramatic as that. *You* are the reason I'm here."

"You said the White House . . ."

Thaddeus paused and grew more serious.

"The president telephoned me the moment he hung up after talking with you three days ago," he said.

"What about?"

"He's concerned about you, Matt."

"I'm fine—look, no cast, no crutches, just a cane! My skull's almost back in one piece. Why, they're processing my release even as we speak!"

"We know all that. It's not your physical condition the president and I talked about, Son. He wants you back on his first team, as he put it, but can tell you're still not altogether yourself."

At last Matthew understood.

"So he sent you over to talk to me, to help me put the past behind me, to make me forget?" sighed Matthew, then added with an ironic chuckle, "My father, the psychiatrist."

"Nothing so specific. Just to visit, to be with you, to help you get back into a normal living situation. Maybe to talk about everything in a more personal way than we have been able to in letters."

Matthew was silent. He had tried to be chipper when talking to the president. He should have known Jack would see through it.

"I suppose I ought to be grateful," he said finally. "He could have just relieved me of my duties altogether."

"He didn't want to do that. He called you his top man in Berlin and he wants you, like I said, on his first team. Things are still hot and changing week to week. He wants you focused and at your best, not distracted."

"I know . . . and he's right," sighed Matthew. "I'm not going to do him any good moping around. It's hard. . . . I've never faced anything like it."

"I understand, Matt," replied Thaddeus. "I lost a wife, remember."

"Yeah, I'm sorry, Dad. I guess you have been through it too."

The room was quiet several seconds. Thaddeus looked over at his son with great feeling.

"I want you to know how sorry I am, Matt," he said at length. "Sabina was someone special. I know what she meant to you. Someone like that only comes along once in a lifetime. I'm just very, very sorry."

"Thanks, Dad. The memories haven't gotten to the point yet where I can look back and enjoy them. But I'll live through it, and hopefully that time will come eventually."

"It will. My memories of your mother are all fond ones now, after the pain of the loss has had a chance to fade a little into the years. I still miss her, of course. But there's a certain feeling of spiritual 'togetherness,' if you can call it that, that comes later, after the anguish, which brings a pleasantness to the memories. I'm sure that time will come for you one day too."

Matthew nodded.

"The thought of Sabina's face will make you cry for a year, maybe two. But there will come a moment, someday, when all of a sudden her smile and the sound of her laughter will break in upon your brain, and lo and behold you'll find yourself laughing too—smiling *with* her again. The moment will be nostalgic, not painful. She will begin to be alive to you again, alive in your memory. It's a transition that will come, believe me, though it can never be rushed. The pain that must be endured before such a time is part of the growth process too."

Matthew quietly absorbed his father's words.

"Thank you, Dad," he said at length. "I'll look forward to that day. In the meantime, you keep praying for me—I need it!"

"I always do, Son—several times every day."

Again it was silent for a moment.

"But . . . guess what!" said Thaddeus all at once. "I haven't told you the best part of my visit yet. Your friend the president has relieved me of my duties in Iceland."

"Huh!"

"That's right."

"But . . . what? Are you retiring . . . ? Did he fire you?"

Thaddeus laughed. "Neither. He offered me a new post, which I accepted on the spot."

"Where?"

"Right here!"

"You keep throwing me surprise after surprise," laughed Matthew. "Do you expect me to have the slightest idea what you're talking about?"

"He appointed me your assistant!"

"No . . . *really!*" exclaimed Matthew.

"I packed my bags that same day. Of course I had to take a 50 percent salary cut. I'm no longer an ambassador, only an assistant to the special presidential envoy. But I jumped at it."

"That's fantastic!"

"Actually, if you want to know the whole truth of it, I asked for the salary cut. The president offered to keep me at the same level."

"Asked for it—why?"

"Because I didn't want to feel I had to be working every minute. I'm still writing my memoirs, you know, and the older I get the more time I feel I need to devote to them."

"So what *will* your duties be here?" asked Matthew, still dumbfounded by the turn of events.

"Whatever you tell me to do," answered Thaddeus with a laugh. "How do you like that? When you were little, you had to obey me. Now the tables are reversed, and I have to obey you!"

Matthew joined him in laughter.

"That's it?" he said.

"Honestly, he just told me to give you all the moral support I could, and to help you in this Berlin thing however you thought I might. Then he told me to spend the rest of my time writing."

"Will, uh . . . will we be going to Berlin?" asked Matthew, feeling a heaviness of spirit even as he asked it.

"Oh, that's another thing I forgot to tell you about," said Thaddeus. "That's the best part!"

"What?"

"Arrangements have been made for us to stay right here!"

"Right where . . . not here at the Chalet?"

"No, here in Bavaria."

"For how long—I'm not sure I get what you mean."

"Indefinitely. We're going to carry out our work from here, not Berlin. With the wall up, things are kind of at a standstill right now. The Russians have their tanks and their guard towers and their soldiers everywhere, but the president says it has relaxed from the day-to-day tension last summer. It's now week-to-week tension. We'll be able to do what he needs from us just as well from here in the Federal Republic as in Berlin, with a trip into the city every so often. Actually, he says, from here on out we may have more business in Bonn, Paris, and London than in Berlin."

"That is a relief, I've got to tell you," said Matthew. "I wasn't looking forward to the city life."

"Not to worry. Your ever-efficient State Department has already rented a house for us."

"Where?"

"Not far from here—up near Oberammergau."

"That's great. I can't believe it!"

"We'll be out in the country, the Alps visible on a clear day, but only five or six kilometers from Oberau and the autobahn straight into Munich. Eighty-five kilometers from the airport—an hour or less."

"Sounds perfect. When do we go?"

"I haven't even seen the place yet, but my things are supposed to be arriving today. As far as I'm concerned, we can blow this CIA scene anytime."

"Then let's be off!" said Matthew, rising. "At least we can go have a look—it can't be more than twenty or thirty minutes from here, once we get down into Garmisch. You have a car?"

"Compliments of the U.S. government."

"They do seem to think of everything, don't they!"

A Christmas Gift to Remember

• • •

WINTER ARRIVED IN THE ALPS SOONER THAN IN MOST places.

By early November the higher elevations were already blanketed in fresh new snow, and ski lifts throughout Switzerland and the southernmost alpine regions of Germany were in full operation.

From the vantage point of their country chalet, Thaddeus and Matthew looked out upon a gently rising slope of green—upon which grazed a dozen or fifteen grey Swiss cattle—which increased in steepness until it gave way to a thick forest of pines, climbing upward at length past the habitations of man toward the remote slopes of the surrounding semicircle of peaks—from Krottenkopf to their west, southward to the Alpspitze and Zugspitze, and back to the Kreuzspitze and Klammspitze to their east, all of which were between two and three thousand meters in height.

The tiny village of which their chalet was a part—comprised of some ten or a dozen homes, a small guest house capable of meal service to fifteen or twenty persons at the maximum, and a bakery—was scattered over a four-hundred-meter-square plateau in the midst of this climb southward and upward out of Oberammergau. The grasses and wildflowers grew luxuriantly in the unwooded oasis. On its gradual slopes the farmers of the village grew a few crops and grazed their cattle. Two or three residents commuted down to the valley daily—when the snows permitted. The others were elderly and retired. Matthew and Thaddeus were the only foreigners, but had already been welcomed warmly into the small Bavarian community.

Indeed, the setting, for the two McCalllums, who loved this land of Germany and its people, could not have been more a dream come true. The pace was more relaxed than in most parts of the BRD, and though skiing resorts and tourist towns surrounded them literally on all sides within ten or fifteen kilometers, the clamor of such activity did not intrude upon the peaceful life of Obenammersfeld—the village whose name meant "Field above the Ammer Valley."

Their chalet was spacious, set on a large tract of land of its own. The nearest other domicile was some hundred meters away. The split-level home had been intended for a family of at least five. Matthew and Thaddeus, therefore, each had a bedroom, an office, and a bathroom of their own.

From their rear balcony, which looked out perpendicularly to the rising terrain, they could gaze either downward upon grassy slopes—broken here and there by small lakes, cultivated fields, and pasture-land—or straight out and upward, when the seemingly ever-present clouds lifted for an afternoon or a day, upon the loftiest mountain peaks in all of Germany. Hiking trails in the region abounded, which they had explored to the extent that Matthew's leg, much better by the time they had been settled in for a month, would permit.

Because of the steady flow of visitors resulting from their work attached to the State Department, they had converted the unused bedroom to a guest room. As the hospitality extended by the McCallums became gradually known, more and more of their diplomatic colleagues took the chance of a visit to Obenammersfeld as an opportunity to remain for a day or two's R and R, removed from the busy life of Berlin, Frankfurt, Munich, or Bonn.

It did the heart of both father and son good to see their tired and careworn associates head out across the fields or into the hills with walking stick in hand, or sit back, shoeless feet resting on an ottoman, mug of hot chocolate or coffee in hand, gazing into a cheery fire on the hearth. Being able to minister in this small way to their associates and friends served as greatly as the peacefulness of their surroundings to stimulate Matthew's soul back to life.

As he gave of himself to those who came—whether by taking coffee to a guest in his room and then cooking him an omelette for breakfast or by sharing about his experience with the Lord around the fireplace in the evening or by taking a book down off the shelf to hand to an intellectual diplomat, a book that explained the tenets of the Christian faith—Matthew found his own spirit reviving from the outgoing flow of his renewing compassion for others who had heartaches equal to, if not greater than his. His earthly loss seemed great, it was true, but then he knew who was the Father of them all. Pity those, he realized, who, suffering from far more minor personal griefs, knew not the Father in whose heart of love all sorrows, large and small, found healing and comfort.

Gradually it began to dawn upon both Matthew and Thaddeus that they were carrying out a similar work, though on a vastly smaller scale, as had the baron and his family.

One man and his wife, saying good-bye in mid-November after a pleasant stay of three days, laughingly referred to the place as "Spa McCallum," saying they would be back again as soon as their schedule permitted. As they drove away, Thaddeus and Matthew looked at each other, then both uttered, nearly together, the words that had come to their mind—"Sort of a spa for the soul."

They broke out laughing together.

"What would the baron think if he saw us now, Matt, my boy!" chuckled Thaddeus.

"I think he would laugh with delight, then smile quietly and say, *'Exactly . . . I like that, McCallum—a spa for the soul. Most well put!'*"

"I can hear him saying those very words," rejoined Thaddeus, "just like he said them on our first visit when we were asking about their estate."

The comparison stuck in both men's minds, and they began calling their simple one-guest-bedroom chalet *Kleines Lebenshaus Süd,* or "Small *Lebenshaus* of the South," in deferent remembrance of their eternal friend and brother, Baron von Dortmann, and his family.

Feeling thus a closer affiliation with the baron's and Marion's lifelong vision of service, hospitality, giving, and personal ministry, both men, especially Matthew, gained a newfound sense of purpose in the midst of their work, and began to weave, even sooner than Thaddeus had predicted, fond and pleasant thoughts into his memories of the past.

Without having planned or even discussed it, the exterior of the house began to resemble—also in miniature—the grounds of the *Lebenshaus* of their fond memories, as both men paid more and more attention to the soil and what might productively grow in it.

Flowers, of course, already grew about the place in abundance, something new, it seemed, blossoming with every progressive seasonal change. One day, returning from a walk high in the hills above them, Thaddeus held in his hand a tiny seedling of a Swiss mountain pine.

"It called out to me," he said to Matthew. "It needed a home; I could tell the moment I saw it."

Several days later Matthew returned from the city with three bare-root roses.

"I don't know if they'll grow here," he told his father. "But what can it hurt to try? If we're going to style our home after *Lebenshaus,* then we *have* to have a rose garden."

"If we put them right next to the house, and keep them covered when it snows, they ought to make it," said Thaddeus.

"Just what I thought—in that little unused piece covered by the overhang of the balcony . . . protected, but with southern exposure to the sun in the spring."

That had been the beginning. Within a month, both men found themselves outside, hands in the dirt, at every opportunity, planting what could survive the winter and already eagerly making plans for the spring, with drawings and plottings to extend their cultivations further down the hillside from the house itself. To their delight, they found one of the rose plants, receiving warmth from the house next to it and apparently not knowing it was the season for dormancy, sprouting tender new leaves and even sending out the beginnings of a new bud or two.

As winter set in with earnestness by the first of December, Matthew took more and more to the chilly and sometimes snowy hillsides and foothill forest paths. He found himself feeling Sabina's presence again. A quiet sort of happy melancholy stole over his spirit, as his father had predicted. He found himself communing in a sad but pleasant way with her memory, conversing with her in his mind, imagining what she would say or how she might react to something, remembering once again all the happiest moments they had shared, smiling often—even laughing to himself occasionally.

It was as he returned from such a lengthy walk, his mood peaceful, his heart full of Sabina, that his father met him at the door. It was four days before Christmas.

"A packet arrived while you were out," said Thaddeus.

"By mail?"

"No—courier from State. Brandeis drove it up from Garmisch."

"Anything important?" said Matthew, removing his coat and hat, shaking a few flakes of snow from them outside the door, then walking in and toward the fire blazing in the hearth.

"It seems routine," answered Thaddeus. "Is it snowing again out there?"

"Starting up. It looks to be a pretty good one. I wouldn't be surprised if we're socked in by morning."

"A white Christmas, eh, Matt."

"Yeah . . . we'll have to break out the Bing Crosby records and the eggnog, just like the old days in Montana! Hey, you got any coffee made?"

"No, but that sounds good," said Thaddeus, heading toward the kitchen.

Ten minutes later the two men eased into their favorite chairs in front of the fire, steaming mugs of fresh coffee in their hands. Neither spoke for some time, sipping at the strong hot brew and staring into the yellow-orange flames. Thoughts of Christmas had turned both inward, toward the two women who were never far from either of their hearts.

"So . . . ," said Matthew, forcing himself to the present and at last breaking the silence, "was there anything urgent the boys at the State Department needed us to attend to?"

"No, nothing much that can't wait till after Christmas."

"No more on Khrushchev's response to Jack's call for people to build fallout shelters?"

"No word on that. Even the Communists seem to slow down for the holidays, though they don't believe in them."

"Berlin's calm?"

"Friedrichstrasse and Checkpoint Charlie are all quiet. There are some reports you need to look at, though," Thaddeus added, rising. "I'll get the packet. Berlin might be expecting a call about a couple of the matters. The decision on passports for Communists is coming up. And the test-ban meetings at Geneva have stalled again."

"Good grief. Can't the Russians get it figured out that bombs kill people!"

"That's what they're saying about us."

"We'll probably have to get over to Geneva right after Christmas and see if there's anything we can do. I know that stalemate is driving Jack nuts. He'll probably be calling me about it any day."

Thaddeus disappeared, returning after a minute with the packet that had arrived during Matthew's walk. He handed it to Matthew.

Matthew opened the black diplomatic case, shuffled through several of the papers, then glanced up at his father.

"What is this?" he asked, holding a thick sealed manila envelope with an odd-shaped parcel inside it. It was stamped with the words "U.S. Consulate, Berlin" and had Matthew's name handwritten across it.

"I don't know," replied Thaddeus. "Neither did Brandeis. Apparently the consulate sent it over to State to have it delivered to you."

"Hmm . . . that's odd—I haven't had any dealings with the consulate in months," said Matthew, holding the package, feeling it momentarily, then unfastening the seal with his fingers. "It's light enough," he laughed. "Can't be a bomb!"

Opening the top of the package, Matthew peered inside, a puzzled expression spreading over his face.

"What is it, Matt?" asked his father.

"I don't know," replied Matthew, reaching inside. "It . . . it looks . . . like a Christmas gift."

He pulled out a small parcel twelve inches long and only some three inches square. It was wrapped with patterned pink gift paper, with a tiny bow, partially squashed from transit, on one side. There was no mark or identification of any kind on it, not even Matthew's name.

An involuntary throb shivered through Matthew's frame as he held the mysterious parcel a moment, turning it over in his hand, with the same puzzled expression still on his face, then handed it to his father.

"You have no idea who it's from?" asked Thaddeus.

"Not a clue."

"You probably have some secret admirer on the consulate staff," said Thaddeus, sniffing the air. "Perfumed paper, too," he added. "You are, after all, one of Berlin's most eligible bachelors."

"A bachelor, perhaps, but not eligible," said Matthew with a sardonic smile.

"Are you going to open it?" said Thaddeus, handing the parcel back to him.

Matthew held it again for a moment, again trembling slightly, then got to his feet, walked across the room, and set it under their tree.

"No," he said, returning to his chair, "It will have to wait with the others. After all, that tree is looking pretty sparse with just the two of us here. We need to save all the gifts for Christmas."

Thaddeus laughed.

"Speaking of which, I still have a thing or two I want to pick up. How'd you like to drive down to Mittenwald tomorrow with me?"

"If we're not snowed in," rejoined Matthew.

• • •

The snow that night came only in flurries, though the temperature dropped several degrees.

Matthew and his father drove down the hill in midmorning, through Garmisch, and on to Mittenwald, one of their favorite towns of the region near the Austrian border just north of the Scharnitzpass. There they spent the remainder of the day, shopping, enjoying lunch together, all the while keeping a close watch on the sky. Its thick dark grey was clear indication that it was only a matter of time before its heavy contents were loosed upon the whole of Bavaria. If they were stranded by the season's first blizzard, they wanted to make sure it was in the cozy comfort of their chalet, with plenty of firewood and ample provisions to enjoy their hibernation.

They arrived back in Obenammersfeld just about dusk, a few heavy flakes swirling about in the descending darkness, drove the final meters to their chalet, hurried inside with their packages, quickly built a fire, then unwrapped from their heavy coats.

"I think winter has finally come, Matt," said Thaddeus, rubbing his hands together as he measured out coffee for a fresh pot.

"Perfect timing," replied Matthew, coming into the kitchen and putting his face and hands to one of the window panes. "It's already coming down faster out there—looks like that white Christmas is nearly on us."

He turned and walked through the room, checking the fire, then ambled toward the tree.

The long, narrow mystery gift caught his eye, and again an inexplicable sensation quivered through him. Now he too caught just the faintest whiff of the paper, as his father had said.

But he was determined not to think about it further until Christmas. He turned and walked back, sitting down in front of the fire.

The blizzard at last arrived.

Half a meter of snow lay everywhere the next morning as far as the eye could see—which was not far. The grey sky hung so low upon the hillside it was impossible to tell where the snow ended and the clouds it had come from began.

Thus it remained all day. Neither of the two men set foot outside once. As long as their supply of firewood on the inside porch remained ample, two more contented hermits it would have been impossible to find.

Christmas Eve dawned with breathtaking splendor.

Every cloud had blown south to Italy, and overhead shone an uninterrupted deep clean wintry blue. Every tree, every peak of the distant mountains, was covered with white. A more perfectly virgin snowfall there could not have been, nor a more perfect setting in which to relish the beauty of the Creator's dazzling white paintbrush.

When Thaddeus wandered into the spacious living quarters not long after dawn, a fire already blazed away in the fireplace. Matthew stood with his back to the room, gazing out upon the vast whiteness.

His father approached and stood beside him a minute in silence, both looking out over the serene landscape.

"This is really some place, isn't it, Dad?" Matthew said quietly.

"You'll get no argument from me on that score. I'm so glad to be here . . . and to have the chance to spend Christmas with you."

"Yeah, me too, Dad."

Again it was silent.

"Sabina's on your mind, isn't she, Son?" said Thaddeus at length.

"How'd you know?"

"I can usually tell."

Matthew sighed. "I suppose a time like Christmas can't help but make you remember."

"I always miss your mother more during the special days."

"The moment I walked by the tree this morning, I was undone," said Matthew. "All of a sudden my eyes were full of tears. I haven't cried in—I don't know, two or three months. All of a sudden, there it was again, just like it had been yesterday."

Thaddeus put his hand on Matthew's shoulder.

"When it happens, let it," he said softly. "It will never go away completely."

Matthew nodded appreciatively.

"When times like this come," Thaddeus added, "I've found I have to let myself grieve awhile, let the tears run their course, so I can get back to enjoying the memories again."

"Can you imagine how wonderful it would be to have them all here? Just think, Dad—Mom, the baron and his wife, Sabina—all of us here around the fire together at Christmastime! What talks we would have!"

"That day will come, Son," said Thaddeus. "I already find myself looking forward to it."

Matthew nodded, understanding his father's meaning well enough.

"What do you think, Dad," he said, "will there be snow in heaven?"

"I have to admit," laughed Thaddeus, "that's one I've never thought about!"

Matthew drew in a deep breath, then let it out slowly. "I think I'll put on some boots and bundle up and go for a walk."

"You'll never get out of the yard!"

"Yeah, but there's something about making the first tracks in the morning after a snowfall."

"That snow's deep out there!"

"I know. But if Sabina were here, you know that's exactly what she would do—go off romping through it!"

Thaddeus laughed.

"Even though I haven't seen her for all those years, somehow I can picture it exactly."

"So you see—I've got to go out," said Matthew. "It's my way of sharing this Christmas Eve snowfall with her."

• • •

The day was spectacular. The sun shone down brightly though cold, turning every drop and every snowflake into a glistening prism. The entire countryside sparkled as though it had been diamonds that had fallen from the heavens rather than crystalized water.

Father and son kept the fire burning and the kitchen busy all day. The two of them could not possibly eat everything their hands busily were getting ready, but it was the preparation they enjoyed more than the anticipated consumption. Most of it they would probably give away anyway.

Baking on Christmas Eve was the way to remember the women of their lives without becoming despondent at the ever-present realization that they were not here to share the season with them. In the kitchen they were able to laugh and enjoy thoughts of how Matthew's mother might have done it, or what they would think of the mess they were accumulating, or how Sabina or Marion would prepare the old German-style strudel they were attempting to fabricate from a cookbook neither could fully understand.

By day's end, every inch of the counter was piled high with dirty pans and dishes. The smells radiating into every corner of the house gave evidence that their efforts had been largely successful. The apple strudel certainly appeared promising, and had already been sampled by both chefs—sampled twice, actually, just to make certain the initial appraisal had been accurate—who gave approval with a kiss of their fingertips. Two large canisters of creamy eggnog were ready for that evening's consumption around the fireplace while they opened the first installment of gifts.

The turkey was ready to be basted and roasted on Christmas morning. And they had given themselves a head start on the all-important turkey stuffing—whose recipe Thaddeus had never been more happy that he had made his wife share with him on their first Christmas together—by dicing the bread for toasting, slicing up the water chestnuts and celery, and readying the wild rice and other ingredients to be mixed up and loaded inside the vacant chest of the great bird bright and early the next morning.

By the time they had the kitchen halfway cleaned up enough to begin mixing the batter for their traditional Christmas Eve supper of blintz pancakes, it was after six o'clock and already dark. Bing Crosby's Christmas album sounded softly from the other room, and a half-dozen candles added their flickering nuances to the Christmassy atmosphere.

"Whew, I'm pooped, Dad," said Matthew. "How about us taking a break?"

"I could go for a glass of that nog, how about you? Besides, I'm not all that hungry yet anyway."

"We did do a little more sampling than was good for us!" laughed Matthew.

"Just a little! Come on, let's see how that fire's doing."

They poured out two tall steins of the thick, frothy, eggy mixture from the canister in the refrigerator, then walked into the living room and sat down heavily in their two favorite chairs, both of which faced the fireplace.

It had been some time since any fresh fuel had been added, and the crackles coming from the hearth were steadily losing their energy. The room was warm, however, and neither man seemed inclined to move.

It fell silent.

Both stared straight ahead into the mesmerizing motion of the yellow flames licking at the wood from which they came. Nostalgic as the moment suddenly seemed, neither was thinking about the two women who had so occupied their thoughts during the day. As if by common unspoken consent, the minds of each had drifted to the Christmas tree behind them.

It was Thaddeus who at length broke the silence.

"Well, Matt," he said, suddenly jumping up, "if you're content to remain in the dark about it forever, I'm not."

He walked over to the tree, knelt down, picked up the long-shaped parcel of pink, rose, walked back to the fire, and handed it to Matthew. "I want to know what this is all about," he said. "It's Christmas Eve. No sense waiting any longer . . . open it up."

He sat back down, as if with authority, and took a large swig from his stein, wiping the milky moustache off his upper lip with his tongue.

Matthew sat still, just holding it, otherwise not moving a muscle.

"Go on, Son. What are you waiting for?" urged Thaddeus.

"I don't know, Dad. I have the strangest feeling about this package. It's almost like I'm afraid to open it."

"Afraid . . . afraid of what?"

"That's just it—I don't know. There's just . . . something odd about it."

"Do you want me to open it for you?" laughed Thaddeus.

"No, no, that's all right," said Matthew, taking a deep breath, then beginning tentatively to tear back the paper from one of its ends. "I don't suppose I can put if off forever."

Gingerly, as if his fingers divined the contents of the box before his eyes beheld it, he carefully tore away the paper and pulled out the long slender box. The two folds of one of the square ends were taped shut. Matthew inserted a finger and pulled away the tape, then opened the two flaps.

Heart beating rapidly, he gently turned the thin box on its end. Out onto his lap tumbled a single wilted rose at the end of a twelve inch stem.

Dumbly Matthew stared down, unable to comprehend the meaning of what had fallen and now lay on the top of his legs.

His brain spun wildly, his eyes blinking back tears of confusion and renewed anguish. His mouth opened as if he were trying to speak, but no words would come.

The crackling of the fire faded from his ears, the images of the room around him blurred and lost focus. Suddenly he was no longer sitting in a Bavarian chalet in the middle of winter but was walking briskly down a Berlin street in the warmth of an early morning, looking over hedges and in yards he passed . . . looking for a rose . . . for the perfect rose to give a special woman he was on his way to see.

In the midst of his recollection, a sound grated upon his consciousness.

He didn't want to hear it, not now. No—he wanted to stay back there . . . back in the past. He didn't want winter to come! He wanted it to remain summer forever!

There was the sound again. But still he refused to heed it. This was the summer of horse rides and laughter . . . and roses. He would not let winter come! He would not let the cruel snows destroy—

"Matt," repeated his father a third time. "Is that all there is . . . isn't there something more in the box—a note or a card or something?"

"Uh . . . uh, no. I . . . uh, think that's all," said Matthew, his brain rudely jarring itself back into reality, though hazily, as the momentary daydream faded.

He held the box up, peered inside it, then added, "That's it, Dad . . . nothing more." His voice was quiet . . . sleepy.

Glancing down at his lap again, now he gently grasped the stem and held it up. The well-formed drooping pink flower was still moist enough to cast its fragrance about a short distance, though its wilting petals would clearly begin to fall within another day or two.

"An odd gift," said Thaddeus.

"Not so odd, really," murmured Matthew, staring at it intently, as if begging the tiny wonder to speak of its origin, to tell the secret only it knew. His brain was still fuzzy with the vain attempt to separate the past from the present. He sat as one awake yet dreaming, caught in that nebulous land between wakefulness and sleep, where nothing is real but everything seems real.

"It's a *Meilland* . . . one of the classic pink varietals," Matthew went on, in but a faint whisper now. His voice was faraway. He had again grown unconscious to his father's presence. "I researched it after I'd given it to her that morning. . . ."

"What does it mean, Matt?" his father was saying.

Yet a moment more Matthew sat in a dull stupor.

Suddenly, as if a bomb had exploded inside his brain, all at once his eyes shot open wide. His body jerked instantly to attention, and the next moment he was leaping to his feet, oblivious to the fragile rose falling to the floor as he did so.

With incredulous agitation he paced the room like a suddenly caged tiger on the prowl, his mind and thoughts flying a hundred directions at once, aftershocks from the first mental explosion continuing to burst within him. He walked down the hall toward his bedroom, heedless of his steps, Thaddeus staring mystified after him.

He reappeared a moment later, eyes still huge, face white as a sheet.

"Matt, what is it all about?" said Thaddeus, growing concerned.

"She's the only one who knew," said Matthew, half to himself, half in response to his father's question.

"Knew what?"

"Knew of the Meilland . . . knew the exact variety of the pink rose. No one else knew . . . no one else *could* know."

Coming again to himself, suddenly Matthew ran back toward his chair, knelt down, and now picked up the delicate flower from the floor with hundredfold increased tenderness, tears flooding his eyes.

"It is a Meilland—I know it! There can be no doubt—the shade of pink, the elongated leaf, the thin stem, the faint but distinctive aroma. *That's* what it means, Dad," he said, glancing over excitedly at his father. "Don't you see—no one else but Sabina knew what the Meilland meant to us. This is the pink rose of the promise!"

"I'm afraid I'm still in the dark, Son," said a baffled Thaddeus.

"Dad, look at it! *This rose was cut less than a week ago!* What can it possibly mean but—"

Matthew stopped, choking on his own words, tears flowing freely down his cheeks by now.

"What can it possibly mean . . . but . . . but that somehow—as impossible as it seems . . . Sabina must still be alive!"

8 8

Following the Fragrance

• • •

THE THOUGHT OF BLINTZ PANCAKES COULD NOT HAVE
been further from Matthew McCallum's mind. Indeed, the fact that
it was Christmas Eve had long since faded into a distant memory of
some former time.

With feverish excitement Matthew paced the floor, bound only
by the length of the cord attached to the telephone.

"There's no one left," he said to his father, hand over the mouthpiece, "a receptionist, a secretary, two guards, and one ambassador's
assistant who's so far down on the list he's probably still in training."

"What did they say?" asked Thaddeus.

"She's looking," replied Matthew, frustration and impatience and
anticipation written across every line of his face. He could hardly
contain the energy threatening to burst out from within him in all
directions at once.

"Yes, the name's McCallum," said Matthew, speaking again into
the phone. "I'm attached to the State Department. The parcel would
have been delivered to you probably five or six days ago. . . . Yes,
possibly the first of this week, maybe last weekend. It arrived here on
Thursday, probably left Berlin Wednesday. . . ."

Again there was silence on the phone, and Matthew glanced over
at his father. "Christmas Eve, and Sunday to boot," he said.

"You might have to wait until Tuesday," put in Thaddeus.

"I *can't* wait, Dad—I've got to find out! I don't care if I have to
walk down off this mountain and drive to Berlin myself on Christmas
Day!"

Matthew continued his pacing. Thaddeus said nothing more for the moment. He disliked seeing his son get his hopes so high with nothing concrete to substantiate them. For Matthew's sake, if only to bring him back to reality, he knew he would have to play the devil's advocate soon enough. First he would wait to find out what the call to the consulate uncovered.

"What?" Matthew said. "Right—the incoming log. I see, good . . . last Monday, six days ago . . . midafternoon . . . and no record other than that—just the signature?" Matthew paused. "And the name?" he added, heart pounding.

Thaddeus watched as Matthew listened keenly to the voice at the Berlin office of the U.S. consulate.

"You're positive?" he said after a moment. "But who was it . . . ? What did she look like . . . yes, of course . . . I'll hold again."

A lengthier silence this time. The fire had burned low. The house was still, quieter than it had been all the busy day. Thaddeus rose and occupied himself for two or three minutes by throwing several more logs into the fireplace and stoking them about into flame. By they time they had caught, Matthew was speaking again.

"Yes, I understand. . . . Thank you—so, describe her as best you can."

Listening with great intensity, Matthew absorbed the words on the other end.

"You didn't ask what it was about?" The frustration began to show in his voice.

A pause.

"Yes, of course. I'm sorry. Why would you have thought to."

Another brief pause.

"Right . . . thank you. You've been extremely helpful. I appreciate it very much. If she should return . . . if you see her again, it is most urgent that you contact me immediately. Try to detain her, get an address or number where I can contact her. It is extremely important . . . yes, all right . . . good. Thank you again."

Matthew hung up the phone with a sigh, then continued to pace the room.

"Not much to go on," he said. "The signature on the incoming log when the package was brought in to them last Monday reads *Ursula*. The lady couldn't read the last name—thought it began with a *W* but couldn't be certain."

"The name mean anything to you?"

"Not a thing."

"A secret admirer, perhaps?" suggested Thaddeus.

"Come on, Dad! Why wouldn't there be a note?"

"If it was Sabina, why wouldn't there be a note?"

Matthew sighed. "I don't know. . . . I just don't know."

Again he sighed. "It wasn't Sabina anyway," he added disappointedly. "The secretary on duty tonight was at the front desk that day. She and I've met a time or two. She remembers the incident. I talked to her just now too. She remembers the lady coming in and saying she had a gift for me, says it struck her as odd at the time."

"Odd . . . why?"

"For the same reason it seems odd to us—no note, no explanation, no nothing. She said the woman seemed nervous and was reluctant to sign the log, just said they had to get the gift to me."

"You're certain it couldn't have been Sabina?"

Matthew nodded. "She said the lady was short, plain-looking, jet black hair, long thin nose, with dark complexion."

"No one you recognize?"

"Dad, I tell you I've got no secret admirers!"

"What other explanation can there be?"

"It's *got* to have something to do with Sabina."

"Why wouldn't Sabina have come herself?"

"Because, I don't know . . . maybe she's trapped on the other side of the wall, in East Berlin."

"How did she get the rose to the mystery lady at the consulate?"

"Dad, I don't know, but there *has* to be a connection?"

"I just don't want to see you hurt again, son. Hope is a wonderful thing, a gift from God. But unrealistic hopes can be pretty painful when they're dashed."

"I know . . . I know . . . but somehow I just feel Sabina's hand in this. I tell you, *nobody else* could have known about that particular pink rose."

"A coincidence perhaps."

"Maybe . . ."

Matthew's voice trailed away.

"You mentioned before a promise in connection with the pink rose. What was it?" asked Thaddeus.

Matthew smiled at the thought. "I promised her that nothing would ever separate us again, that I wouldn't let anything, even another war, keep us apart."

He paused a few seconds, then burst out again. "Don't you see, Dad. This has got to be Sabina's way of reciprocating that promise! She's telling me she's still alive, and that even what looks like a catastrophe *hasn't* come between us!"

"Why didn't she just tell you? Why no message, Matt?"

"Maybe she's still in danger . . . or she thinks I'm in danger. Maybe she's hurt too, or in a hospital. Maybe she knows that if she contacted me I would go after her and find her. She wants me to know she's alive, but doesn't want me to try to find her . . . for my sake! It's just like what she would do! It's exactly what her father told her all these years—to content herself in the knowledge that he was safe, but not to come to him because of the danger it would represent to them both. That's it, Dad!"

"What's it, Matt?" laughed Thaddeus. "I'm afraid you lost me."

"If Sabina is anything, she is the daughter of Heinrich von Dortmann. Don't you see! She's following precisely his footsteps! She's telling me, just like her father told her, that she's safe, she's alive, and she's content—and that I must likewise content myself in that knowledge. To come to her would be to endanger myself . . . and perhaps her as well. That's it—that's why there's no message! Anything else could have been traced. She knew I'd understand the message of the pink rose if I thought about it long enough!"

"There could be a hundred other explanations, Matt," said his father.

"There could be . . . but this rose is from Sabina, I tell you. I know it! And I *am* going to find her!"

"Even though perhaps she doesn't want to be found?"

"I have to, Dad! You said it yourself—she's the kind of woman that comes along once in a lifetime."

"Supposing Sabina is involved in this rose somehow . . . supposing she is alive . . . what can you do? You have nothing to go on. With all this mystery and possible danger, she must be behind the Iron Curtain. There's no way you can get to her, and there's no way she can get to the West. Everything's cut off. You know that better than anyone. Besides all that—you have no clues that would lead you to her."

"I have two clues, Dad—this pink rose, and the mystery lady named Ursula!"

"That still doesn't account for the wall. Khrushchev has cut the two of you off from each other. I don't see any way you could possibly—"

"I'll go to East Berlin. I'll pick up her trail somehow."

"No diplomats of your high level are being let in."

"I'll break in!" interrupted Matthew.

"Break in!" repeated Thaddeus. "People are trying to get out of East Berlin. And you want to break *in?*"

"I intend to find her if it takes me the rest of my life!"

"What about your affiliation with President Kennedy? You've got to be careful, Matt. You don't want to start a war."

Matthew was silent a moment, revolving many new things in his brain.

"You're right, Dad. I've got to think of the implication for Jack . . . and for the whole situation. But," he added, and now his voice had become determined, as if a threshold of decision had been crossed, "I do intend to find her . . . no matter what the risk . . . no matter where it takes me . . . no matter what I have to do."

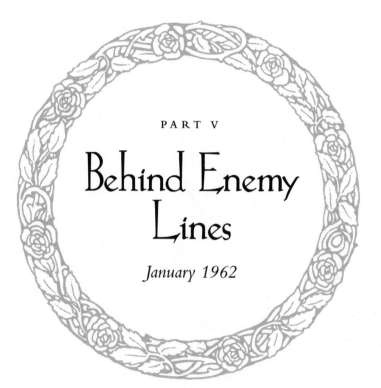

PART V

Behind Enemy Lines

January 1962

89

The White House Again

* * *

THE OCCASION FOR MATTHEW'S VISIT TO THE WHITE House during the second week of January 1962, though related to that of the previous July, was for an entirely different purpose.

After the two old friends shook hands, their pleasantries were kept to a minimum.

"You and your father have a nice Christmas?" the president asked.

"Very nice, thanks. Though by the time Christmas Day came, I had more on my mind than the holidays. But we'd baked enough food for an army, and stuffed ourselves as always."

"I take it that your living together has worked out well?"

"Yes, and I appreciate all you've done for us. I've never seen Dad so happy."

"I'm pleased," said the president. "You took the occasion of the holidays to retire your razor, I see," he added with a chuckle.

"Only temporarily."

"I hope you understand my appointment of General Clay."

"Of course I understand."

"Your responsibilities have been fairly broad. I've had you running all over from Vienna to London. But I needed someone focusing only on Berlin. Had this accident of yours not come up, you would have been my first choice for the position."

"Under the circumstances, you chose the best man for the job. Your mentioning it brings me to the reason for my visit."

Matthew wasted no time getting straight to the point of his hastily scheduled flight to Washington.

"I'm sorry to do this at such a time, Mr. President," he went on, "especially in that I don't feel I've been much help to you these last several months. But I've come to personally deliver to you my resignation. This time not just optional—I *am* officially resigning from your staff."

He leaned forward and handed the president the single typed sheet whose two sentences were brief and to the point.

"I'm sorry to hear that, Matthew," said Kennedy, glancing over it quickly. "Is there anything I can do to talk you out of it?"

"No, sir, there's not."

"It's not a matter of something to do with the duty . . . the pay . . . ?"

"No, nothing like that. It's just like it says there—personal reasons."

"The scapegoat for every resignation in this town!" laughed Kennedy. "Am I correct in assuming that your decision has something to do with our previous talk last summer, and the incident you were involved in at the border?"

"The less you know the better, Mr. President," replied Matthew. "For your own sake, there is a favor I would like to ask in conjunction with my resignation."

"Name it."

"I would like you to make my resignation public."

"No problem. I would do that anyway, with all due presidential regrets and kudos."

"I mean really public, so that the Russians and East Germans are well aware of it."

"All right."

"I flew to Washington to see you in person. Cite the old personal-reasons-and-job-stress gambit, and say that as far as you know I'm leaving for some long overdue R and R in my home state of Montana, which I'm telling you now, on the record, are my official plans at this point."

The president nodded, then eyed Matthew cagily out of one eye.

"What are you really up to, Matthew?"

"Those are my official plans. If I should happen to get waylaid on my way to Montana, well, those are the kinds of things you can never predict."

"Come on, my old friend, level with me."

"Off the record, Mr. President?"

Kennedy nodded. "There are no microphones in this office, Matthew," he said, then added with a sly grin, "and if there were, I didn't turn them on for this interview."

"All right then," said Matthew, "but I never said this to you, remember."

"Agreed."

"Then where I'm going on my way to Montana is behind the Iron Curtain."

Kennedy sat upright in his chair.

"Everybody else is trying to get out, and you're telling me that you're going to break *into* the DDR! How?"

"Don't know yet, but I'll find a way. I have a few connections."

"It sounds crazy . . . do you know what you're doing?"

"No. I just have no choice. It's something I have to do. I'll have to learn as I go."

"Now that you've cut off all your ties with the government, what if you get in a jam?"

"That's a chance I have to take. I can't risk involving you. That's why I want my resignation made public."

"I see your point."

"There are two other things you could do," added Matthew. "I'd appreciate it if Dad could keep the house until I get back, whether on staff or not doesn't matter."

"Of course. I would like to keep him on staff, if he's agreeable."

"I'm sure he will be very grateful."

"You said two things?"

Matthew did not answer immediately. When he did, his voice contained a tone of resignation and foreboding. "If word leaks out about an American nabbed by the KGB and being held in one of their torture dungeons," he said, "you might send the CIA in after me. I'll be using a different name . . . but chances are it'll be me."

90

Undying Embers

. . .

LOLA REINHARDT HAD KNOWN NOTHING OF THE UNDER-lying significance of the incident for her boss, only that he and his Russian assistant were trying to prevent a prison escape.

But during the months of his convalescence she had come to enjoy a much closer intimacy with young Galanov, who, though his wounds had been more severe, had been released from the hospital first. Before he had been called away, she had become privy to what he knew regarding the object of their section chief's personal ruling passion—his *Hauptleidenschaft*.

At first the news crushed her. It was another woman he was pursuing, not an enemy of the state!

How could such a revelation not wound a sensitive spirit like hers? Upon further reflection, however, Lola recognized that perhaps, like Galanov, she could put the knowledge to use for her own purposes. Toward that end she had been busily engaged ever since.

This was not a country where advantages were bestowed on the fainthearted, Lola thought. One had to look for opportunity, then seize it.

She had been lucky enough to obtain this assignment as secretary in the office of the Secret Police. Before his death, her father had known someone in the agency responsible for such things, and he had hired her as a favor to an old friend. Now her father was dead, along with her mother. She was alone in the world. As long as she remained a mere hireling, she would never acquire any material advantages. Few did these days. Even the job was not that secure. She could find herself cast adrift anytime. She had known enough deprivation during the depression years not to relish the thought of facing such again. If it took collaboration, if it took duplicity—well, so be it. Half the people in the DDR collaborated with the government or the *Stasi* in one way or another. Why shouldn't she use her position to her best advantage?

Such was her only way to ensure some kind of future for herself. If the truth were told, she knew she was unlikely to marry if she left events to take their natural course. It was getting late for that. At thirty-seven, her best years had passed her by, and she had never been altogether attractive even in her younger days.

As a teenager, she remembered with bitter inner anguish the day, standing at school with four or five others, when several boys had begun laughing amongst themselves. Cringing in fear that she was somehow the object of their derision, she turned away, but could not help overhearing one of them say, "Who's the ugly one talking to our scrumptious German Fräuleins?"

Brushing away the painful memories from long ago, Lola put the papers she had been reviewing back into the brown manila packet, then rose from the chair.

This is no time to dwell on the past, she thought. Suddenly the present was filled with plenty to occupy her attention!

It had certainly been to her advantage that both the section chief and his assistant had been battered in the crash badly enough to require extended hospitalization. Galanov himself had nearly gone the way of the pilot, who hadn't lived five seconds past the initial impact. But Galanov's stalwart young Russian stock had served him well. Both he and his boss had recovered and were now, with only a few bandages and remaining limps to show for it, about their business again, though Galanov had been subsequently called back to Russia.

Lola had put the weeks of their convalescence to good use, assuming more command of Section Chief Schmundt's office than she would ever have dared in his presence. She had made calls and set investigations in several directions, acting in every case by the authority of Herr von Schmundt himself. She had surprised even herself with the authority she was able to bring to her voice and her bearing and was surprised even further by the obedient cooperation she received. People were more afraid of the *Staatssicherheitsdienst* than she had ever realized.

She had personally visited Potsdam, both the prison and the morgue. She had gone to Teltow. She had familiarized herself with all the principal players in her boss's private little drama, from the baron and his daughter to the American. She had gone over every millimeter of every file connected with the case.

Now, at length, her probings and confidential inquiries had paid off.

Putting to full effect a certain uniquely female version of *Stasi* muscle-flexing bravado, she had discovered facts which, there could be no doubt, the section chief was himself completely unaware of.

He would kill for what she possessed. He had *already* killed for it, though unsuccessfully. To divulge it, however, would be to doom her own chances to turn the inclination of his affections in her direction.

Still holding the confidential packet that had just been delivered to the office a short while earlier—fortunately while Herr von Schmundt was out and she was alone to receive it—Lola continued to walk slowly about the cramped quarters where for so many thankless years she had carried out her menial tasks as the man's secretary.

It was not that she was under any particular illusion about being in love with the man. He was not all that attractive, physically or in any other way. He was neither tender nor sensitive, nor even especially kind. He did possess power by virtue of his position, and there was, she admitted, a certain raw compelling generated by a man of influence. Beyond that, however, there wasn't much passion associated with what might be called her feelings for the man.

But communism made realists of all but hopeless idealists and idiots.

Lola Reinhardt was neither.

Life was not easy in this part of the world. If you wanted to make it tolerable, you accommodated emotional needs by accepting what came your way and making the best of it. She could be content and reasonably secure as Frau Gustav von Schmundt, and she would rather grow old as a taken-for-granted Frau where there was at least a lukewarm body to share one's living quarters with than become a lonely old maid, *alte Jungfer,* who went home to a cold apartment and colder bed at the end of every drab, meaningless day.

She had halfway suspected what the contents of this packet

revealed, but now she had proof positive right in her hands. She had taken measures to ensure that the information came through no official channels and could not be traced. No one knew of it but herself and the two or three peasants who had been bribed, and none of them would talk. They didn't even know who she was. The several dossiers she had had sent to her were not directly connected, and she had masked her reasons for wanting them with great shrewdness befitting her station.

They confirmed everything, including the changeable loyalties of the lackey at the morgue. All the pieces finally fit. She held the solution to her boss's quest.

To hand it over to him would win his temporary praise and gratitude . . . but it would never win his devotion. Until he saw the corpse with his own two eyes, the heart of Gustav von Schmundt would never see her to whom his eyes had long since become far too accustomed.

What should she do? Lola wondered.

One thing was certain. If she did not turn it over to him, the fact of its existence would ever after incriminate her. If found, she would lose her job, her future, and any hope for marriage, and perhaps even find herself in prison.

The decision must be made now, and it was forever irrevocable.

Only a moment more she hesitated.

The next she grabbed up her coat, thrust the packet under it where it could not be seen, and left the building, going in the direction of the river.

She had set her course.

No one's eyes would ever again set themselves upon what Lola Reinhardt's had read twenty minutes earlier. The packet would soon be settling into its permanent grave in the oozing mud under the slow-flowing waters of the Spree.

91

Through the Curtain

• • •

THREE WEEKS WAS NOT LONG ENOUGH TO GROW MUCH of a beard.

Who could tell how long this thing might take? He could well look like Rip van Winkle by the time it was over, though he hoped to be out of here while his face still had a fuzzy and scraggly appearance.

In either event, it should camouflage his identity well enough to keep any officials he should run into—whom he hoped would be few—from recognizing him at a quick glance, and to prevent any descriptions his activities might generate from causing a link to the United States government or the White House.

How guys like Paddy Red made a lifetime business of sneaking around like this he couldn't imagine. They were a different breed of human animal, he supposed—thriving on danger and intrigue.

He wondered if they ever felt fear or if having their life constantly on the line was something they enjoyed.

He was afraid, Matthew knew that much!

Anybody'd be a fool not to be afraid behind the Iron Curtain like this, where one in five or two in five, whatever it was, of the citizenry were actively involved in the business of supplying information to the Secret Police, where the guns had real bullets and those carrying them weren't afraid to use them, where the Kremlin dictated everything, where America was the supreme enemy, where trial by jury was unknown, and where all jail terms were for life and most prisoners wound up far away in the snowy regions of Siberia.

And where things had been so tense for the last year as to have the whole world fearing that nuclear war was about to break out.

Who wouldn't be afraid!

Berlin was a tinderbox, and he was right in the heart of it.

But here he was—there was no turning back now. He'd set his course three weeks ago, on that memorable Christmas Eve when he'd hardly slept a wink, revolving over and over the plan that had already begun, that very night, to take shape in his brain. Between their exchange of gifts and the turkey and the apple strudel, he and his father had spent most of Christmas Day going over the scheme as it then existed. His father had simultaneously tried to talk him out of it and had battered him with questions to help him refine it.

The next day, Tuesday the twenty-sixth, he'd driven to Berlin. He'd talked to the people at the consulate and examined the signature of the mystery delivery lady himself. Then he'd spoken with Bob Clatchen, who had been extremely helpful, off the record, in getting him the several East German identity papers he would need and told him how to contact Paddy Red once he was in.

Then had come the quick flight back to Washington, D.C.—with a one way ticket—and the return to Munich, also one way, under a different name.

The last week he had spent with his father, giving his beard time to fill in. Then the return to Berlin, his new identity papers, East German money, the clothes and makeup—and now here he was.

Slowly, hunched over his cane, he made his way along the final free block of now-famous Friedrichstrasse and approached the uniformed border officer. He had gone over and over the scenario. Even though this was the easiest part of the whole thing, he couldn't help trembling inside. If anything went wrong here, it was all over.

It was dusk, between four and five in the afternoon. The hour had been chosen for the dim light, in case one of the guards should look too closely.

He approached the station known as Checkpoint Charlie. Two guards stood at attention. He hobbled up slowly, pulled out his identity card. The guard glanced at it briefly and with a silent nod of the head passed him on into the small building where the papers were checked and processed.

Inside he took his place in line behind three or four others . . . and waited. At last he reached the front.

He put his identity card and the forged papers Clatchen had obtained for him on the small counter.

"So, old man, you are returning from holidays, no?"

"Ja, mein Herr," answered the gravelly voice from behind the thin but obviously grey beard.

"Visiting your brother in the West, I see."

"Ja."

"How does he happen to be in the West, Herr . . . uh, Herr Liebermann?" asked the clerk, glancing down at the card before him.

"The wall separated us, *mein Herr."*

"I see. And you . . . you are not tempted to *stay* with your brother, Herr Liebermann?"

"Oh *nein, mein Herr.* Berlin is my home."

"You mean *East* Berlin?"

"Ja, mein Herr."

"So, you find the West not to your liking, eh . . . not all the American propaganda would have us believe, eh, Herr Liebermann."

"Nein, mein Herr."

"Then go back to your cold apartment, Liebermann. Next, *bitte!"* called out the clerk, shoving the papers back across the counter and looking up to the next person in line.

Matthew took them and stuffed them inside his coat as he hastened outside and into the descending darkness of East Berlin.

He breathed in a deep sigh of relief, then walked quickly along Friedrichstrasse and away from the checkpoint.

That was the easy part, he thought.

All over East Germany there were plots and schemes to break across the interzonal frontier into West Berlin or the Federal Republic itself. A highly publicized and spectacular escape had taken place in October near Duderstadt, in which fifty-five persons, including fifteen women, one pregnant, and twenty-three children, had made their way dramatically to freedom. Nor had it been the only such escape. All along the wall holes were being found to exploit.

The flow, however, was all one-directional. No one had to plot and scheme to get *into* the DDR, except diplomats. Just last month a U.S. adviser had been barred entrance to East Berlin. Though he had disguised himself as an old man, had it not been for his connections with the president, he could probably have walked straight through with an American passport, and scarcely been looked at twice.

Now that he was in, however, it was a whole new ball game. Getting out and back into the BRD—that would be risky.

It had already cost a dozen or so their lives.

He turned and glanced back briefly.

Even if he changed his mind right now, turned around, and went back to Charlie, told the guards he'd made a mistake and asked to be let back into West Berlin, everything would be changed. They would never let him through. The fifty meters he had just traversed might as well have been fifty miles!

He had walked into the Communist prison. Though the evening was quiet all around him, it was as if a huge clank of iron had slammed the door of his cell shut behind him. He was imprisoned now just as surely as the baron had been at Neustädt!

He wasted no more than a second in his reflections, then turned again and walked on along the street, turned left on Leipzigerstrasse, and was quickly lost to sight from the checkpoint.

He hoped the message had gotten to Paddy Red and that the agent was where he was supposed to be.

92

Nostalgic Streets

• • •

IT WASN'T MUCH OF A PLAN, MATTHEW THOUGHT TO himself as he walked along.

Actually, he didn't have a plan at all. He had two leads—a pink rose, now completely withered, and the name, Ursula, of the lady who had delivered it. Neither had been traceable. Beyond the mere fact that both existed—the rose and the woman—he knew nothing.

A strong sense had grown within him, however, that if he could just *be* here . . . something would come to him, that a sense of direction would follow . . . that God would direct his steps.

The Scripture from Proverbs 3 had come to him on Christmas Day and had never left him since. *Trust in the Lord with all your heart, and do not rely on your own understanding. In all your ways acknowledge him, and he will direct your paths.*

He had thought of it over and over. As he did he seemed to feel the Lord telling him to believe in the promise. Not merely to "believe," but also to *act* upon that belief. If he abandoned himself to God's leading, acknowledging the Father's guidance, his way *would* become clear, one step at a time.

The words came to his spirit: *Acknowledge me, do what you think to do, pursue the options that open before you. Then trust me, listen for my voice, pray continually . . . and the way will be made clear before you.*

He had no understanding of his own he *could* trust in. He *had* to rely on the Lord to direct his paths—there was no other alternative. He had prayed on Christmas Day and given his course, the pathway he felt he had to follow, over into the Lord's hands.

Since then, he had tried to listen intently to every subtle leading that might indicate direction from on high, while at the same time pursuing everything he could think of himself to do.

Over the course of the weeks of preparation, the only direction that seemed clear was that he must *go*. He was reminded of Abraham, to whom God said, "Leave your own country, your own people and your father's house, and go to the land I will show you." The first phase of his journey was simply to "go" to the place where Sabina would be if she were alive—East Berlin . . . East Germany. If that was the first step God showed him, he would take that step and then wait for future "paths" to become apparent.

The only sound in the evening air was that of his footfall along the East Berlin sidewalk.

It was too much to hope for, he thought to himself, to simply find Sabina once again well and living as before in her apartment. She couldn't be there! Yet it was impossible to keep his heart from pounding rapidly as he drew nearer and nearer to the familiar house.

Memories began to flood him as he went—all the times he and Sabina had shared last summer . . . the slow ride by carriage to the ball . . . the morning he had brought her the pink rose . . . the many talks they had had walking peacefully back to her apartment from the West, having no idea what terrible division was to wrench apart this city or what tragedy was soon to come to their lives.

The streets seemed quieter now, quieter than the evening hour could account for. As great as he thought the contrast between East and West had been back then, at least he had had Sabina to share it with. She brought life to any place! Walking the streets of East Berlin now felt like walking inside a gigantic tomb. The only universal in this part of the city was silence.

There was the house up ahead!

Again his heart began to thump with rapidly increasing pace. *Oh, God . . . if only . . . God, please . . .*

He could not even complete the prayer. The thought was too incredible even to contemplate that his eyes might, in spite of all reason against it, soon lay themselves upon that wonderful face again.

Suddenly a terrible thought occurred to him.

What if she was alive and was at home, but hadn't contacted him and hadn't wanted him to find her . . . because the explosion had injured her permanently, disfigured or burned her face beyond recognition. What if she was crippled . . . or worse!

His feelings for her would never change. Oh, but how his heart would ache for her.

He had to tell her! He had to let her know that no external injuries or scars would change how he felt!

He was running now. He was nearly there . . . he turned toward it off the street!

A light shone in the house!

Oh, God . . . let her be there. . . . Let her know, Father . . . let her know that I . . .

Again his prayers fell short. Why had he waited so long to come to her? Why hadn't he come months ago!

Here was the porch. They had stood here so many times talking late into the warm summer evenings. . . .

Matthew paused, perspiring, took in a deep breath, hardly able to contain his mounting excitement . . . then walked the few remaining steps and knocked on the door.

Footsteps sounded from inside! He knew them. There could be no mistake—they were a woman's step.

The door opened twenty or thirty cautious centimeters.

A strange face appeared.

The woman, forty-eight or fifty years of age, stared out at him blankly for a second, then her forehead creased in anxiety and annoyance.

"Ist . . . uh, Fräulein Duftblatt zu Hause?" fumbled Matthew, taken aback by the unfamiliar face.

"Fräulein Duftblatt? There is no one here by that name."

"She used to live in this house. I must locate her."

"She is not here," said the woman roughly, attempting to close the door.

"Please," interrupted Matthew. "Have you heard the name?"

"Never."

"How long have you been here?"

"That is none of your affair," she snapped, again attempting, this time with more force, to shut the door.

"Please," implored Matthew, "were there no . . . possessions, no furniture?"

"The house was empty," she replied with growing impatience. "My brother, who works for the government, obtained this house for us in August. There was nothing here."

"He told you nothing about why the house was empty?"

"Only that the former occupant was dead. I know nothing of the name Duftblatt. Now go away or I will tell my husband to call the authorities. Gottfried!" she called behind her into the house, *"Hier gibt es ein Bettler!"*

"Please," insisted Matthew, "I'm no beggar. I mean you no harm. If I could just perhaps have a quick look inside—"

He never finished the sentence. A burly man, more angry than anxious, suddenly appeared behind the woman.

"Get out of here, old man, or I will call the police!" he growled. "We want none of your kind here."

With rude finality, the door slammed in Matthew's face. In stunned disappointment he staggered backward down the few steps, then turned and walked again to the street, words ringing crassly in his ear—*dead . . . house was empty . . . nothing of the name Duftblatt . . . former occupant was dead . . . former occupant was dead.*

This was certainly no fairy tale—no horse and carriage awaited him to transport him to the princess of his dreams! There was only the cold, dark, silent January street.

Aimlessly he stumbled back in the direction he had come.

God, what shall I do now? he asked. *I have taken the only two steps I knew to take—coming to East Berlin and going to her house. What now, Lord? Guide my steps. I have no understanding of my own that I could trust in if I would. I don't know what to do, Lord. . . . I don't know where to go. I felt you leading me here . . . now guide my steps on whatever pathway you would have me take. . . . I do acknowledge you, my Father. . . . Help me, O Lord, to find her. Lead me to her, Father!*

A quote from the Scotsman came back to him. It seemed especially appropriate right now.

> *We do not understand the next page of God's lesson book, we see only the one before us. It is impossible to turn the leaf until we have learned the lesson of that before us. When we understand the one before us, only then are we able to turn the next.*

Lord, he prayed, *show me the step I am to take now.*

The only thing to do now was to keep his rendezvous with Paddy Red. Hopefully by then some future direction or step would be revealed to him.

93

Liebermann and Red

• • •

BEFORE HE WAS HALFWAY TO THE HOTEL, WHERE HE WAS to spend the night and where Paddy Red would contact him, praying and talking over everything with the Father as he went, the page began to turn.

Where else, indeed, was more fitting to go! As he walked, the sense of leading grew stronger and stronger.

Go to the land I will show you . . . your own people and your father's house . . . your father's house—father's house!

Of course!

It was suddenly so clear and obvious. True, he wasn't exactly taking the Scripture according to its literal intent, but God had many ways of using his Word to indicate leading and direction. What the Lord would show him there, he didn't yet know. But in the absence of any other clues, what other spot on all the earth could put him once again on the trail of those he loved so dearly?

It may have been a cold trail in the world's estimation, but in God's timetable the passage of time gave no concern.

Matthew's heart leapt within him. He had been shown the next step to take! He was certain of it.

Only one step, it was true, but a significant one.

He would go to the father's house!

Then he would simply pray for direction to be shown him for the next step after that!

Thank you . . . thank you, Father! he whispered excitedly, as he walked up to the hotel and inside. *In all your ways acknowledge him, and he will direct your paths. . . . Thank you, Lord!*

•   •   •

"So, Charlie, they tell me you may require my assistance again," said the man known as Paddy Red once they were seated in Matthew's small and dingy hotel room. "I don't know that I'd have recognized you," he added. "First-rate disguise. I'd take you for an old codger of seventy."

"I'm surprised you're not afraid to be seen so openly with me," remarked Matthew.

"Visiting an old bloke named Liebermann, what's just come back from visiting his brother. Who's paying attention? Everything's changed now, mate. For all their spying, you can't imagine how stupid these Communist blokes can be sometimes."

"But why are you still here—on the Eastern side, I mean? Didn't most of the agency's operatives go back to the safety of West Berlin?"

"A lot did."

"You're in even more danger now."

"True enough. But if it weren't for the danger, what's a spy doing in the espionage game anyway, wot? Yeah, they told me I could come in from the cold. But I figured we needed some people over here, and my cover's set deep. Hated to waste all those years getting it in place. Plus, I've got my cyanide pill."

"Doesn't sound very comforting to me."

"But you're not a spy then, are you, mate? Anyway, they told me you needed my help."

"How'd they tell you?" asked Matthew.

"We still got our ways," answered Red. "That wall of theirs can't shut out information from passing back and forth. The less you know the better. Just tell me what you need and I'll see what I can do. You heard what happened to the bloke I put you onto last time?"

"Who, the fox?"

"That's the bloke. We can't use his help no more."

"Why not?"

"Came to an untimely end."

"No, I didn't hear."

"Shot and killed, he was."

"When was it?"

"Back in August, right after you and I had done our business. That's why I figured maybe you had something to do with it."

"What day?"

"I don't know, seems like it was in the first week sometime, around the fifth, sixth, seventh."

Matthew took in the information somberly. That was exactly the time of the escape, he thought to himself. What could have happened to Schlaukopf after they parted in the woods?

"What's the matter, Charlie? You got affections for the sleazy bloke?"

"Uh . . . no, I just hadn't heard, that's all," said Matthew, reminded again how near death was in this spy game these kinds of people played. He would never get used to it and would be glad when all this was over.

"So, what kind of help you need, mate?" said Red. "You got two sets of IDs, I take it?"

Matthew nodded. "Liebermann and Albrecht," he said. "I need Albrecht to become an authorized agent of some kind. A doctor, psychiatrist—or maybe a governmental official who would reasonably be granted access. An examiner, an engineer, perhaps a builder with papers to inspect for repairs or construction."

Matthew told him what he had in mind.

The agent revolved the information over in his mind. "Hmm . . . risky business, that," he said at length. "What isn't over here? Might work. You'll need a car too. What name you want it registered in?"

"Hmm . . . I hadn't thought about that."

"I'll get two registrations, in case you have to become Liebermann again. All I'll be able to get is a run-down little Trabi."

"That will be fine."

"I've got two. I'll get papers showing one of them registered to you. Sure you don't mind a Trabi?"

"I'll fit in with every other car on the road."

"You want me to go along?"

Matthew shook his head. "Something tells me this phase of it I need to do alone. Is there any way I can get in touch with you later?"

"I'll be back here in three or four days. I'll bring what you need. I'll get you some kind of papers. I'll tell you then how to contact me."

94

Back on the Hunt

• • •

THE HELICOPTER CRASH HAD RATTLED HIM.

Being in the hospital so long was bad enough. But as his focus gradually returned, and he realized what he'd done, many realities, long overdue, began to knock upon the soul's door of Gustav von Schmundt, onetime friend of royalty and present *Stasi* agent. The Communist regime to which he had given his allegiance could build walls against humankind. But even the mighty power of Moscow could erect no barriers against that most human institution of all— the conscience of men and women created in the image of their Creator.

Walls are inherent in the human predicament, though their divisions by definition stand contrary to the purposes of God. The wall that had forever changed the history and direction of this city was a symbol and type of that great human wall that men since Adam have been raising against he who would be Father to his own creatures.

Persistent had been the attempts of the heavenly voice to penetrate the thick crust with which a lifetime of self-motivated choices had surrounded what remained of Gustav's heart. The only barrier capable of construction against those soft and never-tiring divine whispers is self-raised from within. It was a wall intrinsically different from that now bisecting this city of his loyalties in this: that the stone curtain of Communism had been raised to keep people *in,* while the purpose of the wall surrounding his heart was to keep the voice of his conscience *out.*

He was a man divided, as Germany was a nation divided, whose core, like Berlin, was surrounded by a suffocating wall raised against that which could give freedom, purpose, and pulsating life to his manhood.

Unlike this nation, which would have to wait another generation to begin healing the scar that now cut across its soul, the wall around Gustav's heart had suddenly been breached. His conscience had awakened and stood at the ready, with hammers and axes, swords and explosives. It only awaited his order—that all-imperative command given from within—to begin the destruction that would allow *life* to flow into the inner chambers of his being.

There had already come many crossroads in Gustav's life, all unrecognized by him as such. How patient had been the Hound of Heaven, how many opportunities he had given, how many forks in the road had been provided that could have changed the direction of Gustav's character.

But Gustav had not done well. The severity of the consequences of his actions thus grew ever more irrevocable.

Now, at long last, he had committed that most heinous crime against life itself. He had looked another man in the eye and, in a moment of passionate rage, had pulled the trigger of the gun borne in his own hand and killed him—a fellow man, a brother of the human species.

Then, while still not recovered from the shock of the first murder, he had killed how many others?—three, perhaps as many as five or six, and almost himself—with his recklessness from the helicopter.

The seriousness of his own injuries had taken its toll on mind as well as body. For weeks he had been but vaguely conscious of what he had done. But once full realization had come back, many and varied were his responses.

Suddenly, as without warning from so many years of silence, his conscience stood at his bedside like a mighty, unwelcome demon, ready to unleash its flurry of accusations.

Pangs of remorse threatened to overwhelm him when he thought of Sabina. *How could he have done it!* He loved her . . . and now—

He turned his head away and blinked back the tears that fain would rise to begin the cleansing.

The sight of the bloody specter at Teltow crossing would not leave him . . . nor Sabina's face . . . the baron's loving countenance smiling down upon him as a boy.

He had betrayed them all. He had betrayed life itself. What kind of foul man had he become!

Could he shed tears of remorse? Or had he sunk so low that true and life-changing contrition could not rise up to remake him?

Two roads stood before him, as they had so many times in the past—the way of self and pride, and the way of relinquishment and surrender. The former would combat the pain of conscience by raising the battlements yet higher, by adding mortar and bricks and wire to the heart-surrounding walls. The latter would allow the pain to do its work, letting the walls collapse and the soothing waters of repentance flow in with their stinging yet soothing balm.

Gustav, Gustav—heed the voice! Whatever you have done, your Father yet loves you. Turn to his face, not away. In him is your only refuge from the sin that has nearly killed you.

Though the consequences cannot be undone in this life, it is still not too late for repentance!

Yours is the predicament of Judas after he had thrown down the thirty pieces of silver at the feet of his temporary allies in the cause of Satan—how to repent when you have betrayed the very Savior of men!

Could Judas have repented even then, after the example of Peter following his own threefold betrayal? Is the entryway into the Father's heart ever closed to any man or woman, however monstrous their sin?

Heed the whispers of the divine Lover of all! You can yet know life. He can save you, as the thief on the cross—now . . . today. Ah, Gustav, let the death you have wrought bring life! Who can tell what good the Father may yet be able to accomplish by your giving your steps, your way, your all to him?

Gustav shook his head, got up from the bed, and began pacing the small room.

This was no time to be getting sentimental, he thought to himself.

All right, he had acted impulsively. He had killed a man. Now Sabina and her father were dead too. It wasn't the end of the world, nor did it have to mean he had failed in everything. He would still gain control of their estate and with it the legendary fortune. He would carry out his father's lifelong dream and get the best of the two of them at the same time!

He shook his head again. *No,* he thought—he would *not* listen to the maudlin voices that would make a weakling of him!

He would not become as that fool, the baron, whom he had killed.

What had he been thinking to give way to such misty tomfoolery? It must have been some dream that had awakened him.

There was only one way out of these mental doldrums, that was to redirect the energy he had devoted to finding Sabina to get his hands on the Dortmann estate, to find the papers, and even the gold if he could.

Besides, he thought further, once Korsch learned that his two chief leads for the locating of the rabbi were dead, he was bound to be more than a little annoyed. He needed to hedge his bets by having something perhaps even more valuable instead.

Who could tell? thought Gustav. Maybe he'd been looking in the wrong direction for the rabbi all this time. The fellow had spent considerable time at *Lebenshaus*. Perhaps that was where to dig up his trail, not from Sabina or the baron at all!

95

To the Place of Beginnings

• • •

MATTHEW STILL WASN'T CLEAR WHAT HE WOULD DO IF HE did get inside. He still had no specific plan. Going *to* the "father's house" had been the only direction he had sensed, not what to do once he was *in* it.

Now here he was. He would just have to wait for what would come next.

Just being here made him feel so close to Sabina again that it would almost be worth it even if nothing came of it.

It had probably been foolish to come so early in the day. But he couldn't just walk in. Something inside him had to commune with the surroundings first, to pray, to think, to allow his reflections to do their work in his heart. It was his way of giving over his steps to the Lord. He had to find a quiet place to calm himself so as to allow the voice of the Spirit to enter more fully into his being.

Even as he had driven north and crossed the East German border into Poland, he knew where that place would be.

He had driven Paddy Red's little Trabi, now licensed and regis-tered under his new alias, into the woods, following the way by various side roads as best he could recall, parked about half a kilometer away, and walked the rest of the way up the hill. He hadn't been here in more than twenty years. He hoped he had the right section of woods and that no walkers or hunters were about.

There it was, just ahead. It *was* still here.

He burst into a jog, reached it, climbed up the ladder, then eased his way into the seat of the hunter's box.

In front of him the plain that had once been the Dortmann estate spread into view. The trees had grown and several obstructed his sight, but he could still make out the house and grounds of *Lebenshaus* clearly.

From this vantage point the house itself seemed unchanged, as did the surrounding countryside. Niedersdorf could still be seen in the distance, with the Schmundt estate between. All the land of both estates had been confiscated by the Communist regime of the DDR. *Lebenshaus* itself had been put to other uses by the state, though the land of the whole region had continued to be worked as part of the giant state-controlled communal cooperative farming system implemented throughout the Soviet satellite nations.

The outline of *Der Frühlingsgarten* could clearly be seen sloping down to the left from the plateau upon which the house stood. High hedges still mostly surrounded it, but they were so overgrown and unkept that they had more than halfway degenerated to the wild state. Approximately halfway down, a tractor path had been cut across the entire width of the garden—creating an ugly scar, as across a once-lovely face—connecting the front of the house with the path next to the oak tree which had also been widened for equipment use. Within the garden itself, Matthew was relieved to see a great deal of remaining greenery, though most of the trees and some of the shrubs were bare from the winter's cold. The garden, like the hedges, had reverted to its wild state. Both bridges across the stream were broken down. He couldn't make out the condition of the rose garden itself. It didn't look good, but he thought he could still tell where it had been, which was a hopeful sign. He wished he had a pair of binoculars. Paths were scarcely visible; grass and weeds grew everywhere amongst the prized plants that had been nurtured by the baron's own loving hands.

But, thought Matthew, at least it had not been destroyed or plowed under. It could hardly more be called a Garden of Spring. If any name fit the jungle inside the hedges now, it would be Wild Garden. But at least there remained some semblance of gardenness to it, and for that he could not have been more pleased.

All the grounds bore the same uncared-for look. The arch into the garden had stones missing. The courtyard at the back of the house looked sloppy. The pond was empty of water, all the plants and shrubs were either dead or completely overgrown, and all the nicely trimmed lawns of former times leading downward from the courtyard had long since been taken over by weeds and wild pasture-grasses. Several large new barns and outbuildings had been constructed on the lower portions of the grounds, though a high fence separated the grounds of the house from the farmland to the north and east, indicating the distinct uses to which the former estate had been converted now that the whole was in Communist hands.

Part of him wished for nothing so much as that Sabina was here sitting beside him again, as they had sat here long before in the season of their innocent youthfulness. Another part of him was almost glad she was not here to see it, for how could the sight do other than crush her spirit. *Ichabod,* he thought—"The spirit has departed." He could feel, even from this distance, that the life had gone out of this place.

So much was here—so many memories from the past, so much pain to be reminded of from the present . . .

There was the balcony where he had shared such joy with Sabina . . . the storm . . . the delight they had both felt . . . and that wonderful moment at her side when her hand had slipped quietly into his . . . then later the exchange of yellow rose and china box to seal their friendship.

Closer to his vantage point still wound the stream he had as a teenager foolishly jumped while clumsily trying to hang on to the white Belgian.

Immediately he was flooded with all the memories of the following week he had spent at *Lebenshaus,* hobbling about on his broken leg, and then discovering the under-portions of the house with Sabina . . . her mysterious tapping on the other side of his wall . . . the legend of the hidden dungeon . . . old Eppie's tales . . . the yet-undiscovered passageway from the garden into the cellar.

And of course . . . the rose garden.

As his eyes scanned it all, they came back to rest in the center of the now-overrun garden plot, just below the tractor-scar through its middle.

If he had to pinpoint a time, a place, a moment when his life with God had begun, it would be right down there, on that fateful, memorable day during the summer of 1937 when he was seventeen years old.

Like it was yesterday, he could hear the baron's words to him: *"If how we view God is new to you, how are you accustomed to thinking of him?"*

That question had opened the door to so many new worlds to him, thought Matthew, as had everything Sabina's father had said to him. That day had led eventually to the pathway of discovery, as the baron had called it, of his own personal faith and walk with the Father. Fragments of the conversation now tumbled back through his mind as he sat gazing upon the site these twenty-four years later. . . .

"God is our Father, Matthew . . . a loving and kind and generous and giving Father. . . . He wants to walk and visit and fellowship with us. . . . He is a good Father . . . a father to call Father . . ."

Tears still standing in them, Matthew closed his eyes. *Lord, thank you for that special day in my life,* he prayed. *Thank you for Baron von Dortmann and his large love for you that he so eagerly and yet gently and compassionately shared with all who crossed his path.*

He paused, taking in a deep breath, opening his eyes once again.

Now, Father, he continued, eyes still open, *guide me in this present time. It is a new day. Help me . . . order my steps . . . fill my thoughts. Help me in all ways to trust you, not myself. Let me rely on your wisdom, not my own insight. Reveal to me what you would have me see, show me where you would have me go, tell me what you would have me do. Protect me, Father . . . and keep your loving hand upon Sabina as well. Lead me to her, Lord . . . lead me to her, I pray.*

He sighed deeply.

It was time, Matthew thought. His spirit was calm. The Lord would direct his paths. Such he had promised. The moment had come for him to put his trust in that promise . . . and move forward.

He climbed down from the hunter's box, then began the walk down the hill through the pinewood to Paddy Red's parked Trabi.

96

Inspector Albrecht

• • •

WITH A BEARING OF CONFIDENCE THAT BELIED THE inner nervousness churning away in his stomach, Matthew walked toward the front door of *Lebenshaus*. If these people didn't speak German, he thought, he was done for. His Polish would not get him past the threshold.

Inside the two vest pockets of the suit he was now wearing rested, on one side, the papers Paddy Red had arranged that he hoped would give him free access, and on the other bulged a flashlight, whose presence he hoped would not be wondered at. In his hand he held a clipboard, already full of many notations and drawings.

Glancing up, he saw that the baron's inscription still remained, though the paint had peeled and fallen away from half the letters. He slowed his step to read the words over the door again, then proceeded forward and rang the bell to the right of the thick wood-slabbed door.

As the great door opened after some thirty seconds, a wave of renewed nostalgia and sickness swept over Matthew, both to see inside the house again, and to visualize what had become of the former House of Life. With great effort he forced his emotions back under the surface, put the most dispassionate expression possible on his countenance, pulled the folded papers from the inside of the suit coat, and spoke authoritatively.

"*Guten Morgen,* Fräulein," he said crisply. "Please tell the man or woman in charge of the facility that I would like to see them immediately. Tell them Herr Albrecht from Inspection Services in Berlin is here to begin his audit."

The young woman disappeared. Matthew was left alone in the entryway, again to contemplate the changes that had taken place since he was last here.

A minute or two later a man appeared, his expression none too congenial. He was a small, slender man, wearing spectacles that gave him something of a scholarly appearance, and a white robe that spoke of the medical profession. He did not seem to be a man acquainted with either humor or compassion—the perfect semi-man to carry out the kind of work to which *Lebenshaus* had been debased. Under the surface of his demeanor, however, also lurked a heavy residual quantity of fear, instilled by both his father and his remembrance of suffering at the hands of the Gestapo—a fear which, though he had never met the man, Paddy Red had anticipated as Matthew's strongest asset in cowing him into complete compliance and docility.

"I am Hans Lengyl. I am in charge of the institution," he said in a medium-pitched voice that tried to carry more authority than his physique seemed worthy of. "What may I do for you?"

"I am here to begin my audit," said Matthew formally. "I assume your people have been informed."

"They have been informed of nothing. I *myself* have been informed of nothing."

"You are not prepared for my arrival?"

"I have heard of no audit."

"Dummköpf!" exploded Matthew in apparent rage, clenching his fist. "This happened at my last inspection as well. I will see the idiots at that office reassigned for their blundering *dummheit!*"

Then, seeming suddenly to come to himself, he turned to the man who stood staring, still not knowing quite what to make of it.

"Ah, I am very sorry, Herr . . . Herr, ah . . . Lengyl. It is of course not your fault. My orders here will explain everything."

He handed him the two papers he held.

A doctor or psychiatrist would have been safer, thought Matthew to himself. *Posing as a Communist official is too dangerous.* What if the fellow called the office in Berlin to check on him! Paddy Red had assured him that the bureaucracy was so riddled with inefficiency and rife with hidden suspicions and fears that the paralysis of inaction and ineptitude was their greatest ally in such cases. "Even if he suspects you for a liar, he will say nothing," Red had told him. "No one wants to rock the boat for fear of losing whatever position they might have. Believe me, Charlie, it will go smooth as silk. I've bluffed these blimey commies like this a dozen times. Just so long as you carry out your half of the bluff," he'd added, "which is bravado. If he challenges you—"

The sound of the other fellow's voice interrupted Matthew's worrying reflections.

"It seems to be in order," the man said. "But, really, today will be impo—"

"*Seems* in order!" barked Matthew. "Of course it's in order. Did you not see the signature on that paper? And today will *have* to do. I cannot make other arrangements after coming all this way out from Berlin."

"Yes, but I still do not understand the purpose—"

"Herr Lengyl, *bitte,*" interrupted Matthew impatiently. "Surely you do not want me to report this impertinence?"

"No, of course not."

"Especially in that my inspection will only improve your lot here. Your record has come to the attention of my superiors in Moscow. They are most pleased. That is why I have been sent—to determine what may be done to improve your complex. Modernization, Herr Lengyl—it is the Communist way. My superiors hope that your facility may become a model for other such units under construction in the Soviet Union. There is money to be spent on research, Herr Lengyl, money whose disposition my report will determine. There are promotions and no little prestige at stake too, I might tell you confidentially."

"I see," replied Lengyl with suddenly heightened interest.

"At present, there is another unit for the criminally schizophrenic, down near Leipzig I believe, which I will be inspecting, and whose records I will audit next week. They too are under consideration."

"Bah, in Leipzig their means are crude," replied Lengyl. "Their research is too narrow to be of universal importance. We do not merely examine the criminal element here, but men and women from all walks of life. We have Jews and Christians, former Nazis, one KGB agent, an American who was captured and then lost his reason, and many intellectuals who suffer from a wide range of mental delusions. I tell you, *Herr Aufsichtsbeamte,* our facility here at Niedersdorf is far in advance of the experiments they are carrying out at Leipzig."

"Ah yes . . . but of course you would think so," replied Matthew with a droll expression. "In any event, my report will make everything clear."

"Then today will be in order. How may I assist you, *Herr Aufsichtsbeamte?*"

"Merely by allowing me free access to the entire facility," replied Matthew, "and by informing your people of my presence."

"What records will you need to see?"

"Nothing just yet. I will inform you, perhaps later. For the present I will inspect the physical layout of the facility and grounds. I must make a detailed report of the uses to which the house is being put at present, and make my recommendations for what improvements can be made and where additional facilities can perhaps be built."

"Very good. I will see that my people give you every consideration."

"Your own office, with all records, will be available to me?" Matthew spoke with a tone that mingled request with command.

"Yes . . . yes, of course."

"Where would that be?"

"Come, I will take you there personally," said Lengyl, eager now to please.

He turned and led the way up the stairs into the baron's former study and office, which was not altogether changed from before. Most of the furniture and bookshelves were the baron's own, although all his possessions had long ago been either crated up or destroyed.

"You may leave me alone, *bitte,* Herr Lengyl," said Matthew.

"Uh . . . yes, certainly . . . uh, Herr—"

"Albrecht," said Matthew with an annoyed expression. "Now please, Herr Lengyl, leave me so I can commence my inspection."

The nervous man turned and left the room, unwilling to turn his office over to a stranger, but fearful to object further. In truth, Matthew had been so nearly overcome with a sense of the baron's abiding presence in and throughout the place, especially here in the office he had so long occupied, that he had had to fabricate some means to be alone in order to regain his composure.

He fell into the man's chair and buried his face in his hands, tears, prayers, and memories all but overwhelming him.

New Danger

• • •

TWO HOURS LATER, AFTER A LEISURELY RAMBLE through most of the sections of the house, Matthew went outside and made his way through the arch and into what remained of Baron von Dortmann's prized *Frühlingsgarten*.

It had been with more than a little difficulty that he had carried out the continued assumption of his official Communist persona in the midst of a veritable flood of emotions and memories. He could not help reliving every moment he had spent in this house and on these grounds. Every centimeter reminded him of Sabina!

Yet it was here—where, though externally it was so changed, the life and spirit of Heinrich, Marion, and Sabina von Dortmann still lived, though the flesh of the place had been given new occupants— that he hoped the Lord and Father of them all would give him direction as to what to do next.

With clipboard in hand, therefore, and making what he hoped would pass as official-sounding comments and plausible-looking diagrams should the papers be seen by the timorous yet crafty Herr Lengyl, he had roamed the memory-strewn corridors, poking now and then into one of the rooms, praying silently as he went, making every effort to keep his expression uncommunicative of his inner-most feelings.

Throughout his sojourns through the halls, the sense had grown that the leading he sought would come from the passageways under-neath the house where he and Sabina had explored together. He had subsequently inspected the ground floor with great care, including the room of his broken-leg convalescence and all the stairwells, to determine if the lower portions were in use. The room where he had recovered from his first broken leg and where Sabina had, after the war, overheard schemes against her, at present housed three patients, all women of extreme age and advanced senility. What they could possibly be doing here, Matthew hadn't an idea. Some aspects of the facility seemed altogether humane, even compassionate, while others seemed experimental and lifeless. All the inmates he had seen were old. From all he could tell, the research was concentrated on the effects of aging upon persons suffering from various mental disorders and imbalances. In his former room, however, he saw no indication of any factors other than age itself. The three women all appeared a hundred or more, with not enough left of their wits to be capable of disorder.

From everything he had observed, not only was the basement corridor not in use, there seemed no known access to the lower regions whatever. Was it possible, he wondered, that they yet remained undiscovered? Even the cellar under the southwest corner was boarded up from below and did not appear to have been used in years. He would attempt to gain access to it through the tunnel from the outside that Sabina had described.

Thus he had made his way to the garden, nonchalantly careful not to be seen, though still carrying his clipboard and papers and continuing to make a profusion of notes and diagrams.

Within moments of his leaving the house and walking across the courtyard to the old stone arch, a second automobile made its way up the tree-lined drive to the front of the house. This was no Trabi, however, but a full-size import bearing an important official of the East German secret police and driven by one who hoped to make this estate his own within a short time.

Unaware of the new arrival, Matthew descended the slope into the ancient and overrun garden. He could not proceed to examine the hidden tunnelway until he had once again seen the rose garden. He had to know whether any of the baron's many prized specimens had survived all these years without care.

The air was crisp, a perfect January day. The sun shone thinly above in the wan blue of the pale wintry sky. The rain and sleet that had fallen from it all week seemed to have drained the color from its depths. The ground was soggy beneath his feet, and wetness was everywhere. The smell of damp earth and decay pervaded the place, not inappropriately, thought Matthew as he made his way slowly along.

Across the tractor-scar he walked, shivering once or twice, trying to remember the exact configuration of the paths and garden byways it had destroyed, and soon came to what he recognized as the rose garden.

Again memories flooded him—faces, conversations, laughter, and bright, lush blossoms blooming in verdant profusion.

He looked around. Weeds, overgrowth, and once-trim but now-wild shrubbery had all but taken over. Many of the roses were still alive, though they had likewise mostly reverted to their wild state. Climbers and ramblers were in their element, and some of the baron's ancient Victorian varieties, more close to the wild, showed leafy evidences of continuing to thrive despite a complete lack of care. The newer hybrid tea species he had cultivated for their showy blooms, however, had mostly gone the way of all earthly things and could hardly be recognized. Most of the tree roses around the perimeter were still recognizable by their thick trunks, but like all the rest were so overgrown that their vines by now extended long and across the ground, many having sprouted suckers that deprived the parent tree of needed energy.

Oh, for an afternoon with rake, hoe, and pruning shears, thought Matthew. What color would explode from this garden in April or May if he was free to work among the vines for a day! He was convinced much of the life of the place still existed and only needed to be rediscovered and cultivated in order to burst forth again.

Walking slowly in the midst of the thorny jungle, suddenly Matthew's heart jumped. He fell to the ground, heedless of the grassy, muddy stain instantly engulfing his knees.

There in front of him, though the plant was yet tiny, stunted from lack of care, a small white blossom had forced its delicate head upward out of the earth toward what light and warmth the sun offered.

Memories came back to him of his last day at *Lebenshaus,* when he and Sabina had each clipped a bud to place in the tiny china box she had given him. Could this have been the very plant he had selected while she was not looking? he wondered.

"Ah, little rose, wherever did you come from?" whispered Matthew, bending low and cupping his hand around it with great tenderness and affection. *Don't you know this is not the season for roses? All your brothers and sisters have gone to sleep for the winter. How do you come to be here, tiny white rose? Are you here just for me, to remind me of that time I was here with her?*

Tears he could not explain came to Matthew's eyes. What was it about the tiny bud that was able to bring forth such emotions from out of his heart? What mystery of life did the little flower contain?

It was such a small little thing. The leaves upon its fragile stalk, too, were almost miniature. Both bud and leaf had had to fight a brave battle against the wintry elements for their existence, and the contest had taken its toll, for neither would mature to full stature.

But this was no ordinary rose. Its perfect tiny bud-shape symbolized the life, even the beauty, to be found in the most squalid of circumstances. How had it found life here, in the midst of so many other varieties that had given up in the fight to retain life?

Here it was, thought Matthew, its tiny, proud head standing up tall, letting the wind and rain and cold and neglect do their worst!

Ah, little rose, Matthew repeated, leaning back to behold it with a smiling sigh, *what story do you have to tell me . . . ? What mysteries do you know? Tell me, little rose, about your master, about your mistress Sabina. Did she ever, long ago, place her nose to your blooms and smile from the pleasure you gave her? Did she pluck you to place in her room? Did she wear you in her hair? Tell me your secrets, tiny rose. I will share them with no one but her! You can entrust your delicate whisperings to me, white rose. I will keep them safe, until . . . until the day when I can share them with your young mistress, she whom you knew many years ago.*

Matthew blinked back a final remaining tear or two, drew in a deep breath, picked up his clipboard where it had fallen from his hand, then climbed back to his feet, still gazing down at the object of his dreamy reverie.

Should he pick this rose, in memory of Sabina?

No, this was no flower to be plucked, but one to live out the brief span of its life to the full. In memory of the baron he would let it remain. It must continue the brave fight to keep the memory of *Der Frühlingsgarten* alive.

Matthew turned and retraced his way out of the rose garden, turning for one more brief look at his tiny white friend, now already nearly lost to sight among the overgrowth, then proceeded upward to the northwest corner of the garden in the shadow of a hugely overgrown hedge where he hoped to find the door Sabina had told him about.

As he approached, he was reminded of his present danger and glanced around to make sure he could not be seen.

The slope here was steep, and the trees and brush and hedge-growth so abundant as to make it difficult even to get through. No wonder, Matthew thought, that no one had found the entryway to the tunnel leading into the cellar.

Feeling and rummaging about through the dense growth, wondering what the curious Herr Lengyl would think to see him with stains and mud all over his suit, Matthew probed deeper and deeper into the hedge wall where he was certain the door must be located.

Forty minutes later, however, he was still no closer to his objective. The mysterious door had either disappeared or else he had mistaken Sabina's instructions.

Suddenly voices sounded fifteen or twenty meters away.

One was Lengyl's. But the other he thought he recognized too, even after all this time! The unwelcome timbre sent a chill through his body from head to foot and everywhere in between.

It could be none other—though the likelihood of such a coincidence seemed incredible!—than the voice of Gustav von Schmundt!

As quietly and quickly as he was able, Matthew was again on his knees, scratchings and pokings innumerable all about his body. Frozen in terror, he listened intently as the voices drew nearer, then proceeded past him down into the depths of the garden.

"I don't understand it, Herr Section Chief," Lengyl was saying. "The man had all the proper credentials."

"You fool," spat Gustav. "He is an impostor, I tell you. I have standing orders that I am to be informed of any and all changes that are proposed to this facility. I have heard nothing of any report."

"He assured me that we were under consideration for—"

"You are as gullible as you are incompetent! How could you fall for such an inane ploy—it was a lie to win your confidence! Why did you not tell me all this the moment I arrived?"

"I am sorry, Herr Section Chief," fumbled Lengyl, struggling to keep to the other's pace, "I did not know you would be interested in his inspection."

"Fool! I am interested in all that goes on here!"

They had already passed the level where Matthew was hiding, and the voices were fading down into the lower regions of the garden.

"Where is he?" spat Gustav, "did you not say he was here?"

"One of my nurses thought she saw the *Aufsichtsbeamte* walking in this direction."

"He is no inspector, I tell you," rejoined Gustav. "When I get my hands on him I will . . ."

Matthew heard no more. Whatever Schmundt was doing here, if he was found, the jig would be up. He could make a run for it and hope to get to his car without being seen. But he would be a sitting duck in that little Trabi. He wouldn't be capable of outrunning a fast goat with that thing!

Suddenly a madcap idea occurred to him!

The next instant he was on his feet and hastening back to the house, glancing back every so often to make sure he still hadn't been seen.

Sweating and disheveled, attempting as best he could to maintain some semblance of an official bearing with expression and clipboard, Matthew ran across the courtyard and into the house through the rear entrance of the west wing he had left about an hour earlier.

Slowing his pace, he took in a deep breath, nodding seriously to two white-clad young women who passed, while walking briskly along the ground-floor corridor to his left. He had bluffed his way successfully at the Neustädt prison. . . . He only hoped it worked so well here!

He stopped. Here he was at the room the ghost of his broken leg now shared with three senile centenarians.

Confidently he walked briskly into the room.

The nurse in charge glanced up. They had seen one another earlier. She nodded, and made as if to continue her work.

"Fräulein," said Matthew, "Herr Lengyl requested me to send you to him. He is in his office."

"I must not leave the patients—"

"Please, Fräulein," interrupted Matthew, "the matter is most urgent. He asked me to watch them until one of the other nurses arrives. He has already sent another down."

With an expression of question still on her face, the woman hesitated but a moment longer, then left the room.

That was stupid, thought Matthew to himself. *There are a dozen things I could have said to get rid of her! Now she'll report to both men that I was right here!*

It was too late to worry about that now. He'd done it. So he'd better make haste to get out of sight!

Hurriedly he glanced around, paying no attention to the three sets of bewildered eyes watching his every move from the beds across the floor.

The old wardrobe was still there!

He ran to it. Its doors were sealed shut. It had not been used in years.

He took hold of its edges and attempted to swing it out of the way. It did not budge a millimeter. He set his shoulder against it, but succeeded only in bruising himself rather than moving or dislodging the wardrobe.

Hadn't Sabina told him that they had sealed off every secret door and passageway that could possibly have been discovered by the Gestapo? What if this opening had been cemented shut? He would be a prisoner of the KGB himself within minutes!

Frantically he glanced about the room, heedless of the mute gestures and expressions now coming from one of the beds.

A croaking sound met his ear.

He looked up. One of the women was staring straight at him, trying to get his attention with wild motions of her thin, white arms. She had finally succeeded in getting some sound out of her aged vocal cords.

He walked toward the bed. Her eyes were wide and stared at him intently, seeming still to have their clarity, and seeming as well to know what he was about.

He looked deeply into her face. If he didn't know better he would have thought he was in the presence of old Eppie herself! The woman was trying to speak.

Matthew leaned close to the bed.

"Other side . . . ," came the faintest of whispers in a voice that sounded as ancient as *Lebenshaus* itself.

"What's that?" said Matthew. "Other side of what?"

"Wrong side . . . in corner . . . ," mumbled the woman, pointing a frail finger toward the wardrobe, ". . . dreamed . . . knew you would come . . . danger . . . saw it move . . ."

Struggling to make sense of her apparent ramblings, Matthew turned and began walking slowly across the floor, still watching her out of the corner of his eye. As he did, her pointing grew more pronounced.

Again he approached the wardrobe. One side of it was wedged tightly into a plastered corner of the room. It was exactly how he remembered it, and yet . . . something was wrong.

Yes, that was it! The woman was right. . . . He had been attempting to swing the wardrobe out from the wrong side. Its concealed hinges were on the side he had been pushing from. It swung out from the corner, not the other way!

He dug his fingers between the wood and plaster of the wall.

It was no use. There wasn't a millimeter's space between them.

Glancing around again, his eyes fell on his clipboard where he had lain it on a chair. Quickly he grabbed it up and shoved the thin wooden end into the space. It penetrated a centimeter or two. With his hand he banged against the other end, succeeding in forcing it a little further into the crack.

He stopped and looked about the room again.

He heard voices in the hall outside—two men and the nurse he had sent out of the room a few minutes earlier! They were coming this way! The new voice sounded eerily familiar, but there was no time to think about it now He had to get out of here!

From the bed his ancient ally was still gesturing wildly. He tried to follow her motions. His eye fell upon a pair of crutches leaning against the far corner of the room.

With one bound he reached them, caught up one of them, ripped off the rubber tip from its end, hoisted it into the air, and jammed it tightly between the wall and his clipboard, which still was sticking out next to the stubborn wardrobe.

With the clipboard for leverage, he leaned his weight against the horizontal crutch. The great wooden wardrobe swung back away from the wall. Released from the crack holding it, the clipboard fell with a crash to the floor. He jammed the crutch well into the newly created space, and the next instant, with a scraping sound across the stone floor, the wardrobe swung the remainder of the way open.

He could hear Gustav's voice raised in anger now, approaching the door!

Throwing the crutch back toward the corner where its mate still stood, he grabbed up the clipboard and jumped through the wall into the black cavity he had created. Behind him, as he stretched out his hand to pull the wardrobe shut behind him, he saw the frail old woman climbing ghostlike out of her bed, her eyes wide as if she were living out the very dream she had spoken of, and approaching.

At first he thought she was attempting to come with him. But then she paused, motioning him as if to close a door. Gripping the back of the wardrobe, he pulled it toward him, again with the scraping sound on the floor. As he pulled, the old woman reached out to help him push the clumsy affair shut. What her strength would accomplish against the weight of the wardrobe was doubtful. But her presence out of bed sufficiently accounted for the crutch on the floor and the sounds they heard as they crashed into the room, so as to distract the three newcomers from searching carefully the corner of escape behind her.

Even as he heard the door opposite open and three sets of footsteps rush into the room he had just left, Matthew pulled the makeshift door the final centimeter back into its former resting place.

The narrowing crack of light from the room disappeared. Damp, cold, silent blackness surrounded him.

Matthew closed his eyes and breathed in and out deeply.

That had been too close!

Through the thick wall he could just barely make out the muffled sounds of angry interrogation. But the incoherent babblings of the old lady about a bearded ghost and secret tombs remained utterly unintelligible to her livid *Stasi* visitor.

98

Memories of Roses

●　●　●

HOW MANY MINUTES PASSED, MATTHEW LOST COUNT OF.
He stood until his arm ached, tugging against the board at the back
of the wardrobe so as to prevent anyone on the other side from
discovering the method of his escape by too easily jarring the
wardrobe away from the corner. If he had loosened the hinges, he
would make up for it by holding it fast from the inside.

Once he was reasonably certain the room was again empty of
both Schmundt and Lengyl, he relaxed his grip. His hand now sought
the flashlight inside his coat.

Switching it on, the thin beam instantly lit up the narrow landing.
Only a foot away, the stairs he remembered so well yawned away
down into the blackness below the house. Gingerly he stepped
forward, then proceeded downward around the tight spiral.

A minute more and he found himself securely upon the damp dirt
floor of the underground passage that extended the full length of the
west wing all the way to the northernmost wall.

Immediately all thought of his present danger left him, and he was
back twenty years in time with the vivid memory of Sabina to
accompany him. Without hesitation he turned left and began walking
down the passageway toward the far room where he and Sabina had
shared so much. The floor underfoot was much wetter than he
remembered it, perhaps because it was winter. In every other respect,
however, nothing was changed.

As he emerged into the earthy chamber under what had once
been the small library, it was as though he had been here with Sabina
only yesterday!

With thoughts of the white wintry rose from the garden still fresh in his mind, Matthew sent the light of his flashlight quickly around the room, then walked straight toward the earth wall that bordered it to the right.

He glanced up. All the shelves and stones and broken pieces of pots were unchanged. Not a day had passed . . . not an hour!

Could he reach up high enough without a chair?

He looked up. The ledge was too high.

He glanced quickly about. There was nothing to help him in the room any more now than there had been then, and he couldn't run upstairs and get a chair this time.

There was the trowel he had used still lying on the floor. He grabbed it and began chipping and pounding at the earth. He would make a foothold in the stony dirt wall itself.

Two minutes later he had fashioned two holes about a foot and two feet off the ground. Setting the flashlight on the floor, he put his foot in the lower of the two, then jumped slightly, attempting to snag the second hole with his other foot and latch onto the high shelf at the same time with his hand.

The first attempt failed. So did the second.

Why did I conceal the thing so well? he said to himself. *Nobody has been here since that day. I could just as well have laid it on the floor!*

Again he set his feet and jumped, this time grabbing hold of the high stone ledge with his right hand. Clinging desperately so as not to lose his balance, he stretched his left hand up over the ledge.

There was the stone he had whacked in half. He took hold of it, pulled it aside, then reached into the cavity behind it.

It was still there!

Careful to get both top and box, he stretched his palm and fingers around the china box and gently pulled it from its hiding place. Making sure he had it securely, he eased back, then jumped down to the floor.

Even as he sat down on the cold dirt floor, picking up his flashlight again to look at the china box with pink roses painted on top, words from their parting came back to him.

"*. . . It's my promise to be back soon,*" he remembered saying.

Well, Sabina, Matthew thought, *it wasn't as soon as I'd hoped, but I did come back . . . though I wish you were here to share it with me!*

For a moment or two more he held the box in his hand, full of so many thoughts.

"*. . . You must promise that you won't open it until I am here with you again,* he had told her. She had agreed to the promise.

He debated within himself. Should *he* open it?

But I didn't exactly make that promise! Matthew thought. *At least I didn't say it in so many words—I only promised to come back! I hope you'll forgive me, Sabina, but I never said that I wouldn't open it if I got back here first! I have to open it!*

Gently he lifted the lid and shined the light inside.

There were the two rosebuds they had put in with eyes closed, now shriveled and dry.

He should have known! he thought, smiling.

They were both white, now faded to a pale, creamy almost-yellow. They had each chosen the same color!

Yet a moment more he gazed down, then suddenly recognized the small folded piece of paper in the box with the roses. He reached down, took it out, and unfolded it. There, in his own handwriting, were the words he had written to accompany the yellow rose: *Friends forever.*

Sabina, laughed Matthew, *you opened the box!*

• • •

While Matthew was reminiscing of happier times in the underground passageways, two and three floors above him *Stasi* Section Chief Gustav von Schmundt led frazzled and terrified Facility Director Hans Lengyl on a hurried but unsuccessful search of the premises for the so-called Herr Albrecht from Inspection Services. No one had seen him for an hour or two, though his car still stood unmoved in front of the building.

99

An Incredible Discovery

• • •

AT LENGTH MATTHEW ROSE TO LEAVE THE EARTHEN ROOM,
carrying the precious china box and the more precious memories
of its contents with him.

As he retraced his steps down the long underground corridor, all
at once the image of his strange dream, of following the candle-bear-
ing, Eppie-like wraith down this same passageway, came to his mind.

The dungeon!

He'd nearly forgotten about it!

Maybe he could find it now. Sabina said her father had located it.
He hadn't seen anything as he'd walked along here. Where could it
be?

Quickening his step, Matthew shined the light all about the floor
and walls of the passage, but it looked no different than the last time
he was here. Presently he found himself at the other end, where the
closed door led out into the cellar.

He turned around to retrace his steps once more, this time slowly
and carefully, trying to recall the details of his dream on the off chance
that there might be some element of reality to be found in them.

As had been the case before, midway through the corridor the
moisture on the floor increased. He paused to look the area over more
carefully. Moving laterally across the floor, the water seemed to have a
slight flow to it. Matthew knelt down and disturbed the water. Grains
of jostled dirt indicated a faint but otherwise undetectable current.

The walls were dry. Where was the water coming from?

Following it across the floor, his flashlight revealed a tiny crack at
the base of the wall where it met the floor. Again he stirred his fingers

in the thin puddle at his feet. As he did, a crack in the floor showed itself as the water faintly washed away the straight outline of a stone in the floor, buried in what otherwise appeared to be mud and dirt. Following its outline with his finger, Matthew began to uncover a second edge at right angles to the first. He appeared to be tracing the outline of a large square stone, inlaid into the floor of the passageway, butted up against the wall at the very point where the tiny rivulet seemed emerging from out of nowhere. He tried to squeeze his fingers into the dirt to dislodge the stone, but with no more success than he had had with the wardrobe in the room above.

Suddenly he remembered the trowel.

Carefully he set the china box on the floor where it was well out of the way. The next moment he was running back to retrieve the garden instrument. Within two minutes he was digging away in the floor of the passageway, attempting to force the trowel under the edge of the stone so as to gain sufficient leverage to pry it upward.

He succeeded in loosening one edge, then lifted it by making a lever of the trowel against the adjacent earth. Holding the handle of the trowel steady with one knee, he now managed to get the fingers of both hands under the raised edge and, with a great effort, hoisted the great flat floor-stone out of the dirt, laying it back out of the way.

He could hardly believe his eyes!

There under the floor, plain as day, lay a large, ornate brass key, wet and discolored, but unspoiled by the years.

With rising excitement Matthew began to poke around further with his fingers. The key seemed to be resting in a depression, perhaps carved away for the very purpose, of a smaller stone or brick that, like the larger slab that concealed it, lay in the wet dirt of the floor.

He picked up the key, then inserted the trowel under the edge of the under-stone, lifting the edge of it with ease, then hoisting it up with his hand and setting it on top of the first.

The sight this time was even more spectacular. Buried thus beneath the two floor stones now showed itself to Matthew's flash-light a flat brass mechanism, in the center of which was an elongated hole, designed for the obvious reception of the key.

His fingers trembling, Matthew inserted it into the peculiar floor lock . . . then gave the key a gentle but forceful turn.

Somewhere, he could not see where, a dull metallic *clank* sounded. To his right, another stone gave way, this time in the wall itself.

It was not a large stone, roughly the size of two hands. But the side of it hidden from view inside the wall had been affixed somehow to a metal plate, with slots attaching it to hooked bolts that, when locked, drew it in to the wall so tightly that it looked like the rest of the wall stones and was utterly immobile. The turn of the key released the bolts, which raised slightly to unhook the slots and release the brick-shaped stone.

This stone Matthew now pulled aside and set with the two others.

Behind it, inside the wall, his amazement continued.

The cavity revealed a complex arrangement of brassworks, the most obvious of which was a thick lever standing vertically in the hole left by the stone, between the two fastening bolts. The use for which it was intended could hardly be mistaken.

With excitement but some trepidation, Matthew stretched out his hand, laid hold of the lever, and pulled.

It gave way easily, rotating down to a horizontal position. At the same instant, more hidden metallic sounds could be heard. Matthew felt movement all about him.

The whole wall seemed to move!

Startled, he half stood and stepped back. Behind the lever, to the height of the ceiling, a huge stone door within the wall of the passageway had been released from the invisible contrivances that had held it securely in place, and was now perfectly apparent. The lever had pulled four thick brass rods, at the top and bottom of each side of the door, inward and out of the empty cylinders set into the wall that housed them. This action released the door to swing freely on the massive rustless hinges which held it on one side.

Matthew stepped to it, set his hand to the free side, and pulled. With marvelous ease and remarkable silence, the great stone door swung toward him, revealing a long black corridor behind it.

With awe and still greater mounting excitement in the midst of his dreamlike disbelief, Matthew poked his flashlight into the hidden hallway. The beam of light disappeared into the blackness straight ahead.

Altogether forgetful now of roses and china boxes, forgetful that he was a spy in a strange, foreign, and unfriendly land, and even forgetful of the fact that somewhere above him an archenemy from the DDR's *Staatssicherheitsdienst* was searching high and low for him and that, if found, he would be thrown into a prison cell probably no wider than this underground passage, Matthew crept into the hole that yawned before him, following the beam of his flashlight forward.

Underfoot the ground was very wet. Whatever underground spring or source the water came from lay obviously in this direction. The tiny trickle moved along this corridor, under the hidden doorway, and into the other, where it had led first the baron, and now Matthew, to concentrate their search for the long-lost doorway.

With ghostly remembrance, Matthew walked slowly along, the eerie sense stealing over him that he had been here before. The beam of his light almost seemed to flicker as if it were from the same thin candle held by the ghost who had led him this same way in his dream before.

All was preternaturally silent. Matthew hardly dared breathe for fear the sound of his own lungs would frighten him so much that he would turn around and flee back the way he had come.

But he could not turn back. He had to follow out the dream, though now it was no dream.

Above him he heard the dull thudding tramp of footsteps.

Matthew stopped, suddenly reminded how close and present danger was. The passage led directly under the main portions of the house. He was probably below what had once been the *Gute Stube* or the family dining room, as close as he could tell. Should he go back and close the door? No, he had no way to conceal the stones and brassworks in the other hall from this side. If Gustav found the lower portions of the house, he would certainly find this passageway too. He had no choice but to proceed.

Matthew continued on, the uncanny sense growing within him that he knew precisely where his steps would lead even before he took them. The only feature unlike his dream was the absence of doors or passageways off this main one.

Gradually the way narrowed. Overhead the ceiling became rounded. His head and shoulders barely kept from rubbing against the enclosure of stones. Any moment he would turn, he thought.

In less than a minute, suddenly his light shone against a solid wall in front of him. Narrow corridors led from it toward both the right and the left. Matthew did not hesitate. From his dream he knew the course he must follow.

He turned his steps to the right.

He found himself, as he knew he would, entering a dead-end corridor, lower and even narrower than that he had been in. Ahead but a few steps further a stone wall blocked his way. He stopped, turning again to the right. The door stood before him, just as he knew it would.

Suddenly the vivid memory of his dream threatened to overcome him with fear. His feet seemed stuck like stone statues into the floor, frozen with terror, yet he knew he could at any moment loose them into flight.

What would he find behind that door!

What but a ghost! he thought, dreamlike shivers pulsing through his body.

Or worse . . . a skeleton, bound in chains . . . what was it old Eppie had said about someone run through the heart with a sword?

What am I thinking? Matthew said to himself, trying to muster up his courage. *This is 1962. There are no ghosts. If old Bismarck's skeleton or that of some count he killed is there on the floor, what harm can it do me?*

Succeeding only partially in exorcising the spooky demon of angst, Matthew lifted his hand and began knocking on the door.

The next instant he stopped.

What am I doing? he thought. *There's no one inside! The knocking was from my dream!*

For the first time he looked the door over from top to bottom. How was he to get in? He shoved against it.

No movement.

There was a keyhole! Low down, no higher than his knees.

He stooped down to examine it.

The next instant he was retracing his steps back along the corridor, running now as best he could, old Eppie and the ghost and his dream and Sabina's knocking against the inner wall of his room all now gone from his mind. Within three minutes he had returned, sweating now from the heat of exercise, not from the cold funk of dread.

Kneeling down, he inserted the key he had found before under the floor stone into the dungeon lock.

It was a perfect fit!

He turned it.

Without a sound the door swung inward and away from him.

Matthew stood and entered the hidden dungeon of the ancient *Lebenshaus* legend.

100

Frantic Search

• • •

TWO FLOORS ABOVE HIM THE THOUGHTS REVOLVING through the brain of the man who would be Matthew's rival, even after her death, for Sabina's affections were progressing along lower and more rutted mental bypaths.

They had searched every floor of the place. The man called Albrecht was nowhere to be found.

Gustav stood in Director Lengyl's office gazing out upon the barren landscape to the west. This office had once belonged to Baron von Dortmann, and one day soon it would belong to him.

Something was up. He could feel it . . . smell it—something alien to his designs.

Fate had put it in his mind to come here on this day. This "inspector," whatever his real identity, had some connection to the former owner of this estate. He knew it. He could tell. Perhaps a solicitor or agent acting on behalf of Otto von Dortmann. Who else could there be that would have any connection to the place?

He sensed the baron's influence. And not just because he was standing in his old office. Some presence friendly to the baron was here, trying to thwart him.

It could not be the baron himself. Dortmann was dead. He himself had thrown onto the van the grenade that had killed the old fool. Later reports confirmed it.

True, his rash actions had killed Sabina along with her father, as well as nearly costing him his own life.

But he had given the naive wench every chance. She should have listened. She should have seen that he was her only chance.

Not that perhaps he wouldn't be a little more careful if he had it to do over again, but he wasn't going to lose any sleep ruing either of their deaths. Their stubbornness had received its reward, and he wasn't about to get sentimental about it all over again.

He would have his revenge by getting his hands on what had once been their estate. He would vindicate the memory of his father at the same time. He had to find the documents and deeds his father had told him about. They would confirm his right to ownership.

Suddenly a thought struck him. What if they were right in this very office!

His mind raced back to the night the Gestapo had raided *Lebenshaus.* He had been distracted by thoughts of Sabina, it was true. But he recalled this office too. All the baron's possessions had been here. He hadn't had time to remove them. What might have happened to them in the meantime?

Gustav glanced around.

Many of the same cabinets and files remained, even to this day. A thorough search might turn up just what he needed to solidify his claim to this estate as well as his father's. There had to be records here about the people they had housed, especially one so important as the Rabbi Wissen—where he had come from, contacts, where he might have been bound. Surely the trail was here, if only he could sniff it out. Sabina may be gone, but it still behooved him to ingratiate himself to Korsch.

Hastily and without any plan, he began riffling through files and drawers and cabinets.

Within five minutes the office was strewn with papers and files. It would take a week for everything to be put back in its place. For all his haste, however, Gustav laid eyes on nothing that predated 1946. There wasn't so much as a scrap of paper to be found that had anything to do with the ownership of the estate prior to its confiscation by the Communists.

What could have happened to all the baron's files?

Their raid that fateful night had come so suddenly, he could not have had time to remove them to some other place. Where could he have taken them, anyway? His brother in the city was a Nazi informant at the time. His pastor friend was by then in prison.

What might he have done with them? There was no evidence

of all the old records being destroyed. When they had taken the baron into custody early that morning, he hadn't had a thing on his person.

Yet he had searched every room since, and there wasn't a trace of them to be found all through the house. What could have happened to them?

Inside the Mystery Chamber

• • •

THE AIR WAS EMPTY AND STILL, YET THICK WITH THE presence of ages lost to time.

Matthew entered the large underground chamber with awe, breathing the dense silence with a slow caution, as if the very motions of his lungs might disturb the ghosts of the past into life.

He took two or three steps, then stopped, panning about with his flashlight. A table stood about three meters to his right. He walked toward it, but before he had the chance to examine any of the objects on it, something hanging in the air above it caught his eye. It was a light bulb, whose socket was hanging from a wire attached to the ceiling.

It couldn't be, he thought. *Electricity down here in the dungeon!*

Leaving the table, he turned back toward the door, scanning the walls near it up and down. There was the switch. He flipped it up. Behind him the bulb brightened and suddenly the room was filled with a dim yellowish light.

Turning off his flashlight, he returned to the table.

It was long and narrow, equipped with several chairs, with papers and books and pens and all sorts of related paraphernalia scattered about it.

Walking beyond it now, he took in the rest of the place.

It was a larger room than he thought could be possible down here, some eight by twelve meters by his estimate. The moment he had entered, he now realized, the low ceiling of the passageway had given way to a much higher vault above him now. Looking up, he judged the ceiling 2.5 or 3 meters in height, which, he thought, seemed high enough to make the dungeon detectable from the ground floor above him. Perhaps the descent of the stairways was of greater height than it seemed.

The room was approximately rectangular, but with several recessed closets and corners into which the light did not reach adequately to see much. One of these recesses was very deep, and after a quick examination with his flashlight, Matthew concluded that it led into what amounted to another small room. He would see what it contained later.

Returning to the center of the room, Matthew continued his cursory examination. Along one of the walls stood a quantity of shelves and cabinets, with many boxes and crates containing what appeared to be books, records, papers, journals, ledgers. Adjacent to it, curiously, thought Matthew, ran a long wood pole upon which hung a great variety of now badly mildewed clothes, mostly coats and outer garments, for both men and women. What could such things possibly be doing here, Matthew wondered. Even though, as Sabina had told him, the baron had discovered the place, why had they used it for the storage of clothes?

Glancing casually along the shelves and files, pulling out now one, now another of the drawers, peering into the boxes, shuffling through some of the files lying on open shelves, it seemed that a great deal of the baron's business papers and important documents had been brought down here, no doubt for safekeeping. As unlikely as the place was, it had the look not only of a workroom but also an office.

He pulled out a box labeled *Lebenshaus* Documents and began sorting quickly through them. One entire file envelope, sealed with string, read Deeds, Purchases, and Notes. Matthew unfastened the string and pulled out the contents.

There were many papers he could not understand, business transactions going back hundreds of years, bank loans, private notes, several documents apparently from Otto von Dortmann's bank, sales receipts, also curiously a few involving the neighboring Schmundt estate, and a variety of other miscellaneous papers. What drew Matthew's attention most of all were four documents labeled on top *Eigentumsurkunde*. He knew the word well enough—Title Deed. Everything was printed in old-fashioned German script, and he could make out very little of their meaning. Two were of very ancient date, the others more recent.

They were of no use down here, he thought, especially now that the Communists had taken over everything. If found, everything down here would probably be destroyed anyway.

Matthew folded the four deeds, put them in the pocket of his suit coat, well soiled by this time, then replaced the rest of the papers in the file, put the file in the box, and continued his walk about the dungeon, searching, rummaging about, examining the contents now and then of one of the files or boxes that interested him.

102
Evil Intent

. . .

AS GUSTAV CONTINUED TO PACE SLOWLY THROUGH THE office he had thoroughly ransacked, there came to him once more the nagging question: Who was the man snooping around here?

There could be no doubt that he was up to something having to do with the estate. What could he be, as he had wondered before, but an agent of Otto, also searching for the papers in order to prevent the estate's falling into Schmundt hands? What other explanation could there possibly—

Suddenly his brain reeled with the seismic jolt of a bolt of lightning.

What if—

The very thought was too incredible!

It could not be! Surely he would have heard something! How could his own reports miss the mark so widely?

But . . . what if it *could* be true!

If Sabina *was* alive, it would be just like her to send someone to look around.

Sabina . . . *alive!*

He leaned against the windowsill for balance, his knees suddenly weak. The revelation of this possibility had staggered him.

What would they be searching for, Sabina and this ally of hers?

What did it matter?

What mattered was that whoever it was could lead him to Sabina! She must have friends he knew nothing of!

He struggled to catch his breath, then slumped down again into

Lengyl's chair, breathing shallowly and trying to assimilate this sudden new rush of thought.

He could only contain himself a moment.

He jumped up, ran back to the window, and looked out. The little Trabi was still in front of the house. The impostor—whether friend of Otto or on some errand of Sabina—was still on the premises!

Calming, still staring outside, the monstrous impossibility of what he had been thinking began to creep over him.

She could *not* be alive. There were the reports . . . he had seen the explosion. Then what could be . . . who was—

Again his brain was seized with sudden revelations in an altogether new direction.

His thoughts raced back several months to the information Galanov had turned up prior to the consulate ball. Who but the U.S. State Department or its meddling CIA would have the clout to penetrate their security like this?

The connection to this family of traitors was more than clear! With Dortmann and his daughter dead, what possible motive could the swine have? Suddenly Gustav's mind was filled with a single name. With the very thought, hate consumed him.

McCallum!

He would find him! The thought that he was so close by, and nearly in the grasp of his power, sent Gustav into a passion of evil delight.

How he would make the baseborn cur pay for stealing Sabina's affections!

He *had* to still be in the house.

He and Lengyl had only left the room where the three idiot women were for a few moments. He could not have gotten far. If they couldn't locate what room he was hiding in, he would post guards at every door. He himself would take up a position in front and wouldn't let the car out of his sight.

He would kill him the instant he made an appearance!

No, he bethought himself. There was no good other than the pleasure of revenge to be gained from that. The fellow *knew* something, and that was of more value even than the joy of watching him die.

When he got his hands on him, he would beat whatever information he possessed out of him one way or another. If he refused to cooperate, there was always prison. The Secret Police had a multitude of ways of making people talk! Even prison might be too good for him. He would kill him later . . . and he would do the deed himself!

In the meantime, while they were waiting for the fellow to surface—whether the American or some other scum of Otto's—he would begin tracing the car and its license. He would find out for certain who he was dealing with!

He briskly left the office, walked down the stairs and outside, where he wrote down what pertinent information he could glean from the parked auto, then returned to the house and sought out Director Lengyl.

"How many men do you have on your staff?" he barked.

"Eleven," answered the timid man.

"Good. Post a man at every exit to the house," ordered Gustav. "If the mysterious Herr Albrecht attempts to escape, detain him and notify me immediately. I will be outside guarding the front, or in your office."

"Yes, Herr Section Chief, I understand."

Gustav turned, bounded back up the stairs, and within several minutes was on the phone to his office in Berlin.

• • •

AS HE GRADUALLY BECAME ACCUSTOMED TO THE MARVEL of his subterranean and earthy surroundings, the purpose of Matthew's visit to *Lebenshaus* slowly returned to his consciousness.

He began to pray, still walking slowly about the ancient excavated chamber known as the dungeon.

What is it you have to show me, Lord? he thought. *What is it you want me to see? Guide my thoughts, my steps . . . direct my paths. Lead me to her, Lord.*

Slowly he returned to the table.

A Bible and several journals were stacked on one end of the long plain wood surface. Opening one of the notebooks, Matthew instantly recognized Baron von Dortmann's handwriting. He read a few lines, and, intrigued, continued to the next page, then the next. Unconsciously he found himself sitting down on one of the nearby chairs, and before he knew it ten or fifteen minutes had passed.

Matthew could hardly believe what he had found. Hastily he flipped through the other handwritten books.

What a treasure he had discovered!

These journals—telling in the baron's own words of his early life, his spiritual development, the early days with Marion, the struggles of his faith, pages and pages of private prayers, his vision for *Lebenshaus,* his thoughts on the mature walk with his Father gleaned from a lifetime's experience, and one whole notebook devoted to his perspectives on the history of his nation and its people—were of far more value than anything he had set eyes on in this place, more valuable than all the buildings and lands of this whole estate.

What a storehouse of knowledge, study, experience, thought, prayer, and wisdom!

This was a legacy indeed—a legacy not won and not passed on without sacrifice, a legacy not of possessions or houses or lands, a legacy passed down, not by the hands of men, but by the mind of God into the hearts of his children.

Here was a legacy of a man's life lived in submission and obedience and relation to his heavenly Father.

The words he had spoken to Sabina came back to him:

"I have asked you to be my wife. That places responsibility for your father in my hands as well. If I am to be his son-in-law, I must now act the part of a son. I will take upon myself the right to make the decision. . . ."

It seemed not ordained that he was to be Baron von Dortmann's son-in-law in this life. But in the spirit, was he not already his son and younger brother?

He would be faithful to his pledge to Sabina.

He *would* take upon himself the role of son, for the sake of them both, for the sake of the baron's legacy, not only to Sabina, but also to him as his spiritual son, and to the untold others who might someday benefit from his words and from knowing about his life with the Father.

He would stand in Sabina's place and do what she could not do. The inheritance contained within these journals—the inheritance of her father's life with God, which the baron most certainly planned one day to pass along to his daughter, this inheritance not of dwindling and corruptible earthly assets and possessions, but of life with a Father who owned all the cattle on a thousand hills and all the hills of the earth—he would keep alive for future generations of God's people.

These writings of the baron he would take with him too.

They must be preserved! He could take no risk that they might fall into the wrong hands or be destroyed.

Thank you, Father, he prayed, *for allowing me the privilege of finding these notebooks. Let me do with them according to your will. Protect them, Lord. Keep them safe, and let the baron's words one day bear abundant fruit in the lives of many others. Accomplish your purpose with them, and let me be a faithful steward over them until you reveal what is to be done with them. And now, Father, what else do you have to show me? Give me direction where you would have my steps go once I leave this place.*

As he set the journals down, Matthew noticed the edge of a loose sheet of paper inside the cover of the Bible. He pulled it out. It was a list of Scriptures, again in the baron's hand, clearly written in haste and probable excitement.

Matthew read the seven entries.

> *Revelation 3:9—They shall know that you are my beloved people.*
> *1 Samuel 13:6—When the people were distressed, they hid themselves in caves, and in rocks, and in high places, and in pits.*
> *1 Kings 22:25—You will find out on the day you go to hide in an inner room.*
> *Psalm 27:3, 5—Though an army besiege me, my heart will not fear; though war break out . . . I will be confident. . . . For in the day of trouble he will keep me safe in his dwelling; he will hide me in the shelter of his tabernacle.*
> *Proverbs 28:28—When the wicked rise to power, people go into hiding.*
> *Isaiah 16:3—Hide the fugitives, do not betray the refugees.*
> *Isaiah 58:6-7—Is this not my chosen fast, to loose the chains of injustice, and untie the cords of the yoke, to set the oppressed free? . . . Is it not to share your food with the hungry and to bring the poor who have been cast out into your house . . . and to not turn away from your own kinsfolk?*

Matthew rose from the chair and proceeded to continue his examination of the table.

Passports . . . identity cards . . . strange clothes . . . pens, printing equipment. The implements of forgery.

His mind began to spin, connecting many vague references he recalled Sabina making about their activities during the war. Suddenly it was more than clear.

What else could this all mean but that *Lebenshaus* had been a clandestine underground operation for hiding Jews and smuggling them out of Nazi Germany!

It all fit with what he knew of the baron and with comments he now recalled from Sabina's own mouth.

He grabbed up the sheet of scriptures again.

This was clearly the baron's biblical basis for this work into which

God had apparently led him during the war. Could it have been this very scriptural study that the Lord had used to reveal to the baron this work he wanted him to do?

There was nothing so mysterious about it. Thousands within Germany had done the same.

Why then had Sabina been so vague? There had been so many times she had begun to speak but had then stopped and looked away. Without wanting to press, it *had* made him curious. The war was long since over. Her father was in prison, she had changed her name . . . what could possibly have been the danger to them in telling him what they had done during the war?

Why had she been so cryptic about their secretive wartime activities? Even nervous at times.

Knowing Sabina as he did, there could be only one possible explanation for her occasional odd behavior—it was not for herself she was concerned, but for others.

Whom could she have been trying to protect? He himself perhaps. If not him, then whom *had* she been protecting?

And why *now* . . . so long after any danger from the Nazis existed?

Eager to know more, Matthew rummaged through everything on the table.

Again he found himself attracted to the baron's Bible. There were a number of papers folded between its thin pages. Absently he glanced through some of them. Here was a letter, apparently from Russia. He didn't take time to read it, though a glance to the bottom showed the name Rostovchev. He sifted through a few other papers. What was this seeming conversation between two people—

Haben Sie Rosen—"do you have any roses?"

Under it, the next line—"Roses do not grow in winter"—had been crossed out. Underneath it had been written the words, *This is not the season for blooms.*

Then followed, "For those of the Father's house, the leaves, the stalks, the petals, even the very thorns themselves give off the perfume of love," but again, the line had been crossed out, and replaced with: *But for those who love, even the petals have fragrance.*

I see you understand the Father's way, was written on the next line, followed by, *How many blossoms do you need?*

Matthew read over the peculiar miniature dialog again. It was very strange, he thought. Yet it sounded like exactly the kind of thing the baron and Sabina would say to one another.

Across the bottom of the page were diagrams and more doodling, some legible, some not.

Vines of Roses . . . the Rose Family . . . the Links of Life . . . Roses Growing Underground . . . the Fragrance of Life . . .

All these had been lined through, as if the baron had been attempting to think of a pleasing phrase having to do with roses. Under them, and circled, were written the words *Netzwerk von Rosen,* followed by an exclamation mark—*Network of the Rose!*

What was it all about, puzzled Matthew, setting down the paper and pacing slowly through the dusky chamber . . . network of the rose?

The name the baron had chosen for their clandestine activities, perhaps? It made sense.

It still failed to explain Sabina's secretiveness now, so long after all these activities had ceased to be—

Suddenly Matthew's brain jolted in revelation.

What if the underground activities begun here in *Lebenshaus* had *not* ended with the war!

What if Sabina—

Yes, of course—everything suddenly fit! *The Network of the Rose still existed!* And Sabina was still involved.

The network . . .

She had let the word slip a time or two, always followed by attempts to divert their conversation into other channels.

More words and phrases she had accidentally dropped now came back to him. More than once she'd made reference to the contacts who had kept her in touch with her father. And there had been that conversation they'd had when discussing what to do about her father, when she'd clammed up.

"I could get word to him through the network," she'd said, *". . . friends . . . contacts I've made . . . You've got to know people in all sorts of walks of life. Please . . . don't ask me more. I promise I will tell you everything . . . soon."*

And that very peculiar ending to the night of the consulate ball! He'd puzzled over that one long and hard. What a strange conclusion to an evening during which a proposal of marriage had been made!

Could her sudden and unexplained urgency to get home have had something to do with the clandestine business in which she was still involved? What else could it have been but a midnight rendezvous? If so, had Sabina carried on the tradition of *Lebenshaus* in postwar divided Berlin . . . even to the hiding of fugitives in her own tiny apartment!

The thought was too incredible. Yet . . . if people were in danger, it was exactly what she would do!

Something he had thought just a few minutes earlier all at once returned to him—*she had changed her name!* Why? he had asked her. Because of Gustav, had been her reply.

Clearly there was more to it!

Were Gustav to find her, the whole network would be endangered! She must be one of its vital links, perhaps the very leader, carrying on the work her father had begun.

Her new name was more than just a way to hide from Gustav and protect her father. It was the link to her private underground responsibilities that she had had to keep secret even from him.

Duftblatt—how could he have been so blind not to see its meaning before! As well as he might know German, he still didn't *think* in German!

She had chosen the perfect compound code name. Gustav would not know its meaning. *No one* would grasp its meaning, not even him . . . except for those who were *supposed* to understand—her comrades in the Network of the Rose.

Duft—aroma, perfume, fragrance.

Blatt—petal, leaf.

Duftblatt—fragrance of the petals.

For those who love, even the petals have fragrance, he mused. *Ah, Sabina, what a clever lady you are! Code names and passwords, all with links to your father and* **Lebenshaus.**

No wonder she had been secretive. How many might she have been trying to protect other than herself, as well as him? She knew his work for the president was too important, and her own work with the network was too important, to risk jeopardizing either by allowing him to know too much.

Matthew could not keep from smiling.

She knew him well, he thought. She knew that he would have wanted to help her and that a conflict of interest with his job would have been inevitable.

None of this answered the most glaring question of all . . . why?

What had been the network's business throughout the 1950s? With the wall now up in the middle of Berlin, people who wanted to escape to the West had to find some way of smuggling themselves across. But before August 13, anyone who wanted to was free to leave. People were leaving East Germany in droves. Twenty-four hundred a day were leaving in the weeks before the wall.

What purpose, therefore, had Sabina's network served?

There were so few Jews left in Poland and the other countries of Europe, and those who wanted to emigrate had mostly gone to the newly created nation of Israel. To his knowledge there had been no underground activities within East Germany since the 1953 uprising.

Even in Russia, now that the Stalinist era was over, many persecutions had been relaxed. There had even been great public gestures of goodwill on the part of the Kremlin toward known Jewish personalities as a demonstration to the world that Communism was kindly disposed toward minority nationalities, especially Jews.

What was the full story? Were the Jews of Russia in more danger than was publicly known? Did Sabina's activities have connections with Israel, where normal channels were not available? What was the *Network of the Rose* about? The passing of information rather than people, perhaps?

More questions filling his mind regarding the *present* than this secret chamber could answer with its histories and evidences of the *past,* Matthew continued to walk slowly about the dungeon, musing to himself.

Guide my steps, Lord . . . direct my thoughts and my paths . . . show me what you want me to do, he prayed silently.

His last hours with Sabina gradually returned to his mind and came into focus.

Suddenly the connections with everything else became crystal clear. Again there had been her vagueness . . . her unwillingness to explain. And the mutiny of what he thought had been a foolproof plan back into West Berlin . . . the uncharacteristic way in which she had commandeered the escape vehicle and then taken off through the fields.

Then suddenly there had been all those people he hadn't known . . . the other car . . . the barn . . . the bakery van. He had found himself caught up in a plan far more complicated than his own, and Sabina was in charge of the whole thing!

It was so obvious now!

Without telling him, as he now remembered her saying, for his own safety, she had employed her network to help with their escape to freedom!

And now, he thought with brain racing, he would likewise employ it in the opposite direction!

He had located the key he was after. As he had penetrated East Germany and Poland, now he had to find a way to penetrate the *Network of the Rose!*

It was the only way he had to get to the bottom of the mysterious pink parcel that had been delivered to him on Christmas Eve!

He spun around, grabbed up the notebooks and the baron's Bible, and, leaving the dungeon as dark and as quiet as he had found it, turned off the light, closed the great door, and retraced his steps along the low narrow corridor.

A few minutes later he was back in the main underground corridor, closing back the door to the hidden passageway in the exact reverse order of steps he had taken earlier.

At length, placing the large, flat, floor stone in place, he picked up the books again, now retrieved the china box from the door, and stood up. Smearing dirt and mud over the cracks of door and floor stones, and satisfied nothing would be soon discovered again, Matthew continued with both hands full and barely able to manage his flashlight, back along the corridor.

This time, however, he would not risk trying to leave through the house. He would be apprehended by the good Director Lengyl in an instant, if not for the things he was carrying, certainly for the mud and grime all over his pants and suit!

No, he would make his escape through the cellar and hope he could get the door open into the garden from this side where he had been unsuccessful from the garden itself. From there, he ought to be able to sneak around the west wing of the house and to the safety of his automobile.

104
Alternate Strategy

• • •

". . . YES, THAT IS THE CORRECT LICENSE," SAID GUSTAV into the phone. "Get me whatever information you have on it immediately. If it is within thirty minutes, call me at this number."

He read the number from Lengyl's telephone on the director's desk, around which he paced with as agitated a stride as the short cord would allow.

"I need the owner of the auto and his address. Any word on Galanov's return?"

A brief pause followed.

"I see . . . another delay . . . ah, family emergency . . . I had hoped to get him back on this case. There are new developments."

He listened as his secretary posed a question.

"Thank you, but I doubt there would be anything you could do. . . . Yes, I appreciate your willingness. I will keep that in mind."

A pause.

". . . Well, in any event I need this information urgently, Fräulein Reinhardt."

Another pause, during which he appeared to be listening to the voice of his secretary on the other end of the line.

"Yes, thank you . . . yes, I'm feeling quite well. You may convey that to the doctor for me if he calls again."

He listened again.

"Ah yes. . . . I will be glad to be back in the city too. I may be detained, however. Something has come up which I must follow . . . yes, to do with the information I need."

A few more questions and replies were exchanged on both sides of the line, following which Gustav hung up the telephone.

It was a puzzling interview, he thought to himself.

The Reinhardt woman had sounded peculiar. There seemed to be something she had wanted to tell him. Her tone had been friendlier than normal too, eager to help with his investigation, and very interested in his well-being.

Of course, what could *she* do? She was only a secretary after all. But once this present business was over, it might behoove him to consider the possibilities afforded by a closer approach to his secretary. She was certainly no Sabina, but she *was* a woman, and that accounted for a great deal in and of itself. He supposed alongside most of the women he saw from day to day she wasn't an altogether unacceptable specimen. And he wasn't getting any younger.

But he couldn't waste time with such musings!

He shook them off. Thoughts of his future amorous inclinations would have to wait.

He hadn't liked it when his assistant had been summoned back to Moscow. He didn't like it now that they continued to move back the date of his return. Not that he couldn't get a half-dozen eager young *Stasi* trainees to do Galanov's work. A shortage of manpower was one problem the DDR's Secret Police did not have. But Galanov was more resourceful than most.

More than that, Gustav had the uneasy feeling of being toyed with. The reminder that all dominion these days still originated in the Russian capital, and that the DDR existed merely by Soviet sufferance, was always galling. Periodically he found himself being lulled into thinking that he possessed genuine prestige and power in his position as section chief of the *Stasi*. All it took was a reminder such as this to bring home the reality of the Kremlin's stranglehold over the whole of Eastern Europe.

What could be the reason Galanov had been called back in the first place? And why now was it being so prolonged? He had been gone for over three months. Perhaps a new assignment with the KGB . . . something to do with his injuries? Had the young zealot taken a turn for the worse?

Whatever it was, Gustav didn't like it . . . not now. It had an unpleasant aroma attached to it. Besides which, he needed Galanov's help in tracking down the McCallum fellow.

Gustav strode again to the window.

The little car was still there beside his own, with one of Lengyl's men stationed beside it. All exits to the building were blocked.

What if he refused to talk once they nabbed him? Or what if he'd already managed to slip out of the house and was waiting for the cover of darkness to make for the woods? And the possibility existed that the licensing information on the automobile wouldn't turn up what he needed.

Gustav's brow wrinkled, running all the options quickly through the not unlimited yet resourceful faculties his brain possessed.

No, he concluded after a moment or two, *it would be most productive to follow the fellow.*

What if it wasn't McCallum at all? The only way to get to the bottom of whatever plot was afoot was to keep the impostor believing that his little charade had been successful.

The torture chamber, drugs, shock treatment . . . that could all come later. First, he ought to try the most straightforward strategy the situation afforded.

He would call off the guards and leave access to the car free. He would take up a vantage point himself just inside the house and would be ready the instant the fellow made his move.

Quickly he turned, left the office, and hastened down the wide stairway and outside, where he hurriedly cleared the area of all evidence of human life.

Away!

• • •

FIFTEEN MINUTES AFTER LEAVING THE DUNGEON, SQUINT-ing from the winter's sun after so long in the hidden bowels of the house, Matthew cautiously emerged through the tunnel, which had meant life to so many, into the unkept upper precincts of *Der Frühlingsgarten*.

Wondering now how he could not have seen the possibility of a door here earlier and taking the hidden key with him, he closed up the bushy entryway, leaving it as obscured from view as before, then crept to the northwesternmost hedge-enclosed corner of the garden.

Peering through the dense growth, the coast looked clear.

Even if he happened to be seen, he thought, the Lengyl fellow wouldn't follow him. The only unknown, now that he noticed it, was another strange car parked right beside his. Another visitor must have arrived after him. That must be whom he'd heard in the hallway.

So much the better, he thought. Lengyl would be occupied, and he could make his getaway without awkward interviews.

Working his way roughly through the scratchy hedge, adding several scratches and tears to the mud and grime and looking more and more unrespectable as an official representative of Inspection Services in Berlin, he glanced around one final time, then drew in a deep breath and stepped out of cover and made for the open ground between himself and the safety of his automobile.

He saw no one. A minute later he was behind the wheel, all his parcels beside him in the passenger seat.

He turned on the ignition, pulled the lever into reverse, turned around, and with as much speed as he dared but not so much as to attract attention, Matthew wheeled his CIA-loaner Trabi down the winding drive toward the road that would lead him toward the next stage of his quest.

• • •

When he was well out of sight, the light brown uniform of the *Staatssicherheitsdienst* emerged from the front door of the house, of which window he had observed the entire escape.

Silently cursing that he hadn't recognized the man, Gustav walked to his auto.

Had it been McCallum himself, he might not have been able to keep from apprehending him on the spot.

But this sloppy, bearded impostor he didn't know from anybody, and he would learn more about his mission first—who had sent him and what his business was. When and if McCallum himself turned up, then he would make his move!

He would follow this so-called Albrecht, which would be easy enough. He would have all the information on the automobile he needed to continue his search for the man's true identity the moment he reached Berlin. Meanwhile, he would be able to overtake the little Trabi within a minute or two.

Gustav climbed into his car, revved the engine a couple times, then sped down the drive. For old times' sake, he ought to drive by the old estate where he had grown up, he thought, glancing right as he reached the main road.

It would have to wait. There would be time for all that later. For now he couldn't let the Trabi get too far ahead.

He bent the wheel to the left, eased onto the road, then pushed down on the accelerator and sped after his prey.

PART VI

The Secret of the Rose

February/March 1962

106

Berlin Again

• • •

HE WASN'T ALL THAT ANXIOUS TO ANGER THE *HAUSFRAU* or her burly *Mann* again.

But he had to start somewhere, and there were only two possibilities. He had opted to try the apartment house again first.

Sure, it was a million-to-one long shot that after all this time the same code words would be used. But any gamble would be worth it, Matthew thought as he walked again along the familiar street toward Sabina's former apartment.

It was midafternoon. Hopefully the big fellow wouldn't be home.

He approached and knocked on the door.

The same woman came to the door as last time. A look of puzzlement came over her. Something about the bearded stranger in front of her seemed familiar, but she couldn't tell what. If it was the same annoying man that had come one evening last week, he had miraculously become twenty-five years younger!

"Please, I mean no harm," said Matthew hurriedly. "I just have one question to ask you."

The moment he spoke, the woman recognized his voice. She couldn't explain the dramatic change in his appearance, but there could be no doubt this was the same beggar. Her face filled with vexation.

Quickly Matthew continued. *"Haben . . . haben Sie Rosen?"* he asked.

"What do you think this is, a flower shop? No, I have no roses!" she said, starting to close the door.

"Even for someone who loves roses?" added Matthew. "Are you

. . . are you quite sure this may not be the right . . . the season for blooms after all?"

"Quite sure. Stand back."

"Please, I need to find—"

The door slammed in his face.

"Good grief!" Matthew said to himself as he backed down the stairs. "I got that thing all mixed up! Though it's certain she didn't care a straw about roses or seasons or blooms or passwords no matter *how* I may have said it!"

Matthew turned and began walking back toward the street. It had been worth a try, but he had obviously run into dead end number one.

"Pssst!" came a sound behind him.

He paused and glanced around.

A portion of a concealed face showed through the half-opened door of the apartment adjacent to that he had just left. The large house had been converted into several separate units, though Matthew had never paid the least attention to any of the others.

He hesitated for a moment, staring, wondering if the sound had been intended for him, or if he was merely the object of some neighbor's curiosity.

A hand now crept through the opening, and a finger beckoned him to come.

Curious, Matthew turned back toward the house, approaching this time the apartment that sat exactly next to Sabina's, also on the ground floor.

He walked up to the door slowly. The partially hidden face backed further away into the darkness, but the door remained opened to the same width.

"Are you . . . do you—," began Matthew, but was quickly interrupted.

"Shh!" the woman's voice inside silenced him. "They must not know I am speaking to you."

"But are you—"

"I overheard that you seek roses," said the woman in scarcely above a whisper.

"Yes!" exclaimed Matthew, forgetting to moderate his tone.

"Shh! You *must* speak softly."

"Do you have roses?" said Matthew, whispering now.

"No, no, I have no roses, it is only that I remember you from before, when you called on Fräulein Duftblatt."

"You saw me!"

"She and I were acquainted. I knew she was fond of you."

"Do you know where Sa—that is—do you know where Fräulein Duftblatt has moved?" whispered Matthew excitedly.

The woman's hand went to her mouth, and Matthew heard her catch her breath.

"Oh, I'm sorry, *mein Herr.* . . . I thought you knew!"

"Knew what?"

"Fräulein Duftblatt is . . . she is dead, *mein Herr.*"

"Oh . . . oh, yes. . . . I had heard something," replied Matthew, ignoring the stab he felt at the woman's words.

"Yet still you come asking for roses?"

"Yes . . . uh, *other* roses . . . ," fumbled Matthew, "uh . . . do *you* know about the roses?"

"Only that she was very partial to them."

"You are . . . *you* are not . . . ," said Matthew with heavy suggestion in his voice.

"No, I was only her friend. She spoke of roses with those who came to visit through the alley in back of the house. I overheard. I heard talk of flowers. I learned much about roses and those who love them."

"But . . . *you* are not one of their number?" asked Matthew pointedly.

"No."

"Can you tell me where I might find any roses at this time of the year?"

"Only that a man called Hermann brought Fräulein Duftblatt most of her roses."

"Hermann?"

"It is all I know."

"Where is this—"

"I only heard his name."

"But—"

"Shh! He is coming! I must go. Leave me—you must go immediately!"

Noiselessly the door shut in his face.

Matthew turned. In the distance he saw the burly man who now occupied Sabina's apartment walking along the sidewalk toward him.

With haste designed to appear casual, he left the house and strode quickly off down the street in the opposite direction. If there was danger from the new occupants, he did not want to bring it upon either himself or his whispering concealed informant next door.

The Barn

• • •

THINGS HAD BEEN HAPPENING FAST, AND HE WAS TOO bewildered that day back in August to have absorbed the details of their route accurately, but he was reasonably certain this was the right place.

All the way down from Berlin he had been racking his brain to remember the names he had heard—on the drive, during the transfer of vehicles in the barn, and in the van. Grossbeeren wasn't that big a village, but even in a place this size, he had to know whom he was looking for.

He recalled the names *Wilhelm* and *Willy,* though whether they were one and the same he didn't know . . . and *Erich* . . . and there had been talk of a baker, though he couldn't remember anything specific.

And how could he forget the mysterious *Hermann* the lady had mentioned in Berlin!

What a tantalizing statement . . . *Hermann brought Fräulein Duftblatt most of her roses!*

There was clearly much more to be discovered!

After two days looking for another opportunity to question the woman next door whose face he had never seen, however, he had finally given up and left his place of hiding down the street.

The burly man and his wife were too close, too observant. If the man worked regularly, Matthew had not been able to make heads nor tails of his routine. His wife was ever on the prowl, about porch and windows, seemingly keeping an eye out for Matthew's—or any suspicious person's—appearance. More and more the sense grew upon him that he ought to avoid further interviews with either of them.

Of the secretive lady next door with the passing awareness of roses, on the other hand, he had seen no further evidence whatever. No drawn curtain, no open door, not even light burning inside.

That she was afraid of her new neighbors there could be little doubt, and Matthew would do nothing to endanger her. Finding out who Hermann was, and where he might fit into the puzzle, would have to wait.

Matthew had, therefore, left Berlin for the farmland just south of the city to follow through on the only other lead he possessed—his own piecemeal memory of the frantic day of the failed escape attempt.

The village was easy enough to find, and as he drove through its two or three quiet streets from end to end he recalled that fateful day after Sabina had taken over the driving from him. They had entered the village from the west, he thought.

Somewhere he recalled her honking the horn lightly. *Where had that been . . . ? Was it a signal of some kind?*

Matthew glanced around as he slowly drove. The place was made up almost entirely of homes, mostly farmhouses. There were but one or two small shops, along with a small *Gasthaus.* Nothing jogged his memory.

It had been as they'd entered the village. After the horn-honk nothing had happened . . . they had merely continued through. On the other side, once they were speeding across the fields toward the barn, they had been following another car.

Where had that other car come from?

It seems they had followed it for some time. Had it been waiting for them on the outskirts of the village, when they had veered off the paved road? No, as he recalled they had been following it even in the village.

That's it! Now he remembered . . . the little car had passed them in the village, and they had then followed it the rest of the way!

How had it gotten behind them? And when?

He tried to picture in his mind the incident from start to finish. There they were, following the other car. An odd-appearing car, he remembered now, with the right portion of its rear bumper twisted upward into a most peculiar-looking position. *What color was it?* Not that it would make any difference. Everyone in the DDR drove a Trabi, and they all looked exactly the same. *Hmm . . . green, that was it . . .* though even in a little town like this there might be a half-dozen green Trabants putting around.

He was out of the village now. He turned off the stony road.

This looks like the place—though there were so many dirt roads and paths across the fields and through the woods in Germany that you could cover nearly any meter of the entire country from the Alps to the Baltic without once setting tires to pavement.

He bounced along for a kilometer or two. He could hardly be sure. They had been flying so fast that day back in August, and the dust flying from beneath the green Trabi's tires had obscured his vision all the more.

There it was just ahead—*the barn!*

It was exactly as he remembered!

Accelerating, Matthew roared up, stopped, jumped out, and ran across to the wide closed doors. No sign of life was evident. There were no animals nearby, no sign of machinery. This was obviously one of the many buildings that had formerly been put to years of use in one of the thousands of small family-farms throughout Germany that had gone the way of neglect under the new cooperative and communal system, which Stalin and Khrushchev had installed throughout the land.

Walking slowly about it, poking and peering here and there, Matthew located a small rear door. It swung open to his touch.

He walked inside. Immediately the smell, the feel, the ambience of farm life assailed him. He paused, allowing his eyes to accustom themselves to the dim light. There were still some implements around and bales of hay and straw. It had not been totally vacated. *Yes, this is the place all right. The white van was waiting for us.*

He continued to walk slowly about.

There was nothing here. No white van . . . no leads . . . no clues.

Fragments of conversation from that frenzied day poked through the outer regions of his skull into the inner portions of his memory. ". . . *Wilhelm, your father says you are one of my great allies,*" he recalled Sabina's voice saying. She was speaking to a boy . . . no, a young man

. . . sixteen, maybe eighteen. He had not accompanied them in the van. He must have gone somewhere else.

Wilhelm . . . could it be the same *Willy* he heard a man's voice say a moment after Sabina's comment?

Leaving the barn, Matthew climbed back into his borrowed Trabi, sat back, and closed his eyes.

What do I do next, Lord? I am out of ideas. I felt your leading to come this far . . . but now what?

He exhaled a long sigh and sat still for several minutes, trying to empty himself of all thoughts foreign to his purpose.

Guide my steps, Father, he breathed. *Again I commit my way, my heart, my thoughts, my direction, my path, my steps to you. Set my feet upon the path of your leading, Lord. I acknowledge you as my Lord and my God, my friend, my Father, the master of my life. Direct me according to your will. Accomplish your complete and perfect purpose in and through me. . . .*

Again he breathed out slowly.

. . . Thank you, Father, he continued. *Thank you for keeping me in your care . . . and in your hands.*

Not knowing where he would go next, slowly Matthew pulled the car into gear, turned around, and crept back across the dirt road through the fields, retracing his way toward the village of Grossbeeren.

108
Willy and Willy's Papa

• • •

AS MATTHEW PULLED FROM THE DIRT TRACTOR PATH onto the rutted pavement leading back into the village, a strange sense of calm came over his spirit. He had nothing that could be called a strategy of his own. Yet he could not help feeling that somehow he was being *drawn along,* into a plan and purpose not of his own devising, toward a destination he could not foresee.

Back through the small town he drove, all the way again to the opposite end, continuing as he went to murmur quiet prayers and requests for direction.

Open my eyes, Lord. Let me see what you have for me to see here . . . direct my paths.

He turned the car around again to make yet another pass through the village of Grossbeeren.

An impulse struck him. He turned and began exploring the side streets as he encountered them at irregular intervals. Some were short, only a hundred meters in length. Others led to houses, then stopped, amounting to little more than long individual driveways. Sabina had ventured onto none of these streets that day when she was at the wheel, but he would now explore every corner of the place.

The fourth such narrow street led away, then left and across a bridge almost too narrow for even a Trabi to navigate. He crept across, then veered with the road toward the right a short distance beside the river. A large building was ahead—a school, by the appearance of it.

He came nearer.

What was that!

Matthew jammed his foot on his brake and stopped.

A bright-green Trabi was parked alongside the building!

Matthew jumped out of the car and toward it. *Yes, and the funny-looking bumper, tilted up at the odd angle! It is the same car that led us out through the fields to the barn!* There could be no mistaking it.

He ran toward the nearest door of the school building. There weren't many automobiles about. It was late in the day and school would have adjourned. He ought to be able to find—

Bounding up the steps, Matthew saw the doors open ahead of him. Two people exited, a woman about his own age and—

Yes, he recognized him. . . . *It's the same young man I saw talking to Sabina!*

He stopped, panting.

The woman paused, staring at him, a look of anxiety beginning to spread over her face as she realized he was looking straight at them.

She turned and began to retreat to the building.

"Mama?" said the young man.

"Willy, please—come!" she implored.

"No, *bitte—bitte,* wait . . . Wilhelm!" cried Matthew.

The boy stopped, heedless now of his mother's exhortations. A sudden look of knowing dawned in his eyes as he recognized the man who had been with them that day.

"He is a friend, Mama," he said. "He was with Fräulein Duftblatt and Papa and me." As he spoke, the boy called Willy proceeded down the steps toward Matthew.

"I want to hear nothing more about Fräulein Duftblatt or roses! It is behind us now, Willy! We are safe from all that now. Willy . . . Willy, please—come with me!"

But Willy and the bearded stranger were by now shaking hands in the joy of reacquaintance with a former comrade of danger.

"I have been looking for you, Willy," said Matthew eagerly. "I am seeking the whereabouts of your Fräulein Duftblatt. Have you seen her since . . . since that day?"

Wilhelm hesitated, seeming to think with himself for a moment, then said, "The reports say she died from the crash."

"I have reason to believe she may still be alive," replied Matthew.

"What kind of reason?"

"I received a message I think may have been from her . . . a message about roses."

The manner in which Willy's face took in the information made it clear he apprehended the significance of the words.

"Perhaps you should talk to my father," he said.

"No, Willy!" sounded the poor woman's voice behind them. "I will have no more of the rose business in our house!"

Willy thought a moment, then turned. "I am sorry, Mama," he said. "This man is no enemy. Papa will want to talk to him."

He turned back to Matthew.

"Wait here," he said. "I will take Mama home. I will get word to Papa that you are here."

"Your father's name . . . is Erich?" asked Matthew.

Willy nodded. "He or I will come to you."

Willy and his mother left the school in the green Trabi. Matthew found a place nearby to occupy himself, then sat down and waited, new excitement nearly bursting within him to have at last made contact with someone who knew Sabina.

• • •

An hour and fifteen minutes later, Matthew was engaged in conversation with Erich and Willy Brumfeldt as the three walked leisurely along a course beside the river that flowed past the school building where the faithful but fearful wife and mother of the two men spent her days.

"I am sorry we cannot invite you to our home," said Erich. "My wife is a good woman, but she suffered greatly from the affair, and she has not altogether recovered."

"I am just glad to find you alive," said Matthew. "The reports I received made it sound as though nearly everyone was killed."

"There were deaths," replied Erich. "One of our number . . . and others."

"I am sorry to hear of it. But what specifically of Fräulein Duftblatt and her father?"

"I myself never saw them after the crash," replied Erich, "though I was unconscious myself. They were taken to Potsdam, and beyond that we really know very little. There is no reason to disbelieve the reports, or to think they are alive. We have heard nothing to the contrary."

"Are there none of your number who might know?"

"The network operates such that every link of the chain knows only about itself and those it immediately touches. Knowing no more than we must offers us our protection and safety. Fräulein Duftblatt, of course, knew much more than the rest. But we were not acquainted with those she knew, nor do we have means to contact them."

"Do you think she *could* be alive?" asked Matthew pointedly.

Brumfeldt thought for several long moments.

"I do not know what to tell you. Would to God that I could answer yes. How my heart would rejoice to discover that she yet lives. But in all honesty I must say that not a whisper of such a rumor has reached me. Of course, if she *was* alive, she would not want us to know—for our own safety. Our involvement in the escape attempt has implicated us very directly, and she would do nothing to endanger us further, which knowing that she lived could only do. Therefore, my having heard no report can prove nothing either way."

"Ah yes, I see," said Matthew.

"Evil men were after her, that much she confided with us," Brumfeldt went on. "If she lived, for the sake of her friends, she would keep news of it quiet. It is possible she would break all ties with the network, change her identity, and begin a whole new life."

"Might she really do that?"

Brumfeldt shrugged.

"These are new and perilous times," he said.

"Someone in your organization must have some idea. I have heard the name Hermann. Does it mean anything to you?"

"He is my cousin—a Berliner."

"Do you know if he has seen her?"

Erich shook his head. "He has not," he said.

"She couldn't start a new life without friends . . . without leaving some trace."

"You may be right. But she would be loathe to endanger anyone. Others of the network, knowing that she was in danger, would only draw the net of secrecy more tightly around any such knowledge they possessed, especially if someone such as yourself began asking questions, even if you knew where to begin. My son and I have seen you before. We know you to be trustworthy because you were with her. Others will not know that."

"If you were to vouch for me . . . ," suggested Matthew.

"Beyond the few with whom we are involved nearby, no one would know the name Brumfeldt. They could mistrust me along with you. My vouching for you would mean only that perhaps we are *both Stasi* agents, looking for her together."

"I cannot imagine anyone would think such a thing."

"Suspicion and mistrust are foundational to life in the DDR. Informants and spies and collaborators are everywhere."

"You do not make it sound encouraging," sighed Matthew.

"What if she is in Poland, with a different name, with new code phrases, and with people I know nothing about—which is all to say *if* she is alive at all, which I have no reason to suspect."

"You hold out little hope of my finding her?"

"None, my friend, unless she *wants* you to find her. The network is founded on stealth. She and the others established it so. Even if she yet lives, I cannot imagine what you would do to locate her."

"What about Bietmann, Papa?" said Willy, who had been listening intently the whole time.

"Hmm . . . he is a possible source," mused his father.

"Who is this Bietmann?" asked Matthew.

"A young farmer. He lives east of here, in a village called Kehrigk-burg."

"He is one of your number?"

Brumfeldt nodded.

"Now that Willy mentions it, I do recall his being involved in a wider sphere of network activities, from Potsdam down to Magde-burg, even into Poland. I have never met him, but Willy worked for him one harvest several years ago. . . . What do you think, Willy?"

"Herr Bietmann had many visitors when I was there, Papa. I think he knows many people."

"If I talk to him, may I use the two of your names to introduce myself?" Matthew asked.

"You may," replied Erich, "though he will have to make up his own mind whether to trust you."

"Then will you tell me how to find him?"

Brumfeldt nodded. "We will."

109

Kehrigkburg

. . .

AS HE DROVE TOWARD KEHRIGKBURG, MATTHEW WAS already beginning to think himself foolish for imagining this was going to be easy . . . or imagining that he had any chance of finding her at all.

He located the Bietmann place easily enough, though when he introduced himself as a friend of Erich and Willy Brumfeldt, the man showed little recognition.

Matthew paused awkwardly.

"I, uh . . . am hoping to find a friend of mine," he said, "a collector of roses by the name of Duftblatt."

Still the man's countenance gave nothing away.

"This is wintertime," he said. "It is cold. I hardly think there are many collectors of roses at such a time."

He looked up, eyeing Matthew carefully.

Suddenly Matthew remembered what he had read in the baron's dungeon.

"Yes, that is true," he said quickly, and showing his obvious nervousness. "Are . . . are you saying that now is, uh . . . the wrong season for flowers . . . I mean, the wrong . . . that is, that this is not the best season for blooms?"

The faintest hint of a smile showed itself around Bietmann's lips at Matthew's fumbling.

"That is something like what I was trying to say concerning your request," he answered slowly. "If I were to reply that this is not the season for blooms, what might you say to that?"

"Oh . . . yes, that, uh . . . let's see," stuttered Matthew excitedly, "I would say that people who love . . . I mean, that for those who love, the leaves also—no, that's not it—for those that love, even the leaves have fragrance."

"How about the petals?"

"That's it—*the petals!*" exclaimed Matthew. "The *petals* have fragrance!"

"Well put," laughed Bietmann. "Come in. Perhaps we should sit down and have a talk."

He led Matthew off his veranda and inside.

Once seated, Matthew explained his situation and his request. The farmer listened intently, but again without divulging anything by expression or manner.

"I may be able to help you," he said at length. "I make no promises. What Herr Brumfeldt has told you is true. Though the fabric is solidly knit, all its fibers are short and of limited extent. No one sees a great distance into the cloth, or how it has been woven elsewhere. Each is concerned only to maintain the integrity of fabric where they happen to be woven into the whole. Do you understand me?"

"I believe so," answered Matthew.

"I have heard rumors," Bietmann went on. "The name Duftblatt has never been mentioned. Still, I have suspicions of my own."

"What can you tell me?" said Matthew, leaning forward.

"Nothing specific, I'm afraid. I can only give you two names—two strands in the fabric like myself that may sometimes have occasion to know things. I have heard that there have been travelers moving among our people, that is all. It is the slenderest of leads, I grant, but it is all I have to offer you."

"I will follow whatever I am able."

"One is far to the north, in Poland, near the Baltic, the other close to the Czechoslovakian border. I know neither individual personally. Neither am I acquainted with whatever means of communication they may be using. There may be dangers I am unaware of. I am sorry I cannot be of more precise help."

"I am deeply grateful for anything," said Matthew. "I will follow and see where the strands of thread lead me."

Bietmann gave Matthew the two names, and the towns where, if they were to be contacted at all, they could be found.

The two men parted with a handshake of firm and slightly prolonged duration.

110

A Long and Circuitous Road

• • •

WITH THE VISIT TO KEHRIGKBURG, AND ARMED WITH
the names from Bietmann, Matthew began a long and wearying
pilgrimage to get onto the track of the mysterious "travelers" said
to be moving through the rose-colored fabric of the network,
though both Bietmann's and Brumfeldt's admonitions against optimism could hardly have prepared Matthew for the discouragement
he would ultimately face throughout his trek.

Weeks passed, then a month.

Matthew followed lead after lead, all of which ended the same
way—with the cold embers of a fire that had seemingly been
extinguished only a few days before.

Whomever's trail he was following seemed to divine his every
move, his every thought, ahead of time. Whenever and wherever he
arrived, they were gone without a trace, the footsteps vanished, and he
was left having, time after heartbreaking time, to begin his search
anew.

If the network was as well organized as he knew it must be, they
probably *did* know his every move ahead of time, and, thinking him a
Stasi or KGB agent, continued to manage to stay several steps ahead.
Just when he thought he had convinced one of Sabina's former allies
of his honest intentions, he would discover that some other had sent
out warnings concerning him, undoing all previous efforts.

He even found himself thinking that it might be Bietmann or
Brumfeldt themselves who had sent warnings out against him the
moment he had gone on his way.

He could not blame any of them. Their lives and families and entire futures were at stake. Why should they trust him? For all they knew, he was the worst kind of spy—one masquerading as a friend. What proof did he really possess that he was what he claimed?

Why would they not be suspicious from all his questions? The closer he probed, the more secretive they became. If it was Sabina, she had to have heard someone was on her trail, getting closer and closer. What else would she do but go even further underground? She probably thought he was Gustav.

He had two or three times been convinced he was on the verge of locating her, only to find the place empty, whoever had been there just ahead of him gone.

The whole search was complicated further by the fact that the *Stasi* were snooping around too. He had had the sense almost from the beginning of being followed. He had therefore had to measure his steps with care, both in front and behind.

The last thing he could do was to compromise the secrecy of the Network of the Rose. A simple carelessness on his part could result in harm to innocent friends of Sabina's. Every move had to be made with one eye in front guarding his steps, and the other watching out over his shoulder. The very thing he was trying to prevent—leading an enemy to any of them—was also the factor keeping him from success: They thought *him* the enemy.

He had caught a glance of the fellow stalking him once, early on.

He could not be sure, especially when he speculated what changes twenty years might bring to Sabina's former neighbor . . . but he dimly imagined that it *could* have been him.

How, Matthew hadn't an idea. He had been so careful. He couldn't think how the fellow could have gotten onto him.

The unlikelihood of it was insurmountable. How could Schmundt possibly have made contact!

Unless, somehow . . . the escape . . .

Could *he* have been the one chasing them in the helicopter! No, for then he wouldn't still be around—hadn't the article from Clatchen said everyone in the helicopter died in the crash? Well, maybe not exactly in so many words, but . . .

His thoughts, as they usually did, drifted into regions where too many unanswered questions left his thoughts fuzzy.

Perhaps, he thought, the shadow lurking about was somebody

from the network itself, following to make sure he wasn't a wolf in sheep's clothing. That made more sense than Schmundt.

Whoever it was, he had taken extra precautions after spotting him for the first time, and then didn't see him again for a couple weeks, though the uncanny feeling of having company on his travels continued.

After leaving Grossbeeren and Kehrigkburg, Matthew had followed the slenderest threads of hope into many corners of East Germany and Poland, even to Niedersdorf itself, to Warsaw, south into Czechoslovakia, northward again through Prague, then Leipzig, where, to his disbelief he had again caught sight of a man following him, though this time he was definitely younger and assuredly not Schmundt.

The Network of the Rose was, if not large, certainly extensive, and utterly devoted to the safety of those involved. He had used bribes, he had pleaded, he had put to use every diplomatic ploy he had learned through the years, occasionally winning confidence only to see it evaporate the moment he reached the next hopeful stage of his journey and still, after so long, had only succeeded in penetrating the remotest outer fringes of the stealthy and furtive organization begun at *Lebenshaus* some two decades earlier.

As the winter of early 1962 drew to a close, success in his quest continued to elude him.

1 1 1

Trust between Brothers

•   •   •

BY LATE MARCH, MATTHEW'S PATH LED ONCE AGAIN, AS
he had suspected it might, to the small village southeast of Berlin
called Kehrigkburg, where the fellow called Bietmann, Matthew
had begun to surmise, might be one of the new pacesetters for the
whole network in Sabina's absence. More and more, as he had
reflected on their initial conversation, the conviction had grown
upon Matthew that his and Bietmann's paths would cross again.

As a result of his brief sojourn there, he was now on his way the
following afternoon to Magdeburg, some 130 kilometers southwest
of Berlin in the DDR.

His supply of East German marks was nearly exhausted, he had
lost fifteen pounds, Paddy Red's Trabi had breathed its last several
times only to be given temporary new life with what patchwork
mechanics he was capable of, and, though he was determined to
pursue the quest as long as it took, he was growing daily more
doubtful of his capability to continue without somehow replenishing
his funds and getting hold of a more dependable automobile. To stop
now, however, was certain to let the trail grow cold all over again.

A confidence began to grow within him, however, as he made his
way along the rutted two-lane road that would lead him eventually to
the east-west autobahn, that the potential postal contact he had
received would at last pay off.

During this second visit with Bietmann, a genuine sense of
brotherhood and camaraderie had sprung up between them.
Bietmann had gone so far as to invite him to participate in a time of
prayer with a small group of believers of which he was a part and then

later to spend the night in his home, notwithstanding Matthew's cautions regarding potential prying eyes that could have followed him from Leipzig.

"There are no religious restrictions in the DDR," said Bietmann. "We do not have to hide our activities. If a *Stasi* agent himself appeared at the door, we would invite him in to pray with us. It is still not so bad here as in Russia."

When they had parted earlier that day, shaking his hand and gazing into his eyes earnestly, the simple German farmer had said, "I believe you will find those you seek in Magdeburg. This new information only came to me last week, and I have been praying that you would visit again. I cannot answer for what your contact will do when you present your request, however. Remember what I told you earlier about the fabric. I am not woven into that region of the cloth, though I have some limited information regarding a few of their strands. If they have reason to doubt you, or if there is danger of which I am unaware, perhaps you will not be given the envelope. I am only giving you the link I have to that area. You must say the words exactly as I have given them. Otherwise, they will not believe your intent to be trustworthy."

"I understand," Matthew had replied. "But if I am being followed, I cannot risk endangering others. Is there any possibility it is one of your people who has been nagging me these past weeks?"

"Very little. We do not engage in espionage, except to protect those we are attempting to help."

"If he is still behind me . . . ?"

"Yes . . . ," said Bietmann, thinking with himself briefly.

"I think we will be able to sufficiently detain him," he added after a moment. "There is a ploy I have put to good use upon occasion. All you have to do is drive through town northward as if you are on your way to Berlin. I will follow close behind you in my own automobile, just far enough back to make sure there is no one between us. If someone wants to pursue, they will have to get in line behind me. I have a friend to the north of the village who will arrange to remove his cows to another field just between our two automobiles. I will telephone him and tell him what we are about. It should prove effective. One kilometer past the cow crossing, a road appears through the fields to the left. Take it. You will be out of sight from the north road within thirty seconds, and it will lead you a distance of some three kilometers straight to the eastbound road, which will take you to the autobahn."

"I am more appreciative than you can ever know," said Matthew with deep sincerity.

"I trust you, my brother, whoever you really are, and whatever your mission beyond what I know. Godspeed, my friend."

As Bietmann had uttered the words, Matthew could not help but be reminded of the trust extended to Paul by Barnabas in vouching for the reality of the apostle's new faith before the church in Jerusalem.

Now—with the cows of Bietmann's friend spread out across the road behind him as he glanced into his rearview mirror—he was on his way, like Paul, to contact a Christian and stranger who may or may not choose to grant him the request he would make.

112

What Price Loyalty?

. . .

THE NIGHT IN THAT FLEA TRAP WAS NEARLY THE FINAL
straw.

He was beginning to regret once again undertaking the pursuit
personally. But when the man he had put on it in Galanov's absence
had notified him from Leipzig that the direction looked to be
heading again straight toward Berlin, he had not wanted to take any
chances. This new lackey did not possess the savvy of Galanov, who
had still not returned from Moscow, and he didn't want to risk losing
the quarry this close to home.

The section chief had therefore opted to take on the case himself in
renewed hopes of finding out what the *Lebenshaus* impostor was up to.

He had been up before dawn, staked out in the frigid darkness to
make sure the Trabi didn't go anyplace without him. In this country
where Trabis were more numerous than barn rats, the particular aging
and ailing specimen that he had kept an eye on across half the region
of the Warsaw Pact ever since it appeared at the Dortmann estate, was
distinctive enough by its dents and rust as to make following it
absurdly simple. He doubted it was capable of more than seventy
kilometers an hour, although it was remarkable how much ground
the fellow had managed to cover.

He had been sitting here the whole morning and past noon. He
was starving. He could have slept for hours and enjoyed a leisurely
breakfast . . . and by now even lunch!

Finally, ten minutes ago they had left the house, both guest and
host, climbed into their two separate automobiles, and left toward the
village. *Where is the other fellow, the local farmer, going?* he wondered.

He bent down out of sight as the two vehicles passed, then started up his own and slowly eased onto the street behind them.

He still was not sure whether it was McCallum in the smoky Trabi up ahead. The beard was effective, he had to admit, and he had only seen the swine once, twenty years ago. He had been drunk himself at the time.

Everyone the man contacted—from hotel clerks and shopkeepers to workers and peasants—that he or his temporary assistant later questioned said the man seemed German enough, perhaps Austrian or Swiss, thought one or two on account of his accent. All had professed utter ignorance of the name McCallum.

So they had continued to follow rather than apprehend him, although Gustav's patience was wearing thin concerning the entire business. He was about ready to drop it all once and for all and just arrest the bearded impostor for impersonating an official of Inspection Services and be done with the whole affair.

He followed the two automobiles through the ridiculous little village that had nothing more to show for itself than the miserable *Gasthaus* where he had spent the night. His information appeared to be correct. They were leaving on the northbound road and seemed heading toward Berlin.

Why was the idiot farmer with whom he had spent the night following him so close?

What is this lunacy!

He slammed on his brakes, nearly crashing into the farmer's car in front of him.

A herd of cattle had suddenly appeared in the middle of the road!

Gustav sprang from his car and ran up ahead, yelling orders to the man standing at the head of the herd. In the distance, he saw the rusty old Trabi, the object of his pursuit, disappearing in the distance behind the thin black cloud of its exhaust.

"I must follow that auto!" he yelled, approaching the man whose countenance was as relaxed and unhurried as the phlegmatic cows under his charge.

"I am sorry, *mein Herr,*" replied the man with a smile, "but my cows do not understand the hurried ways of man."

"How dare your impertinence!"

"Once my ladies start across the road, there is neither stopping them nor speeding their gait."

"Don't you know whom you are speaking to?" cried Gustav, forgetting that he was not wearing his uniform.

"I'm sorry, *mein Herr,* but no, I do not."

"I am the *Stasi* section chief, you fool! I insist you let me pass at once."

"I am sorry, *mein Herr,*" replied the man nervously, his smile vanishing. Immediately he began attempting to clear a way through the herd, but with limited success. Already, however, the puffing exhaust cloud was all but lost to sight ahead.

At the same time, Gustav had spun around and was now shouting at the driver of the car directly in front of his own, who had managed to pull up and stop in the center of the road, turning off his car, just in front of the bovine mass, effectively blocking both lanes.

"Move this car instantly, you imbecile!"

Bietmann nodded compliantly. He reached forward toward the key. The engine turned over several times. He glanced up out of his open window innocently.

"There seems to be something wrong with the ignition, *mein Herr.*"

"Bah, you are an incompetent fool!" shrieked Gustav, grabbing the door and throwing it open. He laid an angry fist on the farmer's chest and yanked him out of the car and to his feet.

"The man was with you last night. I demand you tell me where he is bound!"

"What man?" said Bietmann.

The next instant he lay on the rough pavement, the imprint of Gustav's fist reddening across his jaw and blood beginning to pour from his nose. He had no time even to realize what had happened, for Gustav had already pulled him back to his feet and now clutched him by the throat.

"Unless you want to spend the rest of your life in prison, you low-minded idiot, you had better tell me everything! Is the man's name McCallum?"

"I am sorry, I know nothing of that name."

Another vicious slap sounded across the man's face, though this time Gustav had had the presence of mind to hang onto him with the other so the dolt wouldn't collapse again.

"Why did he come to you?"

"He is a friend."

"You lie! The two of you had never set eyes on one another before yesterday."

"But we had, *mein Herr*—"

"Don't you understand any more than your *muzhik* friend whom you are toying with? I will kill you here and now if you persist in your lies!"

As he spoke, Gustav let go his hold. Fumbling about his person for his weapon, within fifteen seconds he stood over the man, who had fallen again, pistol pointing directly at his head.

"I have killed before, and I will not hesitate to use this again if you force me—"

"Udo, Udo!" cried the other farmer, leaving his cattle and now running up and stooping beside his friend. "Tell this man what he wants to know!"

"*Ruhe,* Micka," whispered Bietmann. "Say nothing."

"Listen to your friend!" shouted Gustav with mounting passion, "or I may kill you both!"

The fallen man's lips began to move. He was speaking, however, to neither friend nor enemy beside him, but rather to his Father, confessing his fear, yet acknowledging his equal willingness to meet the sacrifice if it came to him.

"Udo . . . Udo, please!" pleaded the young farmer called Micka. "Think of your wife . . . loyalty is not worth such a price!"

The next instant Micka found himself clutched at the throat with Gustav's left hand, while his terrified eyes stared into the front of the pistol he held in his right.

"You have spoken truthfully," said Gustav, his voice now low and menacing. "I also speak truthfully when I say that if you do not tell me what *you* know, then you will join your friend, and *both* your wives will be widows before this day is out!"

"Mag . . . Magdeburg . . . ," stammered the man in terror, ". . . He is . . . he is on his way to Magdeburg."

"What kind of fool do you take me for!" shrieked Gustav, beating him against the side of the head. "This road leads straight to Berlin!"

"Please . . . *Herr Hauptmann* . . . I . . . it is true . . . he is—"

"Micka, we must not betray a brother," whispered Bietmann from the ground.

A kick from Gustav's boot silenced him into unconsciousness.

"Continue!" demanded Gustav, waving the point of his gun in the farmer's face.

"He is . . . he is turning back . . . up there ahead—" as he spoke he gestured behind him—"turning back toward . . . going to the autobahn."

"To Magdeburg!"

"Ja, Herr Hauptmann."

"Where in Magdeburg?"

"I . . . I don't know. . . ."

Another clubbing on his ear brought both blood and a further loosening to his tongue.

"I cannot be sure, *Herr Hauptmann,* but . . . but at one time . . . I know he had a friend at . . . at the *Postamt.*"

Already Gustav was running back for his automobile. Let these idiots and their cows block the road as long as they wanted, he would make straight for the autobahn!

The next moment he had wheeled his car around with screeching tires, ground his foot to the floor, and sped back toward the village, from which he would take the most direct route to Magdeburg, while behind him Micka slumped to the ground, buried his face on the breathing but otherwise lifeless chest of his friend, and wept over what he had done.

A Very Special Stamp

•   •   •

MATTHEW'S INSTRUCTIONS FROM BIETMANN HAD BEEN to go into the Magdeburg *Postamt* at either 11:15 in the morning or 4:35 in the afternoon and ask for Herr Fritsch.

He glanced down at his watch. It was a little after three-thirty. He had driven comfortably, for the distance was not far, and ought to be in Magdeburg within forty minutes.

The feeling had grown stronger all day that a breakthrough in his search was at hand and would perhaps even come today. With it, however, also had increased the sense of peril, and he found himself unaccountably glancing about even at other automobiles on the autobahn with the eerie sense that inside one of them was someone watching him.

Less than an hour later, he parked on the sidewalk, opened the door, got out of his car, and walked across the street and into the post office. He went to the window and asked one of the two clerks present for Herr Fritsch. A minute later a man emerged from an office and approached, obviously eyeing him carefully.

"I am Fritsch," he said. "What may I do for you?"

"I understand you are able to offer unusual stamps to collectors," replied Matthew.

Hesitating a moment, Fritsch continued to look Matthew over.

"Occasionally," he said at length, drawing the word out slowly. "What variety of stamp do you seek?"

"The forty pfennig rose."

"The smallest specimen is the seventy-five-pfennig *Luftpost.*"

"Does it show the leaves as well?"

"All roses have leaves. What color do you wish?"

"As long as the petals have fragrance, any will do, though I am partial to red."

"I see," said Fritsch. "In that case, perhaps you would be interested in one that was sent me, though it has already been used."

"So much the better," replied Matthew, "for a rose ought to spread its perfume to more than one person."

The man called Fritsch disappeared, returning a minute later with an envelope in his hand. He handed it to Matthew.

"As you can see," he said, "the stamp has been canceled. But the one who lives at the return address on the back of the envelope is also a lover of roses. He will be able to direct you to the most fragrant varieties of all."

"How will he know that I am a fellow collector?" asked Matthew.

"By that envelope," replied Fritsch. "Show it and you will be welcome. But you must not appear before 6:30."

Matthew turned from the window, checking with a street map of the city on the wall behind him, then left the post office.

He located the address indicated without difficulty, arriving at 6:35. By then night had closed in.

The information he received from the friend of postal officer Fritsch, who seemed expecting him, was enough to send him into a near delirium of impatient ecstasy. Running back to his car to rush that very instant to the new address he had been given, the man called out behind him.

"There will be no one at the Graulinger location until tomorrow," he said. "Shall I make arrangements for a place for you to spend the night?"

"No," Matthew replied, too excited to think clearly. "I will find a hotel."

Attempting in vain to calm himself, he drove and walked about the city for several hours, passing more times than he counted the destination where, the next day, he hoped his search would at last culminate.

He only hoped Bietmann's plan with the cows had worked and that he was alone in this city—and without the presence of whoever had been following him for the last several weeks.

Drawing Ever Closer

• • •

CURSE THE IDIOT WHO HAD OVERTURNED HIS TRUCK on the autobahn! With the traffic backed up for an hour, he would be lucky to make Magdeburg before nightfall.

The *Postamt* would likely already be closed. He would make them open it and give him an employee list if necessary. He would round up every one of them and question them till midnight if he had to!

He glanced at his watch. He might still make it by five-thirty or six o'clock, but it would be tight. He couldn't run into any more tie-ups on the highway!

Fifty-five minutes later Gustav stormed through the door of his destination. It was 5:40. Without the least pretence of ceremony, he blustered past the few customers at the window and barked to the astonished clerk, "I am *Stasi* Section Chief Schmundt! I must speak with your director immediately!"

"Yes, *mein Herr,*" replied the man, turning and hastening toward one of several offices behind him.

The temporarily annoyed customers drew back. They would wait calmly the rest of the day rather than anger an official of the *Staatssicherheitsdienst.*

The postal director appeared, followed by the nervous little clerk who had been sent for him.

"I must question any of your staff who may have had occasion to encounter a man I have reason to believe was here within the last two hours," said Gustav. "How many others have you besides this man here?" he asked, nodding his head toward the clerk.

"One other. We have a woman also," replied the director.

"Bring her!"

The director spoke to the little man, who quickly disappeared down a corridor behind them. A minute later he returned, this time a woman alongside him.

"Did either of you help a man this afternoon, an American I believe, though he would have spoken in German?" asked Gustav, eyeing the two clerks steadily. "He is an enemy of the German Democratic Republic, and I have followed him here to this postal station. I do not know the nature of his request, though it is likely he would have been asking to speak with someone who works in this office. He would have been wearing a beard."

"I remember such a man," said the lady. "He came to your window, Max. . . . It couldn't have been more than an hour ago."

"*Ja . . . Ja,* I remember him now," said the timorous Max. "He . . . he waited in my line, then asked for Herr Fritsch. *Ja . . .* a beard!"

"*Ja,* Max," added the woman, "and did not he ask the assistant director something about stamps?"

"*Ja, Ja!* It was a lengthy conversation, but . . . but of course I . . . I could make out none of what they said."

"Nor I," added the woman, realizing she had already said more than was healthy for her.

"Who is this Fritsch?" demanded Gustav.

"He is my assistant," answered the director.

"Bring him this instant!"

"I am sorry, *Herr Hauptmann,* but he has already gone for the day."

"Gone—why!"

"He asked if he could excuse himself a little early, and I granted his request."

"For what reason?"

"He did not say."

"Then bring me his address . . . and quickly!"

"I am sorry, *Herr Hauptmann,* but you should know we are not permitted—"

The poor director had no time to complete his sentence. The next moment he found himself gasping for breath as Gustav's hand closed about his shirt and neck all at once, lifting his feet half off the ground.

"Listen to me, you imbecile!" he shouted into the man's face. "Unless you desire to be relieved of this position, I suggest you do as

I say. I will find this traitor Fritsch either way. If you do not help me, you may discover the same fate awaiting you!"

He set the trembling man back down, releasing his iron grip. Swallowing hard several times, the director turned and hurried with hasty waddling step back toward his office. Neither clerk nor any of the customers present dared move a muscle nor utter a peep.

A minute and a half later the director returned, bearing the employee folder on his assistant.

Well knowing what betrayal he was committing, yet perceiving no alternative if he would keep his job, he handed it to the *Stasi* agent.

Gustav grabbed it from his hand, flipped through it cursorily, then spun on his heels and stormed out of the building.

Preparations

• • •

THERE HAD BEEN SO MANY DEAD ENDS THAT MATTHEW dared not let his hopes rise too high. Yet he was sure this was it.

It had to be!

Sleep seemed hopeless, his heart was pounding so, his brain filled with so many thoughts and anxieties and hopes . . . and also the lurking uneasiness that all this time he had somehow misinterpreted the mysterious Christmas parcel that had sent him on this long and personal crusade behind the Iron Curtain.

Finding a hotel had not been difficult, and notwithstanding that he might as well not have bothered for all the sleep he turned out to be getting, he had managed to calm himself down long enough that evening to reflect and pray. He knew he had to face the potential reality of coming up empty once again. Intellectually he felt he had arrived at a position he could be comfortable with. Emotionally, however, his heart continued to beat more rapidly than normal, and he could hardly keep a wide smile from breaking out across his face.

More difficult than finding a hotel had been locating a rose.

In some parts of the world they would be blooming in March, but snoop around as he did, he could find no bloom in any flower box or unguarded yard worth clipping. He had finally returned to the hotel, gone to his room, dressed in the best clothes he had, and undertaken an exploration of the city's nicer restaurants, asking merely to have a look at the menu and then furtively glancing about the unoccupied tables.

It wasn't until almost ten o'clock that he had found what he had been looking for. When the maitre d' left him with the menu, he had promptly snitched the long-stemmed rose out of the vase in the center of the nearest table to him, put it under his coat, and made a hasty exit. He hoped he would be forgiven the theft. The cause this once, in his estimation, was worth it.

He was nearly out of money. Ten marks and change was all he had left, barely enough to cover gas back to Berlin or wherever he thought to go if the house he had been spying on this evening turned out to be vacant and lifeless all the next day and the day following that.

Nevertheless, he would play out this hand as if it were his last and throw everything he had, disguise and money and all, into the pot in the middle of the table. If he lost everything in the attempt, so be it—he would have given it his best shot. If he failed and it all blew up in his face . . . he would regroup and begin again.

But for tonight, right now—and tomorrow!—he would hold nothing back. Let the bad guys, let Schmundt, let whoever might know him from diplomatic circles—let them recognize him and do their worst.

Tonight, for her sake, he was coming out of hiding!

Back in the hotel, late now, he walked to the bathroom and set down on the counter in front of him the small bag of purchases he had made from an all-night *Apotheke,* one by one removed them, then slipped a blade into the razor.

"Well, my bearded friend," he said into the mirror, "Albrecht or Liebermann or whoever you are . . . it's been nice knowing you!"

A moment more he paused, then added in a tone that made plain he was now talking to another rather than himself, "It's all been for you . . . and so is this. If we ever see each other again, I want you to know that it's really me."

He bent forward over the sink, wet and lathered his beard, and began the painstaking process of removing it.

Ten minutes later he stood back, drying his face, and looked over his work in the mirror.

"What do you say, paleface!" he said to himself, examining several hairline nicks under his chin and around his Adam's apple. "It ain't no Gillette, that's for sure, but I guess it got the job mostly done."

By now it was late.

Matthew lay down and did his best to sleep, but without much success. He tried to pray again too, but with the same result. He had come all this way, conscious every step of the Lord's guiding. Yet now, the only prayers that came from his lips were sighings and groanings of inarticulate and undetermined focus.

He dozed off an hour or two before dawn.

Dreams ill-defined floated through his semiconsciousness as if continuing the same apparitions that had tormented him after his accident. In all of them he was running . . . running but with agonizing slowness . . . pursuing someone ahead.

He held something in his hand . . . a stick perhaps . . . no—he saw it now!—it was a flower, a rose!

His fingers grasped the stem tightly. He must preserve it . . . he must give it to her. . . . He must catch up . . . he must run yet faster. But his feet were stuck as in thick clay that was steadily drying . . . drying now like concrete. He lifted his feet with great effort . . . laboring . . . still plodding forward.

The image in the distance grew fainter and fainter . . . he must give her the rose . . . she had to have it. . . . It contained the message that would protect her and give her life . . . but try as he might, he could not go faster.

The form ahead began to fade . . . still he clutched the rose in his hand. . . .

He stopped. He could go no further. She had disappeared. He had failed. She would never hear the message.

He glanced down at the rose in his hand. The fragrant blossom was gone.

In its place—aagh, hideous thought!—the end of the stem was covered with a round, slimy, moving mass of slugs and worms and grotesque forms of dreamy unreality!

At the sight, he screamed in horror. But no sound escaped his lips. He was no more capable of voice than his legs had been of speed.

In wretched disgust he tried to throw the ghoulish thing from him. But it would not loosen from his hand. He unclasped his fingers from around the stem. But it was hooked of itself. In panic he shook his arm, but still it remained.

Now first he felt the pain.

The thorns of the stem had stuck themselves so deeply into the palm of his hand that no amount of effort would dislodge them. They were long cruel barbs . . . and now he saw that blood was beginning to flow from them—his own blood!

The words of his own poem reverberated weirdly through the dreamland of phantasmic horrid images—*Einen Dorn geheissen, der wütend mir will das Herze zerreissen*: "It is called a thorn that savagely tears my heart."

Down his hand onto his wrist, then to the elbow—he could not stop the blood!

Ugh! he cried with renewed repugnance, the sound of his terrified revulsion at last breaking the bonds of the dreamworld and sending the first message of wakefulness to his brain.

The gooey mass of foul repulsive bloom was moving down the stem onto his hand! The odious creatures had all become leeches, come to suck his blood!

Along his palm they inched, covering it with a black morbid moving mass . . . then to his wrist . . . along his arm, sucking as they went, increasing the great stinging he felt. . . . They were going to cover his whole body and eventually drain all the life from him!

In fascinated horror he gazed at the ghastly sight, until at length, summoning a colossal effort from somewhere within the semi-wakefulness of his consciousness, he cried out again.

The yell from his own mouth woke him with a start.

He was sitting in his bed, silence and darkness his only companions, perspiring and breathing deeply.

Coming to himself after a few moments, he lay back down and exhaled a long sigh.

That was not at all pleasant, he said to himself, breathing in and out repeatedly.

Sleep did not visit him again.

116
Easier the Second Time

• • •

WHILE MATTHEW HAD SLEPT, THE MAN WHO WOULD
be his nemesis was about a far different errand.

All actions of the human will, whether for good or ill, become
easier the more frequently they are performed.

The *will* is the muscle of growth, the fiber of conscience. What one
makes of those sinews that choose, determines character and, eventually, the entire flow of life.

All muscles, of either physical or spiritual origin, strengthen or
atrophy with each successive use or non-use. Every action makes the
same action less strenuous on some future occasion.

A deed of unselfishness for a proud man may be of epic difficulty
the first time it is faced. Thereafter, similar deeds will become progres-
sively easier, until at length goodness flows from his rejuvenated
character with regularity. Pride has weakened from nonuse, while the
vital muscles of unselfishness and goodness have become strong
through exercise and persistent practice.

Likewise will greed, revenge, bitterness, and anger strengthen and
grow mighty if given regular occasion to flex and exert themselves,
simultaneously causing selflessness, forgiveness, love, and peace to
wither into invisibility.

We are all, every moment of our lives and in every contact with
other human souls, exercising the one set of muscles or the other,
fortifying what character we present to the world and what one day,
when the masks and shields of this life fall away, we will disclose to our
Maker when he asks how we fared with the will and conscience he
gave us.

Gustav had found diligent postal employee Fritsch alone in his apartment at approximately 6:20. Fortunately for the safety of others, Fritsch had already made the telephone call to the colleague who shared his interest in certain varieties of floral stamps not commonly known to the average collector.

Fritsch was just beginning preparation of his simple *Abendbrot* when the *Stasi* section chief burst through the door and strode forward, gun already in his hand.

"I have no time for lies, Fritsch!" he cried. "I know who you are, and I am well aware of the traitorous rendezvous you had with an enemy of the Republic this afternoon. I demand that you tell me all you know!"

"I . . . I am sorry . . . I don't know what you are talking about," replied the poor man with complete honesty.

"Do you deny that you spoke with a man late today in the *Postamt?*"

"I speak with many people, *mein Herr.*"

"This man had a beard!"

"Uh . . . yes, now that you mention it, there was a man with a beard."

"What did he want?"

"He asked about some rare issue floral stamps, *mein Herr.*"

"What did you tell him!"

"I said that the *Postamt* did not deal in stamps for collectors."

"Then what!"

"I referred him to a specialist in rare stamps."

"Why did he ask for you?"

"I do not know, *mein Herr.* Perhaps he had heard that I too was a philatelist."

"Bah! You are lying! He came to you for information . . . not about stamps!"

"I tell you, *mein Herr,* no other subject came up between us. He purchased nothing and was soon gone."

"Why did you leave early, just after his visit!"

"I was feeling ill, *mein Herr.*"

"You have seen no one else since leaving the *Postamt?*"

"No one, *mein Herr.*"

Gustav hesitated momentarily. The man's sincerity had thrown him off his plan. Alas, the muscle of kindness was too far gone. His conscience had forgotten about it altogether.

He spun around and began rudely searching the room, then, to the man's obvious dismay stalked into the adjoining bedroom.

Fritsch rose to follow.

"Please, *mein Herr!*" he implored.

But already Gustav had spotted his small bureau with attached secretary and was proceeding to rummage through the drawers and compartments.

Fritsch hurried forward and tried vainly to stop him. The next instant he flew back onto the floor, a sharp blow alongside his skull from the handle of Gustav's gun rendering him stunned and only half-conscious.

Papers and drawers, letters and pencils and clips and paraphernalia now flew out of the secretary from the stormy hand of Gustav's rage.

"What are these!" he demanded, spinning around and holding a folder toward the floor.

"Uh . . . my stamps . . . ," came a barely audible groan.

Gustav flipped through the book.

"There are no stamps of flowers here, you idiot!"

Fritsch continued to groan in pain, but offered no reply.

"What are these names at the back of the album?"

Fritsch said nothing.

"The names, you fool! Do you care so little for life?" A sharp booted kick in the side of the man's ribs followed.

"They . . . they are my dealers. . . ."

"What dealers!"

". . . Of stamps," groaned the poor man in agony.

Gustav scanned the list quickly.

"There are no shops listed here. Some of these are nothing but little farming villages! What kind of fool do you take me for!"

"Private . . . private collectors . . . ," murmured Fritsch, ". . . please . . . there is no need to bother any of them. . . ."

As Gustav studied the list, a fiendish smile slowly spread across his lips. The simpleton had told him all he wanted to know!

"So . . . there is no need for me to bother any of these people, eh, my good Herr Fritsch?" he said with mocking sincerity.

Gustav broke out in laughter.

"We shall see about that," he said. "I have the distinct feeling that one of the people on this list will be able to tell me all about our bearded friend. Now, if you want to live through the night, tell me which of these *dealers* you sent him to!"

Nothing but silence came in reply. Fritsch realized what he had done.

"Tell me!" shrieked Gustav in a fury, kicking at the disconsolate man repeatedly, now breaking two of his ribs before the cruel foot of his boot found his chin.

Gustav looked down at the wretched excuse of humanity who had now given up consciousness.

"No matter," he muttered to himself. He would interrogate every name on the list. There were only eight or nine. He would do so tonight!

Glancing down again, then thinking with himself about the inconvenience of the thing, even for a *Stasi* agent, he pulled the black cylinder of a silencer from his pocket and proceeded deliberately to screw it onto the end of his pistol. He couldn't afford to have any neighbors snooping around. He had to get on with his business.

Throwing the stamp album under his left arm, without compunction or remorse, he aimed his pistol toward the floor and squeezed the trigger. The body twitched slightly as blood spurted from the dead man's forehead, then lay still.

Gustav unscrewed the silencer, replaced both it and the gun in his pocket, then strode from the apartment.

Curious, he thought to himself as the door closed behind him, murder became easier the second time around.

117

The Diplomat and the Street Urchin

• • •

AT LAST MORNING HAD COME!

Matthew found himself walking with measured exuberance along the street called Graulinger he had reconnoitered in the dark last night.

Slowly he made his way over the thin sidewalk alongside the narrow street. Red-brick and grey-block buildings surrounded him. Small houses and tall structures intermingled. No one else was out at this early hour. It was not a busy street.

The lonely clicking of his footfall along the concrete sidewalk echoed rhythmically in the morning chill. The cadence of its beat seemed too brisk for the silent deadness of his urban surroundings. It was clear he was a stranger, out of place, out of touch with the realities of this place.

The chill was especially crisp on his newly shaven face. He felt exposed, vulnerable—yet ebulliently aglow and tingling with excitement and energy. He wore a broad smile that he could no more have erased than flown to the moon, as his president envisioned that one of his countrymen would do this very decade.

The day had come at last!

Something the man said yesterday suddenly came back into his memory, and unconsciously his step slowed. What had he meant that there would be no one at the Graulinger location until tomorrow?

It was an odd phrasing, now that he thought about it. It sounded like he was referring to a business address. Matthew glanced hurriedly about. This was clearly a residential area, with nothing but houses and apartment buildings.

With sickening dread, a horrible thought occurred to him. His smile faded. What if this was somehow a wrong address? What if it was in fact supposed to be a business location!

No, he was sure this was the number—42 Graulingerstrasse!

There had been no one here all evening, no lights, no sign of activity inside.

It had to be the right place!

Are the occupants due back today? he thought. Is that what the man had meant? If so, what if it wasn't until late in the afternoon . . . or even this evening?

That didn't matter!

He would sit down on the sidewalk or at the door of the house itself and wait. He would wait all day! Nothing mattered any more except to be here and nowhere else. He would not leave this street. . . . He would not let Number 42 Graulingerstrasse out of his sight until he knew . . . one way or the other!

Behind him the yellowish-purple rays of the soon-rising sun extended their fingers farther and farther into the day's growing backdrop of blue. The only other human activity was now a young boy around seven walking along the sidewalk in the distance.

His pace increased again. Glancing about him, he spied a flower box up high on one of the buildings. Somebody had managed to get a rose to bloom up there . . . and the right color too. But it was too high, and besides, he already had the one in his hand that would serve his purpose perfectly.

He was getting closer. Here was number 30, now 34, and at the end of this street the tall brick building boasted a sign with the letters in white: 40.

Suddenly his feet stopped and he caught a quick gasping breath. His body froze.

A light shone from the house across the street!

Someone was already inside!

Only a second before he had been contemplating waiting a full day . . . now suddenly the moment had come!

Schoolboy butterflies assailed him. His stomach and throat seemed to switch locations, passing one another somewhere in the middle of his chest. Suddenly he was seventeen again.

What if . . . so many *what ifs* . . . sprung to his palpitating brain!

He broke into a run, but then almost just as quickly stopped dead in his tracks. He wanted to rush headlong up to the door . . . but an anxiety he could not explain prevented him.

The raggedly clad boy he had seen crossed the street and had now nearly reached him.

Suddenly a wild impulse seized him!

Laughing to himself as he fumbled in his pocket, he dug out what remained of his money. If he failed now, he would have no choice but, like the prodigal, to return to his father, for he would be penniless!

"Hey, young man," he said as the boy approached, trying desperately to calm his voice so the lad wouldn't be afraid, "how would you like to earn yourself a few marks?"

"How?" said the urchin in a high, scratchy voice, stopping.

"Just do me one small favor," replied Matthew.

"You won't make me do something wrong, will you?"

"No, son," Matthew said with a smile. "All I want you to do is deliver a message to that house over there you just passed." He pointed back down the street in the direction the boy had come. "I'll give you—"

Matthew paused and looked down momentarily into his hand.

"Six marks thirty-five pfennigs," he went on, "just to go over there and say one simple thing to the lady of the house."

"What will you do?" asked the boy.

"I'll just be standing here, on the other side of the cross street."

The boy nodded his agreement. Matthew knelt down to one knee beside him, and together they went over the content of the simple message.

Do You Know the Secret?

• • •

THREE MINUTES LATER THE YOUNG BOY KNOCKED ON the door of house number 42.

He waited.

Footsteps approached from inside. Slowly the door opened.

"Guten Morgen, Junge," said a musical voice. "What may I do for you?"

"I am to give you a message," replied the boy.

"From whom?"

"A man?"

"What man?"

"I don't know his name."

"What is the message?"

The boy swallowed, repeating the words slowly to make sure he had them right.

"He told me to ask if you knew the secret of the rose."

It was now Sabina's turn to gasp. Her face went pale as her eyes, drawn as if by the powerful magnet of Matthew's presence, slowly raised themselves from the urchin at her door.

Across the street her dumbstruck gaze fell upon Matthew, leaning loosely against the brick wall of the corner building, his right foot crossed on top of his left. He wore a casual smile, as if this were nothing out of the ordinary and he had just happened by, though inwardly he was trying with the very might of Hercules to keep from breaking out in wild yowls of joy.

In his hand—*oh, Matthew . . . what else would you be carrying!*—he held a single red rose.

For a moment that was thereafter forever swallowed up in the eternity of their memory, both stood motionless, tearful and trembling, numb, stunned, incapacitated by thunderous echoes of the heart, youthfully fearful and ecstatic all at once, each holding the other's gaze.

The next instant Sabina was bounding down the steps as Matthew left the composure of his affected pose and sprinted across the intersection.

They fell into one another's arms in the middle of the street, weeping and laughing together.

"*Matthew, Matthew, how*—" was all Sabina could utter before convulsive sobs of joyful relief burst from her mouth. She buried her face somewhere between his neck and shoulder and chest, letting her tears flow as she melted into his embrace.

"*Oh, Sabina . . . my sweet, precious Sabina,*" whispered Matthew into her ear, tears spilling from his eyes into the golden hair he clutched with the fingers of one hand and stroked tenderly with the palm of the other. "My dear Sabina, it *was* you who sent the pink rose!"

The words sent Sabina into a fresh fit of weeping, mingled now with that unique form of crying laughter of which a woman is so endearingly capable.

"Oh yes," she sobbed, "but I didn't imagine for a moment you'd try to come find me!"

"What else could I do? I had to thank you for it. Besides, I made you a promise—oh, Sabina," he said, suddenly remembering his time in Bavaria, "I thought you were dead!"

"I knew it. . . . I *had* to find a way to get word to you!"

"But without a message?"

"Oh, you'll never know how I agonized! I wanted to say so much! But with all that happened, and the wall up, and with you in your position in the West and me trapped on the other side, I was sure we could never see one another again."

"I knew it had to be from you, but—"

"Anything I said would only have added to your pain. Forgive me! I decided the rose would say enough by itself. I knew you would understand everything, just seeing it, and I didn't want to spoil it, or add to it, with words."

Both now became aware of a third presence beside them. They glanced down. There stood the urchin in the street, gazing up at the two lovers, waiting his chance to speak.

"Bitte, mein Herr," he said timidly, *". . . das Geld?"*

Matthew burst into laughter, released Sabina, and stepped away. Turning around, he spotted the two bills and three coins a pace or two away where he had dropped them. Between them, neglected but not forgotten, was the rose, which had also fallen from his hand.

He stooped down, picked up the money, handed it to the boy, thanked him, and sent him on his way with a pat on the head.

He bent down again and this time retrieved the humble gift that God had created for just this occasion.

He approached Sabina and now handed her the flower.

"Do you know the secret of the rose?" he asked, gazing deeply into her eyes.

Sabina smiled.

"I believe I do," she answered softly. "But I cannot know if I am correct . . . ," she added, pausing, ". . . until I hear it from you."

"Then let me tell you," said Matthew, smiling now also. *"The secret of the rose . . . is that I love you."*

119

The Deeper the Red

• • •

TEARS FILLED SABINA'S EYES YET AGAIN. SHE TRIED TO speak, but all she could do for a moment was gaze into Matthew's face, smiling, weeping, and shaking her head, still fighting her disbelief.

"You make me so happy!" she said after a moment. "You have made it a fairy tale all over again!"

He bent forward and kissed her tenderly on the lips, then took her again in his arms.

"I do love you, Sabina," he said, ". . . more than I have ever loved anyone."

"And I love you, Matthew. I love you so much! Thank you . . . thank you for coming to find me!"

Her face was alongside Matthew's neck. Now she first saw the little nicks about it.

"What are all these?" she said dreamily, poking him tenderly with her finger.

"That's where I cut myself shaving," chuckled Matthew.

"You didn't!"

"Yep. This time yesterday I had a nice full beard."

"No! Why did you cut it off?"

"I didn't want you to have to snuggle up to a scratchy old face."

"I wouldn't have minded. It's *you* I care about, not what you look like."

"I was tired of the thing anyway!"

A blaring honk of an automobile horn reminded them they were still standing in the middle of the street.

Again they laughed, running out of the way. Once back on the safety of the sidewalk, Matthew turned and stood facing Sabina.

"I did not come just to find you, Sabina," he said, softly and seriously. "I came to bring you a red rose. Do you know why?"

Sabina nodded and shook her head all at once.

"Because in the color and fragrance of the red," Matthew went on, "are brought together the colors and fragrances of all the roses."

"Please don't make me start crying again!"

"I meant what I promised when I gave you the first pink rose, that nothing would keep us apart ever again. With all my heart I mean what this red rose intends to say—that more than ever I want to spend the rest of my life . . . with you as my wife."

"Oh, Matthew . . . there is nothing I could want more!"

"And you know what they say about roses, don't you?"

"The deeper the red . . . ," began Sabina, then paused, glancing up at him.

". . . The deeper the love," added Matthew.

For several long seconds they stood, silently gazing fully into each other's eyes.

There were worlds and volumes still to be said. Yet in silence their eyes conveyed what was nearly sufficient, as had the wordless exchange of the pink rose from Sabina to Matthew at Christmastime: that they loved one another—and that it was enough.

Slowly their faces drew together. Their lips met, then lingered a long, tender moment.

When they parted, again their eyes held one another, liquid and shining.

The rose and the kiss, and now the deep penetrating gaze of love, sealed what they had known from the moment at the garden party of their first meeting—that they were meant for one another, to share all life's joys and sorrows, and that nothing would ever part them again . . . forever.

Without another word, they turned and slowly began making their way toward the small house hand in hand, then up the several steps to the doorway.

"Come in, Matthew," said Sabina. "You're just in time to join us for breakfast."

"*Us?*" repeated Matthew.

But already they were walking through the door. Before Sabina could explain her use of the plural pronoun, Matthew was leaping across the room in joyful astonishment.

"Baron!" he exclaimed.

120

The Lost Months

• • •

BARON VON DORTMANN WAS ON HIS FEET THE INSTANT he saw the door open, and now stood with outstretched hands to embrace Matthew as he approached. Neither man gave even passing thought to a mere handshake.

This was an occasion demanding a more intimate and thorough greeting of affection!

Stepping back after heartfelt hugs, now their hands met in a firm manly clasp that did not end until they had exchanged their mutual incredulity.

"It is as wonderful as it is surprising to see you, my boy!"

"And you, Baron . . . you look splendid! You must have put on twenty pounds since I last laid eyes on you!"

"I'm sorry I cannot say the same for you, Matthew. Have you been ill?"

Matthew laughed, stepping back and now stretching his arm about Sabina as she approached, drawing her to his side.

"No, I'm fine. I've just been looking for the two of you for over two months, that's all. My provisions have occasionally been scant."

"Two months!" exclaimed both father and daughter at once.

"It's a long story!"

"I want to hear it," said the baron.

"I've followed you through half of Europe, I think."

"We knew there was someone looking for us," said Sabina. "That's why we kept moving. We received conflicting reports. Some said a friend was trying to contact us, others warned us that enemies to our cause were prowling about. We had no idea. . . ."

"Unfortunately, both reports may be true," said Matthew.

"What do you mean, son?" asked the baron.

"I'm afraid there's been someone tracking *me* rather persistently most of the time too."

Sabina and her father looked at one another in alarm.

"Have you an idea who?"

"I have actually seen two men. I can't be certain—it's been a long time and I did not see him close up—but the older of the two seems to strike a faint resemblance to your old neighbor, Count von Schmundt's son."

"Gustav!" again came two responses in unison.

"We thought the report some of our people managed about our death would have made him finally give it up," added Sabina.

"I don't know that it is him for certain," said Matthew. "Perhaps he doesn't know you are alive. Although," he added thoughtfully, "if he's been on my trail, that means he's been on yours as well. I'm glad I lost him yesterday before driving to Magdeburg."

"Did you lose him for good?" asked the baron.

"Hmm, probably not," reflected Matthew. "Whoever it is has shown himself remarkably resilient about getting me back into his sights after I think I've done with him. No, we'll have to take precautions. I'm certain he's not far behind."

"Enough gloomy news for now," said Sabina enthusiastically. "Come—coffee and bread and cheese and jam are waiting. Matthew, we need to get you fattened up, just like I did Papa!"

They all laughed and adjourned together into the small kitchen.

Baron von Dortmann stretched out his arms even before they sat down, taking the hands of his daughter and their newly found friend, who also clasped hands.

"Our Father," he prayed fervently, *"how thankful we are at this moment! You are so good to us, O Lord! Thank you for bringing young Matthew to us safely. Thank you for answering our prayers for him all this time, though we knew not his errand of mercy toward us. Thank you for this rekindled friendship of the Spirit. We commit it to you, Father. We commit ourselves to you anew, for your service. Let your life and your Spirit flow through us in ever increasing measure. Let us love you, hearken unto you, obey you, and submit ourselves ever more fully to you, our Lord and our good and*

loving Creator and Master. How we love you! Thank you again, Father. Amen."

Amens followed from both Matthew and Sabina.

As they sat down around the small table spread with the wonderful simplicities of a German *Frühstück* or *Kaffee Trinken,* the questions and laughter, explanations and stories, flowed as rapidly as the coffee, tea, and slices of dark rye bread.

The morning was well advanced and two separate pots of coffee already stale, and still they sat visiting with an intensity to make up for the years since Matthew and the baron had spoken in depth, as well as the seven months that had passed between Matthew and Sabina.

"Were you not seriously hurt from the crash then?" Matthew had asked. "The last time I saw you, Sabina, you were lying there. . . . I thought you were dead. I never did see you, Baron. Then I woke up, banged up, severe burns, broken leg, wound in my head, couldn't remember anything . . . until they showed me the article saying that nearly everyone in both the helicopter and the van had been killed."

"The hand of the Lord was protecting us, that is all I can say," replied Sabina. "We probably should have been killed. When the last explosion came—when we were running toward each other—I saw something come flying through the air and hit you. I screamed and stumbled, and then fell flat on my face. The fall knocked me senseless for a minute or two, and I was terrified to move but not injured badly from the blast. Papa fell out of the van in the other direction and into a ditch at the side of the road. He was so weak that he had to be carried away. I was afraid for him for a long time." Sabina glanced over at her father. He smiled and reached out his hand to hers and gave it a reassuring squeeze. "But, thank God, he was not badly hurt."

"What about the others?"

Sabina's face fell.

"Herr Meier, the baker whose van we were in, was killed. It was a dreadful shock to everyone involved."

"But Brumfeldt survived. I saw him again two months ago."

"Yes, but . . . you saw Erich?"

"That's where I went first," replied Matthew, "that is, after your old apartment. I met your neighbor, by the way—a timid and cautious lady."

"Gerta! Bless her—she was a good friend."

"She's terrified of the couple who are in your old apartment."

Sabina's forehead wrinkled in concern, but Matthew went on.

"From Berlin I drove south and tried to retrace your steps. That barn where we made the transfer to the bakery van was the only lead I had to your network people. I tell you, that day when you pulled your mutiny and made me get out and took over the wheel, I didn't know *what* you were doing!"

Matthew laughed at the memory.

"But then as I began to reconstruct it, things began to fit into place."

"So, you did eventually discover all about the network?"

"Not *all,* but enough to begin the process of tracing the threads through to locate the two of you."

"Did you see young Willy?" asked Sabina.

"Yes. He remembered me from the day of the escape and was willing to help. His mother didn't trust me."

"Poor Clara," sighed Sabina. "It has all been very trying for her."

"Willy is the one who saved us all," Sabina went on. "He had followed us and arrived immediately after the accident. He pulled us to safety and got us out of there before any of the men from the helicopter or border guards came. By the time I came to myself and realized what Willy was doing, I insisted he go back for you too. But he said you would only be endangered. I never knew what happened to you."

"He hauled me to the border and left me with the Americans on duty there, though I was unconscious at the time."

"We probably all owe our lives to Willy."

"But he doesn't even know you're alive," said Matthew. "How can that be?"

"He got us to a hospital in Potsdam. After that some others of our number stepped in. Neither Willy nor his father ever knew of their involvement. The *Stasi* were too close, and all had to be managed with the strictest secrecy."

"I owe Willy for finding you too," added Matthew. "He's the one who first brought up the name Bietmann in Kehrigkburg. But what I still don't understand is the official reports about you all being dead."

"We have many friends," Sabina said with a smile. "One of them happens to be a Jewish man by the name of Albert Müller who was at *Lebenshaus* for a short while during the war."

"A nervous little watchmaker from Dresden!" laughed the baron. "Never did we have a guest so anxious to leave us! But we did eventually get him safely to Switzerland."

"He returned after the war, gave up watchmaking, became a rather important official in the DDR bureaucracy, and, through one thing and another also became involved with our continuing work."

"Which reminds me," interjected Matthew. "Very clever with the name—*Duftblatt*. I finally figured it out!"

Sabina laughed.

"Go on about Müller."

"He never forgot what we had done for him, and always made a point of saying he wanted to find a way to repay us. He finally had his chance."

"How?"

"He arranged for the official reports of our deaths, even to the files at the morgue in Potsdam, all of which was reported to the papers. We don't know how exactly he contrived it . . . we don't want to know, do we, Papa!"

The baron laughed.

"At first I suspected it was Gustav chasing us that day," Sabina went on. "I could not believe he had actually tried to kill us. I cannot bring myself to imagine he had sunk to that. We heard the men in the helicopter were killed too, though whether that report is true there is no way to know. In the DDR you *never* know. In the end we had to assume Gustav might still be alive, and, after my father's escape from prison, we knew we would be safer if no one, especially Gustav, knew our true identity or whereabouts. I'm sorry, Matthew—it didn't occur to me at first that you would read those same newspaper reports arranged for by our good Herr Müller. When it dawned on me that you too would think us dead, that's when I decided to send you the pink rose."

"That's another thing—how *did* you manage that!" exclaimed Matthew.

"Do you want the long or the short story?" asked Sabina with a smile.

"Both."

"Which first?"

"The short."

"All right—I asked a friend to wrap up a pink rose in a Christmas package and take it to the U.S. consulate in West Berlin, with instructions that it be delivered to you."

"That's pretty short, but it still doesn't tell me how you managed it!"

"To answer that takes the long story. Do you want it now?"

"Yep, is there any coffee left?"

"A little, but I don't think it's much good after all this time."

"After where I've been and what I've put up with these last two months, I won't even notice." He held out his cup, and Sabina poured out what remained from the pot. Matthew took a gulp, grimaced, then nodded for her to continue.

"We had a family with us for a long while during the war," Sabina began, "a Jewish rabbi, his wife, and their two daughters. Rabbi Wissen was an important man who was hiding some extremely valuable jewels and Jewish relics from the Nazis. He was in a great deal of danger. Papa and he grew close to one another, as Mama did with his wife. And we three girls—myself and Ursula and Gisela—became very good friends as well.

"After the war, we continued to be in touch. Rabbi Wissen was one of the first Jewish leaders to return to Israel in 1948 and was among those who were influential in establishing the new nation. He returned to his family in Russia, where they lived after the war, to help other Jews in danger. He and I were in contact after the war and decided, he in Russia and I in Berlin, to continue the work Papa had begun, helping and hiding Jews, combatting what grew to be a dreadful persecution in Russia, getting families safely either to West Berlin or even down to Israel. After Stalin died in 1953, the silent holocaust began to ease. In recent years our efforts have been mainly aimed at informing the rest of the world about the true state of the oppression in Russia."

"The rabbi and his family are still in Russia?"

Sabina smiled.

"Do you remember the Sunday we spent in the city when I was so tired?"

Matthew laughed. "I certainly do. I thought you were finally getting bored with me!"

"I had been up very late the night before. The Wissens were with me those two nights, and were hiding out in my little house the whole time you and I were together."

"That explains it! But why didn't you tell me?"

"I was just so unsure, Matthew—unsure what was best. Forgive me! I didn't want to get you involved."

"I understand. But go on. How did all this come about? I take it they were finally fleeing Russia?"

"Because of the rabbi's efforts, he continued to be in danger from the Communists. Word may have spread to the Kremlin about what he had possessed during the war. If so, the Communists were as anxious to get their hands on it as had been the Nazis. In any event, he was a threat to their system because he was an important Jew and the Russian link to a network that was exposing the evils of their system to the world. One of his daughters came to Berlin in the 1950s to be with me.

"She and I lived with one another for a while. We had many lengthy talks about God, and especially about Judaism and Christianity. She eventually came to accept Jesus as the true Messiah, became a Christian, and became involved with us in the *Network of the Rose*. All this time she had been betrothed to a young man by the name of Joseph, but also, like you and I, separated by the war."

"What happened? Where was he?" asked Matthew.

"He had been involved in a mission like ours, but in a different direction, helping fellow Jews from Poland escape the Nazis by leading them eastward, into Russia. The Wissens lost touch with Joseph during the war, then afterward there was some trouble with the Communists. The rabbi tried to use his influence to find out where Joseph was and contact him, but he was unable to learn much, especially in that his own situation was tenuous with Moscow and he had to keep in hiding from their spies."

"And?"

"We still do not know any details of Joseph's situation. There have been rumors from time to time. He seems to be one of the many unpublicized casualties of the Communist regime. We think he is in prison, though we do not know where, nor what the crime. Somehow his work during the war led him in directions we are unaware of. Whether it is spiritual or political—we simply do not know."

"Sounds a lot like your own predicament, Baron," remarked Matthew, turning to Sabina's father.

"There are thousands like me, thousands of families still suffering separation. This Communism is an evil thing, Matthew—more subtle, perhaps, than fascism, but no less ungodly."

"There really are thousands still missing, still being held?"

"Have you ever heard of Dr. Rainer Hildebrandt?" asked Sabina.

"The name sounds familiar," replied Matthew.

"He is the leader of another underground organization called the Fighting Group against Inhumanity."

"Yes, I remember hearing of it."

"We've worked together with his people some. His volunteers organize resistance to the *Stasi* and *Vopo* methods in the East. But mostly they're involved in trying to trace fellow Germans, like Papa, who have been swallowed up by Russian prison and slave-labor camps, and free them if possible. He estimates that there are still more than twenty thousand people missing behind what you call the Iron Curtain. Papa is far from the only one."

"Didn't you tell me Müller was involved with Hildebrandt?" the baron asked his daughter.

Sabina nodded. "He had many connections with his people. Erich Brumfeldt too."

"But your Rose Network differs from his?"

"We have been chiefly concerned with Jews, because of Rabbi Wissen, of course, and my own Jewish blood. Our mission, besides helping Jews in trouble, has been to get information to the free world about the plight of our people in the Soviet Union. We've been more an information network than a resistance organization."

"I see what you mean about it being a long story. But I still haven't heard any connection to my pink rose, or what the Wissens were doing in your house!"

"All right, I'll try to tie the pieces together!" said Sabina. "As I said, Ursula and I were involved together in the network. One of the things we were trying to do, in addition to locating *my* father, and get information out about the Russian situation, was locate *her* Joseph. Rabbi Wissen was in the process of solidifying some good contacts in

Russia to work with who were affiliated with the other organization I mentioned, the Fighting Group against Inhumanity—one in particular, a vibrant young Russian Christian by the name of Rostovchev. All this time the rabbi had been in hiding and out of reach from the authorities. Somehow all of a sudden the KGB learned of his whereabouts and he knew his life to be in danger. We think it had to do with some vital photographs he smuggled out of the country. He gave them to me just days before I met you. You do still have the packet I gave you for safekeeping?" asked Sabina.

"Safe and sound. Am I to assume that you passed those same photos off to me?"

"When we decided to try to rescue Papa, I knew they would be safer in West Berlin."

"What about the rabbi?"

"Once he realized how close he was to being located by the KGB, he and his wife and other daughter left Russia, through the network. That's how they came to me that Saturday night after our picnic. The following Monday they were safely in West Berlin with their other daughter. Now they have gone on to Israel."

"An amazing story. And in Russia, no more word on Joseph."

"None. For the moment, those initial contacts with the underground there have been cut off."

"What about your friend Ursula, where is she? Did she go to Israel with the rest of her—?" Suddenly Matthew's face lit up in recognition. "She is still in West Berlin, isn't she!" he said, answering his own question. *"She's* the Ursula who came to the consulate!"

Sabina nodded. "How did you know?"

"She had to sign in when she brought the package! It was the first place I went in trying to track you down—but the name Ursula meant nothing to me."

"Ursula had decided to move to West Berlin in 1956," Sabina went on. "We both had other friends there, and we needed contacts in both halves of the city. And too, we had managed to secure a job for her very near mine, in one of the BRD agencies, so that we were able to see one another easily without raising suspicions. I wanted to remain where I was because of Papa, and we saw no difference with respect to our search for Joseph whether she was in the western or eastern sector. She was in no danger from Gustav as I was. I had to remain deeper in hiding. So she emigrated to West Berlin and has been living there ever since, maintaining network contacts on that side."

"You and she continued your network business together?"

Sabina nodded. "There was a purpose to our work, though at times it became very difficult not to settle into a dull resignation even though we knew it was important. The stress of the division between the Germanys became even more difficult for Ursula once she actually moved to the West. We spoke of it often, but arrived at no conclusion. What conclusion is there? Germany is divided right down the middle of its soul. As long as it persists—at least this is what Papa says—the Germans will be a people ill-at-ease with themselves."

"What do you say, Baron?" asked Matthew.

"It is true. The division is marked by more than a border erected by the Kremlin. It is a division of the very German psyche. I fear we Germans are in for a long night of confusion about who we are, about what it means to be *a German*. It will no doubt be up to future generations to arrive at the answer. My generation brought history's worst war to the world, and we will go to our graves with that sin upon our shoulders. The few men, like my friend Dietrich, who could have prevented it had their voices been heeded, were sadly out of touch with the rest of a generation that allowed its collective conscience to drift off to sleep."

"And Ursula?" asked Matthew at length, still not satisfied with the conclusion of Sabina's "long story."

"Unfortunately, the wall has separated me from her too," replied Sabina.

"Though not completely, right?" suggested Matthew.

"There are still a few methods we have for communication."

"Just enough to tell her to take a pink rose to the consulate before Christmas?"

"I did manage to get such a message to her," replied Sabina, smiling.

The small kitchen grew silent as the three reflected on the years and months that had wrought so many changes in each of their lives.

Next Phase

• • •

"THAT WAS A MARVELOUS BREAKFAST!" EXCLAIMED Matthew at length, as they stood up, stretched, and walked back into the adjacent living room. "I haven't had such a satisfying meal since I walked through Checkpoint Charlie! Now it's time to give some thought to the next phase of this operation."

"It *is* nearly noon, and already nearly time for dinner," said Sabina. "Perhaps I should leave the two of you alone while I put some potatoes on to boil."

"I may need fattening up, but give me at least an hour or two!" laughed Matthew. "I was hardly referring to the next meal!"

"Then what do you mean by the *next phase?*" said the baron.

"And what *operation?*" asked Sabina.

"The operation to get the two of you out of here!" answered Matthew.

"What . . . out of where, Magdeburg?"

"I did not just come to *find* you. I came to rescue you from this place, and to take you back with me."

Sabina and her father looked at one another with astonished expressions.

"I know you were reluctant before, Sabina," Matthew went on, "this being your country and your people and your heritage."

"Yes," sighed Sabina, "but much has changed since then."

"You have your father again. As long as he remains in the DDR, he will be a fugitive, and you will both be in danger. We *must* get to where we can live together in freedom."

"But where, Matthew?"

"Where else but in the West? There is no more freedom possible here. We must start our new life in the West. We have no other choice."

"I don't understand," said the baron. "What can be done? This country is walled up. Do you have connections through your president?"

"No," sighed Matthew. "I quit my job to come here."

"Matthew!" exclaimed Sabina.

"There was no other way."

"But . . . but are you safe?"

"Hardly," he laughed. "No one even knows where I am."

"Then . . . then how—"

"I'm talking about breaking across the border—the three of us."

"Breaking out—I am an old man, Matthew!"

"Not so old as when I saw you last, Baron. You look fit and well. We will find a way. Escape is always possible."

"And dangerous."

"True . . . but possible."

"People have been killed."

"We will manage it . . . somehow."

"But that means you are trapped behind what your people call the Iron Curtain—*just like us,*" said Sabina as the magnitude of what Matthew had done finally began to dawn upon her.

"Just like you," repeated Matthew.

"You risked your whole future, your own freedom, to come find us."

"I never quite thought about it in those terms," laughed Matthew. "I saw the pink rose, and after that I had no alternative. I had made a promise to you, after all."

Sabina smiled at him, eyes filling with tears. How could she have ever doubted his love?

"So you have *no* connections here? You cut all your ties?" said the baron.

"I'm on my own, without as much as a single deutsche mark to my name, driving a broken-down Trabi with half a tank of fuel remaining. It's parked a ways back up the street. Other than that, and a couple forged passports, I've got nothing."

"You're not being encouraging, Matthew," said Sabina.

"What can I say? If we're going to get out of here, we're on our own . . . except, of course, for *Das Netzwerk von Rosen.*"

"You never told us how you first found out about the network?" said Sabina.

"At *Lebenshaus.*"

"You've been to *Lebenshaus!*" exclaimed the baron.

Matthew smiled. "I snuck in, disguised as a DDR official. I don't think I was too convincing!"

"How . . . how is the place?" asked the baron with obvious emotion in his voice.

"It is being used as an asylum or sanatorium of some kind, for research into the effects of aging, so far as I could tell, though it never did seem to make complete sense. In any case, the repairs you spoke of, Sabina, to the house have been done, I assume. Whatever the original damage was, the place seemed in reasonable repair. There are changes outside, however, around the grounds."

"And . . . and the garden?" said the baron, his voice quivering with fearful anticipation of the worst. "Were you able to see the garden?"

"Yes, Baron," answered Matthew. "I'm sorry to say that it was not a pretty sight—though on the other hand," he added, trying to sound upbeat, "I think you would find reason to be pleased. The garden remains intact, in nearly its entirety. It has been utterly ignored, but not destroyed or plowed under. I was able to barely make out some of the paths we used to walk together."

"Thank you, Father!" whispered the baron, obviously filled with a host of deep feelings.

"Did you find the rose garden, Matthew?" asked Sabina.

Matthew nodded.

"Badly overgrown . . . but alive in large measure. Many of the hybrids were gone, but some of the older varieties and climbers and ramblers were thriving. One of the plants even had a tiny bloom."

Both Sabina and her father exclaimed for joy, then asked, nearly together, "Which one?"

"You mean what variety? I have no idea!" laughed Matthew. "It was a tiny little white rose, that's all I know."

"The Pomeranian Ivory!" exclaimed the baron. "One of the hardiest breeds I ever found. An ancient plant that blossomed whatever I did to it, and all year round!"

"A lover of roses never forgets a prize species!"

"Especially not my father," added Sabina. "Did you pick it?"

"No," answered Matthew. "How could I? I left it in the hope that it would serve as a promise that *Der Frühlingsgarten* may yet thrive and blossom again as in days of old."

"You remember what the Scotsman said of old gardens, do you not, Sabina?" reminded the baron.

"Of course, Papa."

"We shall believe it for our Garden of Spring as well!"

All at once Matthew remembered the things he had back in his car.

"How could I have forgotten!" he said, leaping to his feet. "I'll be back in a minute!"

The next moment he was out of the house and dashing along Graulingerstrasse, leaving his two hosts gaping in astonishment after him. Four minutes later he returned, driving this time, parking the Trabi in front of Number 42, and running back inside clutching the books he had retrieved.

"I found the dungeon!" he exclaimed, breathless, as he entered.

At the words, Baron von Dortmann leapt to his feet.

"It had not yet been found . . . wasn't destroyed!" he exclaimed in incredulity.

"Not a bit."

"The key in the floor . . . the brassworks . . . the concealed lever!" he exclaimed. "You discovered them all . . . on your own. And got into the hidden room itself!"

Matthew nodded. "From all I can tell," he said, "it was just as you had left it. The worktable, all the things you were using to smuggle people to Switzerland. It was in the dungeon where I put it all together, with things you had said, Sabina, and realized the network still must be active. I had no idea you were alive, Baron," he said as he walked across the floor to where the baron stood, "but I knew I could not leave these behind."

He handed Sabina's father the stack of journals and his old Bible.

The old man slumped into the chair behind him in disbelief.

Speechless, all he could do was gaze down at the books now sitting in his lap, great tears falling from his eyes. Slowly the fingers of his right hand began to move across the old and weathered leather cover of the Bible he had studied daily for more than thirty years, with the fond and tender caress due an old friend.

At length he glanced up. Matthew and Sabina both stood looking lovingly down upon him.

"Oh, Matthew, my boy," he sighed, "what joy you have brought an old man's heart! You will never know how much your thoughtfulness means. I thank you, from the depths of my being!"

He lifted his right hand toward Matthew, gazing intently into his eyes. Matthew took it.

Again the two men shook hands.

As Sabina witnessed the exchange, she could not help thinking that the spiritual torch was in that moment being passed from one generation to the next. The aging patriarch—who had led both daughter and the man who would be her husband through their first fledgling years of faith—now gave the right to share authority over the family Dortmann to the younger protégé, who was in truth, if not fully in fact, a son now entering the prime of his spiritual manhood.

A long silence followed. Sabina and Matthew took chairs, while the baron slowly thumbed through the journals, pausing here and there to read a line or a phrase, nearly fifty years of memories filling him with untold wellsprings of emotion.

"I never dreamed I would see these again," he murmured softly. "We left in such haste and had a long walk ahead of us that night; I knew they could not be managed if I was to be able to help the others. So I had no choice but to leave them behind. The thought of these journals has caused no little grief to my flesh over the years, though at the same time has motivated me to diligence in new writings. Ah, what crumbly vessels are these tabernacles filled with self," he exclaimed. "All those years in prison I thought God would prompt me to recreate much of this. Yet whenever I set pen to paper, my thoughts went off in far different directions. Now I see that he had *new* things for me to say during that season of my life, because he had preserved all this, awaiting your arrival. Ah, Matthew . . . Matthew," he said, glancing up, eyes full of tears, ". . . how could you have known?"

"Do not forget, Baron, I had occasion to know your daughter quite well. The two of you are very much alike."

"It makes me more happy to hear you say that than to hold these books you have brought me."

1 2 2

Another Proposal

• • •

SUDDENLY THE BARON'S COUNTENANCE BRIGHTENED. He set down the volumes and glanced up with expression full of exuberance and life.

"That reminds me, my boy," he said, "Sabina told me the two of you planned to be married!"

A sheepish expression came over Matthew's face.

"We spoke of it, yes, sir," he said. "Such was my hope . . . except for one thing."

"What could that possibly be?"

"I felt it was only proper . . . that is, I wanted to speak with *you* first, and tell you of my intent, and ask for your consent to make your daughter my wife. Unfortunately, things got a little mixed up before I got a chance to talk to you."

"There's no time like the present," rejoined the baron, throwing Sabina a quick wink.

Taken by surprise at the suddenness of it, Matthew glanced over at Sabina, then back toward the baron, who had risen forward in his chair and now sat as one waiting expectantly.

"Then here goes," said Matthew after a moment. "But I've never done anything like this before, so you'll just have to let me stumble along."

"Stumble ahead!"

"All right," said Matthew, pausing to swallow, then going on. "You have called me your son. Now I would like to request that you allow me to inherit that title by right of marriage. Would you, Baron Heinrich von Dortmann, consent to allow me the honor of proposing to your lovely daughter, Sabina?"

"Request granted!" boomed the baron with delight, rising to his feet and striding forward to shake Matthew's hand vigorously.

"Thank you, sir."

"Well, what are you waiting for, son . . . there she is, right over there, tears running down her face. Don't keep her in suspense any longer!"

Matthew grinned, then turned and walked the few paces to where Sabina stood, face wet, smiling from ear to ear. He took her two hands in his.

"Sabina," he said seriously. "I love you so much! So I'm asking you now, again, with your father's approval, if you would marry me . . . and be my wife."

"Request granted," whispered Sabina softly, still smiling through her tears.

Matthew took her into his arms, and they stood together several long moments.

"Well then," said the baron boisterously, enjoying the role of elder gadfly to the romantic moment, "what I want to know is when this wedding is going to take place. I've never given away a daughter, or had a son of my own for that matter, and I'm getting older every day!"

Matthew and Sabina laughed.

"We can't proceed without *my* father," answered Matthew, "and he's in Bavaria."

"I presume what you're suggesting is not that we bring him here?"

"No, sir. For more reasons than a wedding, I believe, as I said before, that it is imperative that the reunion take place there . . . in the West."

The Secret of the Rose

• • •

THE REMAINDER OF THE DAY THE THREE VISITED, laughed, prayed, and talked over plans together, though most of the time was spent reminiscing and catching up on the months since they had so calamitously parted. In the case of the baron and Matthew, a whole new relationship of adulthood, equality, fatherhood and sonship, and most importantly of Christian brotherhood, was rapidly being formed.

That evening, after they had eaten, Matthew took two chairs out onto the small veranda, then asked Sabina to join him. The night was chilly though not unbearably cold, and, though they bundled in sweaters, the nip of the March air felt refreshing against their faces.

They sat down and allowed the stillness of approaching night to settle over their spirits. It had been a day neither would ever forget.

"I have something for you," said Matthew at length.

"Nothing could surpass the gift you gave me this morning," said Sabina in a contented voice.

"Nothing?" repeated Matthew.

"It is the first red rose I've been given in my life. I should say, it's the first I've *accepted.*"

They both laughed lightly.

"I will keep the rose you gave me this morning forever. I will find some special place of honor to preserve it. Do you still have the box we bought in Berlin?" she asked.

"It is safe and sound with my father," answered Matthew. "But," he added pointedly, "I have another gift for you. Are you absolutely certain nothing could surpass this morning's red rose?"

"Positive."

"Not even something from *Lebenshaus* itself?"

"I don't know what you mean."

"Not even . . . this?"

As he said the words, Matthew pulled out from where he had kept it concealed in his clothing the rose-painted china box.

Sabina gasped when she realized what it was.

"I didn't only visit the dungeon when I was there," he said. "I had this one other errand to attend to as well."

She took it tenderly from his hand, holding it for several moments.

"We said we would not peek inside until we could open it together, remember?" said Matthew coyly.

"I . . . I remember," said Sabina, reddening slightly and trying to keep from smiling.

"We said we would enjoy the roses we put inside . . . *together*," Matthew added, emphasizing the last word with deliberately feigned innocence.

There was a moment of silence.

"I don't know how to tell you this, Sabina," Matthew went on, his tone now sounding contrite and apologetic, "but . . . well, when I was there, down in that dark room with only my flashlight . . . and not knowing if I would ever see you again . . . I'm sorry, Sabina, but I'm afraid I could not help myself."

She glanced over at him.

"You . . ."

"Yes . . . I opened the box. I hope you'll forgive me."

At first Sabina's expression was blank, not quite grasping the full implications of his humble and repentant tone.

"But . . . then, you *know?*" she said, more in statement than inquiry.

"Know what, Sabina?" replied Matthew, eyes wide in pretended ignorance. Gradually a smile played at the edges of his mouth, and she finally realized the game he had been making of her.

"Oh, Matthew, I couldn't help it!" she said with apologetic exclamation. "I didn't know either if I'd ever see you again, or *Lebenshaus* either for that matter! You can't imagine how badly I wanted to take it with me that night. When Papa went down to seal up the dungeon and the whole bottom part of the house, I went to look one last time at our box. I decided to leave it, hoping that somehow it would be safe. But I *had* to look—I had to know! I said to myself, 'Oh, I hope Matthew will forgive me this once!'"

Matthew laughed.

"All is forgiven! On both sides?" he added.

Sabina nodded.

"It would appear we both broke the promise," he said.

"Only out of love."

"Perhaps . . . then we are excused."

Again silence fell.

Without another word, Matthew reached over and placed his hand on top of Sabina's. Together they removed the white lid and peered inside, sharing now together the sight they had both already seen alone, of Matthew's small note and the rosebuds.

"Two white roses," said Matthew after a moment.

Sabina sighed. "Two white roses," she repeated.

After a moment Matthew leaned close so that he could see deeply into Sabina's eyes even in the scant light from inside the house.

"Friends . . . *forever,*" he said.

"Ever," she repeated, holding his gaze.

Their lips met, each holding the other's for several long seconds.

They eased away, both sighing with pleasure, and sat back beside one another, Sabina still holding the china box on her lap and now slipping the fingers of her right hand through those of Matthew's left.

Contented enough to spend two years sitting as they were, neither moved nor spoke for some twenty minutes. Both their hearts were too full to give expression to words.

"I won't soon forget what you have done, Matthew," said Sabina in scarcely more than a whisper, after a long time had passed and the night seemed deepening around them. "What am I saying? I won't *ever* forget! First you let me be *Aschenputtel* herself, complete with horse-drawn carriage. When I told my father about the ball, he couldn't believe it! 'You found yourself quite a man there, Sabina!'— those were his words!"

Matthew laughed, and the mood between them lightened.

"And just when I'm beginning to get adjusted to the fact that I'm not going to be able to spend my life with the man I'm in love with, who should show up at my door but a little urchin, asking me if I know the secret of the rose!"

Sabina could not keep away a few remaining tears of quiet joy.

"Not only was my fairy tale not yet over," she went on, "but what should my *schöner Prinz* have done but risked his own life, charging into the very camp of the enemy on his white steed—"

"I would hardly call that rattletrap Trabi a white steed!" laughed Matthew.

"Make light of it if you want," chided Sabina. "To me you *are* a knight in shining armor who braved the very den of the dragon to rescue me. Your coming here is every bit the fairy tale as was the *Maskenball.*"

Again Matthew laughed.

"What else could I do! The lady I loved was in prison behind the walls of the Communist dragon! I had to rescue her!"

He stopped and became serious, though still with humor in his tone.

"Now all I've got to do is figure out how to get us *out* of the dragon's lair!" he added.

"Oh, Matthew, you have such an imagination . . . , you are so full of fun—and you never stop finding new ways to try to make me happy! I am just . . . so grateful. You make me feel so loved . . . and . . . and my heart is so full. Even if we should never . . ."

She looked away without finishing, but weeping happily, unable to keep the tears from flowing in earnest.

After two or three minutes, Sabina wiped her eyes, then glanced up at Matthew.

"Do you mind if I ask you a question?" she said.

"Of course not—what about?"

"Roses."

"I can't think of anything better to be asked about."

"As I was growing up," Sabina began, "I always remember my father telling me about what he called the 'secret of the rose.' But whenever I would ask, he wouldn't tell me what it was. He said it was a secret whose meaning every man and woman had to discover for themselves. For a long time I thought it was some huge mysterious truth, having to do with what he used to call the 'mysteries of the garden.' I thought the secret of the rose was a great mystery to be discovered about God and growing things.

"By the time I was older, and began to sense that it was much simpler than that, though perhaps just as profound in its own way . . . by then I thought it was too late. Once I knew what he'd meant by the secret of the rose, you were gone, and I didn't think I would ever hear—except maybe when I dreamed about you—those three words that *are* the secret of the rose."

"I understand what you're trying to say," said Matthew. "For a long time I suppose, having heard the phrase while at *Lebenshaus* when we were young, I misunderstood too."

"That's my question," said Sabina. "How long did it take you . . . I mean, when did you finally discover what the secret of the rose really is?"

"I don't know," replied Matthew. "Maybe sometime last June and July when I was bringing a rose to you every day . . . although I'm not sure I thought about it so concretely then. It might have been last fall when I was rehabilitating from the injuries from the accident. I sat, one day in particular for hours, holding the box with the dried petals in it, thinking about you and our time together. I can't say *when* the secret of the rose really dawned on me. . . ."

He pondered quietly for a moment.

"It might not have even been until this morning, as I was walking along holding the rose I'd found, thinking of what I would say when I saw you. I thought of fifty things, but none of them *said* it—do you know what I mean?"

Sabina nodded.

"I don't know that I ever really settled on what I would say, until all of a sudden, there we were, and the words came out of my mouth—*the secret of the rose is that I love you*. I suppose it grew into my consciousness slowly, from all those things."

"Papa used to say that the secret was only given to those who came to understand the depths of the red rose."

"Do you think *I love you* is all your father meant by the secret of the rose?" Matthew asked.

"Yes and no."

"How do you mean?"

"There are millions of secrets—about life and growing things, about God and love and his creativity and his love of beauty and his gifts to his creatures. He was always talking about secrets and the hidden meanings of everything. But *the* secret of the rose that Papa spoke of, that I so often remember him whispering into Mama's ear as she smiled, was so much simpler. How can anyone understand it fully until they have shared it with that one person meant for them to share it with? So, yes—perhaps that is all he meant by it. He knew that if you and I were those two people for each other, eventually we would discover it."

Matthew glanced down at the china box, then removed the lid again. He pulled out the two white buds they had picked in the baron's Garden of Spring over twenty-one years earlier.

"Even dry," he said, "it is easy to see why God gave these amazing little blossoms to mankind. What more perfect window into the very heart of the love that grows between a man and a woman. I see why your father never would tell what the secret was. For the secret of the rose can only be known and grasped by one who discovers that love blossoming, just like a rose, in his own heart."

"How blessed we are to have been able to discover it together," said Sabina, "first as friends, like your little note said, and now . . ."

She hesitated.

"You know what I mean," she went on, "being able now to discover the full secret of the rose together after all these years. God has been good to us to have blessed us so!"

She took Matthew's hand and pressed it between her own two.

"I do love you, Matthew!"

"And I you, Sabina. I'm so happy that God allowed me to discover the secret of the rose . . . with you."

About the Author

MICHAEL PHILLIPS is the author of more than fifty books, with total sales exceeding 4 million copies. He is also well known as the editor of the popular George MacDonald Classics series.

Now launching a new series with Tyndale House, *The Secret of the Rose*, Michael Phillips is one of the premier fiction authors publishing in the Christian marketplace. His newest non-fiction title, *A God to Call Father*, will be released in the fall of '94.

Phillips owns and operates a Christian bookstore on the West Coast. He and his wife, Judy, live with their three sons, Patrick, Gregory, and Robin, in Eureka, California.

Books by Michael Phillips

A God to Call Father

The Secret of the Rose
The Eleventh Hour
A Rose Remembered
Escape to Freedom
TYNDALE HOUSE

The Journals of Corrie Belle Hollister
My Father's World★
Daughter of Grace★
On the Trail of the Truth
A Place in the Sun
Sea to Shining Sea
Into the Long Dark Night
Land of the Brave and the Free
A Home for the Heart
Grayfox (Zack Hollister's Journal)
BETHANY HOUSE

The Stonewycke Trilogy★
The Heather Hills of Stonewycke
Flight from Stonewycke
Lady of Stonewycke
BETHANY HOUSE

The Stonewycke Legacy★
Stranger at Stonewycke
Shadows over Stonewycke
Treasure of Stonewycke
BETHANY HOUSE

The Highland Collection★
Jamie MacLeod: Highland Lass
Robbie Taggart: Highland Sailor
BETHANY HOUSE

The Russians★
The Crown and the Crucible
A House Divided
Travail and Triumph
BETHANY HOUSE

The Works of George MacDonald
(Selected, compiled, and edited by Michael Phillips)
BETHANY HOUSE

★with Judith Pella

GRIFFIN
©'93

BERLIN, 1961.

Karin Duftblatt walks the streets of Berlin on a secret mission. She is weary and tired, much like the metropolis she inhabits—a city that still carries the ravages of the war some two decades earlier. Even so, her new name and identity can't conceal the blonde hair and blue eyes of the beautiful young girl she once was.

She is pursued by an evil man, once her suitor. Her father remains a captive in a dark cell, with little hope for freedom. And she herself feels imprisoned—her life a secret in a city of secrets.

SUDDENLY she sees a face. Familiar. Can it be? No . . . but it is!

Is the fairy tale to be believed—or will the explosions and gunfire on the lonely field just outside of Berlin bring a premature end to the secret of the rose?

Historical Fiction

ISBN 0-8423-5929-X

0 31809 05929 6

9 780842 35929